Weird Canyon

A.M. Jordan

Published by:
Thursday Night Press
an imprint of
DX Varos Publishing
7665 E. Eastman Ave. #B101
Denver, CO 80231

Book cover design and layout by
Thursday Night Press
using images

ISBN: 978-1-955065-44-3 (paperback)
ISBN: 978-1-955065-45-0 (ebook)

Printed in the United States of America

To Laura
and to high school nerds everywhere

INTRODUCTION

"Oh, for a muse of fire--"
Shakespeare—Henry IV

As the late afternoon October sun beat down indifferently, the town of Mohawk, Colorado, burned to the ground.

Daniel Jael and Siegfried Shultz had ringside seats for the festivities. They were wearing lab coats, Sieg's pristine white and Danny's...not. Both of them had been born and raised in Mohawk, both were seventeen and both were seniors in Mohawk High. Sieg was dating their best friend, Courtney James, but Danny wasn't dating yet. Sieg was about five and a half feet tall and had been chubby his entire life. Danny had been over six feet tall before he was fifteen and could hide behind a stalk of corn. Most people considered Sieg to be a genius but few, if any, would think the same of Danny.

The intersection of Mohawk Avenue and Main Street was normally the busiest in town, and now it was even busier. The sounds of sirens, yelling people and crackling flames filled the air. The smell was of fire, burning wood and fear. Danny and Sieg stood in the center of the intersection and looked around with an increasing feeling of dismay and panic. The fire ravaged the aspens and evergreen along Mohawk Creek as it wound its way through the center of town. The giant, red-brick, three-story Mohawk Hardware Company had stood for over a century and was now burning merrily in sheets of multicolored flame. At the corner the Imperial Hotel announced it was closed as a loud explosion shattered all of its windows.

In later years, it would be known as the Great Mohawk Fire. Eventually, six different fire departments would answer the call to fight the flames consuming twenty square blocks of the town. Almost two hundred buildings would burn, not counting those merely scorched or water-damaged. That's what happens when a town has survived since the gold mining days without a fire and so was never completely rebuilt in brick. In the space of a single afternoon, one of the state's historical treasures was reduced to a pile of ashes.

Danny and Sieg stood there and watched, frozen in place. A hand landed on each of their shoulders and they turned to find a Mohawk County deputy sheriff standing there.

"You boys are coming with me," he said.

Danny looked over at Sieg, who was standing there wide eyed, his mouth moving with no words coming out. Tears were beginning to show at the corners of his eyes. Danny understood. He felt like crying, too. Instead, he essayed one last dark joke.

"So, what are we going to do for an encore?"

ONE

I guess you could say it all began in Mr. Harrison's classroom in Mohawk High. Mr. Harrison didn't have anything to do with the disaster except possibly allowing the Mohawk Science Club to meet in his classroom after school every Wednesday.

I liked Mr. Harrison. He was balding and he always wore a vertically striped shirt and suspenders. He was also the only teacher brave enough to sponsor the Science Club after Sieg and I had joined. I suspect his willingness stemmed more from wanting to avoid his wife, Ivana, than the fact he lost the fight in the teacher's lounge.

As an English teacher, Mr. Harrison probably couldn't have told the difference between Einstein and Edison but he was the best sponsor we could have hoped for. He didn't care what we did as long as he could stay behind his Rocky Mountain News and didn't have to referee our fights.

If there was a drawback to meeting in his classroom, it was the fact he absolutely refused to open the windows and he always had the radiators going full blast. He could have grown tropical plants in there. When I was a dumb frosh, I tried to cross the line one day.

"Can't we open a window?" I asked.

His paper never moved, however one of his index fingers gently wagged back and forth.

"Fresh air kills," he said.

And that was that, since there was no way to breach his newsprint Fortress of Solitude. So year after year we just sweltered along every Wednesday, dripping sweat and stepping out into the hallway from time to time for air.

So, on this particular day, when the trees were still green and the hot smell of cut grass crept under even the tightest window, Sieg opened our second meeting of the year. The week before, he'd managed to be elected our new Grand Pooh-Bah, and now he was bouncing up and down and just aching to flex his presidential muscles.

I was slouched in a chair off to one side with my notebook and pen, ready to take notes. While Sieg had grandiose ambitions, I was content to just be the club's secretary, taking notes and filing a dispatch with the school paper the next day.

We started with the requisite amount of screwing around. We talked about girls, cars and the latest comic books. Sieg finally stood up at the front of the room and smiled broadly.

"Good afternoon," he said. "I'd like to welcome all of our new members who joined us last week. I appreciate you've decided to come back even after the unfortunate argument—"

"Get on with it, Shultz!" said a voice from the back of the room.

I glanced back to see Randy Binderman sitting back

down and putting his feet up on the desk in front of him. Randy was taller than Sieg and always dressed in expensive clothes. Today he was in a pair of black jeans and one of those stupid shirts with the little animal stitched on it. He and a couple of his friends had been the other side of the "unfortunate argument" the week before. After losing his bid for club president, he'd made a few ugly claims, and it degenerated from there. It didn't help that Randy had loathed us since before kindergarten and the feeling was mutual.

With the smile of a snake-oil salesman, Sieg raised his hands to forestall any more argument.

"If we can keep the interruptions to a minimum," he said, "I can get to the point."

"Slow down!" I said. "I have to write this crap down!"

The Rocky Mountain News moved slightly and one of Mr. Harrison's fingers began wagging at me.

"Jael!" he said. "Language!"

"Sorry, sir," I said. "Slow down, Sieg, I have to write this dog strudel down."

That earned me a contemptuous snort from the Fortress of Solitude. Then Sieg held up his hands again.

"If you will bear with me," he said, "the point is we have to make a float for the Homecoming Parade next month."

Randy snorted and tossed his head. Behind his back I liked to call him "Horse-face." It wasn't that I was afraid of him, I just didn't want to see his horse-face cry. He probably couldn't beat me up, but why chance it? As it was, he apparently wasn't impressed by Sieg's announcement.

"Big freaking deal," he said. "That's something we do every year."

Sieg's smile changed to that of a shark who had just found out it had wandered into a school of fat, slow-moving mammals in Speedos.

"You're right, Randy," he said. "Every year we build a float for the parade. Every year our float has a totally lame theme. What did we do last year? We rode on the back of your Dad's flatbed, wearing our lab coats and holding up microscopes. We called it *Better Science with Mohawk High*. The year before, if I remember correctly, it was *To the Stars with Mohawk High*. We all wore our lab coats and held up telescopes."

"What's wrong with that, Mr. Shultz?" Miguel Herrera asked from the front row. He was a freshman, and he found Sieg and I were easier to get along with than Randy, who spent a great deal of time hazing him. I didn't mind a bit of poking fun at someone, but Randy always overdid it.

We heard the newspaper rattle and, to our surprise, it lowered to reveal our sponsor.

"You have to admit, it *is* a tradition," Mr. Harrison said.

You could have heard a pin drop. Beyond critiquing our language usage, Mr. Harrison had never, ever, spoken at one of our meetings. Up to this time, he had always been content to stay behind his paper. We all stopped and stared at him. It was as if we had been hunting for a goat and ran into a burning bush instead.

"With all due respect to our esteemed patron," Sieg said after regaining his composure, "we jolly well can argue with tradition. For one thing, it's boring. The same thing every year with a slightly different dress is dull. You know this, I know this. Heck, even the football team knows this."

We all laughed. If there was one group the Science

Club always seemed to have trouble with, it was the football team. Why the players felt we were good targets for their pranks and their insults was beyond me.

Apparently either the discussion was interesting or Mr. Harrison was up for a fight, because he rattled his newspaper again.

"So, Shultz," he said. "You get bored with turkey, dressing and borscht every Thanksgiving?"

We all just stared at him, afraid to even move. Sieg, on the other hand, was fearless, and he smiled broadly and began nodding.

"Yeah," he said. "Just like that, especially when you can have ham, duck or even roast beast. We're the Science Club, and we're supposed to have more imagination in our little fingers than the rest of the school has in its collective body."

"Even the art class?" I asked in my most naïve tone.

That brought him up short. He turned to glare at me and I grinned back at him like a loon. I enjoyed poking fun at him in public, if only to prove I was my own man. Sieg merely shook his head and looked at the ceiling.

"Besides," he said, "I have an idea."

Thinking back on it, when he said he had an idea, we should have made a run for it. Mr. Harrison should have hit him with the News and put a stop to it. I should have jumped up and throttled him before another word escaped. Randy should have thrown something at him. Anything to interrupt the train wreck we were heading for.

None of that happened, though. We just looked at Sieg with curiosity and wariness until Malcolm finally broke the tension.

"Okay, smart guy," he said. "What is this big idea of yours?"

"If you guys will shut up for half-a-second, I'll be glad to." Sieg said "Mr. Secretary, who are we playing at the homecoming game this year?"

"I think we're playing Fairview, from Boulder."

"You are correct, sir. Do you know what their team is called?"

"I do!" said another freshman in the front of the room. He had short hair, button down collars and a pocket protector filled with pens and pencils. *Nerd* screamed from his very pores, yet I found I liked him, even if he was bouncing up and down like a very tiny dog. His hand was raised like a battle flag, and Sieg stared at him as if he were an octopus in a punch bowl.

"All right," he said. "What are they called, uh...?"

"I'm Orville, sir. We're playing the Fairview Knights."

I could see it coming from a mile away and was awed not only by its simplicity but by the fact I had missed it. A groan of appreciation spread through the room, and I shook my head.

"And we're the Dragons," I said. "It's too perfect."

Sieg grinned at me.

"Isn't it, though?"

"It's so bloody obvious," Randy said. "Why didn't I think of it?"

Neither Sieg nor I chose to answer. For once we were going to keep the peace.

"That's one of the reasons I'm up here," Sieg finally said when we had calmed down. "I'm a genius, and the rest of you are common, run-of-the-mill, brainy types."

A shower of spitballs was launched. Raspberries, cat-calls and Brooklyn cheers filled the room. I shook my head, and then a little light went on, and I decided to bring him up short.

“Did you remember to ask Courtney to the Homecoming Dance, smart guy?” I asked him.

He turned around and the blood drained from his face as he stared at me in horror.

“What?” he whispered.

I just shook my head sadly. Courtney had been his girlfriend for a year and this kept happening.

“You always forget to ask her, and she always ends up asking you. That’s going to get you in trouble someday, smart guy. She’s even running for the Homecoming Queen this year. You’re such a freaking super-genius.”

For a few seconds all he could do was stare at me with his mouth hanging open. When the initial shock wore off, he took on a look of supreme confidence.

“I’ll ask her when she gets out of volleyball practice. Look, this Homecoming parade needs a knight-eating dragon. I think we’re just the guys to provide it.”

“What do you plan to wear on your float, Shultz,” our sponsor asked.

I imagined all of us wearing suits of armor. During our sophomore year, I had made a robot costume out of a couple of cardboard boxes, lots of aluminum foil and some of the big, old, Christmas lights. I would have won the Halloween costume contest if I hadn’t forgotten my extension cord at home. Randy won the contest by dressing like a box of cigarettes.

“Oh,” Sieg said, grinning and backing away, “we’ll just wear our lab coats. You can’t go against tradition, you know.”

* * *

We were standing in front of Mr. Harrison’s room after the Science Club meeting. Sieg had assigned projects to our fellow members and decided to meet at Malcolm's house for the actual build.

"Sieg!" Courtney's voice said from behind us. Sieg and I both stiffened at the sound of her voice. It was amazing how much menace could be stuffed into a nice, feminine contralto.

As one we pivoted to face her. She stood next to the school's trophy case with her arms full of books and one foot tapping impatiently. The school was almost deserted. You could hear the sounds of squeaking sneakers coming from the gym and the occasionally slamming door. The janitor was making his rounds, and I could smell his disinfectant and paint remover.

"What are we going to do now?" I whispered to Sieg even as we slowly walked toward Courtney.

"Shut up, you idiot," he replied. "Don't make eye contact."

His face suddenly melted into the same idiotic, pleased expression it carried every time he was near Courtney. It had to be the way she smelled. I didn't know what kind of cologne or perfume she wore, but it was a heady hormone-carbonating mixture.

"Darling," he said to her, "what a surprise! I thought you had volleyball practice today."

"I did," she said, "but after what happened at the Homecoming meeting, I'm not in the mood for volleyball right now."

"Then what can I do for you?"

I winced at the amount of smarm in his voice. There were definitely times when he managed to ooze insincere charm, mostly when he was in trouble with Courtney or his mother.

"You could start by carrying my books," she replied.

She handed them over and Sieg had to juggle for a

second. To his credit he didn't try to hand them off to me. I had already made it understood that Courtney, best friend or not, was his girlfriend and it was his job to do those little errands boys do for girls all the time. I convinced him of this when he once tossed her books to me and I stepped aside and let them hit the floor. He never tried it again. I'll admit, Courtney was my other best friend. The three of us were like characters out of a Dumas book, but I wasn't going to carry books for her once she started dating Sieg.

"You know they were counting the votes for the Homecoming Queen today?" she asked after Sieg finally got himself balanced.

"I heard something about it," I said, "Kenny came by and said something about Patsy winning."

The temperature of our immediate area dropped several degrees and Courtney tossed her hair to one side.

"By winning it," she grated, "you mean she had fewer votes and then managed to con the Committee into going with the so-called 'pretty' girl instead of the 'athletic' one."

I had to admit *athletic* was a good description of Courtney. I wasn't romantically entangled with her, so I could see her objectively, or as objectively as any teenager could see a member of the opposite sex. She had long dark hair with red highlights, a trim body with narrow hips and small breasts, and as I said earlier, she smelled wonderful. In the back of my mind, I damned Sieg. With effort I kept my face under control.

Then again, if I or anyone else for that matter tried to get frisky with her without permission, she could break us in half. Mr. James had been a Marine and now worked as the foreman of a road crew for the state. He'd always wanted a boy, but Courtney was, like me, an only child. In consequence, Courtney could probably kill with her bare hands, slam-dunk a basketball over my head and had a 'winner takes all' attitude when it came to games like Risk and Monopoly. I could never figure out what she saw in my short, baby-fat-carrying, partner in crime. Maybe he made her laugh.

Sieg laughed and pointed a thumb back at me.

"If they wanted pretty," he said, "then they should have nominated Danny."

"If I could reach you, Sieg," I said genially, "I would hurt you. That doesn't seem fair, Court. If you got more votes..."

"There's some stupid clause in the Homecoming rules," she said, "that lets the Committee pick a winner from the top three candidates. I checked with Mrs. Garvey and she told me the rule was made when some guy managed to get elected Queen back in the '70s."

I blinked. Neither Mom nor Uncle Ray had told me that story and both of them had attended Mohawk High in the '70s."

"So," she said with a pout, "I'm just a bit put out with the world right now."

We'd reached the stairs and I stopped because Sieg had stopped. Courtney and I turned around and saw him standing behind us, one hand on the water fountain, with his lips moving soundlessly and his eyes staring at the ceiling. Slowly he lowered his eyes and blinked.

"I guess I'm going to break tradition again," he said.

Court and I exchanged alarmed looks. The last time Sieg had that light in his eyes, he "borrowed" his mother's car and drove all the way to Denver to complain to the Denver Post about a story they had printed about Mohawk High winning the State volleyball tournament. When he had that look, he was capable of anything.

"What are you going to do?" Courtney asked.

"Like I said," he replied, "I'm going to make a break with tradition. As president of a sponsored school club, I have a seat on the Student Council. That ought to cut through an ocean of red-tape."

"So?" I asked.

"So, the Student Council can ask Mrs. Garvey to review the decision. I'll go to the meeting tomorrow afternoon and persuade them to take steps."

"It seems like a good idea," I said. "Do you need any moral support?"

"Nah, it'll be hard enough without everyone having to wash the smell of 'nerd' out of their hair. I'll be a big enough nuisance."

"That wasn't nice, Sieg," Courtney said, "Danny is the club secretary. He should be there."

"He's the comic relief. Forget it."

"Oh, come on," I said. "Besides, if you don't let me come with you, I'll just go by myself and stare at you. I know you hate that when you're trying to speak in public."

"All right," he said, "come along if you want to. You'll be bored though."

"Not around you, Sieg," I replied.

TWO

The Student Council met in the conference room next to the principal's office. I'd never gone to a meeting, so I was surprised how cramped the space was. A single row of chairs lined one wall and another row sat behind the table. Sieg and I were a bit early, and I took a spot near the door, in case we were going to have to flee for our lives.

"I still don't know why you had to come with me," Sieg said.

"Trust me," I replied. "It'll be helpful to have a friendly face in the room. I can practically guarantee I'll be the only friend you'll have in here."

With a sigh and a shrug, I got comfortable and waited for the circus to begin. The rest of the Council arrived in little groups, with John Dodge, the president, entering last. Mary Beth Tiernan, the vice-president, looked surprised to see us when she entered. Then she smiled at me, and I felt warm all over. I wanted to ask her out on a date since forever but I couldn't get up the courage.

I'd never gotten along with most of the Student Council members. Dodge was a pretentious twit who made Randy look humble. Today he was wearing a maroon polo shirt with blindingly white jeans and sneakers. You could almost see an aura of pure smug glowing around him as he took his seat. I should have seen that as a warning.

Everyone else, including Mary Beth, had made a double-take when they found Sieg sitting at the end of the table, calmly reviewing his notes. He had disappeared into the principal's office all during lunch and came out chortling, which is even less attractive than it sounds. He refused to tell me what he found, and I gave up asking about five minutes before the meeting began.

"What are you doing here, Shultz?" Dodge asked with a sneer.

"I can be here," Sieg replied with a sneer of his own. "I am a member of the Student Council."

"That's well and good," Dodge said, "but I have to ask, specifically why are you here? I'm pretty sure that no other club president has ever decided to join our deliberations."

"Candy Wallace," Sieg said, "she was president of the Sewing Club back in 1976. She got the Student Council to ask the principal to keep the club even though they didn't meet membership requirements."

"Ah, I see you've been studying up," Dodge said. "However, I don't think there's much for us to discuss."

"I want to ask for a review of the Homecoming Queen decision."

Dodge looked down for a moment and then looked up with a slow smile. I felt sick and could see what was going to happen from a mile away. I remembered something I'd heard some of the other kids talking about earlier in the day.

"Very well, Mr. Shultz," Dodge said, "we'll add this to the agenda. However, as President, I have some new business of my own to add. I move to revoke the Science Club's charter and have its officers removed."

"On what grounds?" Sieg asked standing up.

"On the grounds that your little club is obsolescent and adds nothing to the daily life of the student body."

Sieg shot a panicked look at me. Unfortunately, not only was Dodge's maneuver legal, it would mean Sieg would no longer be a member of the Student Council and could only petition it at a future meeting. We were sunk.

Dodge knew his vote. His motion passed five to one, Sieg's being the only dissenting vote. Dodge turned toward him and waved toward the door.

"I'm sorry but since you are not a member of the Student Council, you'll have to petition us at our next meeting. I'm sorry, we're very busy right now, and you'll have to come back then. We'll be sure to put your petition at the top of our agenda, even if only to reject it."

Sieg stood up slowly and looked down the line. Mary Beth refused to meet my gaze and was the only member to have the grace to look guilty. The rest of the swine were smiling at us as if they'd just eaten a canary.

"Dodge," Sieg said, "as I live and breathe, I'm going to make sure you regret this."

"Everyone needs a hobby, Shultz," he said with a little wave.

I followed Sieg out of the room.

"You didn't know that Dodge is Patsy's boyfriend, did you?" I asked him.

"No. If I had, I would have tried something else."

"I've got an idea," I said and caught his arm at the

front door, steering him toward the principal's office.

"Let's go talk to Mrs. Garvey," I said. "Maybe she'll overturn this."

Mrs. Garvey had been the principal of Mohawk High for only a few years. Her office was decorated in institutional modern. Unadorned file cabinets, torturously uncomfortable plastic chairs, and a dull, beige-colored, steel desk were the only fixtures. She looked up as I knocked on the doorframe.

"Hello, boys," she said. "What can I do for you?"

"We've got a little problem," I said. "The Student Council just took away the Science Club's charter."

"I'm sorry, boys," she said with her hands folded. "I've always made it my policy not to interfere with the Student Council as long as their decisions were within school policy. Unfortunately, this one is. To tell you the truth, I really haven't seen a purpose to the Science Club since I came to Mohawk High. You hardly ever participate in school functions beyond the Parade, and frankly I think we could use your help on other things. If you're technologically adept, the A-V Club is always looking for members, and maybe you'd fit in a bit better. I don't think it's a good idea to encourage the anti-social streak running through the Science Club."

"That's not exactly fair, Ma'am," Sieg said.

"That's life, Mr. Shultz," she informed him. "This is as good a time as any to learn that."

Sieg's eyes widened. "What if we were to get an outside sponsor for our float? Would we be allowed to participate then?"

"I guess so. Where will you find a sponsor this late in the game?"

"I'll worry about that."

She narrowed her eyes and stared at Sieg. He just

looked back blankly.

"I'll tell you what," she said. "If you boys can prove to me that your club is worth saving, proving it by winning the 'Best in Show' award, I'll consider reversing the Student Council's decision."

As we left her office, Sieg was still so angry I could see steam rising from his ears. Our compatriots were standing around in a knot under the big elm tree on the front lawn. They followed us over to the bike racks and stood there as Sieg and I unlocked our bikes.

"Is it true?" Randy asked.

"Did they?" Malcolm asked.

I held up my hands to stop the questions.

"What have you guys heard?" I asked.

"We heard the Student Council was going to yank our charter," Malcolm said. "Karen told me Dodge was bragging about it at lunch."

Now I was pissed off. Dodge had planned this from the start. I knew neither he nor the bunch he hung around cared much for the Science Club. We were outcasts. We were the guys too socially inept or too smart to play their games. I was surprised, though, at the amount of venom he had applied in his planning. I was beginning to wonder if the whole thing between Patsy and Courtney had been a set up.

"Yeah, they took the charter," Sieg said. "They want us to petition for reinstatement at the next meeting."

"That'll be after Homecoming," Randy said.

"I know," Sieg replied.

"We've already got a truck and the stuff to build the body," Randy said. "What are we going to do?"

"Keep on building the float. I'm working on an idea," Sieg said.

"Another idea like the one that got our Club

wrecked?" Orville asked. "No thank you."

Randy gave him a shove in the back. "Shut up, kid! If Sieg has a plan, then maybe we have a chance."

"I thought you didn't like him," Orville said.

"I don't," Randy said with a smile. "I'm just not dumb enough to bet against him."

Sieg wanted to say something but shook his head. We pulled our bikes from the rack and started walking them toward the street.

"Hey!" Randy called after us. "What are we going to do, Sieg?"

"Build that damned dragon, Randall! I told you I have an idea."

* * *

My Dad had been the middle of three brothers. All of them, and I for that matter, had the same brownish blonde hair, the wide Prussian face, the dark blue eyes and the flashing smile. If I had a best friend besides Sieg and Courtney, it would be my Uncle Ray.

Ray was the youngest, the baby of the family. He had been old enough to be drafted during the Vietnam War. He'd gone in as a medic and came back from Da-Nang as a different man. I didn't know if he had flashbacks or screamed in his sleep or had any of the other problems that plagued Vietnam vets. I did know he was a member of both the VFW and the American Legion and went to meetings religiously. He marched in the Veteran's Day parade every year.

However, for someone who had been born a millionaire, he rarely cared about wealth. He lived in a tiny, white, frame house standing in the shade of the willows along Mohawk Creek. His location was perfect for a landscaping company, being in a little oasis near downtown Mohawk and just below School Hill with all of its mansions, big gardens and huge lawns. He ran all three of his companies out of his garage, which was larger than the house. From there he drank beer, read pin-up magazines and basically ignored the world outside Mohawk.

One time, when we were mowing the Millholland lawn, I complained about something President Reagan had done. Ray took a long drag, blew out the smoke and waved the cigar at the three-and-quarter acres of grass we were mowing.

"What does any of that have to do with what we're doing?" he asked.

This afternoon we found him sitting on his front porch wearing a stained tee-shirt and tattered blue jeans.

"Why don't you wear work shirts, or at least buy some new jeans?" I asked him as I parked my bike next to his pickup.

"I'm just doing my best to keep the property taxes low," he said, slowly smiling. "You boys remember to park those contraptions next to my truck, not behind it."

The two of us nodded. We had learned that lesson right after my tenth birthday. You wouldn't believe the amount of damage an ancient Ford Apache can do to a bike when it rolls over it. The truck itself was pale blue with giant rust spots and hand-painted signs advertising Ray's businesses on the doors. I had a warm feeling for that truck, since it was the vehicle I learned how to drive in, about an hour after Ray had backed over my bike when I was ten.

As we walked up to him, Ray took a long drink from his beer and set it down on the porch next to him. Then he took a long drag from his cigar and blew a stream of smoke at us.

"What brings you boys down to me today?" Ray asked. "I've got nothing on the schedule until Saturday, if you're looking for work."

"Ray," Sieg said, "we come on bended knee to ask a huge favor from you."

Ray groaned. One of his favorite aphorisms was "A favor is nothing more than money out of your pocket." He was about to say no and send us packing when Sieg held up a placating hand. I think Ray was generally amused by Sieg, as he would let him get away with stuff even I couldn't do. Sieg changed his expression to a lost puppy-dog look that didn't work on Courtney and wasn't going to work on Ray.

"This won't cost you a thing," Sieg said, "and it'll be good for business."

"I've been told that before, Kiddo," Ray said. He blew a smoke ring at us.

He muttered something I didn't catch and then looked at his cigar. Finding the cigar had gone out, he let out a curse and tossed the stub into a sand-filled coffee can. He then picked up his beer and emptied it.

"All right," he said, "I'm fortified. Shoot."

"You know how it's autumn?" Sieg asked.

"Get on with it, Sieg," Ray said. He fumbled around and finally pulled another cigar stub from a back pocket.

"It seems," Sieg began again, "the president of the Student Council is dating a certain girl. Because of this, this girl was chosen—not elected—for Homecoming Queen."

"I think they're doing more than dating," I added.

Sieg shot me a quelling look, a look that I ignored. Ray laughed loudly.

"That's something I've heard before," he said. "If I'm not mistaken, that's how both of you came about. It's not exactly something new."

I stood there and blinked in surprise. No one had ever told me that story before. Then again, you'd think Mom and Dad would be pretty reluctant to tell me. Ray, of course, had no such inhibitions, and I was about to ask for more information when Sieg continued his story.

"Courtney was the elected Homecoming Queen. She was cheated out of it by Patsy and her boyfriend."

"Now if that don't beat all," Ray said. "You're not letting them get away with it, are you?"

"It's a bit complicated," Sieg replied.

"Kiddo, it's always complicated. I'd ask some snot-nosed looie about when I was going home and he'd tell me it was complicated. Now, I'm going to ask you one more time. Are you going to let them bastards get away with cheating your woman?"

"There's not a lot we can do," Sieg explained, "since Mrs. Garvey won't overturn the decision without a petition from the Student Council, and they won't petition because John Dodge owns their asses. He managed to pull our Club's charter, and now we don't have official standing for the parade."

"What's the parade got to do with it?" Ray asked.

"If we won 'Best in Show,'" Sieg said, "it would be a punch in Dodge's nose, since the principal would give us back our charter."

"Okay, so what do you want from me?"

"We want you to sponsor, with just your name and signature, the float we're building. That way we can get into the parade which is half the battle."

Ray reached into his cooler for another beer and then put his cigar back in his mouth. Sieg and I managed to step upwind before the potent fumes got to us.

"Is that all you need?" Ray asked. "All you need is

my permission to use Ray's Landscaping as a sponsor for this float?"

"Actually," Sieg said, "there's something else."

"Ah," Ray said, "there is a catch. What else do you need?"

"Do you still have that old Weeble weed-sprayer?"

Ray almost lost his cigar in his confusion. He put it down in the coffee-can.

"That piece of crap?" he asked. "Yeah, it's probably hanging in the garage. Why do you want it?"

"I have a plan," Sieg said, "and it's a major part of my plan."

"I'm hoping this plan is better than that damned robotic lawnmower of Danny's," Ray said with a laugh.

"Hey!" I said. "We fixed Mrs. Farris's begonias!"

"Only because you had turned them into begone-yas," Ray said. "So anyway, what you are giving me is free advertising for the use of my name and a piece of shit weed-sprayer that I don't use anymore?"

"That's it," Sieg said.

"You drive a hard bargain, Kiddo," he said. "Where do I sign?"

* * *

"What did you want that thing for, Sieg?" I asked.

We were riding up Main Street towards home. Sieg had the weed-sprayer strapped to his back and I had the hoses wrapped around me like a bandoleer. I had to veer around an old man who stepped out from the doorway to the Mohawk Hardware Company and then almost collided with Sieg when he stopped for the light at Main and Mohawk Avenue. He was smiling to himself, and as he looked at me, his eyes grew wide as if he was surprised at the question.

"There's only one thing our dragon is missing," he said. He looked at the light and reached over and started punching the crossing button over and over.

"What's that?" I asked him. "I thought our design was complete. I think I can even get the neck and tail to move, and with Randy's stereo speakers, the roar ought to be spectacular."

He stopped pushing the crossing button and turned to me.

"What are the most salient features of dragons, Danny?"

"What do you mean?" I asked.

"What makes a dragon a dragon?"

I thought about it for a moment as we watched the passing traffic.

"Well," I said finally, "they fly, eat cows and unwary knights and they—oh...oh, no!"

"They breathe fire," Sieg said finishing my sentence for me.

"No," I said. "Our dragon is not going to breathe fire! We'll get in trouble!"

"Danny," he said staring across the street, "we need something unbelievably spectacular for this parade. We need to show everyone in this town what we're capable of."

The light changed and he took off across the street. I pedaled like a demon to keep up as he sprinted around planters, pedestrians and sidewalk signs. We left downtown behind us, and I finally caught up to him after he made the corner at Maple and started up the hill. He could beat me on a flat track any day of the week but when we hit a hill, I usually took charge. I could almost make my bike climb a tree.

He was halfway up the first block of the hill, his

pedaling was slowing and his face was turning a dozen different shades of red and purple. I had to give him credit, he had taken off so fast that even I was gasping for breath now that I had caught up with him.

"Give it up, smart boy," I hissed through my teeth.

"Oh, to hell with it," he gasped. He stopped the bike and got off while holding the brakes with a death grip. We were in front of the Gundersons, and Mr. Gunderson was watering his lawn. He waved at us as I got off my bike and the two of us started staggering up the hill toward Sieg's driveway.

We stopped at the end of the driveway for a few seconds to catch our breath. I had to admit he had definitely come a long way from the days when I would race past him and up the hill in third gear.

"So," I said, gasping, "why do we need something spectacular? Just getting into the parade will stick it to Dodge and the rest of the Student Council."

"It's bigger than that," he replied. "You heard Mrs. Garvey. They think the Science Club is obsolete. Do you really want to spend the rest of your senior year schlepping AV stuff around? If all we ever do is win 'Best in Show,' we'll have proven there's still a place for our club at Mohawk High. We're doing this for pride and for all the nerdy kids who'll follow in our footsteps."

"So we're doing this for some unknown future kid who likes science? Is that what's driving this?" I asked him.

"I don't like being treated like this, Danny," he said seriously. "We deserve more respect and we're going to get it."

"You're taking this personally, Sieg."

"You better believe it. We have something to prove," he said.

I sighed. If there was one thing you couldn't do with Sieg, it was smack his ego around. I had to admit I was pretty pissed off, too. If they had just held a vote at the council meeting, Dodge would have won anyway. He controlled everyone there and if they had defeated us there, within the system, they would have gotten away with it. Dodge just had to be the big-shot and rub our noses in it. He was going to pay for his *hubris*.

We wheeled our bikes down the driveway, past his house and into the garage.

"Okay," I said, "what's with the damn weed-sprayer? I don't understand why we need it."

Sieg put the sprayer on the workbench while I hung the hoses up with their garden cousins.

"Ray might know about this, I didn't ask," Sieg said as he picked up an oilcan and started working on the tanks. "I was reading an old book on Vietnam War weapons. I found out what a wonderful little gadget this is." He picked up a wrench and started removing a fixture from one of the tanks. "The Weeble Corporation made a bundle back in the '60s when they built the M-227 flamethrower for the Army. After the Fall of Saigon, they found they had plenty of flamethrowers but no one to set on fire, so they converted them into Green Thumb Weed-sprayers."

He held up Ray's Green Thumb Weed-sprayer. I looked at it for a moment as dawn appeared in my mind. I was dumbfounded.

"Oh," I said slowly. "Oh, my."

"All we have to do is come up with an igniter," he said, "and something a little less destructive than napalm. We want a small flame, not a line of burning petroleum. Butane or propane will probably work. We'll have a fire breathing dragon and that'll get everyone's attention."

"Yeah," I said, "I guess that would do it."

THREE

Saturday, October 5, 1985, dawned bright, clear and warm. It was the big day and the members of the Science Club were ready. We gathered together at Malcolm's and he drove the truck carrying our masterpiece and the rest of us riding on the back.

I thought our effort was pretty impressive. A seven foot long Fairview knight of cardboard and aluminum foil lay under one of the dragon's feet. The dragon's other foot rested on the roof of the truck, giving our creation the illusion that it was about to take flight.

The dragon was a bright, enameled red that glinted in the early autumn sun. It had a pair of canvas wings that we would unfurl for the judging and later during the parade. I'd spent an entire weekend building the structure of the neck that stuck out a full six feet ahead of the truck's grill. With the motors and controls I'd installed, the neck could go up and down and left and right. The tail stretched a similar distance from the rear and could also move from side to side. Sieg and I were at the neck controls and Randy was running the tail. Orville had installed the lights behind the eyes and we were running a continuous-loop tape of the roar.

The night before the parade, Sieg and I had snuck into Malcolm's backyard and installed the flamethrower. We had tested the equipment the day before; the butane and oxygen mixture working just fine to produce a reasonable flame. The gas was very expensive but we got a good three foot flame out of the deal and thought it was worth it.

"Should we tell the guys?" I asked Sieg as we crouched over our creation.

"Nah," he replied. "I want to make it a surprise for everyone."

Thinking about it later, I think Sieg just didn't want them to physically restrain him from using it.

In a final fit of pettiness, the Homecoming Committee barred Courtney from even being a member of the Homecoming Queen's Court, citing "a difference of feeling." We thought it was a bunch of crap, and Courtney decided to watch the parade from the second floor of the Imperial Hotel, where she worked on the weekends.

When we rolled into the school parking lot, Dodge was leaning against the convertible carrying the Queen and her Court. He and Patsy were lip-locked, and I thought he was going to bite her tongue when he saw us roll through the gate. He came running over as Malcolm parked us in an open spot.

"I thought we banned this float from the parade," he yelled.

"The Science Club was disbanded," Sieg said, drawing himself up and glaring down at Dodge. "This float is the entry from Rays Landscaping Service."

"You're not going to be in the parade," Dodge said,

"if it's not a student float."

"You need to go back and re-read the parade rules," Sieg said. "They clearly state any student group with an outside sponsor is permitted entry as if they were a club or regular organization. I've already submitted the paperwork to Mrs. Garvey, and now you're stuck with us."

"It won't matter. You'll be bringing up the rear."

Sieg started laughing.

"You know," he said, "as well as I do that position in the parade is determined by the judges. We're going to be following your girlfriend down the route, right on her bumper."

I thought Dodge's head would explode with that. His face turned bright red, and he turned on his heel.

"We'll see about that," he shouted over his shoulder. Patsy came over to him and they were whispering together. If looks could kill, Sieg and the rest of us would have been disintegrated.

"He's going to make it impossible to get the club charter back," I whispered in Sieg's ear.

"After this parade, we'll be in clover," he whispered back. "Dodge won't stand a chance. We have to have faith in ourselves."

He turned to the rest of the club and raised his hands.

"All right, guys! Let's suit up."

We all started putting on our lab coats and everything was just fine and dandy until I pulled mine from my backpack and put it on. The entire club stopped what they were doing and stared at me in horror.

"What the hell did you do to your lab coat, Danny?" Sieg asked in a croak.

"Uh, well," I said, "you remember when I was in

Joseph and the Technicolor Dreamcoat last year? This was the Dreamcoat."

Sieg shook his head and looked as if he couldn't decide whether to strangle me or just start crying.

"You tie-dyed your lab coat," he said with a tragic catch in his voice.

"I thought it looked pretty cool," I replied.

"Danny," he said, "when this is said and done, you and I are going to have a very long talk."

"Okay," I said. "Whatever turns your crank."

Sieg turned to the rest of our compatriots. "All right, guys, take your positions. Danny, should we open the wings now?"

I eyeballed the parking lot gate carefully. I wasn't sure of the width between the posts so I shook my head.

"We'll have to unfurl them for the judging," I said, "but we'll have to roll them back up to get out. Malcolm, after we hit the street, you're going to have to stick to the middle of the road. As it is, I think we're going to be clipping the lampposts."

"I'll be careful," Malcolm said. "I guess we should have taken a few measurements before construction."

"Build first," Sieg said, "modify later."

Randy and Orville unfurled the wings and we heard an appreciative moan from the crowd. I climbed on board and turned the head so it faced Dodge and Patsy and hit the button for sound. The roar was almost as gratifying as the look on their faces.

"You know what, Mr. Shultz?" a voice said from behind us. Turning around we found Mr. Harrison standing at the edge of the float looking up at us. "I think you were absolutely right. This is the best float in the parade."

"Well, we hope so," Sieg said.

"It better be," Mr. Harrison said, "because I just nominated it for 'Best in Show.'"

"Won't they throw your vote out?" I asked.

"Why would they do that?" he replied with an innocent look, "I have no connection with Ray's Landscaping Service."

He touched the side of his nose and walked off. Sieg looked at me and I found myself grinning with him. For the next hour the rest of the judges came by. A few stopped and asked questions about various details. My lab coat was the subject of more than its share of attention, but I ignored it. Finally, the crowd that gathered around us parted and Mrs. Garvey walked up.

"Boys," she said, "I have to admit your entry in this year's parade is imaginative. This is the best float I've ever seen, and I love what Daniel has done with his lab coat."

I turned and stuck my tongue out at Sieg. Mrs. Garvey ignored us as she reached out and stuck a big blue ribbon on the door of the truck.

"I guess we're going to have a discussion on Monday morning, boys, she said. "The Science Club may not be as out-of-date as I thought. Congratulations, boys, you've won 'Best in Show.'"

As she walked off to catch her ride downtown, I found myself slowly sitting down on the edge of the float. Everyone around us was cheering and dancing around. I looked over and saw the rest of the club looking back just as stunned as I was. Orville walked over to Sieg and shook his hand.

"You were right," he said, "we're going to get the club back!"

"I hope so," Sieg said.

A few minutes later we were in position and the

signal was made. A couple of teachers motioned for us to fall into line right behind the car carrying the Homecoming Court. With a start, I realized that I recognized the car. It usually sat on a rack in the front of Big Ed's used car lot. He'd bought it on a whim and hadn't been able to unload it since. Over the summer, Sieg and I had washed it daily and silently cursed it for all the nooks and crannies we had to scrub out.

"At least Uncle Ed's finally getting some use out of that damned car," I said to Sieg.

"Yeah," he said, "and we didn't have to wash it this time."

We rolled out onto Highway 340, which went down the hill and turned into Main Street at the bottom. Sieg and I unfurled the wings and set them up. Sure enough, we were just barely clearing the lampposts.

Sieg ducked around and took up his position on the far side of the dragon. I opened a panel in my side of the dragon and hit the sound button. As the dragon began to roar I found myself with a warm feeling all over.

"How is the neck control working?" Sieg shouted over to me.

I swung the head back and forth and then up and down.

"We're good," I said with thumbs up. "Everything is copacetic."

"Good!"

"When are we going to show our surprise?" I asked him.

"Not until downtown," he replied. "I want to surprise everyone."

We rolled down School Hill and into downtown Mohawk. Thanks to the dragon, people were coming out onto the sidewalks to see what was making all the noise.

It was gratifying to watch them cheering and pointing at us. We were the hit of the parade.

After crossing the bridge near Ray's house, we turned onto Mohawk Avenue. There were hundreds of people crowding the sidewalks and I saw the huge crowd up at City Hall. Looking up, I saw Courtney standing in the window of the Imperial Hotel waving at us. We waved back, and Sieg hit me on the shoulder.

"Okay, now!" he said.

I raised the dragon's neck and he pulled the trigger on his side. What happened next was not what we expected. Instead of the nice little three-foot flame that we had gotten in our experiments, a five-foot fire ball erupted from the dragon's mouth and sailed out in front of us. Someone screamed as another fireball soared out.

"Sieg, stop it!"

"I'm trying to," he yelled back, "but the trigger's stuck."

Ahead of us, Patsy's hair caught fire. She always used too much hairspray, and it went up like a torch. We could hear her screams as she jumped out of the car and into the Fire Department. Fortunately someone there quickly put her out.

I guess Malcolm panicked about this time and tried to slam on the brakes. They weren't as good as we thought because the truck lurched and then kept going but only after the entire Science Club found itself on the ground.

Sieg and I rolled to our feet and took off after the truck. Malcolm bailed out and the truck was rolling on its own. The dragon continued to whip its head around, spouting flame. The truck finally came to a rest against the now evacuated bleachers in front of the courthouse.

The world became a nightmarish blur of flames and

people screaming. Downtown Mohawk had been built during the Gold Rush and was one of the few mining towns to not suffer a devastating fire during its heyday. Its luck ran out as the town went up like a tinderbox built of mostly very dry, very old wood.

The dragon itself was now ablaze as the head whipped around and around. Fireballs were spewed everywhere and the float was burning merrily like a Viking Funeral. Later I would give serious thought to the idea that Sieg and I should have jumped into the blazing ruins as some kind of funeral pyre.

Before the afternoon ended, at least half a dozen fire departments were called in to fight the fire. By then, Sieg and I were already cooling our heels at the Mohawk County Sheriff's office.

FOUR

"I told you it was going to be a dump," Sieg said. He was standing next to me in a cloud of dust, staring out of those beady, little, blue eyes behind their Coke-bottle-bottom glasses. I began to wonder if there was any way for the two of us to escape from this prison we had been exiled to.

The Lake Weir Resort stood before us. It was a gigantic, rambling, three-story Victorian monster standing on the shores of a long lake. A tower stood over the center of the building, while two wings stretched north and south. At one time the entire building had been painted some long-lost shade of white, but now weather and time had taken their toll. The paint was cracked and peeling off in giant scabs. There were places where it had been repainted in odd colors, and the missing pieces of the front porch railing gave it the impression of a giant, gap-toothed, flower child lurching out of the Sixties. Just beyond it, on the lakeshore, stood a forlorn-looking boathouse and a dock that had seen better days.

Behind us, Uncle Ray was busy tossing, or I should say throwing, our bags out of the back of his truck. Done and without a single word, he slammed the tailgate, climbed into the driver's seat and roared out of the parking lot in a cloud of dust leaving us in a coughing fit. Sieg caught his breath and shook his head.

"He's still pissed off at us," he observed.

"I can't blame him," I said. "Because of us he lost his home, his business and a complete cherry run of *Playboy*."

"Hey, I'm a bit miffed about the *Playboys*, too. You can't imagine some of the things I've learned over the years by reading them during rainy days. I just hoped he'd get some kind of perspective. With all the landscape work needed during the Mohawk reconstruction right now, he'll make a mint and be able to replace his entire collection."

"Sieg," I said, "the only reason you and I are even alive right now is because everyone got some *perspective* and didn't lynch us on the spot when they had the chance."

He paused while he considered this and then nodded. "Good point. Shall we go on, Macduff?" he asked bowing before me.

"Whenever you're ready, Macbeth," I replied bowing back.

* * *

The fire's aftermath had become a long ordeal stretching through our senior year. First had been interview after interview as the authorities tried to understand exactly why we had done what we had. Then came the trial, which was mercifully short. Sieg tried to take all the blame himself but I stopped him, and we both ended up pleading guilty. The judge was a kindly man, mostly because he hadn't lost any property in the fire and perhaps because he was secretly amused by the story of the Mohawk Dragon. He put us on probation and suspended our driver's licenses for six months.

Then Sieg received a registered letter from Harvard. I received a similar one from Miskatonic. We were informed that, while we had been previously accepted by both universities, they would no longer allow us to join their institutions. No other college that we applied to would touch us with a ten-foot pole, or even a fifty-foot one. Educationally, we were at a dead end.

We'd been allowed to finish our senior year at Mohawk High. However, while the Science Club had been given a new charter, neither of us were permitted to rejoin our comrades-in-arms. Randy became the new club president, something he managed to tell Sieg at least once a day until graduation.

Another blow for Sieg came after Prom. For some reason, Courtney broke up with him, and neither would talk to me about it. Courtney refused to say anything at all, preferring to walk away rapidly whenever I approached. I gave up chasing after the third time it happened.

Neither of us could find an after-school job to save our lives. Even Ray wasn't speaking to us. Everyone else treated us like pariahs. We tried to go back to work at Big Ed's Used Cars, but in protest customers quit coming, and Ed didn't have a choice but to let us go. After that I spent most of my time in my room feeling sorry for myself.

Finally, about a week before the graduation ceremony that we were banned from, Big Ed paid me a visit. True to his nickname, he was big, like the Nebraska linebacker he had once been, and the years had been relatively kind to him, as nothing had gone slack. I could still chin myself on one of Ed's upraised arms. Since he and his wife, Vera, didn't have any kids, Sieg and I sort of ended up their *de facto* children.

He arrived at the house and pulled me out into the garage. There, surrounded by my Dad's power tools and a Pontiac under an old sheet, he told me about an opportunity he had come upon.

"Danny, you have to think about the future," he said

"I know, Uncle Ed, but what kind of future can I have when I can't even get started. After graduation, there's nothing for me to do. I can't go to school. I can't get a job. I don't know what I'll do."

"You'll come work for me."

"We tried that, remember? No one wants to buy a car from the lot that employs the kid who burned down his own town."

"You've got to quit thinking like that." he said. "Unfortunately, you're right about the car lot. So instead, I want you to work for me at the Lake Weir Resort."

"Where?"

"Lake Weir Resort. I won it in a card game." He grinned. "Any idiot can bluff and make people think they're not bluffing. It takes a real pro to make people think you're bluffing when you're not. My straight beat his three-of-a-kind."

"You won a resort?"

"Yup. It's up past Lake Fork. From what I understand, it's fallen on tough times lately, mostly because of the aforementioned idiot. I think with the experience you've gained by working on the restoration project here in Mohawk, you could make a go at it."

"You can thank Sieg for that, it was his idea."

He nodded. "I have to admit it was a stroke of genius to ask the governor to declare Mohawk a disaster area. If Sieg hadn't come up with that one, I think both of you would be down in Cañon City right now making license plates."

"Yeah, maybe you ought to give Sieg the job up at your resort."

"I did," Big Ed said with a smile. "He's already accepted a position."

"You offered Sieg a job before me?"

"Yes, I did. He's going to take the job if you're going along. He made it clear you're a package deal. Your mom and aunt wanted me to try to keep you at the car lot. They thought that without Sieg, maybe we wouldn't have as much trouble. Sieg convinced me otherwise."

"You went to Sieg first?" I realized that I was pissed off. Sieg was my best friend, but I was family. I didn't know whether to be relieved or angry about the whole deal.

"Are you going to take the job?" Big Ed asked.

I thought about it for a moment. "Why not? It might be fun." I shook his offered hand. "All right, Uncle Ed, you've got yourself a deal."

* * *

Sieg retrieved his bags, and I slung my duffel bag over my shoulder and grabbed my grandfather's old leather suitcase.

"I should never have listened to Ed," he said. "This place looks positively haunted."

We stopped at the bottom of the front stairs and looked up at the resort's crumbling façade.

"Oh, come on," I said. "For one thing, any ghost

willing to harass you would have to be pretty dumb. Besides, did you have a better choice?"

"No," he replied, "I guess I didn't. I'm probably too pretty for prison."

"Sieg," I said with a laugh, "you look like a humanized penguin. I don't know what you've been reading lately, but you are definitely not too pretty for prison. The other convicts would run away from you."

"Oh, like you would know," he said. "You're not so hot looking yourself, bean-pole."

I grinned at that. He was beginning to sound like the Sieg I knew and loved.

"Hey," I said, "I'm not the one who was dumped by his girlfriend."

"That's because you've never attracted a girlfriend."

"Not true, and you know it," I shot back.

While we were busy with our banter, someone came out onto the porch and looked down at us. He was a few years older than us and was almost as tall as I was. He had curly black hair and dark eyes. He wore blue jeans and a black polo-shirt with Lake Weir Resort stitched over the breast.

"So," he said, "are you two going to come on in, or stand there tanning your tonsils?"

"Who the hell are you?" Sieg bristled.

"I'm Mike Orr," he replied, "the head houseman. I'll bet you two are Jael and Shultz, my new minions."

"I ain't nobody's minion, pal," Sieg shot back. "As to your question, yeah, we're the new housemen."

I shook my head slowly and pointed my thumb at Sieg. "Trust me," I said. "You don't want him as a minion."

"Look," Mike said patiently, "just come inside. We've been waiting for you, and Cap has some forms you need to fill out. The new owner is waiting for you, and there's some woman who wants a word with you."

A worried look crossed Sieg's face, and we exchanged a glance.

"That doesn't sound good," he said.

"You don't think it's...?" I asked.

"I don't think so, but you never know."

"Come on guys," Mike said. "How bad could it be?"

* * *

The morning dawned when Mom swung the door open and slowly danced into my room. She swung the tray she carried onto my desk and then shook my shoulder. I was already awake, having not slept a wink, instead thinking about what I was about to do, but I didn't want to worry her.

"Come on, Danny," she sang out. "Your uncle will be here soon."

With a groan I rolled out of bed and swayed to my feet. She had a sympathetic look on her face, even though she acted as if this was the happiest day of her life.

"I made your favorite," she said, indicating the tray, "oatmeal with raisins and toast!"

"Thanks, Mom," I mumbled.

"Oh, come on, dear," she said. "This is the first day of the rest of your life! You have to seize the day! Remember, *carpe diem* and all that jazz!"

"Okay, Mom," I mumbled. Then I sat down at my desk and played with the food for a minute before getting to my feet and stumbling into the shower.

About an hour later, showered, fed and dressed, I finished packing my duffel bag and carried it downstairs. Just as I got there, Ray pulled up in the driveway. Sighing, I hoisted the bag over my shoulder and went out to where he was waiting.

"Where's the other one?" he said, jerking his head to indicate Sieg's house. Ray hadn't spoken more than a dozen words to either of us since the fire, and it was apparent he wasn't going to change that now.

"I'll go get him," I said and started across the lawn.

I dodged through a hole in the shrubbery separating the properties and walked up to Sieg's open back door. I knocked on the screen.

"Come in," Sieg's sister, Melinda, said. She was sixteen and annoyed the hell out of me by being right all the time. I hadn't caught her out on a fact in years, and it unnerved me. I wished I was smarter, but she always seemed to be one step ahead of both her brother and me. Without pausing, I opened the door and gave her a quick noogie on her head as I passed the Shultz's kitchen table. Melinda stuck her tongue out at me and then turned back to make sure little Frederick wasn't throwing his bottle away again. I noticed she was wearing one of those off-the-shoulder sweaters and had her hair up in a big poof that added almost a full foot to her height.

"How are you doing, Squirt?" I asked.

"I'm okay. Sieg's not doing so well, though."

"Oh great, what's going on now?"

"Mom's having one of her little moments."

I shut my eyes and grimaced.

"Yeah," Melinda said as she cleaned spit from the baby's face. "She's in full voice, too. Bring your earmuffs."

"Thanks."

"No problem," she said, keeping Frederick from putting his bottle in his ear.

I wandered upstairs to Sieg's room and found the rest of the Shultz family. Mr. Shultz was standing in the hall, staring at the ceiling in an almost catatonic state.

From inside the room came the roar we all had grown to know over the years.

"You can't be leaving me!" Mrs. Shultz screamed. I stuck my head in the door and pulled it back out almost immediately.

Mrs. Shultz was a big woman. She was taller than Sieg, and normally she wore business suits that she had made herself. She worked as a seamstress and clothes buyer for a department store and was considered one of the best in the country. Why she chose to live in Mohawk was a mystery, one she never cleared up.

Mr. Shultz worked at the First National Bank as a mortgage manager and had been busier than usual since the fire. He told everyone how surprised he was with all the mortgages taken out to improve properties being rebuilt or just on the edge of the burn zone. As a result he was always tired, and even now he looked as if he had climbed out of his grave to be there.

"You ought to go to bed, Mr. S.," I said.

His eyes wandered down from the ceiling and focused on me with difficulty. Then he smiled. I'd always liked Sieg's dad, he would always act as if life was a joke he was sharing.

"What?" he said, "And miss the show?"

We both laughed at that. Then Mrs. Shultz stormed out and we stopped laughing. If you could say someone had a stormy expression, the one on her face was a category five hurricane with a name and a title. It didn't get any better when she saw me standing there.

"You!" she shouted. "This is your entire fault! My poor little Sieg is going to get eaten by bears or crocodiles, and it'll be your fault, you little bastard!"

I didn't get angry, mostly because when you've seen this on a regular basis you sort of become inured to it.

"Hi, Mrs. Shultz," I said with a grin. "Is Sieg ready? Ray's waiting for us."

"Of course he's ready," Mr. Shultz said.

She pushed past her husband and started jabbing me in the chest with her index finger. "You can't take my baby! I won't let you. He's staying here!"

Mr. Shultz slowly stood straight up and turned to face his wife. Normally, you had the impression that he was smaller than she was. When he decided to have a direct confrontation with her, you found out just how tall he really was. He had at least a foot on his wife.

"Agatha, dear," he said in a voice that cut right through her histrionics, "the boy's eighteen and able to make his own choices. He's made up his mind and he's going. You're not going to unmake it for him."

Mrs. Shultz looked up at her husband for a moment and somehow...broke. There was no other word for it. Her face just fell, and suddenly she was pushing past us and into her bedroom. She slammed the door, and we heard her sobbing. Mr. Shultz turned to me.

"Go get Sieg. It's time for you guys to go."

"Right," I nodded.

I went into Sieg's room just as he was closing his suitcase.

"Where's Mom?" he asked.

"She's in her room, crying."

Sieg had the grace to blush and shook his head. "Let's go."

I grabbed the other suitcase, and we went back into the hall. Sieg silently shook his father's hand. Mr. Shultz refused to release his hand until he had pulled him into an embrace. He whispered something into Sieg's ear. Sieg nodded and whispered something back. Then he went to his mother's door and knocked.

"Mom, I'm leaving," he said. "I love you."

The door flew open, and Mrs. Shultz stood there with red eyes and tears still running down her face. Without another word she grabbed Sieg's face and kissed him. Then she closed the door and went back to sobbing.

Downstairs, Melinda was holding Frederick in the kitchen. Sieg stopped and kissed the baby on the forehead.

"Good luck, Kid," he said. "You're the man of the house now."

Melinda threw her free hand around Sieg's neck and pulled him down for a kiss.

"Take care of yourself, Sieg," she said.

"I'll try."

"You'd better," she said as we went on through the back door.

* * *

Mike looked perplexed as we started up the stairs. His natural ebullience took over though and he spread his arms wide as if to take in the entire resort.

"Welcome to the Lake Weir Resort along the shores of lovely Lake Weir. The resort was built in 1889 and is in immaculate condition."

"What do you mean by immaculate condition?" I asked.

"Don't ask me," he replied. "I'm just quoting the brochure. The place is actually a cesspool of filth and vermin just waiting for the final nudge to be given to send it into a heap of collapsed garbage."

"Really?" Sieg asked.

"Nah, I'm just quoting Cap on one of his more depressed days. I have to admit it looks pretty bad, but Todd and I have been fixing the place up. With you two, we ought to be able to get a lot more done. After we're done here, I'm going to take you over to the house so you can find someplace to crash. Then we're going to start training you."

"I thought we'd have a day or two," Sieg whispered in my ear.

"Not a chance," I replied.

I looked at the stairs as we climbed them. The treads looked so damaged that I was sure Sieg was going to fall through one. What was left of the porch rail was so rotten that it was worth your life to lean on it. On impulse, I gave a section a quick shove and watched in horror as it fell away with the sound of breaking balsa wood. The revealed surface showed more worm and termite damage than I thought possible. The deck wasn't in much better shape, having been patched with all kinds of scrap wood, plywood and even a couple of pieces of what looked to be old hardwood flooring. Mike watched me with a slightly amused look on his face. I looked back blankly.

"I guess we're going to have our work cut out for us," I said.

"What was your first clue?" Sieg asked.

* * *

Even if the exterior looked like the Taj Mahal, it couldn't possibly do justice to the interior. Darkly stained paneling covered the walls, while matching timbers and pillars held up the ceiling. Huge, richly upholstered, overstuffed chairs and couches were scattered everywhere. On almost every wall and pillar surface was some kind of hunting trophy, photograph or painting. It was kind of like walking into a genteel museum. Despite the fact they had let the outside go to hell, it was obvious a lot of care had gone into the interior. Sieg was like a kid in a candy store.

"Hey! Look!" he said pointing toward the far end of the lobby.

There was a huge fireplace, and near it stood the largest stuffed polar bear I had ever seen. This time, Mike wasn't as amused.

"Come on you two," he said. "Let's get a move on. I'd like to get this done before lunch today."

The front desk was built into the wall with a polished wood arch holding up the ceiling above it. The front of the counter had a matching arch built into it. Behind the counter was a tall woman that anyone would call beautiful. She had long, auburn hair and wore a dazzling white blouse and a dark blue blazer with the resort's logo over the pocket. As we walked up, she was busy talking on the phone and taking notes in a huge ledger laying on the counter in front of her. Glancing up at us, she merely nodded toward the door behind her. Without a word, Mike went over and knocked.

"Come in," said a muffled voice.

Mike opened the door, and we entered Cap's office for the first time. It was the lobby all over again except in miniature and of a nautical theme. Shelves filled with various naval doodads and ship models were interspersed with a few seascapes. A polished oaken desk dominated the center of the small space. Behind it, in a green-leather upholstered office chair, sat our new boss.

Cap Hayes was probably somewhere in his early to mid-fifties. He had wind-burned skin and pale, almost colorless, eyes. His hair was very short, in a flat-topped cut, and he wore a blue shirt under his blazer with a silver and red striped necktie. He looked over half-rimmed glasses at us as we came in.

Across the desk from him, in one of the matching

office chairs sat Big Ed. Today he was wearing his gray "going to see the banker" suit, the one he used when negotiating loans with car buyers and the bright red power tie he always liked to wear on those occasions. He was sitting in a comfortable position with his legs crossed and a notebook across his knee.

My heart dropped when I saw who was sitting next to him. I had hoped for a moment it would be my mother—I'd feared it was going to be Sieg's—instead it was Helen Shapely. She was a gigantic woman with dark gray hair and bright blue eyes that seemed to bore their way into my brain when she looked at me. She wore a muumuu made of miles of shapeless flowered print. She also wore a badge and held down a desk in the D.A.'s office. She'd been our probation officer ever since the trial, and she smiled when we came through the door. Sieg let out a little groan when he saw who it was. Helen merely smiled.

"Well if it isn't my two favorite delinquents," she said.

* * *

"So what are you going to do, Daniel?" Helen asked me. Besides Mom, only Helen called me "Daniel," as in "Daniel, clean your room" or "Daniel, what are you going to do with your life now that you have completely destroyed it?"

"I'm not sure, yet."

Every Monday after the trial, Sieg would meet with her in her office and a half-hour later I would meet with her. She watched us like a hawk, just waiting for a screw-up. While she hadn't lost a house or something in the fire, she made sure we were as uncomfortable as possible during the meetings.

"You graduate on Friday, Daniel," she continued. "I'm afraid if you do not have a job and a place to live by then, I'm going to recommend to Judge Spears the revocation of your probation."

"Then I would have to go to jail," I said.

"That's correct. I'm sorry but it's the way it works."

"That's not fair! I've done everything you've asked of me. I did the community service, and I've spent most of my free time helping to rebuild the town. I kept my grades up, and in order to stay out of trouble, I've stayed home on the weekends. I even missed the Senior Prom!"

Mom had talked me out of going to the Prom, which pissed me off. She pointed out how much trouble teens usually got into on that night, and after two weeks of fighting, I'd given in. Sieg and Courtney had gone, and they ended up with their relationship in tatters.

"Life isn't fair," Helen said, unmoved. "If you do not have a job and a place to live by Friday, you will be remanded to the Mohawk County Jail for processing and then transferred to the Colorado State Prison in Cañon City. My hands are tied, Daniel."

* * *

Now I had the job and a place to live, and here she was checking up on me. I should have expected her. Before I could say anything, though, Big Ed rumbled and stood up.

"Ah, glad to see you boys made it," he said. "Cap Hayes, this is my nephew, Daniel Jael, and his friend, Siegfried Shultz."

Sieg winced at the use of his full name. Then we shook hands with Cap. He motioned us into another pair of office chairs. He nodded to Mike, who stepped into the lobby, closing the door behind him. Then he turned to us.

"Boys, I understand from Big Ed and Officer Shapely that you're in a bit of a bind right now."

I looked down at the floor. Even in a friendly situation, talking to Cap was a lot like being called into Mrs. Garvey's office.

"Yes sir," I said.

"What happened down in Mohawk has been explained to me," he said. "From this point forward, the two of you will be under my supervision instead of Officer Shapley's. I don't give a rat's ass if it was an accident or not, if you're guilty or not or whatever. I'm taking a chance on the two of you. I hope you can appreciate the opportunity. If either of you screw this us, I'm going to boot both of you back down the hill and into Officer Shapley's waiting arms. Have I made myself clear?"

"Yes sir," Sieg said.

"Now," Cap continued, "the terms of your probation are as follows. You will remain on Lake Weir property at all times unless given leave otherwise, which means I can ground you. You may have to go down to Lake Fork or Weir for supplies now and then. I understand they pulled your driver's licenses when you were convicted so you'll be riding with someone else, probably Todd. With any luck, if you two keep out of trouble, we'll be able to drop the probation by the end of the summer. Are there any questions?"

"No sir," Sieg said, answering for both of us this time.

"Good. Now sign the forms on the marked lines and then I'll send you out to Mike."

We signed on the dotted lines, explaining to the government that yes, we were citizens, and yes, we had a right to work in the country, and yes, we were single, and yes, we had no deductions. Cap looked over the forms and placed them in a manila folder on the corner of his desk.

Thank you, gentlemen," he said. "Is there anything you wish to say to them, Mr. Jael, Officer Shapely?"

I don't know if I'd ever heard anyone, and I mean anyone, call Big Ed, "Mr. Jael" before. Everyone, including his wife and dog, called him "Big Ed." I saw a slight smile flicker on Big Ed's face as he stood up.

"Call me 'Big Ed,' Cap. 'Mr. Jael' is dead twenty years," he said, turning to us. "Boys, I want to thank you. I really need your help at Lake Weir, and I think you'll do just fine."

"I don't know what we can do, Uncle Ed," I said looking down at my hands, "we're just a couple of housemen."

"It's a start," he replied. "Don't forget you're now on the front lines of my latest enterprise. I think you two will do just fine."

We all stood up together, and Helen Shapely shook our hands. "Good luck, boys, and stay out of trouble, or at least as much as you can."

We opened the door and found Mike waiting outside with our bags. He was busy talking to the front desk clerk. He looked up as we came out and grinned.

"I guess you're all done in there," he said.

Sieg nodded. "Yeah."

Mike nodded toward the desk clerk. "This is Lisa Collins, our day clerk. Later on you'll meet Gwen, the night auditor. Lisa, this is Danny Jael and Sieg Shultz, my new housemen."

"Not the Jael and Shultz from...?" she said with a wary look.

"Yep," Mike said, "and now they're all ours."

"I guess this won't be a boring summer then," she

said and shook our hands.

"I hope not," Mike said laughing, "I've got five bucks with Todd on whether they survive the summer or not."

"Oh, that's nice," I said, unimpressed. I reached into my pocket and pulled out a five and placed it on the counter in front of their surprised eyes.

"I'll take a piece of the action," I said. "I'll bet five we both survive the summer and beyond."

"Danny," Sieg said, laying a hand on my arm, "maybe you ought to..."

"No," I said, shaking him off. "If people want to bet against us, I'm going to bet on us. You remember the last time a bunch of people bet against us?"

"Yeah," he said. "Look where we ended up."

"But we still got the Science Club's charter back," I said. "That was what we set out to do and we did it. People who bet against us seem to always lose."

"Just calm down, Danny," Mike said, holding up his hands. "I'll take the money. I'm just not telling you which side Todd or I are on. Does anyone else want a piece of this? Sieg? Lisa?"

Sieg merely smiled and stepped back. Lisa shook her head slowly and smiled a ten-thousand watt smile.

"I don't think so," she said. "I usually lose when I bet, and I wouldn't want to lose this one. I want them both to succeed."

* * *

The back hallways seemed to be abandoned. It felt like we were walking through a graveyard. The air was stuffy and smelled of dirt, grease and dust. Some of the doors still carried old, tarnished brass plates, while more than one looked as if they were standing only through some fluke of gravity. Mike's expression was sad as we paused at the top of the basement stairs.

"It used to be a great hotel," he said. "Mr. Jael thinks we can turn it around, but I have to wonder."

Suddenly an eerie voice echoed down the hallway behind us.

"Miiike! Miiike!"

"Oh, not now," he said shaking his head.

The door behind us flew open, and someone jumped out. Startled, Sieg and I stepped back. A tall, busty, red-headed woman pinned Mike's hands above his head and was busy kissing him on the mouth. We looked away in embarrassment.

Eventually Mike was able to free his hands. He embraced her and continued the kiss. After Sieg and I were totally disgusted by this display and tried to figure out how we could escape gracefully, he pushed her away and wiped his mouth with the back of his hand.

"Please, dear, not in front of the children. Penny, this is Sieg and Danny, our new housemen. Guys, this is Penny Tyrell, our head housekeeper."

"It looked like she was keeping something else," Sieg said.

"Would you like to keep your teeth, Shultz?" Mike countered. Before Sieg could answer back, Penny put a hand over Mike's mouth.

"Don't worry about him, boys," she said with a voice that made me tingle. "Mike's a big pussycat. I just like to show him who's boss from time to time."

Mike pulled her hand down.

"Right, we'll have to discuss that on Friday, dear."

"Promise?"

"Get out of here! I've got work to do."

"Bye, boys, don't forget to write."

She winked at us, and we all watched as she

sauntered away. I'd never seen a woman strut like that before, like a lioness walking away from her kill. I felt my heart start beating faster and face started getting hot. Mike finally turned back to us.

"All right you two, back to business. If either of you mention this to anyone..."

Sieg sighed and shook his head.

"Yeah, yeah, whatever you say. Let's get going."

* * *

The basement felt like a dungeon from somewhere in the Middle Ages. The deeper we went, the louder the machine sounds became and the earthier, more elemental, the air smelled. There was an odd chill seeming to sink right into our bones. Mike led us through a door and into the laundry.

I had been in smaller hangars than the laundry. The smells of the rest of the basement were displaced by ozone, detergent and sweat. Out of the thick cloud of steam filling the space, we began to see figures moving about. As we approached, they turned out to be uncountable men and women working at machines or pushing carts from one place to another. Everyone was wearing blue cotton smocks and spoke rapid-fire in languages I couldn't decipher.

At the heart of the swirling, dancing chaos was the most remarkable figure I had ever seen. He stood over seven feet tall and appeared to be a skeleton with pale colored parchment stretched over it.

At first I thought he must have been some kind of manikin or statue. Then one of his hands made a quick gesture and he turned his head to bark a command to someone in their own language.

I noticed both of his hands had long, red lacquered

fingernails. In one he held a streaming cigarette in an ivory holder. He was dressed from head to foot in a green and red embroidered silk robe and wore a matching silk cap. His pale green eyes glinted as we entered and his scowl changed to a wide smile. With shock, I realized his teeth were jade green.

"Greetings, Michael," he said in a melodious voice, "what brings you to my humble domain?"

"Good morning, Mr. Chang. May I introduce Danny Jael and Sieg Shultz, our new housemen?"

Mr. Chang bowed, and I was amazed how low he could bend. When he straightened, the glint had come back to his eyes, and he looked at Sieg and me as if measuring our worth.

"I suspect these two will need raiment worthy of their duties. Is that not so?"

"That would be the size of it," Mike replied.

"Let me see," Mr. Chang said, stroking his chin with his free hand. "Black and dark blue are too formal and should only be worn by those in supervisory positions, such as you, Michael. Green would not go with their skin tones and the brighter blues would look ridiculous on them. Ah, I think I have the perfect color for them."

He waved a hand and a tiny, wizened woman stepped from somewhere in the crowd and stood silently next to him. He leaned down and said something we couldn't hear into her ear. She cackled as if it were the best joke she had ever heard. She came over and began circling both of us. Occasionally she would stop and make a tiny chuckling sound. Once she reached over and pinched my thigh and then did the same to Sieg. We both jumped at this. Just as I started to wonder about what this ritual was all about, she stopped and disappeared into the crowd.

There was surge of traffic. People started rushing from one side to another, and the sound filling the room took on a completely different tone. I was about to say something when the tiny woman stepped out from behind a machine and handed me a brown paper package. After she had given one to Sieg, she turned to Mr. Chang and chattered in her own language. He smiled slightly and bowed to her. She went back to work, and the laundry resumed its normal course.

With a serene smile, Mr. Chang turned and barked another order. Then he came to us.

"I believe you will find this is what you require. I must humbly remind you the employee laundry is done twice a week, on Monday and Thursday. I shall expect you will make sure your laundry bags are brought down to us before noon on both days. I am afraid I cannot allow any of my employees to venture over to your disgusting hovel and place themselves at the mercies of that demonic feline."

He turned away. I started to ask Mike a question, but he stopped me with a raised hand.

"You'll find out soon enough," was all he would say.

As we began to leave, I glanced back and saw Mr. Chang watching us with a mysterious little smile. He waved his cigarette in farewell to me.

* * *

"Okay," Sieg said, "I stand corrected. *This* is a dump."

The three of us were standing in front of the most dilapidated house you could ever imagine. The resort was a palace compared to it.

At three stories, it was still dwarfed by the surrounding evergreens. If it had been painted sometime in the past century, the color had faded into a nondescript gray and brown mix. I couldn't count the number of broken windowpanes and the porch roof was sliding away toward the east. The porch itself, complete with a swing on rusty chains was slowly migrating its way toward the west and freedom. I nodded in agreement with Sieg.

"Yeah, I think the only thing keeping it standing is the termites holding hands."

Mike rolled his eyes at this.

"Oh, come on guys. Unless you two want to live back at the resort, next to Cap's room by the way, this is the only place for you to stay. We have electricity and running water, what else do you need?"

"A tetanus shot," I replied.

"It's not that bad!" Mike said.

"I think you are protesting too much."

Sieg pasted a big smile on his face and stepped into the argument.

"Maybe he's right, Danny. Maybe this house is actually another opportunity. Maybe we can take this termite nest and turn it into the very best house on the mountain."

"Do you think so?"

"No, not really, but I thought I should at least try to stay positive."

"Oh, you two are very funny," Mike said. "If you don't like it, find somewhere else to stay."

"Whoa!" I said holding up my hands, "Hold on there, Tex! Sieg and I didn't say we weren't going to stay. Is there anything else you need to tell us?"

"Like what?"

"I don't know. Is there a big pile of glowing green goo in the basement, or is the place haunted?"

"For one thing, it doesn't have a basement. As for

haunting, I have to admit there are a few things—"

"Hi!" a voice interrupted before Mike could finish his thought.

We turned around to find a guy coming up the trail behind us with bags of groceries in his arms. He was wearing a bright, eye-catching, yellow, resort polo shirt, blue jeans and mirrored sunglasses. His hair was bleached blonde with long sideburns threatening to crawl down his jaw. His smile was almost as bright as his shirt. Mike stepped down and took one of the sacks from him.

"Guys," he said turning back to us, "this is Todd McGowan. Todd, this is Danny and Sieg, our new helpers."

"Groovy. How about you all let me inside before all the ice cream melts?"

Sieg opened the door for him and we quickly followed along. Just inside the door, Mike stopped to give us a quick orientation.

"Bedrooms are up on the next two floors. You'll have to find a couple habitable ones." He pointed to his left. "The dining room and kitchen are over here, while the living room is over to the right."

He pushed the door into the dining room and disappeared inside. Sieg and I shrugged and started poking around. I opened the door across the hall and found the living room stocked with a pair of black, steel, folding chairs, a brassy-colored black-and-white portable television looking as if it had escaped from the 1960s, a bookcase built from old apple crates and the worst rug in the history of habitation. The rug actually looked as if a giant ant migration was covering the floor. I hurriedly closed the door before finding out for myself. Sieg had been looking over my shoulder, and I kept my voice down as I spoke to him.

"Now it's getting worse."

"Maybe the upstairs is better," he whispered.

"Wanna bet?"

"No."

Mike still hadn't returned, so we decided to go exploring on our own. Sure enough, Mike and Todd had commandeered the only two habitable rooms on the second floor. The other two reminded us of the living room rug. The first one had some kind of rat's nest in the ruble scattered across the floor, while the other had an extra "window" created when someone had broken a hole through the wall.

"Onwards and upwards," I said, biting my lip.

"Right," Sieg said unenthusiastically.

The third floor was slightly better, although neither of the inhabitable rooms were as good as the ones Mike and Todd had taken. I fumbled around in my pocket and pulled out a half-dollar.

"Call it," I said as I flipped it into the air.

"Tails," Sieg said.

The coin bounced on the floor and came to a rest next to my feet.

"Ha!" Sieg said. "I'll take this one."

"Gee, thanks awfully."

"Quit whining, you big baby."

There was sort of a bed in the middle of my room. It needed a mattress, and nothing with more legs than I had came rushing out when I kicked the frame. There was an old desk with a scarred top and no drawers against one wall. I went over to the matching wardrobe and opened the door, wincing at the alarming creak. It was completely empty except for the cobwebs filling it. I gagged a bit and slowly closed the door. The disappointment welled up as I dropped by bag and tossed my uniform package onto the desk. Sieg stuck his head in and looked around.

"Oh cool, you've got a wardrobe."

"Forget it, Sieg, I've already checked."

"Damn."

"Besides, if any faun comes out here, I'm going to clobber it."

"You're not being very nice."

"So?"

Mike came up the stairs and looked in at us.

"Okay guys, put on your shirts and we'll go back to the main building and see if we can find whatever we need."

"We're going to need some heavy stuff for the bathroom," Sieg said, "I think there's a growing civilization in the shower. I swear I saw something building a pyramid near the drain."

"Trust me," Mike said, "whatever you need, we'll have it. Penny absolutely insists on it."

"So tell me, Mike," I said, "why haven't you guys at least fixed the holes in the walls or some of the other stuff?"

"Because Todd and I have been the only housemen around here until you two showed up. The resort takes all our time. I have to admit Penny came over a few times and helped me with my bedroom, but for the most part we've been on our own."

"I'm sure she helped a lot," I said.

He looked at me. I don't think he could detect the sarcasm in my voice but I just returned a blank stare.

Suddenly I felt something rubbing against my leg. Looking down, I found a large, mackerel-striped, tabby cat. He purred as I reached down to pet him.

"Hello there, little fellow. What's your name? Aren't

you a loveable little cuddle buddy?"

I scratched him behind his ears and his purr became louder.

"Uh, Danny," Mike said, alarmed, "I don't think—"

Without warning the cat jumped in the air, spun around and managed to latch onto my arm with every single claw. I started thrashing around with my arm, trying to dislodge my furry assailant.

"Owww! Get it off! Get it off!"

Mike and Sieg were of no help whatsoever. Their laughter filled the air even as the cat changed its purr to a horrendous growl. I thought I could feel the claws digging into bone as I tried to fling it from me. After a few seconds, after probably deciding he had had enough of a ride for an "E" ticket, the cat let go, landed on the floor and strutted down the stairs with a contemptuous flick of his tail.

I caught my breath and assessed the damage. The scratches were superficial, and I began to think I was going to survive. I had suffered worse recently. I looked down at Mike and Sieg, who were both holding their sides and laughing.

"Would you like some assistance? I mean, before I toss you down the stairs?"

They just laughed harder, if that was possible. Finally, Mike got control of himself and straightened up. Looking at my expression sent him back into a paroxysm of laughter. By the time he had calmed down, Sieg had also managed to stand up. There were both gasping as they tried to catch their breath.

"Sorry, Danny," Mike finally said, "but I've never seen anything so funny. The look on your face when Edgar got hold of you..."

"Edgar? You named that monster, Edgar?"

"Todd's grandmother left him after she was killed in a motorcycle accident."

"Oh, how old was she?" Sieg asked between gasps.

"She was about ninety. It fell over on her as she was walking past it on her way to the post office. They think the kickstand collapsed."

Despite myself I began to laugh. I tried to stop, but it was too much, and it just boiled out of me.

"It's not funny," I said, "It's just not funny."

"It's true!" Mike protested. "Todd's got the newspaper clipping and everything. Edgar's so mean we have to drive into Lake Fort to pick up the mail every day. Edgar used to hide inside the box and attack the mailman. I once saw him chasing a bear up by the lake, and I think he likes the taste of human flesh."

"What does Todd feed him?" I asked.

"Tender Vittles."

I looked at him for a long moment. When he didn't smile, I stepped into my room and opened my uniform package. Inside were several polo shirts, each with a Lake Weir logo stitched over the left breast. Each one was a bright, almost corpuscle, color. Something about the color disturbed me, as if it symbolized something I knew was bad. For the life of me, I couldn't figure out what it was. Shrugging, I pulled one on and stepped out into the hall where Mike and Sieg were waiting for me. Sieg's shirt was exactly the same shade of red as mine, just a lot larger. He grinned at me.

"We just have to remember to not be the first ones down to the alien planet."

Mike looked embarrassed and held up his hands as if to say it wasn't his fault.

"Uh, Mr. Chang likes to go to conventions, a lot. I once caught him looking into a mirror while wearing pointed ears."

"Well," I said, "I'll be damned if I'll be turned into a little gray cube and crumbled into dust. I guess we now know which way Mr. Chang is betting."

"You're taking this well," Sieg said. "I would have thought you'd have gone off like a skyrocket."

"Frankly, I don't care anymore. It's not important. I just want to get to work and prove everyone wrong."

"Okay," Mike said with a shrug, "it's your funeral."

"Not yet it isn't," I replied.

* * *

Back at the resort, we waited at the polar bear while Mike talked to Cap about what we were going to need for the house. Sieg and I examined the bear from every angle as we walked around it.

"I'm not sure I like this resort," I confessed to Sieg when we were in the corner away from the front desk.

"You're the one who kept yapping about what a great opportunity it was. What happened? Cat got your guts?"

"Not funny, buddy. There's something weird about all this. Honestly, we've got someone who dresses like a Sax Rohmer villain and loves television science fiction, a murderous cat and a resort filled with more taxidermy than the Natural History Museum.

"You're just letting your imagination run wild. Just calm down and go with the flow."

"Go with the flow? Look, there's something strange working around here. I don't know what it is. I don't care, but I know I don't like it."

"As you once pointed out, Danny-boy, we don't have a lot of options."

"Yeah, I know. I know."

"Then calm down. You're making this worse on us."

"You sure have room to talk."

Mike and Todd came out of Cap's office. Todd was carrying a piece of paper and Mike waved us over to them.

"We're going up to the attic to grab a couple of spare mattresses. I figure the four of us can carry them over to the house. Then we'll come back for cleaning supplies."

"Sound good to me," Sieg said. I stayed silent.

"We'll take the elevator up," Mike continued. "I don't think we're going to want to climb the stairs all the way up and then carry mattresses back down."

"Cool," Sieg replied.

The elevator was an iron and brass contraption right out of the middle of a Jules Verne novel. Just as it arrived, we heard a voice behind us.

"Oh. My. God! Ed didn't tell me you'd be here!"

Turning around, I saw Courtney standing there. I wasn't anywhere as shocked as Sieg was. He just stood there with his mouth open as she walked up.

"What are you...?" he said.

Courtney ignored him with a toss of her head as she passed him.

"Nice to see you again, Danny," she said as she passed me.

I turned to Sieg as she walked up to the front desk and started talking to Lisa.

"She's still not talking to you. What happened?"

"I'm not talking about it."

"Sieg, she's going to be working here. You're going to see her every day one way or another."

"I don't care. I'm not talking about it."

"Fine, be that way."

"I will. Is the elevator ever going to get here?"

As if on cue, the doors opened. I was about to step

forward when a blonde goddess hurried out and ran into me. She had been reading some papers as she exited. The collision caused the papers to fly all over as her momentum caused both of us to lose our balance and start to fall to the floor. She tried to grab me as I desperately attempted to catch myself. It was too late. With a loud crack leaving me seeing stars, my head hit the floor along with the rest of me. The blonde used me as a landing pad.

"Glah..." was all I could say. I have to admit it wasn't the most urbane thing to say. I just laid there for a moment, hoping the world would quit spinning around. The girl, on the other hand, had other ideas. She struggled in my grip and slapped my face.

"Let go of me, you weasel!" she shouted.

I had a hold of her? I checked my hands and tried to think through the ringing inside my head. Then I realized what while I didn't have a grip on her, she had a grip on me. She was holding my shirt with on hand and shaking me hard.

"Let me go!" she said.

Overwhelmed, I pushed her aside and rolled to my knees. I shook my head to clear the bells and stars. Sieg took a hold of my arm and tried to help me to my feet. I shook him off and found myself face to face with the goddess. She was trying to stand up, too. I took her hand in an attempt to help her, and then I looked into her eyes.

The universe came to stop as I peered into a pair of deep blue eyes that went on forever. I wanted to look into them forever. She had other ideas.

"Let go of me!"

She yanked her hand from my grip and stood up. She brushed down her skirt and blouse. Then I noticed she was wearing a resort blazer. This time I didn't fight as

Sieg helped me to my feet. I wasn't really thinking then and could only stare at her as she started picking up her papers. She saw me staring and glared at me.

"Why don't you look where you're going?"

"Uh..."

She snatched her remaining papers out of Mike's hand and stomped off toward the front desk. I stood there and watched her walk away. Mike grinned and laughed.

"Wow! You sure have a way with the women, Danny."

I didn't say anything. I just stood there. Sieg reached out and shook my shoulder.

"Are you all right?" he asked.

He shook me again and I ignored him. I watched as the goddess handed a bunch of the papers over to Lisa and then entered an office just past the front desk. I kept watching, hoping she would come back. Sieg finally got tired of all this, I guess, and poked me in the arm, hard.

"Earth to Danny! Are you all right?"

I turned to reply, not really seeing him.

"Wasn't she lovely?"

FIVE

Clouds of steam ran from my mouth like the exhaust of a steam engine. The morning air was icy with the past winter still hanging on. Spring in Colorado was sometimes like stepping backwards in season. I shivered violently as I stretched and prepared for my morning run.

Ever since my dad died, running had become less of a hobby and more of a therapy. He'd died when I was sixteen, and I needed some kind of physical activity to burn away the anger sometimes. I didn't want anyone trying to help me or console me or even to talk to me, so I started running every morning.

I started with a quick trip around the block. In a few weeks I found myself ranging all over Mohawk. I'd run down Maple Hill, then across the Main Street bridge. Sometimes I'd run up to the High School and back. Usually, though, I ran past Ray's house and eventually all the way out to Big Ed's Used Cars. My aunt would wave as I ran by, even though I never stopped. Even after the fire, during the trial, I sometimes managed a good twenty miles a morning.

This morning had been different. It was the first one at the resort, and I awoke to the fact I was not alone. My pillow had sprouted fur, and I realized Edgar was lying on my pillow, using my head as a chin rest and purring. I was about to reach up when a series of needle-sharp claws gently touched my scalp as if to tell me I'd need a toupee for life if I continued. Brute force was just going to get me hurt, so I tried sweet reason instead.

"Listen, you stupid cat, I have to get up. I need to pee, and if you don't move, I'm not going downstairs to feed you."

Those must have been the magic words, because the claws were withdrawn and he stood up, pulling my hair in the process, stretched and jumped to the floor with a thump shaking my window. I rolled out of bed and padded down to the bathroom. Edgar sat at the top of the stairs and alternated between washing his rear end and watching me as if I was going to escape without feeding him.

I pulled on my shorts and a tee-shirt and started downstairs, dodging Edgar as he continually tried to trip me to my death. Detouring to the kitchen, I took just enough time to carve some food out of a can and throw it onto a plate for Edgar. He sniffed at it for a second, looked up at me and then went face-down into the plate. After I drank a glass of water to the sounds of his devouring, I went outside and wandered down to the parking lot to stretch.

The parking lot was filled with a lot of emptiness. There were a couple of cars parked near the resort along with the company truck. Courtney's Cadillac was parked in splendid isolation near the center, with the rest of the lot deserted. I went over to the Caddy and used one of its gigantic chrome bumpers as a brace to stretch against.

"Oh, hi," came a voice from the other side of the car. Standing up, I saw my blonde goddess coming towards me. She was wearing a pair of red shorts and a gray sweat-shirt doing nothing to hide the fact that she was a female of the species. She came to a stop about a dozen feet away.

My first instinct was to turn and run away as fast as I could. I didn't have a whole lot of experience with women, and I'd already screwed things up with this one. Instead, I decided to answer her.

"Uh, hi there," I said.

Her face lit up with a smile that would have launched an entire navy.

"Hi! I want to apologize for yesterday. I'm so sorry. I wasn't watching where I was going when I ran into you. You were a convenient target, and I'm embarrassed."

"Oh, it could have happened to anyone. I'm Danny Jael, by the way."

As she walked closer, I held out my hand. She shook it, and it felt like I was touching lightning. I had to tell myself to breathe as I again looked deep into her eyes. I could drown in them, and I didn't care who knew it. Gently, she pulled her hand free and smiled.

"I'm Anna Charles, the new bookkeeper. I just started last week. I saw you out here and thought I should at least apologize. Do you like to jog?"

From the parking lot, there was a paved pathway winding itself around the lake. Up near the falls feeding the lake, the path went around and up until you crossed the creek on the cliffs above. Mike had told me about it the night before, and I was itching to try it out. Anna and

I started off, following the trail clockwise. I found she was as good as I was and maybe a hair better.

We were almost to the base of the climb up to the top of the falls when we both stopped and stared at each other. A noise wafted across the lake and assaulted our ears. Because of the canyon's acoustics, you couldn't tell what direction it came from or from how far away it came. I started to look around in alarm.

"Do you think a wild animal got caught in a trap?" I asked Anna.

"It doesn't sound urgent. I think it's coming from up ahead."

We continued our run, keeping our eyes peeled for any obvious causes of the noise. After another half-mile we stopped again.

"I think I can hear words," she said.

"I think you're right."

Sure enough, the noise resolved itself into an incredibly obscene version of *The Road to Mandalay*. Anna blushed crimson at some of the words, and I knew my ears were turning red. It was worse than some of Ray's drinking songs I'd heard over the years. Anna grinned sickly at me.

"I think we've found some old prospector taking a bath in the lake," she said.

"He can stay in there for all I care," I replied. "I'm pretty sure I don't want to meet someone who sings like that."

"Oh, I don't know," she said with a little smile, "I think it's kind of cute."

"Yuck," I said, shaking my head in disgust. "I hate cute."

"Why?" she asked.

"It seems to be used to describe just about

everything. I've heard women use it for pit bulls, fluffy bunnies and cars. Whenever I hear it, I feel all pink, sugary, bouncy and...well, you get the idea. Sometimes I feel like just using the word is going to give me diabetes."

"Oh, grow up!"

She started running again and I stood there for a moment, feeling embarrassed.

"Good going, boy blunder," I said to myself as I took off running after her.

I caught up with her and we ran side-by-side across the creek and down the trail back to lake level. Near the base of the cliffs, we stopped again because the singing had stopped. We looked around and then heard something moving through the bushes just ahead of us. Anna turned to me and smiled.

"See, I told you it was..."

She never finished the sentence. The bushes down the path from us parted and something came out onto the trail. It was large, hairy and of a deep brown color. It moved quickly across the path and into some more bushes. We could hear it moving around in a grove of aspen trees. We went down to where we had seen it and looked toward where it had been but didn't spot it again. Anna drew up close to me with her bare arm rubbing against mine. I was surprised not to see electric sparks flying from the contact.

"What was that, Danny?" she whispered.

"I don't know. Do you think it could have been Bigfoot?"

She stepped away from me and slapped me on the arm.

"Oh, right! Now all we have to do is start looking for Elvis as he eats a burger while sitting on a log. Let me guess, you and your friends somehow knew I was going to be out here. One of you, probably that fat, little pervert, dressed up in a costume to scare me, right?"

"No. If that's true, then the joke's on me, too."

"You don't know anything about this?" she asked, rolling her eyes.

"No, I don't."

"Baloney! I don't believe you. I should have expected a despicable trick from you frat-boys!"

She took off at a dead run, and somehow I didn't want to catch up with her. I wondered if it had been some kind of joke. Could the guys have set me up? I wouldn't put it past Sieg, but how would they do it? Sieg didn't know the territory, and Todd and Mike didn't have enough time to prepare such a hoax. As I ran I tried to think if I'd told anyone else of my plans to run around the lake. It was like a loose tooth I kept worrying at all the way back to the house.

* * *

After a quick shower, I went to my room to dress for the day. We'd spent the afternoon before cleaning, polishing and repairing what we could of our rooms. I smiled to myself when the wardrobe door emitted no sound as I opened it and ran through my options for clothes.

"Let me see," I said to myself, "blue jeans and red polo shirt, blue jeans and red polo shirt or possibly blue jeans and red polo shirt."

As I went down the stairs, a part of me felt like a fool wearing my blue jeans and the spanking new red polo shirt. The shirt was tightly woven and felt something like an itchy second skin.

"Are you ready for breakfast, Danny?" Mike asked me as I entered the dining room.

"I guess so. What's cooking?"

By default, Mike was our cook. Sieg could set water on fire, and I was even worse. I could probably make canned soup or a bowl of cereal, if I had help. When we asked him about Todd's culinary abilities, Mike just laughed.

As I sat down and poured a glass of orange juice from the pitcher, I looked around at the guys. None of them seemed to be out of breath from running all the way home from where I'd seen the Bigfoot. On the other hand, I only knew Sieg's athletic ability and there might have been a shortcut.

"How do you like the morning air?" I asked Mike as he passed a plate of pancakes over to me. He raised an eyebrow at the question. I felt a flash of irrational jealousy because I knew I couldn't raise just one eyebrow.

"What about the morning air? I mean, besides the fact that it's freezing and I won't go out in it at any cost."

"I thought I had seen you out there."

He blew milk out of his nose.

"There're only three reasons for me to leave my nice warm bed before seven in the morning. The house has to be on fire. Even then I'll only consider leaving if it's obvious we can't put it out. Cap could call me and demand my presence to serve some customer's whim, which is unlikely, since Cap is even less likely to be up early. Finally, if Penny decides to get frisky, then I might venture out of doors. Even then it would take some serious persuading, though Penny is quite capable of such."

The pancakes were good and I've always been a sucker for buttermilk. As I sat there, slowly chewing, my mind spun around trying to figure the riddle out. I rejected the idea that we had an actual Bigfoot wandering around. Colorado is not the Pacific Northwest. I had to admit I was stumped. I also knew there were other things I needed to worry about and soon.

* * *

"Cap wants to see what you can do about this railing," Mike said. We were standing on the resort's front porch and I looked at it forlornly.

"Why me?" I asked.

"Why not? Besides, Sieg and I are going to be setting up the ballroom for the dance tonight. Penny wants to go, so maybe he can show me a couple of moves."

"Yeah, right, I know for a fact he can't dance."

"How do you know?" Mike asked.

"I told him," Courtney said from behind us. We turned around and she was standing with the door held open. She was wearing a blue resort polo shirt pulled tightly across her chest. She noticed where my eyes had wandered and snapped her fingers at me.

"Keep your eyes up here! Mr. Chang and I are going to have a little talk about what clothes I should be wearing for work."

"Doesn't look too bad from where I'm standing," Mike laughed.

"Shut up, or should I tell Penny you're ogling me?"

"Uh..."

"Yeah, I didn't think so. Mr. Chang is probably sitting in his dungeon, laughing his ass off."

"You don't look as funny as Sieg," I said with a smile. "He looks like a little blonde sausage."

She didn't say anything, and after a few cold seconds, Mike decided to leave.

"Danny," he said at the door, "the stuff you'll need is in the storeroom behind the front desk. See if you can get this job done today, okay?"

"Yeah, it shouldn't be much of a problem."

"Right."

Courtney just stood on the porch and watched me as I worked. She had to move out of the way when I went inside. She followed me to and from the storeroom and then continued to watch silently as I measured the railing and counted the spindles. Once, when I looked up, I found her staring at me and biting her lip."

"What's up, Court?"

"Nothing."

"It's been a while since we hung out together," I said as I slathered glue in all the right places.

"Yeah," she said in a monotone.

I didn't mind the one-sided conversation. The rail was replaced between the roof supports, and I was busy slotting the new spindles in place. I looked up at her again for a moment.

"Are you going to talk about it?"

"I don't think so."

She stayed there and watched me work for almost an hour until Penny came out.

"Oh, so this is where you are, Courtney."

"Huh?" Courtney said, looking around at her. "Oh, sorry, I stepped out for some air and forgot the time."

"That's all right. Mr. Chang just called up about the sheets. They're ready, and we'll have to go down and get them."

Without a word, Courtney went inside and Penny stood there looking back at me. I could only shrug.

"Do you need something?" I asked her.

"No. I'm just trying to figure out what makes you so fascinating. She stood in the hall window upstairs and watched you running with Anna this morning."

"That's news to me," I said as I stood there and

blinked. For the life of me I couldn't figure out why she'd do that. Penny watched me with a slight smile on her face.

"Poor boy," she said and went inside. I was left to wonder what the hell she meant.

* * *

"Not bad at all," Mike said as he came out later in the afternoon. I was putting a coat of primer down and he grinned like a loon when he saw my progress.

"Where did you get those twisty spindles?" he asked.

"I made them on the lathe in the workshop. They're like the ones in the Imperial Hotel. I must have done a million of them during the rebuilding project."

"It's looking really good. We'll have to have you do some of that over at the house when we've got time."

"I'll think about it. I'll admit there's something about the state of repair over there making my hands itch."

Sieg waddled out onto the porch and looked around. He let out a huge sigh and shook his head.

"I don't suppose you've seen Courtney lately?" he asked.

"Yeah," I replied, "she was here for a while this morning while I was putting in the new rails. I think she and Penny went off to pick up some sheets from the laundry."

"Oh."

"Yeah, we only have her and Penny working as housemaids right now," Mike said, adding to our meager store of information. "We just don't have enough business to need more."

"What happens when we do have guests?" I asked.

"We don't have a whole lot at one time," Mike said.

"Usually, two housemaids are enough to handle things. The entire south wing is closed up."

"That doesn't sound good," Sieg said.

"Not much we can do about it right now. Hey! It looks like a guest coming up right now."

We looked and saw a Mercedes sports car, painted British racing green, roaring into the parking lot with an obligatory cloud of dust. It slowed to a stop. I noticed its New York license plate read "Sven One".

The driver slid out of the car and jogged up the stairs toward us with a black leather briefcase dangling from one of his narrow hands. He was tall, thin and had brown hair looking as if he spent a great deal of time brushing it. He wore a conservative blue suit I could tell was expensively made, and he wore it like he knew just how expensive it was. His expression was pleasant and friendly. I hated him from the moment I laid eyes on him.

"Good afternoon," he said with an East Coast accent in his pleasant voice, "I'm looking for Cap Hayes."

"Good afternoon," Mike returned as he opened the front door. "Welcome to the Lake Weir Resort. If you will check with the front desk, I'm sure they'll know where to find him."

"Thank you," the man said as he went inside and Mike let the door close. Sieg was the first to speak.

"Not a guest."

"I guess not," Mike replied, "Danny, how long are you going to need to finish the porch?"

"Let me see," I said, rubbing my chin, "the primer needs to dry and then there are a couple more coats of paint. Since it'll take a while to dry, I'd have to say it'll be ready sometime this evening. Why?"

"Sieg and I need a referee. I think he's been seeing things."

"I am not!" my chubby best friend protested. "Those chairs moved by themselves. I swear it!"

"Right," Mike said with a shake of his head, "a huge stack of banquet chairs just moved from one side of a table to the other all by themselves."

"Now what are you two blathering about?" I asked as I looked from one to the other. Sieg let out a big sigh.

"Mike was showing me how to set up the ballroom," he said, "and when I turned to pull a chair from my stack, the stack had moved to the other side of the table from where I was standing."

"Are you sure it moved?" I asked. "I mean, you could have moved and forgotten the stack wasn't behind you."

"Danny," he said, looking at me over the tops of his glasses, "I just pulled a chair from the stack. I'm sure it was right behind me but when I turned around, it was ten feet away."

"Are you sure?" I asked.

"I don't know. Maybe I used my last chair and didn't realize it."

"Well," I said, "let's go look. I've got nothing to do until the primer dries and maybe we can figure this out inside."

I hung up "Wet Paint" signs even though I knew full well human nature would dictate someone was going to walk up and put a big old fingerprint in my work sometime before it was dry. Shaking my head, I followed Mike and Sieg back inside the building.

As we entered the lobby, I could see Anna having an animated discussion with the man in the blue suit. Once again, I felt an unreasonable hatred of him. I ignored it and followed the guys into the ballroom.

The ballroom was in the northeast corner of the building. It had an expensive parquet floor and a huge crystal chandelier electrified with flame-shaped bulbs. Hundreds of chairs were scattered all over the place in haphazard fashion. A bunch of round tables were thrown about, some on their sides, some upside-down on top of others and some sitting with a leg up on a stray chair. Sieg and Mike looked dumbfounded.

"So, what do you call this design?" I asked.

"This isn't how we left it," Sieg said.

"No, it isn't," Mike said as he turned around with an angry look on his face. "We had twenty tables and two hundred chairs set up in a box formation for the dance. Everything was right where it was supposed to be when we left."

"Maybe someone is playing a prank," I said.

Sieg shook his head.

"Who'd do that? Come on, Danny, there isn't anyone else in the building. There has to be something else going on. I know that stack of chairs moved."

"You know," I said slowly, "this sort of reminds me of those coffins in Barbados. They would move around when the crypt was sealed. If I remember it right, they finally discovered sea water was getting in and floating them around."

"Uh, Danny," Mike said with a long look, "we're thousands of miles from the sea and there's no way the lake can come up here."

"I'm just saying it reminds me of the story," I replied.

"It reminds me of something else," Sieg said as he stared off in the distance.

"Like what?" Mike asked.

"Like the stories my mother used to tell me about poltergeists. Maybe something supernatural moved the chairs and tables around."

"Oh, come on you two," Mike said as he threw his hands up in the air. "Are you guys for real? Danny's talking about floating coffins, and you're talking about polter-somethings? Give me a break. What are you two, nuts?"

"Do you have a better theory?" Sieg asked as he turned on Mike.

"I have," Cap said from behind us. We turned around and saw Cap standing there with the man in the blue suit.

"My theory is you three are too busy screwing around to get this dance set up," Cap said with a deep frown. I knew he wasn't happy. Mike grabbed a loose chair and moved it into place.

"We're on it," he said.

"Good," Cap said. "When you're done, I've got a couple of other jobs for you, if you're not too busy. Where's Todd?"

"He's helping Penny and Courtney move sheets up from the laundry."

"Excellent. Oh, and by the way, this is Sven. He's going to be our new Sales and Banquets manager."

Sven nodded to us. Then he and Cap turned and left. Mike looked at us with wide eyes.

"Yow!" he said. "We're in trouble, guys."

Sieg pulled a table off of a chair and grinned at us.

"You can say that again."

SIX

"Hey! Wait up!" I looked behind me and saw Anna running up the lake path. I slowed down and she caught up, falling into step with ease.

"I'm sorry. I forgot you only arrived up here the day before."

A week had passed since the two of us had seen the mysterious figure in the woods. Each morning I would go down to the resort and stretch in the parking lot. Every day, I left disappointed because I failed to catch a glimpse of Anna. I changed my route a couple of times and went down the hill and ran along the highway for a few miles. I found I preferred the truck-free lake path. I also found I was stretching a bit longer to avoid the strange bather at the falls. Who could blame me?

"I should have known you didn't know about that stupid prank," Anna said as we cruised along side-by-side.

"I'm willing to chalk it up to us just imagining something. How about if we just forget about it? We'll probably never see anything."

"Sounds like a plan. What if we encounter it again?"

"We'll burn that bridge when we get to it," I said.

The mornings were becoming glorious as we moved into early June. It was the time when the cold dulled its bite, and we put quite a few miles under our sneakers. The only noise we heard was the singing of the birds, and we didn't encounter our mysterious bather. However, at the end of our run, we did encounter an unforeseen difficulty.

We came jogging down the path and found Sven leaning against Courtney's car. He was wearing a green, pin-striped suit and had a cigarette dangling from one hand with the smoke slowly trailing away. He strolled over as we stopped at the front stairs and began our cool-down.

"Fancy meeting you here, Anna," he said, "I see you have a new boy-toy."

"He is not a boy-toy."

The words were flat and angry. I could sense a history behind them, a history I didn't know. I almost said something, then realized I needed to stay out of the way. Anna's glare seemed to broaden Sven's smile.

"Oh, come now," he said, "I seem to remember you toyed with my heart once. Why not his? It's what you're good at."

"You were my fiancé," she replied.

What? I thought. *When did that happen? What am I getting into?*

I took a step back, seemingly unconcerned as I did a series of calf stretches. Sven took a long drag from his cigarette and let the smoke stream from his nose.

"Ha! You toyed with my affections and then left me at the altar."

Anna advanced on him, shaking a finger in his face. He took a step back, his hands up to defend himself. When Anna spoke again, the words came out between clenched teeth.

"For one thing, you've never been to an altar in your life. The holy water would boil if you entered a church. For another, I caught you screwing my cousin in the pantry during the engagement party! Talk about toying with someone's affections."

"She meant nothing to me," he said.

"Which is my point exactly," she exclaimed. "Apparently I didn't mean anything to you either!"

She turned away and stomped up the stairs. With an angry flourish, she slammed the door behind her. I finished stretching and began to jog across to the trail leading to the house. Sven tossed his cigarette away and called after me.

"You should watch yourself, boy! She'll break your heart like she did mine!"

While I wanted to pretend I didn't hear him, some devil in me caused me to stop and turn. I slowly looked him up and down as if examining something Edgar had dragged in.

"I'll keep it in mind," I said before turning back and continuing up the trail.

SEVEN

While we found Sven to be really annoying, we also had to admit he was a genius at bringing business to the resort. One of his ideas was to advertise a weekly dance in the ballroom. The first of these turned into a gala affair, with a buffet and live music from a local band, Claude Willie and His Mountain Men, a bluegrass combo with steel drums and electric guitars.

However, when Sunday rolled around, we had to be up early to clean up the remains from the ballroom. After the encounter with Sven, we were working and Mike was wincing and growling under his breath every time we made any noise. Sieg finally got tired of this and stopped working.

"What's your problem, Mike? You sound like a bear with a toothache."

Todd laughed as he swung another chair onto a stack, making sure the sound would cause Mike to cringe.

"Dude," he said, "Penny dragged him to the dance last night. She made him buy her champagne. I think our groovy leader is feeling it this morning."

"It was her birthday," Mike said quietly as he gently stood a table up and began folding the legs.

"Hey," Sieg said, "maybe you ought to try some of the hair of the dog that bit you."

"Maybe you ought to shut the hell up, Shultz," he replied.

I started to laugh. Just the thought of Sieg giving drinking advice to someone was hilarious.

In our junior year, before the fire, he had managed to get his hands on some alcohol. I don't know if he raided his parent's liquor cabinet or what. All I know is that he showed up with a couple of six-packs of beer and a huge bottle of vodka. Thinking about it now, I think the vodka was pilfered from his mother.

Anyway, during the Junior Prom, the three of us, Sieg, Courtney and I, sat outside of the gymnasium under a big maple tree and drank the stuff. At least, Courtney and I drank some of the beer, which I didn't care too much for. Sieg, on the other hand, not only drank an entire six-pack by himself, but downed half of the bottle of vodka.

By the time the dance was over, he was thoroughly snockered and couldn't stand up. When Ray showed up to give us a ride home, Courtney and I had to throw him bodily into the back of the pickup. I can remember him trying to pull himself up to apologize for getting drunk and having half his face covered with dirt from the floor of the truck bed.

He puked twice on the way home.

I couldn't help it, I laughed hard and then a thought occurred to me.

"There's something you could do, Sieg."

"I don't need any," he replied. "I haven't been

drinking."

"No, I mean, you could ask Courtney to one of the dances."

"Forget it, Jael," he said, turning his back on me.

"But—"

"I said, forget it!"

I desisted but kept the conversation in the back of my mind. *What was going on between Sieg and Courtney*?

EIGHT

On the other hand, I had been given an unwelcome glimpse into Anna and Sven's relationship. I was pretty damn sure I wanted to stay out of the middle of it. The more I was with Anna, the more I *wanted* to be with her. I found her in more and more of my dreams, both day and night.

My question was, *did she see me just as someone nice to run with or was there more?* While my thoughts didn't affect my work, I was becoming moody, snapping at guys and grumbling around.

Could there be more to this relationship? I was desperate to know. I was afraid to say anything, to make any move, because I was afraid I'd screw it up and ruin everything. Then one morning, while we were out jogging, these thoughts came to mind and I started running faster. I started running as fast as my thoughts whirled around, the world around me forgotten.

"Hey! Slow down," Anna called from somewhere behind me. I turned my head and saw she was a few yards behind me. For a moment, I saw her sheer beauty and my breath caught in my chest. My heart raced and I had to look away. Distracted by my hormones, I wasn't paying enough attention to where my feet were going and I suddenly tripped. Something held my foot as I tried to catch my balance. A lightning strike of pain shot through my leg as I felt something wrench in the ankle and I fell hard onto the trail. Anna sprinted toward me.

"Are you all right?" she asked as she reached me and I was sitting up and holding my ankle.

"I'm not sure, I think so. What the hell happened?"

She looked around and suddenly knelt and picked up something from under the bushes along the edge of the trail.

"I think it was this," she said holding up a piece of fishing line. The remainder of the line trailed off into the bushes toward the lake. Another remnant hung from a bush on the far side. Anna gave the line a tug. Somewhere, down in the bushes, there came the metallic rattling of old cans.

"Can you help me stand up?" I asked her.

She came over and helped me to my feet. As I put some weight on my twisted ankle, another shot of pain lanced through me.

"Ow!"

"Do you think you can walk?" she asked.

"Not like this," I answered. "Help me sit back down. I'm going to need you to go get Sieg and Mike."

"I can't leave you by yourself," she said. "What if a bear comes out? What if that—that—whatever it is comes around again?"

"What if they do?" I asked her. "A bear is going to run away from me and our bathing friend has shown no interest in seeking us out. Just go and get some help."

“I’m not leaving you here, Danny,” she said sticking her chin out. “It’s just too dangerous. We’ll have to work together to get you back home.”

She took my arm and put it over her shoulder to help me hobble along. I realized I was actually touching her, with her permission this time and sort of holding her close. It kind of destroyed any incentive I had to say no. She managed to help me to the house and up the stairs to the front door.

When she raised her hand to knock, I lost my balance and we staggered back to the edge of the stairs. She caught us in time and pulled us back to the door.

“Kick it,” I said.

I was tired and my ankle was throbbing. Anna wasn’t in any mood to argue after helping me for almost a mile. She kicked the door so fiercely I thought it was going to fall in. We staggered around for a second as Sieg opened the door and looked at us.

“What happened?” he asked.

“Just get out of the way, stupid,” Anna said as we pushed our way inside. He backed away hurriedly as we limped into the living room and I was able to collapse onto one of the folding chairs. While I was busy trying to unlace my shoe, Anna looked around.

“You guys don’t have much in the way of furniture,” she said.

“Ha!” I replied. “You should have seen it when we first arrived. The rug alone would scare you into fits.”

I took off my shoe and sock. My ankle swelled like a balloon and changed color. The room spun around and I could hear myself babbling along without a thought of how to stop.

“Before Sieg and I started fixing things around here, I think Mike and Todd were living in a damp cave somewhere. I can just see them as the original cavemen."

Mike came in from the dining room and saw me sitting there as pain built up into a crescendo. Without a word, he knelt next to me and gently poked my ankle with a finger. Then everything went black.

When the world came back, I was flat on my back and my whole body was beginning to feel cold.

"What the hell?" I whispered.

"You're going into shock, Danny," Mike said. "Todd! Go over to the resort and call Doc Clark. He's going to have to make a house call."

"It's not that bad," I said. Then I tried to sit up.

Another sharp pain shot through my leg and I fell back with a yell. My other leg hit the chair and sent it skidding across the floor. Anna bit her lower lip and said nothing but I could see the tears shining in her eyes. I looked up at the ceiling because I was trying to keep my own tears back.

"Hey," I said, "I don't think it's as bad as it looks."

"If I hadn't distracted you," she said, "you would have seen the line."

"It was fishing line, Anna," I said, "I wouldn't have seen it if I'd been alone. Then where would I be, stuck out on the trail by myself?"

"What's this line you're talking about?" Sieg asked.

"I don't know," Anna replied, tears rolling down her cheeks. "It was connected to a bunch of old cans and was strung across the trail."

"Could it have been an old snare or something?" he asked.

"I don't think so," I said. "It wasn't there yesterday."

"Are you sure?" Mike asked as he pulled his jacket off of the rack and laid it over me.

"No. I twisted my ankle yesterday, too," I said. "I

decided to save it all up this morning because I wanted the attention."

"You don't have to be sarcastic," he said.

Man, my ankle was throbbing. Sieg left the room. When he came back, he had an ice-pack wrapped in a dish towel in his hands.

"Here," he said, "put this on it."

"You guys are making this out to be more than it is," I said. Anna knelt and held the ice-pack to my ankle. Mike sneered at me.

"Yeah," he said, "I just love coddling you. Now shut the hell up."

Anna smiled at me.

"Listen to the man," she said.

Sieg picked up his jacket from the rack and put it on. Mike looked over at him and stood up.

"Where do you think you're going?" he asked.

"I'm going to go and find this line of Danny's," he said. "Anna, will you come with me and show where it is?"

"Do I have to?" she asked.

A wave of stress washed through me. I knew I needed her to leave before I started crying.

"Please, Anna," I pleaded. "We need to find out who put that tripwire out there and make sure there aren't any more for a guest to fall over."

"All right," she said with tears welling up again, "I guess I can go with him."

They left and Mike pulled the chair over and put my foot up on it.

"Now just sit there and wait for the doctor," he said.

"I could—" I began. He cut me off.

"You can't even wiggle your toes, Danny. I'm just hoping Doc won't have to take you down to the clinic."

The front door crashed as Todd came back inside. He shucked out of his jacket and pulled the other chair over to sit on.

"Doc's on his way, Dude," he said. "Cap saw me and asked what was going on. He wasn't too happy to find out we don't have a phone over here."

With everything else going on, this just made me start laughing. Mike and Todd joined in and it took a couple of minutes to calm down before I could speak again.

"Gee, I wonder why," I said.

"Probably because it would cost money," Mike choked out. "Just like your leg is going to."

"If it's a problem, I'll pay for it myself," I said. "I wouldn't want to cause any trouble since I was off duty at the time."

"Don't worry about it," Mike said. "Cap's always like this before he's had his morning coffee. As soon as he fills up, he'll probably be down here to see how you're doing."

"I won't hold my breath," I said.

Ten minutes later, Cap came inside. After looking at my ankle, he gazed around with a thoughtful expression on his face.

"I see you boys haven't been screwing around when you're off-duty," he said. "I like that, it shows initiative."

A few moments later, Doc Clark knocked on the door and Mike ushered him in. He was an elderly man with snow white hair cropped close to his scalp, and he wore a plain brown suit. As old as he seemed to be, he had to be in fantastic, almost perfect shape. At first I didn't think he was a large person until I realized he dwarfed Cap. He knelt next to me and peered through a pair of bifocal glasses. Gently, he prodded and turned my leg, which brought an involuntary gasp to my lips. When he spoke, he had a voice sounding like controlled thunder. Somehow I found it reassuring.

"I don't think there's anything broken," he said. "Still, I'd like to get some x-rays to be sure. I'm going to take you down to the clinic."

"Oh, man," I groaned.

Just then, Sieg and Anna entered and the room started getting crowded.

"What's the verdict," Sieg asked.

"I guess I'm going down to the clinic," I replied.

Before anyone else could move, Doc knelt down and picked me up into a fireman's carry as easily as if I were a child. Waving to clear a path, he bore me out of the house and down the trail.

* * *

The trip to the clinic was a terrifying, breathtaking experience. Doc carried me carefully down the trail to where his Microbus sat idling. He must have customized it sometime in the past, because he was able to slip his huge frame behind the wheel effortlessly. He put it in gear smoothly, and we rolled out of the parking lot and onto the highway. The ride down wasn't too bad if you ignored Doc's habit of taking the curves on two wheels. While I was strapped in pretty well, I still didn't want to end up at the bottom of a ravine or wrapped around a tree.

"Hey, Doc," I said, "maybe you ought to slow down!"

"Just relax and let an old man indulge himself."

I held on for my life and prayed I would live long enough to get x-rayed. I don't know or care if it was a record, but I do know we arrived in Lake Fork a lot quicker than I found comfortable. Doc let up on the accelerator on a curve just above town and we coasted the last mile or so, coming to a stop at the traffic circle in the center of town where the "Peak-to-Peak" Highway met the Mohawk Turnpike.

Then Doc drove with decorum as he followed the "Peak-to-Peak" a couple of blocks and turned into the rear of a sprawling shopping complex at the heart of town. At the back, built into the mountain, were a series of offices, one of which had a sign reading "Clark's Clinic: A Medical Facility". We pulled into a parking spot, and Doc went inside and returned with a pair of crutches.

"Here," he said, "you'll be able to get around with these. I have a couple of other patients inside. I'll have to check on them first. Your little accident came at just the wrong time, which seems to be the way of the world."

With his help, I managed to get inside. He left me at the door and disappeared into an office off to one side. I stood there and stared at the odd character sitting behind the reception desk.

He was the most pleasantly ugly, ape-like, old man I had ever seen. He had a low, barrel shape and extraordinarily long arms. His kindly, twinkling eyes peered at me through glasses thicker than Sieg's. His smile wouldn't have frightened the most timid person, and when he spoke, he had a tiny, child-like voice. I found myself liking him despite myself.

"Don't just stand there gawking, Kid," he said. "Come on in and grab yourself a seat."

When he left the reception desk, I found his legs were badly bowed and he walked with a rolling motion, adding to the ape-like image he created. He smiled again as he brought over a clipboard that fit in his stubby fingers like a playing card would in mine. He was wearing bright orange pants with rainbow suspenders and a multi-colored Hawaiian shirt.

"Howdy," he said as he thrust the clipboard at me. "You must be the casualty from up the hill. I've got a couple of forms for you to fill out, so you just sit yourself right there and relax."

He pointed to a comfortable overstuffed chair sitting near the front door. I gratefully sank into its embrace and put my sore foot up on a tiny ottoman. I took the clipboard and pen just as the door behind the desk opened and another old man stepped out. The receptionist turned around and gave a loud squawk as he hurried back to the desk.

"Teddy!" he said, "You've got filing to do, you reprobate."

The newcomer looked down at the receptionist coolly. He looked like he had been a handsome man in his youth, maybe even verging on pretty. His thinning hair was iron-gray and slicked back and looked as if he spent a good part of his day combing it before a mirror. His dark-blue suit was expertly tailored to his thin, whippet-like frame, and he leaned heavily on an expensively carved walking stick. In one hand he held some manila folders. He sneered at the receptionist before speaking.

"What do you think I've been doing, Andy?" he asked in a mild baritone. "Of course, if the Alzheimer's is getting worse, I can talk Doc into sending you to the Old Fools Home..."

"You ought to talk, you disbarred shyster!" the receptionist said as he shook a fist at him. Teddy drew himself up, ram-rod straight and glared down at his sparring partner.

"You...you...you ape! You became so fumble fingered in your dotage ACME Chemical had to let you go. I was never disbarred, you skunk! I retired from my law practice when Doc opened the clinic. He needed someone to handle the malpractice and Medicare forms."

"Yeah?" Andy said as he moved around the desk, "You learned all that by chasing ambulances."

As entertaining as this exchange was, I had to interrupt.

"Uh, excuse me," I said, "I'm done with this form."

Andy turned around with a broad smile and came over to take the clipboard. He glanced at the forms while Teddy went back inside. He noted my look of concern and smiled.

"Oh, don't mind us. We've been fighting like this forever. Back before the Spanish-American War he managed to graduate from Harvard. He thinks it's a great thing. I, on the other hand, graduated from a much more prestigious university."

"Oh?" I said, "Which one?"

"Yale, of course, is there any other?"

For some reason his words made me remember the registered letter from the winter before. Somehow I felt incredibly sad.

"I was going to go to Miskatonic."

He rounded the desk and placed the forms in a folder. With a few deft slashes, he wrote something on the label.

"Miskatonic is a good school," he said. "What happened?"

"I got into some trouble and couldn't go."

He stopped with a suspicious look on his face. I began to feel uncomfortable as he opened the folder and examined the form again. Soundlessly he mouthed my name and then smiled.

"Uh, huh," he said with a smile, "I should have recognized you. Teddy, Doc and I were keeping up with the case in the *Courier*. Wasn't there some other kid involved, too?"

"Yeah," I replied, "he works up at the resort with me."

"That ought to keep things interesting around here, as if we needed any help."

"What do you mean?" I asked.

"Oh, nothing," he laughed. "Every weekend, I end up being called into the clinic because some idiot managed to get into a fight down at Devon's Tavern or hit a deer or something. At least the winters are pretty quiet though. Summers are murderous with all the tourists wandering through. You would not believe how many can't find the grocery store on the other side of the mall. I guess they know up at the resort."

"I don't know," I said. "We haven't had any guests yet."

"Oh, you will, Kid, you will."

Teddy stuck his head through the door and slapped Andy across the back of the head.

"Hey, Knuckles! Doc is ready for the kid."

"Jerk," Andy said as he rubbed the back of his bullet-shaped skull.

Teddy jerked a thumb over his shoulder.

"Come on, Kid," he said. "Doc wants to see you."

The next hour or so was pretty painful with my time in the x-ray machine and another examination by Doc. I found myself sitting in a chair in his office and he turned on a light frame and put the pictures up on it. He tsked to himself for a moment and then turned to me without a trace of a smile. I felt like I was sitting in Helen Shapley's office again, about to get an interrogation about my week.

"Your ankle isn't broken, Daniel," he said as he sat behind his desk. "I think you'll be up on your feet again in a few days."

"*A few days*? Doc, I've got work to do!"

He looked over his glasses at me with a serious expression. His eyes were yellowish with golden flakes spinning around in them. I felt as if he could read my mind and know if I was lying.

"I'm sure they'll find something up there that doesn't require you to stand up."

"I'm a houseman," I said. "Everything I do is standing up."

"Daniel," he said, "you have a bad sprain. If you want it to heal before the Fourth of July, you're going to have stay off it for at least three days, maybe more. I'm going to write Cap a note explaining it. He'll find something for you to do even if you can't stand up."

"Geeze," I said, "I hope so."

While he was writing I looked around at the photographs he had on the shelves behind his desk. In one there was a picture of Doc with five men. Two were obviously the younger Andy and Teddy, the others I didn't recognize. He noticed my interest as he finished the note and slid it across the desk to me.

"They were old friends, gone now," he said. "Do you mind if I ask you a question?"

"No," I said, "go ahead."

"Knowing what you do now," he said slowly as if trying to find the right words, "would you do it all over again? I'm speaking of the parade."

"You know, Doc," I said, "we had our reasons. If I had to do it all over again, I think I would have tested the flamethrower more before the parade. Then we might have figured out it was too much. Then I might have persuaded Sieg into giving it up or found a better way. We thought we were doing something harmless that would impress people and fix a couple of problems. I don't think I would have let Sieg use the flamethrower knowing then what I know now."

He nodded and stood up.

"Well, good luck, Daniel," he said, holding out is hand to shake. "Try to stay out of trouble."

"I don't think there's much trouble I can get into on one leg, Doc," I replied. He smiled as he helped me to the reception area.

Anna and Sieg were sitting in the waiting room, leafing through ancient copies of National Geographic. Andy was pretending to read the newspaper, but I caught him looking at Anna with a wistful smile on his face. The way Sieg was looking through the magazines; I knew he was hoping to find nudes. I reached out with a crutch and knocked it out of his hand.

"It's not a *Playboy*, you idiot," I said.

"So?" he replied. "Nude is nude."

"You're disgusting."

"You're stupid, so I guess we're even," he said.

"Children," Andy said as he put down his newspaper, "go play outside. There's a certain rhythm to the well-turned insult and all you two are doing is scaring the other patients."

Outside, I found they had come down in Courtney's Cadillac. There wasn't any sign of its owner though.

"Where's Court?" I asked.

"She didn't come," Anna replied as Sieg clambered into the back seat. "She let me have the car and stayed at the resort."

I glared at Sieg. He was staring out the window and ignored me pointedly. After I had climbed inside, he took my crutches and laid them across his lap. Anna slid behind the wheel and we rolled out onto the road. As we left town, Sieg finally decided to break the silence.

"We went back to where you fell," he said.

"Yeah?" I asked.

"There was a slight problem," he said.

"Oh? What?"

"We couldn't find the line or the cans," he replied.

* * *

Back at the house, we were sitting in the dining room, where I was finally catching up with breakfast. Sieg and Anna told their end of the story to me and Mike.

"You found nothing?" Mike asked.

Sieg took a swallow of milk. He and Anna were snacking on an apple pie Mike had baked a couple of days before. I was half afraid he was going to choke when he talked with his mouth full. As it was, we had to dodge the geyser of crumbs.

"We found nothing," he mumbled, "Nada, zip, zilch. I couldn't even find where the line had been tied."

"It was there," I said.

Sieg ate another bite, this time swallowing before answering.

"Hey, I believe you," he said. "I think someone removed the line."

I speared a sausage and crammed it into my mouth whole. Anna had to look away. After swallowing, I turned to Mike.

"What am I going to be doing with a sprained ankle?"

"Cap and I have already talked about it," he said with a grin. "We decided to give you something new to work on, something with a pretty girl involved."

"Sounds promising," I said. "Why am I worried?"

"You're going to learn how to help out at the front

desk," Mike laughed. "Lisa is going to be your trainer."

"Why do I have the feeling this isn't going to be fun?" I asked.

"It isn't."

NINE

Lisa started out by carefully explaining the Lake Weir system and then handed me a batch of fake invoices. I was to put them into the fake register she had helpfully prepared. However, while standing close to her, I became so distracted, I screwed up. When I was done, Lisa checked up on me and quickly found out I hadn't paid enough attention.

"No," she said, tapping the page with her pen, "You have Mr. Black staying from August until July of the same year. Fix it."

Further down the page she lightly circled another entry that was wrong. "Think! Does it look right to you? Fix it."

Near the bottom of the page I had wandered out of the field of the English language and she sneered at me as she pointed it out. "You cannot possibly be this dumb. I think you're just trying to annoy me. Fix it."

For days I could hear her voice in the back of my mind, "Fix it, fix it, fix it." It made me want to start hitting my head against the desk.

After several long days of this I was able to register a reservation without error. I could even run the credit card "knuckle buster" without injuring myself or destroying the receipt. After working on a small stack of real reservations, Lisa looked at her watch and yawned.

"Now that you're finally paying attention, I'm leaving you here for a few minutes while I run to the dining room for some coffee."

"You're leaving me?" I asked. "Me? At the front desk by myself? What will Cap say? What if someone comes in? What if...?"

"It's not as if anyone is going to show up while I'm getting some coffee," she said. "If they do, I'm confident you'll be able to screw it up without any help from me."

"Gee, thanks awfully."

"Don't be snide, Danny," she said. Then she wandered off. I struggled to keep blind, unreasoning fear from climbing up my spine and taking hold of my brain. It didn't help that I was sitting on a borrowed barstool and had my bad leg propped up on a cleared shelf. The dining room door had barely closed on her when the front door swung open and Mike appeared, rolling a cart of luggage.

Behind him was a beefy old man with a shock of white hair and the face of a leathery apple. On his shoulder he carried a small, white monkey that looked around excitedly at his new surroundings.

"Welcome to the Lake Weir Resort," I said in my most professional manner, the one Lisa taught me. It was a balance between human interest and personal disinterest. The guest came up to the desk and held out a wrinkled old hand for me to shake.

"Howdy! I'm Dr. Anton Sybel from Pasadena. I

believe you have a reservation for me."

"Let me look," I replied.

Sybel smelled of cheap aftershave, sweat and monkey. He wore a Hawaiian shirt, tan shorts and a pith helmet. The monkey kept trying to groom him, and he irritably swatted at it. While I was looking up his reservation, he perused the trophies, paintings and photographs cluttering the lobby.

It didn't take long to find his reservation, it being the only one currently in the ledger. I felt somehow disappointed there was a reservation, and I began to think I had been set up by Lisa. Also, there was something about him that didn't sit right with me. I couldn't put my finger on it. Was it the way he looked at the trophies as if they belonged to him? Or was it the feeling he was acting as if the whole resort was some new playground? I kept my misgivings to myself and pulled the correct keys from the board. I slid the register around for him to sign.

"Here you go, Dr. Sybel, room 202."

He signed the register and then reached over his shoulder to stroke the monkey's head slowly. "This is Mr. Monkey. He's my only friend anymore since my family all died or moved away. Sometimes, though, he gets really angry and he stands up and spits at me. Most of the time, though, he's such a good monkey, aren't you, Mr. Monkey?"

Mr. Monkey merely looked around. He stared at me as if trying to figure out how to escape from his owner. Heck, I wanted to escape from his owner. His aftershave smelled strongly of mothballs and liniment.

"This is for you, youngster," Sybel said and handed me a banana. Then he handed a five-dollar bill to Mr. Monkey. "Oh, silly me, what was I thinking?"

Mr. Monkey and I traded tips, and Sybel followed Mike over to the elevator. As the door closed, Mike flashed me a quick thumbs up. For some reason, though, I didn't feel like smiling as I finished the paperwork and filed the credit card slips. As I was bent over the file, I could smell a particular perfume. Turning my head, I found Lisa standing at the edge of the desk, wearing a broad smile and carrying one of the dining room's thick ceramic coffee mugs in one hand.

"Good work, Danny," she said. "I knew you could do it. I think you're a natural."

"After all the grief you've given me," I replied, "I'd better be."

A slight frown crossed her face. "Is there something bothering you?"

"Be careful of the old man in two-oh-two."

"I think Sven said something about him being some kind of doctor or something, a crypto—something."

"A cryptozoologist?" I asked with alarm bells going off in my head.

"Yeah, something like that."

I sat there in shock for a moment. Was it a real Bigfoot we had seen out on the trail? I asked myself. If it wasn't, was it a coincidence that a cryptozoologist was here now? Then another thought occurred to me like a bolt out of the blue. Was there a connection between Sven and Sybel?

"Danny!"

With a start I realized Lisa had been trying to get my attention. I looked at her and smiled.

"Sorry," I said, "I was just thinking about our doctor from Pasadena."

"That's only to be expected," she replied as she passed over a couple of pages. "I want you to check out these old registrations from last summer. You need the practice. Try to figure out how many rooms were in use each day of July."

"Now you're giving me busy work," I said.

"You need the practice," she answered and went back to her work.

The possibilities of why a cryptozoologist would be on the mountain ran around and around in my mind. I barely acknowledged Mike when he came back down from delivering Sybel to his room. He waved at me as he came over.

"Was he a good tipper?" I asked.

"Nah, he just gave me a banana. I traded it for a fiver."

"Are we supposed to allow monkeys in the resort?"

"Ask Lisa. I just work here."

He headed back out through the front door. I was still deep in thought when the door opened again and Doc Clark entered. Once again he was wearing a plain brown suit and a bright yellow tie. I noticed his skin was deeply tanned, almost bronze. He was carrying a little black bag and smiled when he spotted me behind the desk.

"I'm glad to see you're up and about. I didn't want you atrophying. Have you been keeping off your sprained ankle?"

"Yes sir," I said.

"Good boy. Come over to this couch and I'll take another look at it."

"I thought I was going to have to take another trip down to Lake Fork to see you," I said. I hobbled across the floor on my crutches and flopped onto the couch. "Do you normally make house calls?"

"Up in these mountains I do," he said. He removed

my shoe and sock and carefully examined my ankle. "A lot of people depend on me and some can't get to town. I have storefronts in Weir, Eldora and Wall Street. I'm sort of like a circuit judge. People tend to wait for me if they have non-emergency medical issues. I usually have Andy or Teddy along for the ride, unfortunately today they're busy with one of their immortal feuds."

I smiled at the thought of the two old men who seemed to hate each other and also seemed to be inseparable.

"They sound like a couple of characters," I said.

"You ought to have to live with them. You'd learn just what a precious commodity peace-and-quiet really is."

Doc removed the bandage and from behind us I could hear the elevator opening. Looking over my shoulder, I saw Dr. Sybel stepping out. He spotted Doc working on my leg and started crossing the lobby. Suddenly he stopped and stared at Doc. Doc serenely continued to poke and prod at my ankle.

"Does any of that hurt?" Doc asked.

"No," I said. "I didn't even feel a twinge."

"Oh, you'll probably feel a twinge," he said, "when you return to your normal duties. I want you to take it easy and slow down a bit to let your ankle get used to working again before you start running all over the mountain."

I stood up and tried my weight on it. He was right, there was a twinge. I thought I could handle it though. We shook hands as the front door opened and Sieg came in. Sybel was still standing behind us, watching the entire exchange.

"I saw Doc's van," Sieg said, "and thought you might be a free man." He tossed me my unused shoe and sock.

"As free as either of us is going to be for a while," I said.

"So you must be the mysterious Mr. Shultz," Doc said. He was busy repacking his medical bag. Then I saw something I had never seen before. Sieg was blushing.

"I'm not all that mysterious," he said in a low voice.

Doc laughed and patted him on the shoulder. You would have thought God Himself had granted some minor grace on my chubby buddy. As Doc was about to go, Sybel stepped over and held out a hand to shake. Doc ignored it. Mr. Monkey peered around Sybel's head at Doc.

"Excuse me," Sybel said, "do I know you? I'm Dr. Anton Sybel of the California Institute of Cryptozoology."

Doc smiled warmly, however the warmth didn't seem to get into his eyes and the gold flakes in them swirled around like a vortex.

"I don't believe we've met," Doc said. "Have you been a patient in my clinic?"

"I don't think so," Sybel said. "This is my first trip to Colorado. I have to say you seem to be very familiar."

"I'm sorry," Doc said. He picked up his bag. "I can't think of where we could have met." He reached into a pocket and pulled out a bronze colored business card. Sybel slowly turned it over and read it carefully as if filing the information away for later.

"If you're sick or injured," Doc continued, "feel free to visit one of my clinics. The one in Lake Fork is closest. I do stop by the resort on Fridays, especially now that they have dancing." Doc smiled shyly at that and started walking away. He smiled to me, and this time it reached his eyes.

"Well, Daniel, as much as I've enjoyed meeting you, I hope I don't see you for a while."

"Same here, Doc," I said.

He waved and went through the door. I sat down to pull on my shoe and sock. Sybel watched the door with a look of serious concentration.

"There's something going on here," he said to no one in particular. "I'm sure I've seen him before. I just can't think where."

"Can I ask you a question?" I said.

"Shoot, youngster."

"What brings you to Colorado?"

He turned to me and smiled. Mr. Monkey just looked bored.

"Someone called the Institute and told us that there was a Bigfoot in the neighborhood. So I came out to have a little look around to see if there really was one."

"You've got to be kidding."

"Oh, no," he said. "The *Midnight Star* is offering a reward for a Bigfoot, alive or dead. We could use that money to pay for a lot of research."

"You're going to kill a Bigfoot?" Sieg asked. His eyes were wide, and it sounded as if he was as horrified by the idea as I was.

"What?" Sybel said, startled. "No! Whatever gave you that idea?"

"You just said..." Sieg began.

"Look," Sybel said. He sighed and shook his head. Mr. Monkey glared at us as if we'd upset his owner. "Never mind the dead or alive stuff. That's just their way of generating tension for their stories. No one is going to kill a Bigfoot. Besides, do you think I know which end of a gun is which? Come on now."

We both just stared at him and his monkey. Mr. Monkey stared back while Dr. Sybel closed his eyes as if trying to gather the strength to deal with us.

"Let me tell you, kids," he said, "my hands are innocent of ever handling a firearm. People want to know if Bigfoot is a menace, though and it's the duty of the California Institute of Cryptozoology to find out. Honestly, if innocent hikers are in danger from a ravening beast leaping out at them, we need to know that. That's why I'm up here."

"Why not search in Oregon or Washington?" I asked him.

"Kid," he said, "do you realize how many people are wandering around Oregon and Washington looking for Bigfoot? I can at least work here in Colorado without having to elbow my way around a bunch of rainbow colored idiots who are trying to 'feel the Bigfoot's aura.'"

Mr. Monkey kept swiveling his neck around as if trying to see the entire lobby at once. He suddenly stopped, and I realized that he had spotted the moose head with the Mickey Mouse ears. Sybel reached up and stroked him.

"No, no, Mr. Monkey," he said in a calming tone. "I'd love to hang around this lobby for a while. I've never seen such a huge collection of exhibits outside a museum before but Mr. Monkey likes to climb. We're going to go out and see what we can find. Mr. Monkey can smell a Bigfoot from a mile away. I'll soon know if there's one in the area."

Sieg had started edging away from him, and I was about to start, when Lisa spoke from behind me.

"Danny," she said, "go to lunch. I need you to come back in about an hour so I can go."

I caught up with Sieg at the door, and we fled the building together.

* * *

We had grilled cheese sandwiches and salad for lunch. As we ate, Sieg spoke at length about the reporters and their quarry. He thought the whole idea was hilarious and kept breaking up in laughter over the idea of a Bigfoot in our canyon. I, on the other hand, just stared at my plate and pushed the lettuce around with my fork. It became quiet suddenly, and I looked up to see all three of them watching me.

"What's the matter?" I asked.

Sieg looked at me with shuttered eyes for a second before speaking.

"You're awfully quiet today, Danny. It's almost as if you were too quiet. All right, give it up."

I looked down at my plate.

"Uh," I began, "remember back a couple of weeks ago when I started asking if you guys had been out in the morning?"

"Yeah," Mike said, "I remember. I also remember all of us telling you we didn't go out early in the morning."

"When I first met up with Anna," I said slowly, "we were out on the trail, and we saw something cross the path in front of us. I thought it was a Bigfoot. Anna thought it was some kind of prank you guys were pulling on us."

"And you think this might be the Bigfoot this guy is hunting for?" Todd asked.

"You've got to be joking," Mike said. "There's no such thing as a Bigfoot. Some guy already admitted he'd been faking those footprints for years."

Sieg leaned his chair back on two legs and began staring at the ceiling. Alarm bells and sirens went off in the back of my mind. I'd seen that look once too often to be comfortable with it. I was ready to run for it when he sat up and looked at us with an unholy light in his eyes.

"Now we have evidence," he said as if trying a new idea for the first time, "there may actually be a Bigfoot in the canyon. I'll be damned. One thing's for sure, we're going to be the ones to find it before this idiot and his monkey does."

"Why would we want to do that?" Mike asked.

"We want to do it for the reward," Sieg answered, "or for the publicity or for the chance to make something of ourselves. That's why. Besides, *we* have an advantage over him."

Mike and Todd were both looking at him as if he had grown an extra head. I was trying to figure out a way to head him off at the pass.

"What advantage would that be, smart guy?" Mike asked.

"Weren't you listening to Danny?" he replied. "I'll bet money that Bigfoot is bathing in the lake every morning and singing. I'll also bet it set the alarm trap that nailed Danny. If we can get out there early enough, we can catch it long before Dr. Sybel."

"What do you mean by *we*?" Mike asked. "I think I've made my views on getting up early pretty damn clear. It isn't going to happen."

"Oh, come on, Mike," Sieg protested, "this is a once in a lifetime opportunity."

I shook my head. I could see the disaster as if it was already happening.

"No, Sieg," I said in a low voice. I was surprised to see everyone looking at me.

"What?" he asked, startled. "Not you too, Danny. Come on, this is the break we've been waiting for."

"Look," I said, "if there is a Bigfoot in the canyon, and if he is bathing in the lake, we're going to leave him alone. He's been living peacefully for who knows how long, and we're going to leave him in peace."

"Well," Sieg said, "if you're all against me, I'll just do this myself. If you're not helping me hunt the Bigfoot, then you can all go to hell."

I let out a huge sigh and shook my head.

"No, you're not," I said. "You know better."

"Why do I know better?" he said. "What do you think you're going to do about it?"

"I'm going to do what I should have done last year," I replied. "I'm putting my foot down and stopping you."

"Oh, come on, Danny," he said, "what's the worst that could happen?"

I closed my eyes in pain. Nothing good ever comes after that phrase.

"The mind boggles, Sieg," I replied. "Remember Mohawk?"

"As if I could forget it," he said. "But come on, that was an accident."

"It was a preventable accident, you chowder head!" I said. "It was an accident I could have prevented, and learning from that mistake, I'm stepping up to prevent this one. If we screw up, you and I will be viewing the world through the bars of a cell in Cañon City. Don't forget about that!"

"Then this yahoo and his monkey are going to find the Bigfoot," Sieg said bitterly. Hearing the disappointed tone of his voice, I almost thought I would see tears in his eyes.

"I have to agree with Danny," Mike said. "Technically, since the resort owns the entire canyon from the highway all the way up to the Continental Divide, the Bigfoot is our guest. This is a resort, and all of our guests should be afforded every consideration."

Sieg looked from Mike to me and from me to Mike.

He then sat back and folded his arms.

"Nobody ever lets me do anything!"

* * *

After lunch, Todd and Sieg went out to work on the dock. It had been getting pretty ratty, and they were going to spend the day scraping and painting it. There was some grumbling from Sieg as they went off.

I started down the front stairs, holding onto the rail. It was time to go back and let Lisa go to lunch. Mike looked down at me as I took the steps slowly.

"Were you actually serious this morning?" he asked.

"About what?"

"Were you serious about the Bigfoot? I mean, you weren't kidding around, right?"

"No, I wasn't kidding," I replied. "You can ask Anna, if you like. She still thinks the three of you were screwing around or something."

"Wonderful," he said. "One thing's for certain, we're going to have to keep an eye on your buddy. I'm half afraid he's going to Sybel to tell him everything. Then we won't get a minute a peace around here."

"I wouldn't worry about it, Mike," I said at the bottom of the stairs.

"Why shouldn't I worry?" he asked. "You saw the look on his face."

"Weren't you listening?" I shot back. "Sieg wants the glory of finding the Bigfoot for himself. He's not going to share the glory, and he's not going to help someone else get the glory for love or money."

"I hope you know what you're talking about."

"So do I," I said. "I think you can trust me on this one."

"I sure hope so."

* * *

Mike came along with me, which was a good thing, because I stumbled twice on the trail and he caught me before I fell. Lisa smiled as we came through the front door.

"Mike," she said, "Cap needs to speak to you right away. Danny, I've got another project set up for you."

I groaned. Over the past couple of days, I had found every "little project" was actually a big pain in the ass. Confirming my suspicions, she held out a sheaf of forms. Mike laughed as he walked past and into Cap's office. I took the forms and sat down at the small table behind the desk and turned on the lamp.

"Don't be such a baby," she said. "I want you to figure out exactly when these two groups are due in. Then I want you to find out how many rooms they're going to need. It'll give you something to do while I'm at lunch."

"Why am I doing this?" I asked.

"Mostly because I told you to," she said. "Also, because we need to figure out just how many resources we have to have on hand for the duration. It wouldn't look good if we ran out of cleaning supplies or food while we have guests."

"All right," I said with a sigh, "I'll get right on it, slave driver."

She blew me a kiss, and I got to work. It was obvious people other than Lisa had made the reservations. I had a hard time deciphering the spidery script scrawling across the page. After a while I began to put together a picture of what was going on, and it troubled me.

Lisa came back and was sipping yet another cup of coffee as she worked on a crossword puzzle. I looked up and without saying a word, turned the pages around so she could read them.

"What's the matter?" she asked.

"I think we're in trouble," I said.

"Why?"

"Look at this," I said, using my pen to point. "From what I can figure out, these two tour groups aren't arriving one after the other. They're arriving simultaneously. In fact, they're going to be here within minutes of each other."

"What?" she said. "That can't be right!"

"I'd appreciate it if you can find my screw up, then. If I am right, we do not have nearly enough active rooms available to cover both groups."

She started checking my numbers and making small marks on the papers with a pencil. A frown creased her face. She stood up and walked over to Cap's door. A muffled voice answered her knock. She went in and closed the door behind her.

"What!" Cap said through the door.

Sven came out of his office and glanced at the door. We could catch only bits and pieces of the conversation within.

"What's going on?" he asked.

"I think we've managed to book two groups in at the same time," I replied.

"That would be correct" he said. "Both groups are going to be in the state at the same time. I managed to land the contracts. We have the rooms."

"Uh, you do know one entire wing of this resort is closed down? I don't think we have the room."

"Oh, crap. I thought we should grab all the business we could."

Cap's door jerked open. Cap stuck his head out and spotted Sven standing across from me.

"You!" He pointed at Sven. "Come in here now!"

Sven gulped.

"I may have made a miscalculation," he said as he passed the desk.

* * *

That afternoon I had a "fly-on-the-wall" view of Cap's war council. After Sven had been thoroughly chewed out, Cap had come out of his office and started yelling orders to Mike and me. We didn't say a word or ask a question. We merely obeyed.

Sieg and Todd soon arrived, and we spent the better part of an hour pulling a pair of couches over to where the polar bear stood. Mike disappeared to issue Cap's summons to the other members of the management team while the three of us continued to pull overstuffed chairs across the polished floor.

Lisa ordered me back to the front desk, which was where I remained during the meeting. Mike had to stay for the discussion, and he made it clear he wanted Sieg and Todd where he could grab them at a moment's notice.

Everyone else arrived slowly, one at a time. I had met most of them during my sojourn at the resort, but it was really quite impressive to see how many people it took to keep the place running smoothly, or at least as smoothly as we ran.

Sven stood off to one side. He wasn't his usual self and stayed very quiet. While I wanted to exult in his screw up, I had to feel sorry for him because *I* certainly wouldn't want to be the target of Cap's ire.

After a while, the circle was filled. Cap sat in a huge red leather chair we had placed right in front of the polar bear. Lisa sat on a couch to his left. Sven stood behind the couch to his right. Mike and Penny were sharing the couch and unconsciously holding hands.

Facing Cap was Mr. Chang. Today he wasn't dressed like an escapee from a Sax Rohmer novel and instead had opted for an excellently tailored blue silk suit. Sitting there, with his legs crossed and an open notebook on his knee, he looked more like a Hong Kong banker than the head of our laundry. I wondered if the changes happening to the resort had prompted this change in him.

Gwen Collins, Lisa's sister, was sitting on the couch next to her. Gwen was a tall platinum blonde wearing a black dress and the ubiquitous resort blazer. While everyone else was looking back and forth, she kept looking down as if afraid of meeting anyone's glance.

As night auditor, Gwen did everything Lisa and Cap did during the day and ran the telephone system too. I didn't know her well, only meeting her the few times she had arrived to relieve Lisa and me in the afternoons.

I sensed an air of infinite sadness about her. However something about the way Lisa spoke of her sister kept me from satisfying my curiosity. I chalked Gwen up as yet another resort mystery, possibly one I didn't want an answer to.

Karl Quintana sat in one of the overstuffed chairs to the left of Mr. Chang. He was the manager of the dining room and the bar. His black hair was slicked back, and his pencil-thin mustache was immaculate, as was his gray suit, which was almost a match for Mr. Chang's. He watched the rest of the group with half-closed eyes, as if he was tired and wanted to take a nap.

Anna sat across from Karl and, like Mr. Chang, kept a notebook across her lap. I caught Karl sneaking a look at her a couple of times. I suspected he was trying to get a peek down her blouse. I didn't get jealous, because I knew if he got too friendly, Anna would shut him down fast.

After they were all seated, Cap came right to the point.

"Due to the business acumen of our brand-new catering director," he said, glaring out of the corner of his eye to where Sven had the grace to look guilty, "we're in the position of having to open the north wing. Under the old management, in this situation we would have just tendered our apologies to one of the groups and refunded their money. However, Big Ed is more interested in making money. Our aforementioned catering director has assured me this is the best way to build our business."

Karl raised his hand. "Cap, I think I speak for all of us when I say while opening up the north wing is a great idea, I don't think we have the time or the staff to do the job."

Cap nodded as a murmur rolled through the circle. "I understand we're going to be strained, probably to the limit with this. On the other hand, I just got off the phone with Big Ed. He told me to spend anything I needed to get the job done. We're going to have to hire and train extra crew to help. Housekeeping, laundry and food services are authorized to get anyone they know who can do the job. I mean that. You can hire whomever you want as long as they know what they're doing. We don't have the time to do a whole lot of training on this job."

Mike raised his hand.

"What about the housemen? Are we going to get some more help?"

Cap made a sour face. "You wish. The four of you are going to be damned busy. Danny's going to spend most of his time on the front desk in order to relieve Lisa and Gwen. The rest of you are going to schlep luggage while the groups are checking in an out, handling any set ups we need in the lobby or ballroom, and work on a whole bunch of small projects we need done. You've done a damned good job fixing things up around here, and you're going to continue. Mike, I don't think you're going to need much more help than you already have."

Then he turned to our head housekeeper. "Penny, I don't have time to interview people. I just need you to find people you think you can trust. We'll fill out the forms when we can. Which goes for you, Mr. Chang, and for you, Karl."

Chang and Karl nodded, and Penny smiled wolfishly.

"Great!" she said, rubbing her hands together, "Courtney and I have already made plans."

Cap looked at her incredulously. "You have?"

"I've been planning on this ever since Big Ed took over the resort. There was no way he was going to let us run around with one hand tied behind our back. I didn't know you were going to give me free rein. I was prepared to fight for the people I wanted. Courtney used to work for the Imperial Hotel down in Mohawk. The maids there are still out of work since they're still rebuilding the hotel. We think we can pick up a pretty good group with just a bit of head-hunting."

For a fleeting moment, I tried to imagine Penny and Courtney in nothing but loincloths and body paint, carrying spears and jumping out at unfortunate maids. I quickly managed to repress the vision created.

"How soon do you think you can get them?" Cap asked.

"Oh, we could get them in a day or two. We just need

some time to go down and..."

"Then go! Get down there and get them! We don't have time to screw around here, Penny. We've got less than five days before we have to be up and running at full speed. We'll need a lot of help to refurbish the north wing. The same goes for you too, Mr. Chang."

"I understand," he replied.

Cap looked around at each of his people and then nodded to himself. "All right, meeting adjourned."

TEN

The next day found us running all over the place. The resort's north wing hadn't been used in years, and we found ourselves hauling everything from tattered furniture to shaggy linen. Sieg was grumbling to me as we moved a mattress through a dusty hall.

"I can't believe this is happening to us."

All over the place came the sounds of fifty construction guys moving around, fixing what they could as they tried to make the north wing inhabitable for guests. I shook my head as we threaded our way past a couple of carpenters. They had removed a door from one of the rooms and were busy sanding it down and using a plane on the edges.

"You can't believe it?" I said. "I can't believe they haven't been in the attics here for over a century."

"Oh, come on Danny, just because we found a newspaper with an article about the Scopes Monkey Trial in it doesn't mean they haven't been up there."

"It means they haven't been up there since the Jazz

Age," I said bitterly.

Fortunately for the two of us, the mattress we had was the last one needing removal. We headed upstairs to the third floor, where we found Mike and Todd replacing yet another cracked window. Mike wiped his hands after they had finished and turned to us.

"Just like the house," he said.

"Yeah," Todd said with a grim smile, "at least we're getting paid for this, Dude."

***

Because of the lack of furniture in the living room, our dining room table had become the social center of our universe. While there were two steel folding chairs in the living room, the other five chairs were around the table. It was here we would play board games like *Risk* or *Monopoly* on slow nights. The room was almost empty except for the table and chairs. Some ancient Lake Weir monogrammed towels served as curtains, and the floor was in desperate need of sanding and polishing. Mike and I had discussed that little project a couple of times, but we just hadn't found the time for it.

On the Friday before the tour groups were expected to arrive, the four of us were gathered together in a state of exhaustion. Mike absolutely refused to cook, so now he was on our newly installed telephone, ordering a few pizzas. We were starving, and each of us had wildly differing tastes. I couldn't understand how anyone, especially Mike, could stand ham and pineapple on their pizza. Todd loved anchovies, which didn't bother me too much, though I preferred them in a Caesar salad. Sieg liked pepperoni, and while I could tolerate it, I preferred good-old Italian sausage and green peppers. The argument was threatening to take all night, so Mike ordered four large pizzas with everything, including anchovies, on them. When we tried to argue with him, he merely put his hand over the mouthpiece and glared at us.

"If you don't like something, pick it off," he hissed.

At one end of the table, Todd and Sieg were busy counting our funds. There was a pile of crumpled greenbacks growing between them. I couldn't believe how they abused the bills being unearthed from their pockets. They stopped counting at one point and looked over at me expectantly. With a small sigh, I pulled out my wallet and took a couple of crisp, brand-new fives and tossed them onto the pile. They looked like fresh green tents pitched over a hill of brush. Then I leaned back and propped my feet up. Mike hung up the phone and knocked my feet off the table.

"We have to eat here, idiot!" he said. "Besides, I don't want you breaking that chair. We don't have enough as it is."

"Haven't you talked to Cap yet," I asked him. "You said you would."

"With what time, Danny?" he asked. "You've been as busy as I have and you haven't talked to him either. Todd, I want you and Sieg to go on down to the highway and meet the pizza guy. Your cat's reputation is faster than our telephone."

"Cool," Todd replied.

"I think we need to do something with that cat," I said. "He's beginning to wear out his welcome."

"Dude, leave my cat alone," Todd said, pulling on his jacket. "It's not his fault how he's made. I don't know what you have against him."

"Well, let's see," I replied. "He uses my head as a pillow, and he wakes me every morning by purring loud enough to scare a bull-moose."

"He likes you because you feed him."

"Wonderful," I said. "It's just what everyone needs, a stupid killer cat fan club. Fan-freaking-tastic! You know something? I'm going to feed him. I'm going to feed him to a woodchipper!"

Mike shook his head. "Oh, would you just calm down, Danny? What are you two waiting for? The delivery guy won't hang around forever and we're hungry."

Sieg grinned. "I'm waiting for Danny's head to explode."

"Get moving," Mike ordered.

Sieg stood at attention and saluted.

"Sir, yes sir! O Captain, my captain!"

They left, and as I sat there shaking my head Mike went over to the fridge in the kitchen. He opened it and tossed me a beer. I looked at it and then looked at him and back to it.

"What's the matter?" he asked.

"It's been a while since I've had one. I've been under what amounted to house arrest since before I was eighteen. I think I haven't had one since the junior prom."

"Well," he said, "you're now old enough and no longer under house arrest. You might as well have one now; you've earned it."

I took the bottle opener from him and popped the top. After a swig, I looked up at him.

"Not bad," I said.

"It's good beer," he said. "Remember, life is too short to waste on bad beer, Danny. If you ever learn anything, that is something you should know."

Someone knocked on the front door. I looked at

Mike and he looked back at me.

"Were you expecting someone?" I asked.

"That was what I was going to ask you," he replied as he went out and opened the door. Anna, Penny and Courtney came inside. Mike stepped back with a smile and ushered them over to the table.

"Ladies," I said, "what brings you here?"

I stood up, and they took seats around the kitchen table. I brought back the two folding chairs from the living room and set them up. Mike took one of the chairs and I sat on the other next to Anna. She was wearing some kind of perfume; it reminded me of cotton candy. I had to control myself, or I would have tried to kiss her just because of the scent. Penny poked Mike in the stomach, and he jerked back and laughed.

"We thought we'd drop in and share your beer," she said.

"And I'll bet it's just a coincidence we've got pizza on the way, too," Mike said.

I rolled my eyes. "Oh brother, you two are completely transparent."

Penny turned her eyes on me.

"Oh, really?" she asked.

"Yeah," I replied. "Why don't you two go get a room?"

"Well excuse me!" she said. "Maybe we'll just do that. I'm going to borrow your boss for a while."

She took his hand, and they left the room. I stuck my head out the dining room door as they started up the stairs.

"Hey! He's not my boss!"

I could hear them laughing as they galloped upstairs and just shook my head as I went back into the dining room. Anna was laughing, and Courtney was smiling. It was the first time I had seen her smile since she had arrived at the resort. I grinned back at her and then sat down across from her.

"All right," I said. "Do you finally want to talk about it?"

"Talk about what?" she said.

"I think you know what."

"No," she said, "I don't."

"Okay, that answers my question. My next question is this: are you going to keep avoiding me like I've got the plague? You could at least give me the courtesy of telling me what the hell I did."

"It wasn't you, it was Sieg."

"It's always Sieg, Court," I said. "Sieg is the center of our particular universe. We orbit around him whether we want to or not. I mean, seriously, everything we do is predicated on either something he has said or something he has done."

"Hah!"

"Tell you what," I said, "if you finally decide you want to talk about it, come find me. I'll listen."

She looked down at her hands for a second. "Okay," she said in a voice barely audible.

Anna was watching us with her lower lip caught between her teeth.

"Is there something I can help with?" she asked.

"Nah," I said. "Don't worry about it. This is about old friends and all that."

"Oh."

I reached across the table and squeezed Anna's hand. Courtney watched us and then looked back down at her own hands. I decided we needed a change of subject.

"So," I said, "what have you two heard about how

everyone is handling the invasion?"

Courtney looked up and smiled slightly.

"Chuck can't wait because he's hoping for big tippers, or at least bigger than he's used to."

Chuck was the dining room attendant, and he also ran room service orders.

"Yeah," I said, "I guess all those old ladies coming up for Sunday dinner don't exactly tip that well."

"He says he usually gets a dime," Courtney said. "If they give him a quarter, it's a real fortune. On the other hand they do have interesting conversations right in front of him. You'd be surprised how many octogenarian sluts hang around those Saturday dances looking for a man who can give them a thrill. I think they scare Chuck half to death."

I snickered. "Don't tell Sieg, or he'll be trying to become a gigolo."

Courtney looked at me in horror. "Oh, ick! That's disgusting!"

"Yeah, but you have to admit it's very Sieg Shultz."

"It could have gone without saying," she said.

"And it probably should have," I said. "You have to admit, though, I've changed the subject."

"Did you have to do it that way?" Anna said. "Just thinking about it makes me itch all over."

"Oh, come on," I said, smiling, "some of those women would welcome a bit of chubby love."

"They'd never be satisfied," Courtney said. "Then they'd demand their money back. I should know."

"I don't think I needed to know that," I said.

While I thought it was good to get Courtney to talk, the conversation was heading down avenues I thought we should avoid. When she saw the expression on my face, she laughed. The laugh was nice.

"That's right, *you* don't want to know."

Anna started laughing and I just sat there, red faced and watched them for a moment before I started to laugh along with them. For a couple of minutes we were laughing together and pointing at each other. When we had ourselves back under control, Anna turned to me.

"What do you think Mike and Penny are up to?" she asked.

"You've got to be kidding," I said.

Courtney and I looked at her, and she started to blush, which I found utterly charming.

"Oh," she said in a small voice.

"That's all right," I reassured her, "You'd be used to it if you lived over here. Penny comes over a lot, and they disappear for a time and then—"

I was interrupted by the front door flying open. We looked up to see Sieg standing in the doorway, breathing heavily with his eyes wild. I noticed right away his hands were empty.

"Where's the pizza, dummy?" I said.

"Forget the pizza, Danny," he said, "I saw it!"

"Saw what?" I asked.

"I saw the Bigfoot!"

"Oh, yeah, right," I said and held up a hand. "I'll bet you saw it. Where's Todd?"

"I'm right behind him, Dude," Todd said from the hallway.

Todd pushed his way past Sieg into the dining room. He placed the pizzas on the table and handed me a plastic shopping bag holding a couple bottles of pop. He didn't look his usual happy self. Courtney stood up and took the pop out of my hands and headed for the kitchen. Anna followed her.

"What happened?" I asked Todd.

"Dude, the pizza guy gets down there by the road and I was paying him when Sieg suddenly started shouting and raced off into the woods. I had to carry everything by myself."

"I saw the Bigfoot," Sieg said, "and I decided to go after it!"

I slapped him across the back of the head.

"Ow!" he said, rubbing where I'd hit him. "What did you do that for?"

"You moron," I said. "You could have gotten lost in those woods, and it would have been days before you were found."

Courtney came out of the kitchen and glared at him.

"Assuming we'd even bother looking," she said.

"So?" he asked. "I didn't get lost, here I am."

I frowned at him. "And you let Todd carry everything up the hill by himself. While I wouldn't put anything past you, this would be a pretty low stunt, even for you."

"I don't know why you're all against me today," Sieg said.

Anna came back from the kitchen with a stack of paper plates and plastic cups. She put them on the table and sat back down.

"Maybe," Todd said, "because you went running into the woods instead of helping me carry the pizzas, Dude. Our priority list is sex, beer, food and fun, in that order."

"I notice work doesn't appear on the list," I said.

"You're learning something, Dude," he replied.

Courtney and Todd went back into the kitchen and I opened one of the boxes and grabbed a piece of pizza. Sieg looked around in confusion.

"Where's Mike?" he asked.

"I'll give you one guess," I said.

The dining room door opened, and our missing friends came in. They were both freshly showered, as shown by the dampness of their hair.

"Oh," Sieg said. "I should have known."

Mike opened one of the boxes and pulled out a couple of slices. He put them on plates and passed one to Penny.

"We're going out on the front porch," he said.

It sounded like a good idea, so we gathered up the pizzas, pop, plates and cups and trooped out onto the porch. A cool breeze was wafting through the trees from the lake. Crickets were chirping, and for a moment I was able to forget most of my troubles.

Sieg leaned against one of the porch supports and picked off something from his slice and tossed it into the bushes.

"Now this is the life," he said.

Penny and Mike had appropriated the porch swing and were busy whispering and giggling to each other. I didn't know if I was disgusted or jealous. I sat down on the stairs with my pizza and a cup of cola. Anna sat down next to me.

"Is he always like this?" she asked.

"Who?"

"Sieg," she said. "I mean, does he always seem to explode all over the place like this?"

"Of course," I said. "Let us just say whatever it is he suffers from, he makes sure it's very contagious."

"Is it?"

"Oh, yeah," I said. "If it wasn't contagious, I'd be on my way to Miskatonic University and downtown Mohawk wouldn't be a pile of ashes."

"You were going to Miskatonic? I didn't know."

"Well, I was," I said. "I had their acceptance and

everything until about a month after the fire. They claimed I didn't live up to their code of conduct, which was a bunch of garbage. I think they just didn't want a convicted arsonist traipsing around their pure and unsullied campus."

"You're bitter," she said.

"You better believe I'm bitter," I said, "especially about that. A ten-second perusal of the trial transcript would show I'm no danger to anyone."

"Except you," she said. "What were you planning on studying?"

"Promise not to laugh?"

"Why would I laugh?" she said.

"Promise not to laugh?" I asked.

"No, I can't promise," she said. "I've known you too long."

I mused for a second and decided I could stand a bit of ridicule.

"Oh, all right," I said. "I wanted to be a nuclear physicist. They have a great program at Miskatonic."

She started choking and held a knuckle up to her mouth. Her plate of pizza dropped to the stair, fortunately pizza side up, and loud snorts were forcing their way out of her nose.

"It's not funny!" I said.

"I know, I know," she said, gasping. "It's just I'm trying to imagine you working with nuclear stuff."

I guess with my history, I would laugh too. I was about to protest some more when I heard Edgar yowling from somewhere behind the house. Sieg looked around, annoyed.

"Now what?" he asked.

I stood up, my pizza hanging dangerously from my fingers.

"Damned if I know. Let's go and find out. Maybe he's got a poor bear trapped in a tree or something."

Mike stood up from the swing and shook his head.

"There aren't any bears dumb enough to come down the canyon anymore," he said.

"Dude," Todd bristled, "my cat isn't that bad!"

"Tell it to the bears," Mike said.

With the girls trailing behind us, we four intrepid adventurers walked around the house to where the tool shed stood. At least we thought it had once been a tool shed. It was the only explanation we had for a structure too big to be an outhouse and too small for a garage. By this time, it was doing its damnedest to imitate a termite mound with windows and a door.

Edgar was standing on his hind legs, with his forepaws up against the door, and yowling. Suddenly the door shook from something inside the shed.

"I say," came a cultured, British voice, "go away you beastly cat!"

Oh, just our luck, I thought, the killer cat has trapped an innocent tourist.

I cupped my hand around my mouth and shouted to the prisoner.

"Hold on, sir! We'll get the cat!"

The door quit shaking. "You will?" said the voice. "Thank you."

Todd walked over and picked up Edgar, something none of the rest of us would have tried. He flipped Edgar around so that the cat was draped over his shoulder and Edgar merely started purring. He opened his eyes and looked at us as if to say, "Try this and I'll eat your liver." Absentmindedly, Todd scratched Edgar behind the ears as he strolled toward the house. I was waiting at the back door. For a blinding instant, I thought about forgetting to open the door, then realized it would put me in the vicinity of a very angry Edgar. With one fluid motion, I opened the door, and Todd chucked him into the kitchen. I slammed the door shut and immediately Edgar started howling and scratching to be let out again.

"No way, Dude," Todd told him, "Eat your food and take a nap!"

Anna leaned close to me as I stepped away from the house. "I can't believe he did that," she whispered. "He's very brave."

"Tell me about it," I whispered back. "He does it all the time. I don't know why he isn't dead or at least getting stitches."

Courtney had been standing behind Anna and heard us.

"It's his cat," she said.

For someone who supposedly hated Sieg, Courtney was spending a great deal of time near him. I was going to say something when Mike walked up to the shed and I decided to follow him instead.

"Okay, sir," he said, "we put the cat inside. You can come out now."

"I...I...I must stay here and compose myself," the voice said. "My nerves are completely gone after that horrid creature attacked me. I did not think there were any dangerous animals in the canyon and suddenly..."

Mike turned to me. "Great," he said in a low voice, "we're going to get sued again."

"What do you mean *we*?" I asked him. "Todd's the one getting sued. Sieg and I have made our feelings for that cat known long before this."

Mike sighed and turned back to the shed.

"Sir," he said, "you can't stay inside there."

"Why not?" was the querulous reply. "It is safe in

here, unlike out there where great rampaging beasts seem to proliferate."

"Sir, the shed is old and it's about to fall down."

"I am quite comfortable here," the voice said. "I am staying here until I feel that it is safe to leave."

Mike just looked over at me, and I knew what he wanted. I stepped over to the shed and grabbed the door handle. He held up his hand as I awaited his signal.

"Sir," he said, "you've got to come out of there!"

"I refuse to leave this refuge!"

Mike dropped his hand. I grabbed the handle and yanked with all my strength. Ordinarily, I would have either pulled the door open or pulled a muscle. This time, with the wood so rotten, I ripped the door completely off its hinges.

Standing there, holding the remains of the inside handle, was the Bigfoot.

"Oh, I say," it said, looking at us.

The Bigfoot was well over eight feet tall and was crouched inside the cramped interior of the tool shed. It was covered in long, fine, brown hair, and it had beady black eyes and a tiny button nose. What really caught my attention was the green, red and silver striped tie hanging around its neck and the small, gold-rimmed spectacles dangling from a bright red ribbon disappearing somewhere into its fur.

I looked over at the guys and saw that Sieg's eyes had grown to the size of dinner plates. He slowly pointed to our visitor with a shaking hand.

"It's the Bigfoot," he said in a low whisper.

The Bigfoot, for its part, turned around with a confused expression. Then it brightened up as realization dawned, and it turned back to glare at us.

"I will have you know," it said in an even tone, "I am

not now nor ever been what you would call a Bigfoot or a member of the *Homo Americus Bigfoot* species."

His voice had a very distinctive British accent and for a moment I felt I was being lectured by some learned don. My mind reeled as I tried to make sense of such a voice coming from such a being.

"Huh?" I asked in my usual wittily urbane manner.

"That is the species designation for an American Bigfoot, young human. While a worthy species, they are not as cultured as my own *Homo Canadian Abominable.*

"And that is?" Mike asked in a puzzled voice. The *Homo Canadian Abominable* looked at him levelly for a moment before sighing.

"In the vernacular, I am a Sasquatch. A Canadian citizen, if you will, from British Columbia."

"Oh, I guess that makes sense," Anna said rolling her eyes. "If anything about a Sasquatch inside a tool shed makes any sense."

The Sasquatch turned around and slowly studied the shed for a few seconds.

"*This* is a tool shed?" he asked. "I had thought I had taken up refuge in the remains of an antediluvian woodpile. However, now I can see the Victorian charm of the construction..." He reached out and touched the edge of the roof and a small piece fell off. "Then again..."

"Is there a difference?" Courtney asked. "These idiots just haven't had the time to tear it down."

"That sounds like an excellent plan," the Sasquatch said with a toothy grin. "I have to admit, though, the structure has certain charms of its own. You might wish to consider some plan of preservation."

"Right," Sieg said, recovering from his shock. "So what the hell are you doing hiding in our tool shed, dilapidated or not. And what's with the accent?"

"Obviously," the Sasquatch said, "I was endeavoring to escape that vicious beast of yours. This was the only sanctuary available. As for my accent, what is so objectionable about it?"

"Nothing," Sieg said blinking, "How should I put it? It's a bit *educated*, for a Sasquatch."

"Of course I'm educated," the Sasquatch said. "What else would you expect from an Oxford graduate? I believe it was Epictetus who said *Only the Educated are Free*. I like Epictetus in the evening, he always seems perfectly civilized for such a civil time of day."

"Good quote," Sieg said, "I'll have to remember it."

The Sasquatch began to edge away, keeping us in front of him.

"Now if you will excuse me..." he said.

"Where are you going?" Sieg asked.

"I'm going back to my lair, young human. All of us educated monsters have lairs, though mine seems to be a bit more rustic than most."

"I have to warn you," I said, "there is a doctor from the California Institute of Cryptozoology up here and he's trying to find you."

"That would be the chap with the monkey?"

"Yeah, that would be him," Sieg said.

"I was aware of his interest. *I* was following *him* at a discreet distance and watching his monkey's antics with much amusement."

"Wait a minute!" Sieg suddenly said. "Why haven't we found any of your footprints? I thought Bigfoots and Sasquatches and whatever always left footprints all over the place."

A deep rumbling laugh rolled from the Sasquatch.

"Do you seriously believe we are that clumsy?" he asked Sieg.

He started to back away again and I held up my hand. I just had to ask him a question.

"Are you the person singing in the lake every morning?"

"Why, yes I am," he said. "I like to sing *The Road to Mandalay* when I'm bathing. I learned it during my second year at school. Is there a problem?"

"Frankly, it's alarming. We're about to have a lot of guests at the resort, so you might want to change your song. Did you also set the snare I tripped over?"

The Sasquatch had the grace to look down and shuffle his feet a bit.

"I must apologize for that. I didn't think of the risks inherent with such an experiment. I shall refrain from repeating it."

With that, he stepped into the shadow cast by a giant ponderosa pine. After we blinked we discovered he had disappeared. We looked around in surprise. Sieg and Todd went over to the tree and peered into the woods to see if they could spot him again.

"Well, Anna," I said when I could speak again, "now do you think we're messing with you?"

"No," she said distantly. "I guess not."

Sieg came back to us and punched the palm of his hand.

"Now we can make some money!"

"What?" Mike asked.

"I can see it now, 'Bigfoot Tours: Come up and we'll show you the trail of the primeval savage of the Colorado forest.'"

"No, Sieg," I said.

"But--" he said.

"No, Sieg!" we all said in unison.

"You guys never let me do anything," he said with a

pout.

"Now guys," Mike said, "we have to keep our friend there a secret."

"Why?" Sieg asked. I could almost see the dollar signs behind his eyes.

"One, because we don't want everyone to think we've lost our minds, which would be bad for business. And two, because we don't want uncontrollable crowds wandering around the canyon, which would also be bad for business."

"How could that be bad for business?" Sieg asked him.

"If the canyon becomes flooded with Bigfoot hunters," Mike said, "it'll drive our regular guests away. Then when they don't find the Bigfoot, they'll get bored and leave, and we'll be stuck without customers."

"I didn't think of that," Sieg admitted.

We let out a collective sigh and then Todd spoke up. "So, do we have to hide the Sasquatch Dude?"

"Yeah," Mike sighed. "It looks like it."

"Oh, Dude," Todd said, shaking his head.

"I know, man, but it's just what we're going to have to do."

Penny grabbed Mike's arm and pulled him against her.

"Let's go in and try to figure this out," she said in his ear. "Nothing's going to get decided out where everyone and their kid brother can hear."

* * *

Mike stood at the head of the dining room table and clapped to bring us to order. After coming inside, we'd sat around and talked about the Sasquatch and tried to figure out what we were going to do when the resort was filled up.

"So," Mike said, "are we decided? We're going to try to hide evidence of our new Sasquatch friend?"

I noticed Courtney was sitting pretty close to Todd now. Glancing to my left, I saw Sieg watching them intently. Mike and I were staring at him, and when he didn't answer, I reached over and nudged his shoulder.

"What?" he asked.

"Are we agreed we have to hide the Sasquatch?" Mike asked him.

"Oh, I guess so," he said. "It's not like I really have a say in this."

"You could screw it up, Sieg," I said.

"No, I can't," he replied. "Mike was right. We need to keep him a secret. If the resort closes, you and I end up in Cañon City, as you so recently reminded me."

I blinked. Helen Shapely and our Mohawk troubles seemed to be a thousand miles away. I had managed to forget about them. I looked at my buddy and he smiled sourly.

"So," he said, "in the name of self-preservation, I agree."

"What about our friend and his monkey?" Mike asked. "They're wandering all over the canyon."

Sieg frowned. It was obvious he, as well as the rest of us, had been thinking a great deal about them during the past few minutes.

"Good question," he said. "With any luck, our Sasquatch friend will be able to stay away from them. If something else happens we just have to figure it out then. If we deflect Dr. Sybel, he'll just try harder. Right now, I think our biggest problem is going to be keeping our new friend under wraps with a full house of tourists."

"That's going to be the big problem all right," I said.

"According to the estimate, we're literally going to be full. Lisa was telling me about it earlier."

"I volunteer to stay in Mike's room," Penny said. "The other girls could stay in your spare rooms."

"Thank you," I said. "You cannot imagine the problems that will cause. The extra rooms upstairs aren't inhabitable yet. We just have not had the time to fix them."

"How bad could it be?" Courtney asked.

"You couldn't possibly imagine," Mike said.

ELEVEN

The Saturday before the invasion dawned very bright, very clear and very, very cold. As soon as the sun climbed into the sky, it would warm up, but it still felt like mid-winter during our run.

Later in the day we spent our time following Cap around as he went and personally inspected every guest room. I think he'd read something in a trade magazine about how a big hotel chain's owner did that. As it was, Cap made a few of his famous "suggestions," and we immediately took action. After a while we gathered in the lobby. He looked at the four of us and slowly smiled.

"Not a bad job overall. We're going to have to do something with those attics eventually. I didn't know they had gotten that bad."

"They've been closed for a long time," Mike said with a shrug.

"Yeah," Cap said, "but the William Jennings Bryan headline was ridiculous."

"It was probably up there long before they closed up

the attics, Cap," Mike said.

"You're probably right. By the way, Danny, you did a good job on the banister on the third floor."

"No problem," I said with a self-conscious smile. "Fortunately, the moldings up there match the rest of the resort. I was able to find a couple of extra."

"Monday's going to be the big day," Cap continued, "so I have a few more projects for you."

He fished some slips of paper from his shirt pocket and handed them to us.

"We're having a luncheon in the ballroom at three o'clock. The Intermountain Chamber of Commerce is coming up for a tour. Sven invited them."

"Yeah," Mike said, "I thought I smelled him in that."

"I'll tell him to use a better deodorant," Cap said. "Todd, I want you to take Sieg with you and buy the supplies on our new list."

"No problem, Dude. We'll be back before lunch."

"You'd better be. Danny, I want you to go out there and fix the damned dock. I also want it sanded and varnished before nightfall."

"I thought Sieg and Todd did that a while ago," I said.

"So did they," Cap said with a glare at them. "I want it done right and you seem to be our woodworking expert."

"I hope it'll dry in time," I said.

"So do I. It won't look good with people stuck on it."

* * *

It turned out Todd and Sieg *had* done a lot of work on the dock. However, some of their repairs were sloppy since they had no idea of what they were doing. I made a close examination of the whole structure and then replaced a couple of boards they'd missed.

After taking a belt sander to the whole deck, I slapped a coat of varnish on it and waited for it to dry.

The day had indeed turned warm, and I was sitting in the shade of a pine tree with a piece of grass twirling between my teeth. I became aware of someone behind me. I glanced up and found Courtney standing there.

"Hi, Court," I said. "What's up?"

She pointed up and then sank down on the grass next to me. She plucked a small flower and started shredding it.

"The new girls are driving Penny crazy, and I wanted to get the hell out of there before they started getting to me. It's bad enough that Dr. Sybel *and* that damned monkey keep staring at my ass."

"What's wrong with the new girls?" I asked.

"Nothing, really," she said. "I used to work with most of them back at the Imperial. Now, I just don't know. They're all talking about their boyfriends and how cute Todd and Mike are. Every time one of them talks about Mike, Penny starts getting frantic."

"She shouldn't," I said. "I'm sure Mike only has eyes for her."

"It's a girl thing, you wouldn't understand."

"You're probably right."

We sat for a long time and watched the cloud reflections as they scudded across the surface of the lake. The wind was calm and hardly a ripple disturbed the water. Finally, Courtney let out a long, sad sigh and leaned against me and put her head on my shoulder.

"Have you ever had to apologize and didn't know how?" she asked.

"You're asking me?" I said. "When I was sitting in the courtroom during the trial I wondered what to say."

"I forgot about that. Other than the stupid dragon float, you seemed so normal. Sieg was the weird one."

"Oh, I don't know," I said. "He's got his problems too."

"Yeah, I don't think I helped him much. Then, you'd know all about it."

"I'd know about what?" I asked. "Neither of you will talk to me about what happened."

She sat up and looked at me, startled.

"Oh," she said, "and here I thought you knew everything. I thought Sieg would have told you."

"Until this past year, I would have agreed with you," I said. "Then again, until this past year, I would have thought you'd have told me everything, too."

She looked out over the lake as if trying to see somewhere into the past.

"It all started when Sieg forgot to ask me to the Prom," Courtney began. "He ended up going by himself, and I think he was jealous. He forgot to ask me, but Nick Wills didn't. The Prom was right around the corner, and I didn't want to miss it. I was kind of flattered by the attention, especially after losing the Homecoming Queen in the fiasco and then being known as someone close to you two. It wasn't improving my social life, let me tell you.

"You and Sieg were so wrapped up in the problems caused by the fire, which I think is why Sieg forgot to ask me to the dance. Anyway, when Nick asked, I said 'yes.' Sieg found out right away and then went nuts. We had this huge fight out in the parking lot with his mother sitting right there.

"Well, Sieg couldn't con any poor girl to go with him, small wonder. So he showed up all by himself and hung around the punch bowl until a bunch of football players made him go away. I think I should have been suspicious. I thought they were still smarting from losing the parade contest. Boy, was I wrong."

She looked away for a moment. "Nick then invited me to Mary Beth Tiernan's after-prom party. I didn't think anything of it and went along with him. That was my big mistake.

"At the party, Nick offered to show me another part of the house. I should have been more cautious when he led me upstairs. I didn't figure it out until he pushed me into one of the bedrooms. There was a bunch of them there, the same football guys who'd chased Sieg off. 'This'll show you little geeks what happens when you burn down our town,' Nick said. It turned pretty nasty then. They tore my dress and...I...I thought I was going to beat the crap out of them and then get away. There were just too many of them. Norman managed to push me against the wall and then...then...they ganged up on me.

"The next thing I knew, they had me on the floor, one on each of my legs and two holding my arms.

"'Let's move her up on the bed,' Kyle said, and they lifted me off the floor. I kept trying to get free but I just couldn't get loose. They...they used their belts to tie me to the bed. Then Fred grabbed the hem of my dress and ripped it all the way to my waist.

"Nick said, 'You're going to remember this night for a long time.' Then he started taking his shirt off."

She stopped talking and started crying. I didn't know what to do. I didn't know whether to hold her, pat her or just stay back. Instead, I stood up. I was clenching and unclenching my hands.

"I'll kill them," I said. "I will kill every single one of them."

She stood up and put a hand on my arm. I looked at

her, and I could feel tears welling up inside me. She shook her head.

"No, it's okay," she said. "It didn't happen."

"What?"

"Just when Nick took his shirt off, the door opened and Mary Beth and Sieg were standing there. Mr. Tiernan was right behind them with his shotgun. 'I want you boys to start running right now,' he told them. 'Maybe you'll live to see dawn.'

"I've never seen people move that fast. If those guys had been that fast on the football field, Mohawk would have been undefeated last year.

"Anyway, they started running down the stairs. Mr. Tiernan called after them in a loud voice, 'You want me to shoot them, Courtney?' Then Mary Beth and Sieg came in and untied me.

"When I stood up, I turned on Sieg. I told him it was entirely his fault. I was so mad and scared that I locked myself in the bathroom and didn't come out until Dad came and got me. I cried all the rest of the night and all the next day. Dad wanted to call the cops and prosecute all the boys. I just...just didn't want to go to court and have to relive it all over again and—"

"I understand," I said. "Why didn't you tell me? We've been friends forever, since kindergarten!"

The tears welled up in her eyes again as she looked up at me.

"I...I...I thought Sieg told you everything and you weren't talking to me anymore."

"That's silly, Court, why would I, of all people, not want to talk to you?"

"I thought it was because I blamed Sieg for the whole thing. I knew it wasn't his fault, except for not asking me to the Prom, but I still blamed him."

I reached over and put my arm around her shoulders and pulled her over for a long side-hug. She buried her face in my shoulder and started crying again. Then I thought of something.

"You're still going to have to sit on Sieg and make him listen to you," I said, stroking her hair. "You forgot about something."

"What's that?" she asked, pulling away from me.

"He's got an infinite capacity for self-martyrdom, Court. Remember when he wanted to take all the blame for the dragon? If his lawyer hadn't talked him out of it, he was going to claim I had nothing to do with it. He's always been like that. I think the reason he's not talking to you is because in that slab of lard is a heart and he believes he really is at fault."

She looked at me with widening eyes as realization dawned.

"Oh my God, I never thought of that. I was so busy—"

"You were busy dealing with the most traumatic moment of your life, Court. Hell, I should be blamed for this, too. I was so wrapped up in what was going on with the fire and everything else. I didn't think of coming over and trying to find out from you. I thought you were pissed off at me and I didn't want to—"

She placed a finger on my lips, stopping me.

"Shhh," she whispered. "It's okay."

Suddenly she pulled my face down to hers and slowly kissed me. There are moments you hold deep in your heart, and I suspected this one would always remain there.

After kissing me, Courtney stepped back and smiled.

"Wow. Maybe I should have dated you instead."

"What?" I asked, confused.

She laughed an evil little laugh.

"Don't worry, Danny. I wouldn't do that to Anna."

"What?"

She stopped and looked in my eyes for a moment. "Oh, I should have known, especially after knowing you all these years. Poor, clueless Danny, you have no idea. Oh well, I won't spoil the surprise."

"What are you talking about?" I asked her.

"Don't worry about it," she said and hugged me again. My thoughts were roiling around too much to appreciate it.

TWELVE

Sunday evening arrived early at Lake Weir. Even now, on the leading edge of summer, the sun faded behind the mountains early, turning the sky into a kaleidoscope of reds and purples. After I had managed to put another coat of varnish on the dock, Cap had come up with a bunch of extra chores needing to be done before Monday. We ended up cleaning out the coatroom adjacent to the ballroom, which we were doing in record time.

I was returning from the dumpster when Lisa called out to me.

"Danny, your mom is on the phone."

I stopped and looked at her.

"What?" I asked, unable to believe what she had just said.

She held up the phone and nodded toward it.

"Your mother is on the phone."

I walked slowly across the lobby. I didn't know what to think. Mom hadn't called me since I'd left Mohawk. I knew she was excited about my having the job and she knew Big Ed was looking out for me, but she'd left me on my own ever since I'd gotten into Ray's truck for the trip up the mountain.

I took the phone from Lisa and put it to my ear.

"Hello," I said.

"Hi, Danny. How are you doing up there?"

"I'm fine, Mom," I replied. "Is everything okay? What's going on?"

Mike came out of the coatroom to look for me. I waved at him with my free hand.

"Everything's fine, dear," she said, "but I do have something to tell you."

It was the tone of voice she had used when she told me Dad wasn't going to survive his cancer. It was the voice she used when she told me Sieg had refused the plea bargain. I knew something was happening, and I wasn't going to like it.

I let out a deep breath. "Okay, shoot."

"You remember my friend, Frida, right?"

"That lady you used to go to school with? I think she came to Dad's funeral."

The lady in question had been a large, brassy blonde woman who had seen better days and knew it. She was loud, profane and had terrible taste in clothes, at least to me. However, she'd been very sympathetic about Dad, and I found I liked her despite all that.

"That's her," Mom said. "She works for the Lemon Drop Kid Hotel and Casino in Las Vegas. When she was here, she mentioned they were looking for another seamstress to help with their floor show costumes. I'm pretty good with costumes you know."

"Yeah, I remember," I said. She was good at costumes. I always had the best costumes at Halloween every year. Even Sieg's mother would come over to help out in order to get his costumes made. Mrs. Shultz worked for Yerkin's Department Store as a dressmaker. If you had to ask the price of one of her dresses, you couldn't afford it. Somehow, I could feel my heart sinking even as I listened to my Mom's enthusiasm.

"Well, after you went to work, I sent them a copy of my resume and a sample of my work."

"What sample?"

"Just a couple of your old costumes," she said. "Guess what."

"What?" I asked.

"They called me and interviewed me over the phone. They want me! I've got a job in Las Vegas!"

"You've got what?" I asked, not believing my ears.

"I'm taking a job in Las Vegas, dear. I'm leaving Mohawk."

"You're leaving Mohawk?" I said, my voice going up about a thousand octaves, "What about the house?"

"I'm selling the house. I was going to do that anyway."

"You can't do that! That's Dad's house!"

"Danny," she said in a reasonable and calm voice, "there's no reason to keep this house. I'm moving to Las Vegas and you're going to be wherever you are. It's just a pile of bricks and wood."

"But it's our house. Dad died there!"

I could feel my world collapsing around me. As long as I knew I had a home to go to, I could handle whatever Lake Weir handed me. Now my support was being ripped out from under me. Thinking about it now, it was probably the best way to break the news.

"Danny, Matt is not this house," Mom said. "He's gone. He's not going to one day walk through the door. You have to realize this. He lives in our memories, not in this house."

I knew she was right but my knees buckled anyway, and I sank to the floor, still holding the phone. I felt something wet on my cheek and realized I was crying. Until that moment, I had pushed all thought of my father's death away from me. I'd ignored it, even at the funeral. In the back of my mind, Dad was going to appear again one day.

And now he wasn't.

"Danny," Mom's voice went on, "I know this is hard but you have to move on. It's time for both of us to move on and get lives of our own. While your father was alive I could live for him but since he died, I've felt there was something more in life for me. I don't want to live in this big old house all alone. Matt and I were going to start traveling after he retired. He didn't make it, but I'll be damned if I'm not going to. I've waited too long and damn it, I want something to retire *from!*"

I felt as if I had been punched in the heart. It hurt so much that I could feel the numbness rising up my body.

"Okay," a voice sounding like mine said, "if it's what you want then do it. I don't have anything else to say about it."

"Ed's going to put your stuff into storage. He promised to look after the house and try to find a buyer for it. With this economy I don't know how he's going to do that."

"Ed will figure it out," I said. I sighed deeply.

"We all have to grow up some time," she said. "I'm proud of you, Danny. I know Dad was proud of you."

"So, this is going to be goodbye?"

"I'm not dying, Danny," she said. "I'm just moving to Nevada. It's only a couple of states away. You can visit anytime you like, and I'll probably visit you, too."

I was trying not to sniffle. I didn't want her to know I was crying even though she probably knew from my voice. I closed my eyes and felt the past leaving me.

"Okay, Mom. I'll see you later."

"Goodbye, Danny. You must come and see me in Vegas when you get the chance. I'll leave a number and address with Ed when I find out where I'm going to live."

She hung up, and I reached up behind my head and dropped the receiver onto the desk. Lisa must have returned it to its cradle. The calmness I had been feeling faded and I put my head between my hands and sobbed.

"Do you think you can help him home?" Mike said from far away. "We don't have much else to do tonight, and he's not going to be much of a help."

"I've got him," Anna's voice said.

Two pairs of gentle hands carefully helped me to my feet, and I realized they belonged to Anna and Lisa. I wanted to shake them off but I couldn't see through the tears. It was as if all the grief I had bottled up when Dad died finally came out all at once. I fell into Anna's arms and sobbed like a child with a broken toy.

* * *

I don't remember the trip from the resort but the next thing I knew, Anna and I were in my bedroom. She was holding me in her arms and the door was closed. Before I could say anything, she pushed me down onto the bed and started pulling my clothes off.

"What are you doing?" I asked her.

"Shut up," she explained. "You're a mess."

Then I was naked. She pushed me down the hall and into the shower. Sieg and I had spent over an hour cleaning the tile and it was now a cool, white and blue area. She reached in and hot water cascaded over me. I leaned against the wall with my eyes closed. The tears kept coming. I couldn't, I wouldn't, stop them. Then I felt a presence, and a slim, naked body joined me.

"Come here," she said. She pulled me to her. I didn't know where to put my hands and just held them out, helplessly. Holding me with one hand, she pushed my hands against her back. She held me fiercely.

"Go on," she said. "Let it out."

It didn't occur to me I was holding a naked woman in my arms. It didn't matter. I was living in a dream. All that mattered was the great black void that opened up somewhere and swallowed my life. I found the void was somewhere between my heart and stomach, and I couldn't have stopped crying if I had wanted to. All the grief, all the pain came boiling up only to be washed away by the water.

My father died when I was sixteen. I helped burn down my hometown. My college career was over before it started. My mother was leaving to have her own life. The house I grew up in was being sold to strangers. One of my best friends had almost been raped. My other best friend was being consumed by guilt. I had seen a living, breathing Sasquatch. All this rose up in my vision and I felt myself washed away with all of it.

When I opened my eyes again, I was flat on my back and staring at the ceiling in my bedroom. For a second, the only thought I had was, *You know, I think I could fix those cracks with a bit of spackling*. I was dry and naked. Suddenly, Anna's face appeared above me and I could feel her straddling me.

"Now relax," she said in a gentle voice, "you need this."

In that timeless period in my room, Anna changed my world. I would never see it the same way again.

Afterward, I was still staring at the ceiling. Anna was curled up against me with her head on my shoulder. She had pulled my blanket over us and my hand trailed over her back with a mind of its own. When I spoke, my voice was small and distant.

"Wow."

Her lips kissed my ear. "Yeah, that was pretty intense," she whispered.

I don't know how long we were lying there but eventually Edgar started scratching at the door. Anna rolled away for a second I could hear a shoe hitting the door.

"Go away, cat!" she said and then cuddled up against me again.

"Does this mean something?" I asked.

"What do you mean?"

"What we just did, does it mean something? Are you my girlfriend now?"

"Danny you have to be the only man in the world to get philosophical after sex. This was something you needed. It was something I wanted. Let's just enjoy the moment and shut up."

I hugged her to me and she sighed. As she adjusted herself to my side I thought of something.

"I'm going to have to talk to Sieg," I said.

She sat up and looked down at me.

"About this?" she asked.

"What?" I said. "Oh, hell no! This is none of his business. No, there's something between him and Courtney, and I think I'm going to have to fix it."

"Why should you fix it? Can't they fix it themselves?"

"If they could," I said, "they would have done so a long time ago. They could have fixed it when they both came to work up here and they haven't. No, I'm stepping in and pushing the issue."

"Why is it any of your business?" she asked.

Maybe I shouldn't have told her about Courtney and the party. However, I needed someone to talk to who wasn't immersed in the problem. Anna lay back in my arms as I spoke.

"All this time and Sieg's been blaming himself?" she asked.

"Yeah, he's like that a lot. Courtney feels guilty about blaming him. He feels guilty because he thinks she's right in doing so. They're both too embarrassed to talk to each other. If I'd known what was going on sooner, I'd have stepped in a long time ago."

"Are you going to be able to fix it?"

"I hope so. However, right now, I don't feel like getting out of bed."

"I hope that's an invitation," she said with a wicked little laugh.

"Come here and find out."

* * *

Later, Anna and I were still entangled on the bed when someone knocked on my door.

"Danny?" Sieg said, "Are you in there?"

Anna rose up next to me.

"No! He's gone to Key Largo, go away!"

I began to laugh and tried to untangle from her. I was amazed how our legs fit together so well. She sat up and looked on while holding the sheet to her chest.

"What are you doing?" she asked.

"He's worse than the damned cat. If we don't leave, he'll do something stupid like picking the lock or climbing the side of the house."

"I can't believe it. Maybe you ought to have him neutered."

"Sieg or Edgar?"

"How about both," she said.

We stood up and kissed.

"Thank you," I said.

"No dear," she said, "thank *you*."

After dressing, we came downstairs to find the guys out on the front porch. Sieg was slowly rocking on the swing. His lips were a thin line as he glared at Todd and Mike who were casually standing nearby as if to prevent him from leaving the swing. Mike winked at us as we came out onto the porch.

"Are you all right?" he asked me.

"Yes...no...I don't know," I replied with a shake of my head.

"You've got to pull yourself together, Danny. We're going to have a lot of work tomorrow."

"Yeah," I said, "I know. I'm just not sure what I'm going to do."

Sieg stopped his rocking and glared at us.

"What were the two of you doing in there?" he asked.

Anna raised her eyebrows and shook her head slightly.

"If you have to ask," she said, "you're too young to know."

Mike and Todd started laughing. I just shook my head. Seeing Sieg sitting there made me decide on something.

"Guys, Anna," I said, "could you take a hike for a while? I need to talk to my associate here."

Mike looked at me with a startled expression. Anna took one of his arms and one of Todd's and led them down the stairs and around the house. Sieg watched them go and then looked at me.

"Oh, come on, Danny," he said, "I knew what you two were doing. I was just..."

"We need to talk about Courtney, Sieg."

"It's none of your business, Jael. I've told you that before. I don't want to talk about it."

"You don't have a choice and don't cover your ears. You look like an idiot. Don't give everyone more evidence than you already have."

He lowered his hands and looked at me with a scowl.

"I don't know why you're taking this tone with me."

Silence filled the fathomless void between us as I walked over and sat down next to him.

"I talked to Courtney today down at the lake."

"Oh, so now you know."

"Sieg, it wasn't your fault."

"Oh yeah, were you there?" he asked. "I don't think so. Why don't you just shut the hell up and go away?"

"Will you calm down?" I said. "The three of us have been friends too long for that crap. Look, if anyone is to blame, it's those bastards. I wish you'd have told me about it. Then we could have gotten even with them."

"You forget about Shapely," he replied. "If we did anything that would have done any good, she would have revoked our probation and sent us off to jail."

"You're right, I did forget about that."

"And you're the one who keeps reminding me. I'd love to get some revenge on them after what they tried to do to Courtney. They're lucky I wasn't carrying the shotgun. They wouldn't have gotten the choice of running or dying."

"You're still going to have to talk to Courtney," I said.

He looked away. “I can’t.”

“Sieg, you’re going to talk to her whether you like it or not. If I have to drag you...”

From somewhere behind the house, I could hear Edgar yowling again.

“Oh, for gosh sakes,” I said, “You don’t think that...”

“I can’t even begin to imagine,” Sieg said shaking his head. We both stood up from the swing.

“After you, Dr. Shultz,” I said bowing.

“Oh, no, after you, Mr. Jael,” he said bowing even lower.

We left the porch and started around the house.

“Does wanting to *do* something to those bastards make me a monster, Sieg?”

“You, a monster? Excuse me? Do you ever look in the mirror? You’re so squeaky clean it’s embarrassing to be seen in public with you.”

“Gee, thanks a lot.”

Sure enough, when we came to the back of the house, Edgar was standing at the tool shed door again. We could hear the Sasquatch’s voice coming from inside.

“Go away, you beastly cat!”

It showed how distracted I was when I grabbed Edgar. Before he could do anything, I chucked him inside the house. I paused only long enough to yank the back door open and then slam it closed. Considering I didn’t get a scratch, I think Edgar was just as surprised.

The remains of the tool shed’s door slowly moved aside and the Sasquatch looked out at us.

“Is it gone?” it asked.

Sieg stood there and shook his head.

“I can’t believe you’re afraid of a stupid cat.”

“Have you ever been attacked by it?” the Sasquatch asked. “It’s a killer.”

"I don't know," Sieg said. "He attacked Danny, and he's still alive."

"You're hilarious, Sieg," I said. "I'll admit it's not a whole lot of fun, Mr. Sasquatch. You'll have to excuse my friend here, he lacks empathy."

The Sasquatch cleared its throat. "You may call me Howard, since we are neighbors. My full name is Howard Edward Richard Henry Winston duSasquatchi. No one except Mother calls me that."

"When she's mad at you, right?" I asked.

"Usually," he replied.

When the idea hit me, it was like a thunderbolt from Zeus. It was so brilliant and elegant that I was surprised I was the one who came up with it. Sieg was usually our local genius but for once, I was the one with the great, grand and bad idea.

"Howard," I said, "we need to talk."

"I'm so sorry," he said edging toward the trees, "I'm very busy. Perhaps I can fit you in sometime next year. That Dr. Sybel is around here somewhere, and I need to find somewhere to calm my nerves."

"Seriously," I said holding up a hand, "the resort is going to be filled to capacity starting tomorrow. You're going to have tourists underfoot everywhere as well as Sybel."

"I'll take that into consideration."

"It's more like an invitation," I said. "I know right now the shed isn't in great shape, and it's a bit small—"

Sieg grabbed my arm and pulled me back.

"Come here," he said.

He pulled me a couple of feet away and then turned on me with his back to Howard.

"What do you think you're doing?"

"Listen and find out," I said.

"Excuse me, I'm the crazy one, remember?"

I smiled broadly, I couldn't help it.

"Trust me," I said. The look in Sieg's eyes was hilarious, but I managed to suppress my laugh. Howard was waiting expectantly, and I smiled my biggest smile.

"If we could fix the shed up," I said to Howard, "could you use it as a shelter?"

He turned around and examined it with a critical eye. He held his paws out to frame it like a movie director.

"I think so. The structure has possibilities. With a bit of Sasquatch know-how, we could make a very charming cottage out of it."

"Right," Sieg said, rolling his eyes.

"Are you actually offering this to me as a domicile?" Howard asked.

It felt almost like the time when Sieg explained the flamethrower to me. The creative forces were boiling up inside me, and I felt a heady flow in the back of my mind.

"Yeah," I said, "I think so."

"I have to admit," Howard said, "it would keep me out of the rain and give some protection from that blasted animal."

"That was kind of the idea."

Howard crossed his arms and began to look as if he were pondering the matter. Then he raised a finger. "I accept," he said. "If you gentlemen assist me in making a home here, I shall assist you in the same."

"Deal," I said, holding out my hand. Howard reached out and shook my hand with a leathery paw.

"When shall we start?" he said.

"We'll start as soon as we can," I said. "We are going to be a bit busy for a few days, you know."

Howard smiled and then faded back into the trees. I

was about to leave with Sieg when Howard returned with a cardboard box and calmly entered his new house.

"Don't worry about me," he said. "I'll keep a sharp lookout when those pesky tourists arrive."

He closed the door, and Sieg and I started walking away.

"Well that took care of that little problem," I said.

"Really, smart guy?" he asked. He looked at me as if I'd lost my mind.

"Yeah," I said. "What's the problem?"

"What's the problem? What are you going to tell Mike?"

"I'll think of something."

"You do that. Me, I'm going to bed," he said.

Inside, I found Anna and the others sitting around the dining room table drinking iced tea. Just as we came in, Anna excused herself and went down the hall to the washroom. I cleared my throat and they looked at me expectantly.

"I think I've fixed our problem with Howard," I announced.

"Who?" Mike asked.

"The Sasquatch," I told him. "His name is Howard."

"Oh, so now he has a name. That's good. How did you fix our problem?"

"I invited him to live in the old tool shed," I said.

Mike jumped up from his seat. "You did what?"

"I, uh..."

"I heard what you said," he said, "I was just wondering if *you* heard what you said."

"I thought it was a good idea."

"Did you think by moving the Sasquatch even closer to our guests he'll stay under wraps? That was your good idea?"

“If he’s here,” I said, “then there’s less of a chance of him being spotted by the guests.”

“I just don’t see it,” Mike said. “It’s bad enough we have that idiot and his monkey running around. We have to tell people there’s no Bigfoot in the canyon and then you turn around and move it in next door. It’s got to leave.”

“No,” I said.

“What?” Mike asked. His eyes were wide and he looked surprised at what I said.

“I said no,” I repeated. “We’re going to keep Howard out of trouble and we’re going to keep things quiet until we figure out something better.”

“You could get fired if Cap finds out,” Mike said with his hands up to plead with me. “You’ve got to get rid of him.”

Helen Shapely’s face came to mind, and I thought I could hear a cell door slamming shut. Mike was staring at me in disbelief.

“Right is right,” I said, “We can’t just let him wander all over the place. By knowing where he lives, we can deflect investigation.”

Anna returned and stared at us as she came in the room.

“What’s going on?” she asked.

Sieg turned to her with a broad smile. “It seems my *compadre* here has just developed a spine at the most inconvenient time. He’s letting the Sasquatch move into the tool shed. Now Mike’s afraid Cap will find out and fire us.”

“He can’t fire you,” she said.

Mike stuck out his chin and glared at her. “Oh yeah, why can’t he? If Cap finds out—”

“There are several reasons,” she said. “Big Ed owns

the resort, and Danny is his nephew. Big Ed's not going to fire him. Also, if Cap could fire Danny, I'm pretty sure he'd be without any housemen the next morning."

"He can always hire new ones," Mike said.

"In less than twelve hours?" she said. "Good luck with that. Besides, I don't see how Cap is going to know. He's only been over here once."

"There is that," Mike admitted.

"On top of that," she added, "if Cap fires Danny, *I'll* quit. Trust me on this, the resort doesn't work without me."

We were all surprised. She let go of my arm and stood there with her hands on her hips.

"Howard is a person," she informed Mike, "the sooner you figure that out, the better off you'll be. Even if he wasn't, you let Todd keep the damned cat around, so I don't see what the problem is."

"I just know it's a mistake," he replied.

"You don't have to like it," she said. "You just have to live with it."

"What if someone—"

"Let's deal with the 'what ifs' when they occur," she said.

Someone knocked at the door, and Todd went to open it. Courtney was standing there. Before anyone could say anything, I grabbed Sieg and launched him at her.

"What the hell?" he asked.

"I don't want to see either of you until you sit down somewhere and talk. Don't come back until you do," I told them.

"Hey!" Sieg protested, "You can't—"

Courtney laid a hand on his arm and started pulling him outside.

"Sieg, we have to talk," she said.

He looked back at me helplessly as she pulled him out the door. Mike came up and put a hand on my shoulder.

"All right," he said, "maybe you're right. It's against my better judgment, but I think you're in no condition to be making decisions right now."

"He still isn't," Anna said with a wicked smile.

I stuck my tongue out at her and stepped out onto the porch. There was no sign of Sieg or Courtney. Anna followed me, and we sat down on the swing together.

"So, tomorrow the balloon goes up," she said.

"Whatever that means," I said.

"It's just something Grandmother Charles used to say when something was supposed to happen."

Mike stuck his head out the door and looked at us.

"You'd better get some sleep, Danny. You're going to need it."

THIRTEEN

The Western Travel Group rolled in just after breakfast. We met Cap at the bus. Each of us had a baggage cart in hand. The tourists headed inside as the driver pulled the luggage from under the bus. Cap read the names on the bags while consulting his clipboard.

"I'll organize the baggage," he told us. "I want you to take the carts inside the lobby and then up to the rooms as the guests are checked in. All right, let's get on with it."

Penny and Courtney helped us as we rushed load after load through the lobby and onto the elevator. Cap had the list of the reservations and managed to keep us working from one end of each floor to the other.

"Hey! Be careful there, Shultz," he said one time. I looked up to see Sieg struggling with a cello case almost taller than he was. The cello's anxious owner, a very nice looking willowy blonde in a white pantsuit, stood to one side with wide eyes. Her hands kept twitching as if trying to grab the case out of Sieg's hands as he fought to maintain his balance.

"Do you need a hand?" I called out to him.

"Nah, I've got it," he said.

Those words usually preceded a disaster, but this time he made it inside and eventually onto the elevator. I shook my head slowly and turned to see how many guests were left to help.

There was a lull in the action, and I found myself with the last person, Mr. Robert Dixon. He was a tall, dark-haired man wearing a conservative blue suit and a yellowish necktie. He stood next to a stuffed buffalo head and watched Sieg and the cello getting onto the elevator.

"Do you need some help?" I asked him.

"No," he said. "Actually, yeah. I'm sorry, I'm just a bit distracted."

"That's okay," I said. "Are you ready, Mr. Dixon?"

"I guess so. Let's go upstairs."

We found his room on Three South. As we approached, Sieg was closing the room across the hall. His cart was empty, and he was whistling an airy tune. At least he thought he was whistling an airy tune; he couldn't carry one in a bucket.

"Did you have any problems?" I asked him.

"No problems," he said with a smile. "She's a great tipper, too."

As I unlocked Dixon's door, we heard the sound of the blonde tuning the cello. Dixon stopped and turned to stare at her door.

"I can't believe I came on this trip," he said distantly.

"What's the matter, sir?" I asked.

"Nothing," he said and passed me a twenty. "There's nothing wrong that you can fix. Do you think I could get another room?"

"I'm afraid not, sir. We're packed."

"Damn."

"Is there a problem?" I asked him.

"Not really," he replied, "if you don't count staying across the hall from your ex-fiancée."

He closed the door quietly, and I pushed the cart back toward the elevator to the sounds of her playing.

* * *

When I had gotten back downstairs I found Anna standing in the middle of the lobby being confronted by an older woman. The woman had blonde hair with a touch of gray at the temples and wore an expensive-looking dress and hat. I thought she must have gotten Godzilla to cough up the pearls that made up her necklace. I was struck by how much she looked like Anna and vice-versa.

"Mother," Anna said, confirming my suspicion, "that's not necessary."

"But I understand Sven is working here, too," her mother said. "We could hold the wedding right here."

"I'm not getting married, Mother."

"Oh, Anna, you are so stubborn. Don't you worry, Mother will take care of everything."

"I don't—" Anna tried to say, but another woman, who could have been her dark-haired twin, came through the front door.

"Are you sure this place is safe, Aunt Barbara?" she asked. "Oh, Anna, it's so good to see you!"

She rushed forward and attempted to enfold Anna in a hug. Anna pulled back and folded her arms across her chest. The look on her face was as cold as the water in the lake. Putting two and two together, I realized that Sven was in for a surprise, too.

I was dragging my cart out the front door when I heard Sven's voice from behind me.

"Oh! Mrs. Charles!" he said. "What a nice surprise!"

I'll bet, I thought as the door closed behind me. Cap was folding his paper as I arrived at the bus.

"This is the last of it, Danny," he said. "Good work this morning. Be careful with this load, it belongs to Anna's mother and cousin."

I smiled broadly. "I wouldn't miss this for the world."

"I was afraid you were going to say that," he said. "Don't get involved."

"I don't plan to, but I'm probably already involved."

He closed his eyes and raised his face to the sky. "Why me, oh Lord?"

"Why not," I shot back before rolling the load inside.

The atmosphere in the lobby was about two degrees below that of Antarctica in mid-winter. Anna was standing back, glaring at her mother, cousin and Sven.

"Hi," I said brightly. "Whose luggage do I have here?"

"Oh, that would be ours," the cousin said. She had an annoying nasal voice, which didn't help the fact that I already hated her.

"Anna," I said, "I'll need the key."

"Of course, Danny," she said. "Come on over to the Front Desk."

I trailed after her while Sven chatted to the other two.

"What am I going to do?" she hissed to me.

"Why are you asking me?"

"Because you're my boyfriend," she said.

"I am?" I asked. "That's news to me."

"You're asking that after yesterday?"

"Hey," I said, "I thought we already had this discussion. You didn't want to talk about it."

"That's not important right now!"

"You're right, I'm sorry," I said. "I think I've already sized it up. Come over to the house tonight and we'll talk about it."

"Fine! Just get them out of the lobby, now!"

I retrieved the keys from Lisa and led Anna's mother and cousin to the elevator. Sven tagged along with us.

"So, Mrs. Charles," he said, "what brings you and Brittany to the Lake Weir Resort?"

"I wanted to bring Brittany on a trip to celebrate her graduation," the older woman said. "We had no idea that Anna was working here."

I'll bet, you old biddy, I thought as I stared straight ahead.

"Yes," Brittany added, "it was such a surprise."

Sven smirked at me. I ignored him.

They didn't tip, not that I cared. Sven caught up with me at the elevator and rode down with me.

"You don't stand a chance," he said. "We're educated, wealthy people and you are..."

"I am what I am," I said as the door opened, and I wheeled the cart into the lobby.

* * *

That evening, while I was sitting on the porch swing, a large, hairy figure vaulted over the rail and sat in the shadows near my feet.

"Howard?" I said, startled.

"Shhh," he said, "I'm hiding from that damned cat!"

"Good idea," I said. "I added a hasp to the inside of your shed this afternoon."

"Thank you. What are you doing here?"

"I'm waiting for a lady," I said.

"Ah," he said, "we all spend a great deal of our time

waiting for ladies."

"Give me a break," I said. "We've been waiting for women since we first walked upright. Heck, I'll bet Mr. T. Rex had to wait for Mrs. T. Rex all the time too."

Howard started making some strange snorting noises. At first I thought he was choking or something. Then I realized that he was laughing quietly.

"That was a fair observation," he said.

Thinking about why he was there, a thought occurred to me and I stood up.

"Wait here," I said, "if Anna comes by, tell her I'll be right back."

"Where are you going?"

"I'll be right back," I said.

After a quick search, I found what I wanted under the sink. I pulled out an almost empty squirt bottle of window cleaner. I dumped it out and washed it in hot soapy water.

"Daniel," Howard yelled, "I need your help!"

I had a pretty good idea of what was going on and quickly finished washing out the bottle which I then filled with plain tap water.

Sure enough, I found Edgar sitting on the porch rail hissing at Howard. The Sasquatch had backed into the far corner behind the swing. Edgar looked as if he was going to jump to the swing in an attempt to attack the Sasquatch.

"Bad cat," I yelled and squirted him right in the face with water. He quit hissing and sat back. He wore an expression that clearly said, *What the hell did you do that for?* "Bad cat," I repeated and squirted him again. With a yowl he jumped to the ground and tore off around the house.

"Oh, thank you," Howard said as he came out from

behind the swing.

"What's going on?" Anna asked from the foot of the stairs.

I held up the squirt bottle. "I'm trying to teach Edgar that Howard is not prey. My Aunt Rhonda keeps one around if her cat, Chuckles, decides to act up. Howard, take this, and if he makes another try for you, just squirt him."

The Sasquatch wrapped a paw around the bottle and gave it an experimental squirt. A bright smile spread across his hairy face.

"Thank you very much. With any luck I'll only have to use this sparingly. If you'll excuse me, I had some cocoa on the fire."

I spoke to his retreating back as he lumbered away.

"Oh, sure," I said. *Fire? Cocoa?*

He was already out of earshot and I shook my head and looked to see Anna coming up the stairs to me. She gave me a quick hug and we sat down on the swing.

"Where are the rest of the guys?" she asked.

"I don't know," I replied. "I think Sieg's in bed. He might have snuck out with Courtney, though. Todd's sawing logs, you can hear him all the way down to the kitchen. Mike is off with Penny, and I'm here with you."

"So," she said, "you've met my family."

"Was your cousin the one...?"

"Yeah," Anna said, "she's the one. Anything I've ever wanted, she's taken. Her brother is pretty decent, but I think she's a greedy slut."

"She can't be that bad," I said.

"She can't? She's managed to steal every boyfriend I've ever had. Sven was just the latest."

I grinned. "Well, here's one she isn't going to get."

"Don't bet on it," she said. "She's probably dreaming

of how to get you in her bed even as we speak."

"It's not going to happen," I said.

"Watch," she said. "Do you have any idea of how depressing it is to know that every boy I'll ever want, she'll steal and then dump?"

"Did she dump Sven?"

"Probably," she said, "but I've never bothered to ask. They're just a bit too chummy for my taste."

Edgar came running around the house, screeching at the top of his furry little lungs. With a whoop of joy, Howard came bounding after him, the squirt bottle held high.

"Take that you nasty little beast," he shouted as they disappeared around the house. I turned to Anna.

"I think I've created a monster."

Her lips were tight, and snorts of mirth were still escaping from her nose. I felt my own rising up.

"Go ahead," I finally gasped, "your head will explode if you hold it in any longer."

We both fell into each other's arms, laughing our heads off.

"What the hell's so funny?" Mike said as he came up the trail. I struggled to regain my control.

"You'd better..." I gasped, "get up here! You don't want...to be...in the way!"

"Are you all right?" he asked.

He came up the stairs with a concerned look on his face. Todd, wearing just a pair of baggy surfing shorts, opened the screen door and came out.

"Dude, what's going on out here?" he asked.

Suddenly, like a refreshing shower on a sunny day, Edgar and Howard appeared again.

"There!" the Sasquatch said. "How do you like that?"

We all collapsed in laughter, which is where Sieg

found us as he came up the trail. Before he could say anything, Edgar dropped down from the porch roof and streaked into the house. Sieg looked at us in consternation.

"What's going on?" he asked.

"Show's over," I barely gasped out, which sent all four of us back into paroxysms of laughter.

"Man, you guys are losing it," he grumbled as he went inside.

FOURTEEN

"Is he still hiding in there?" Sieg asked me as I peered into the depth of our linen closet. Behind a pile of towels I could see a pair of pointed ears and a single flash of eye.

"Yeah," I said, "he's still in there."

"Do you think he's going to have kittens?"

"If he is," I replied, "I think he's already had them."

"So what are we going to do?" Sieg asked.

I sighed. "We'll leave him in there for now." I reached in and pulled a towel from the stack while Edgar hissed at me.

"Danny," Sieg said, "he's going to destroy our towels."

I glared at the ears, which seemed to twitch in embarrassment.

"He won't if he doesn't want to get wet!" I said with a sadistic grin.

"Hey," Sieg said, alarmed, "don't do that! We're already going to have to wash all of the towels to get rid of that wet cat smell. What do you think Mr. Chang is going to say?"

I shut the closet door just enough to leave room for Edgar to leave if he decided he was hungry enough or if hydraulic pressure moved him. The towel, I hung over the bar in the shower, and then I clumped down the stairs after Sieg.

"I don't know," I said as we made the turn at the landing, "I almost feel sorry for the little fellow."

"He got what he deserved," Sieg said. "You did the right thing. It's about time someone showed that cat who's boss."

"Yeah, but embarrassing him like that?" I asked.

"He'll get over it."

Breakfast was the usual affair: oatmeal, juice, pancakes. You know, the breakfast of champions without the vodka. We had just sat down when there came a knock at the back door. Mike went into the kitchen to answer it. When he came back, he had a guest in tow.

Howard was much more impressive indoors. He had taken his morning bath and his hair was carefully groomed. His necktie, which resembled Mr. Dixon's, looked freshly pressed. Anna and I had lately taken to jogging along the highway because we didn't want to disturb him while he bathed. A Sasquatch was one thing, a naked one would have been worse, sort of. In one of his paws he held a thick newspaper.

"I thought I might join you gentlemen at your breakfast," he said.

Sieg pulled one of the spare chairs up to the table and patted it companionably.

"Have a seat, Howard," he said.

"Thank you," Howard said with a nod of his head.

Mike looked over and smiled.

"Would you like something to eat?" he asked the

Sasquatch.

"Just a little orange juice, if that is not too much."

In some ways it was a demented domestic scene with the five of us sitting around the table, the Sasquatch at one side presiding like a father over his children. Howard perched his pince-nez delicately on his nose and began to read his newspaper. I saw that it was the current *New York Times*. He noticed me staring at it.

"Well," he said, "it's not the *Times of London*, but it will do in a pinch."

Todd swallowed some cereal and then spoke to Mike.

"Dude, what are we doing today?"

"We're going to be taking care of the guests and whatever else Cap wants. Of course we're going to be busier now that the resort is full."

"That is going to be a deuce of a problem," Howard said, looking over his paper at us.

"Yeah," Mike said with a grimace, "and we're not going to be able to get Cap to back us up."

"Why not?" I asked.

"They're paying guests," he explained. "Right now, with the resort's very existence on the line, he's not going to alienate any paying customers. In fact, he might fire all of us if they go and complain because we're not being helpful about something or other."

"What we'll do," Sieg said with an evil grin, "is if anyone starts asking about a Bigfoot or whatever we'll start talking about *Weiry*."

"Dude," Todd said, "Weiry?"

"Yeah," Sieg said, "you know, the monster in our lake. If Loch Ness has *Nessie*, and Lake Champlain has *Champ,* then Lake Weir is going to have *Weiry*. It'll easily deflect any questions, and everyone will just assume it was an urban myth or whatever. If worse comes to worst, we can always tell people the straight truth with a wink and they'll think we're lying."

Howard laughed softly at that.

"There's a quote from Congreve that covers this situation," he said. "No mask like open truth to cover lies, as to go naked is the best disguise."

* * *

After breakfast, I headed over to the resort to check in with Lisa. I didn't think there was going to be much for me to do but I arrived to find the lobby in turmoil. Fighting my way through the crowd, I stopped at the front desk.

"What's going on?" I asked Lisa, who put down the phone she had been dialing.

"It's a good thing you're here," she said. "Apparently the ballroom wasn't set up for this morning's breakfast meeting for New American Tours. I think Cap's about to hit the ceiling."

"I happen to know for a fact that we set up for that," I said, frowning.

"Well, you'd better go and look now."

Sure enough, when I fought my way through to the ballroom I found the chairs were all stacked neatly and the tables were leaning against the walls. Cap was standing in the middle of the room with Sven. He crooked a finger the minute he spotted me.

"I thought I told the lot of you to set this room up."

"We did. It was the last thing we did yesterday."

"Could it have been your 'ghost'," Sven sneered.

I knew exactly what had happened and I wanted to wipe the sneer from Sven's kisser. I couldn't with Cap standing right there so I decided to merely go into smart-ass mode and perhaps tell Cap exactly what I thought happened.

"I don't think so," I said. "The ghost isn't this neat."

"Then you must have forgotten to set up the room," Sven said. "That's too bad. I'll try to calm them down, Cap. If Mr. Jael can be bothered to actually do his job, maybe we can get started sometime this morning."

With that, he strolled out of the room. I would have launched myself at him if Cap hadn't suddenly thrown a hand across my chest.

"Yeah," he said, "I think I do know what happened. You guys are sure you set this up?"

"Yes sir," I said. "The guys set it up and I came in and added the extra table like you asked."

"And then I double checked it," Cap said. "I think you've made an enemy, Danny."

"I can handle it. I think Mike's on his way, now."

"Good," Cap said, "let's get this fixed."

Mike showed up a few minutes later, and Courtney followed with an armful of tablecloths. She looked around at the three of us.

"What happened?" she asked.

"I don't know for sure," I said. "I think a certain someone is messing around with us."

"Who?"

"Don't worry about it," I told her. "We'll take care of it when we have the time."

Actually, eleven tables with ten chairs each isn't a big deal. Cap and I laid out the tables and then helped Mike drop the chairs into place while Courtney threw the tablecloths. I opened the door and peered out into the lobby. Sven was talking to Mr. Peabody, the tour manager. One of the new waiters, whose name I hadn't learned yet, rolled a table of food through the lobby. He stopped and looked at me, and I nodded.

As the waiter came in, Courtney, Mike and I slipped out the back door. With the double doors between us and the ballroom closed, I started swearing and pacing up and down.

"Are you going to be all right," Mike asked, concerned.

"Oh, eventually, I guess," I said.

"What's wrong with you?" Courtney asked. "I haven't seen you this angry in a long time."

Just thinking about it set me off, and I couldn't answer her. I was too busy making up new curses on the spot. I was all the way up to Sven's great-grandmother's dallying with a weasel.

"I think he suspects our Catering Director of sabotage," Mike said with a scowl. "The only reason I'm not cursing, too, is because I have to maintain my dignity."

"Dignity, schmignity," I said. "We need to get even with that son-of-a-bitch for this."

"I'm sure we will, Danny," Courtney said.

"Stay out of this, Court. This is between me and...and...weasel boy out there!"

"You're wrong," she said, "because if he is messing with you, he's messing with all of us."

Mike grabbed my arm.

"Come on," he said, "let's get him out of here before he explodes."

Courtney grabbed my other arm.

"Right."

We were heading back to the lobby when a door opened. Anna came bursting into the corridor. Her face was bright red, not the red of a blush but that of sheer uncontrollable rage.

"Do you know what they've done now?" she demanded of us.

"Uh..." I said.

"They've set me up on a date with Sven! Without even asking! How dare they? How dare they?"

The door opened behind her and her mother entered the hall. She looked right through us as she approached her daughter.

Mike knew when it was time to retreat. He and Courtney resumed propelling me out of the corridor and into the lobby. By this time, it was deserted, except for Sven, who was seated in a large, overstuffed chair next to a stuffed alligator. A tiffany lamp hung over his shoulder and he seemed to be reading a newspaper.

"Are you having problems?" he asked sweetly.

I shook loose of Court and Mike but managed to keep my temper in check.

"Not really, just another day at work," I said.

"You should think about the quality of your enemies," he said.

I turned toward him even as Mike and Courtney caught my arms again. I just smiled my biggest, sunniest smile. It's the one that makes me look like I'm about to bite your ear off.

"As should you," I said in a soft voice. Sven flinched at my tone if not my smile.

"I've got to get you out of here," Mike hissed in my ear. "Neither Cap nor I need you blowing up on Sven right now."

Without another word, they pushed me out of the lobby. I stood on the front porch and gripped the rail tightly. I slowly took in copious amounts of sweet mountain air.

"I don't think that's going to be a problem," I finally

said.

"Why isn't it?" Mike asked.

"I've already figured out what I'm going to do to Sven."

"God, now what?"

"I'm going to consult with Sieg," I said, smiling. "If the two of can't think of something, then no one can."

"I knew I wasn't going to like that," Mike said. "Look, Danny, just do me one favor, huh? Run whatever you come up with past me before trying it, okay?"

"Sure," I said. "Believe me, I think you'll like whatever we come up with."

"Are they going to kill Sven?" Mike asked Courtney.

"No," she said. "They like their victims alive to appreciate what happened to them. Sven might *wish* he was dead, but embarrassment rarely kills."

"I'm taking you back to the house," Mike said, "and I'll have Todd take your place at the front desk until you've calmed down."

They tried to help me to the house and I kept trying to shake them off. They just kept holding my arms and pushing me along which made me feel like I was an insane asylum escapee. Thinking about it later, maybe I was exactly that.

Todd and Howard were sitting on the porch, with the Sasquatch slowly drifting back and forth on the swing. Todd was seated on the stairs. Each of them had a large clear tumbler in hand. Todd's obviously held lemonade but Howard's held something greenish.

"What are you drinking?" I asked him as I came up on the porch.

"This is a mint julep," he said. "I acquired a taste for them during my graduate studies at Cornell. I was staying with a very nice old lady from Louisville and she showed me how to make them."

"I'm not going to comment on that," I said. "However, I am going to ask you to make me one. I need it."

"Dude, what happened?" Todd asked.

We explained it to them, or rather, Mike and Courtney explained it. I was too busy inventing cuss words to be bothered. After they were done, Todd handed his lemonade to Mike and stood up.

"Dude, I'll go over and try to hang loose."

"You do that," Mike replied. "Where's Sieg?"

"He said he was going to look for you," Howard rumbled.

"Well, he didn't find us. Can you do me a favor, Howard?"

"What do you need?" the Sasquatch asked.

"Will you take care of Danny for a while? I don't know what the hell is going on or why Sven is deliberately baiting him but I can't let him inside the resort for a while."

"Shall I accede to his choice of beverage?"

"Do you mean give him a mint julep? Yeah, you might as well. The alcohol might mellow him out. See if you can calm him down."

"I am calm!" I said. "I'm wonderful except for the fact that you're talking about me as if I'm not here."

"I'm beginning to wonder," Mike said, slapping me on the arm. "Don't worry. If Lisa needs any help, I'll fill in for you. Try to stay somewhat sober, I might need you sometime today."

He and Courtney had to run to catch up to Todd. Howard disappeared into the house, and I slumped down on the swing and started slowly rocking back and forth. *What the hell was wrong with me, anyway? For a while there I really wanted to punch Sven's lights out. Was it Anna or something more?*

There was a scratching noise, and Edgar pushed the screen door open with his nose and stood there glaring at me.

"You have only yourself to blame," I told him. Without further ado, Edgar leapt into my lap, draped himself over my thighs and promptly fell asleep.

"Oh great," I said to myself. "Now I'm cat furniture."

Howard came out onto the porch, and before he could say anything, Anna came stomping up the trail. She stopped in front of the Sasquatch and looked at the drink in his hand.

"Is that alcohol?" she asked.

"In part."

"Good," she said and snatched it out of his paw and drained it in one gulp. "That was pretty strong," she said and stood swaying for a moment. Then, like a cut tree, she started falling forward. Howard caught her, and I managed to push Edgar off my lap and catch the glass before it hit the ground. Howard looked at me in surprise.

"I wouldn't have expected that," he said.

"Neither would I," I replied. "Here, take the glass, I'll deal with her."

"What are we going to do with her?"

"I'll put her on my bed until she wakes up," I said.

"Wait a minute. I'll help you," he said and stepped into the house. He returned without the glass and took one of Anna's arms.

"I could just carry her," he said.

"All right, I'll follow," I said.

Despite the fact that an unconscious adult is substantial dead weight, Howard carried Anna as if she were a small child. After placing her on the bed and covering her with my blanket, we went back down to the porch. Howard made a quick detour to the kitchen and made mint juleps for both of us.

"Do you know what this house really needs?" I asked.

Howard gazed over his drink at me. For someone who was a mythical creature from British Columbia, I had to admit he made the best alcoholic drink I'd ever had.

"Furniture," he said, putting his drink down.

"There's that," I admitted. "I think an air-conditioner or swamp cooler would be nice, too."

"What, pray tell," he said, "is a swamp cooler?"

"What it is," I replied, "is the most incredible invention in the history of climate control. Whoever came up with it should be canonized as a saint, especially here in Colorado."

"But what is it?"

"Some genius realized that if you put a damp towel in front of a fan, the air coming out is cooler," I said.

"That would be evaporation, of course."

"Of course," I conceded. "The genius part was that they realized the towel could be on either side of the fan. If you made a big square box and covered three or four of the sides with pads that were kept perpetually damp, then pulled air through them, you could blow copious, and I mean copious, amounts of cold air through a building."

"It sounds useful in this climate," Howard said.

"Of course it would be nice if the roof of this piece of crap could actually support the weight of the cooler, which I doubt."

"You would have to..." he said and stopped. He

stared at the door, and I turned and saw Anna standing there. As I stood up, she came out onto the porch. With an inarticulate wail she threw herself into my arms.

"Oh, Danny, what am I going to do?"

* * *

"Are you going to be all right?" I asked Anna as I held her and tried to calm her down. Howard, the big coward, had fled at the first sign of her tears. As he passed us, he muttered something about "delicate sensibilities and all that."

Anna pulled away from me and collapsed onto the porch swing with her face in her hands.

"I don't know if I'm going to be all right," she said in a muffled voice. "I thought I had gotten away from all of them when I dropped out of Vassar and took the job here. I guess I was just running away from them."

She raised her tear-streaked face to stare blearily at me.

"I meet you," she continued, "the first guy who isn't interested in me because I'm one of the Park Avenue West Charleses. I meet Lisa and Courtney and Penny and all sorts of new friends who don't care who my parents are, and I thought my life was getting better. Then that bastard Sven shows up and ruins it all. I thought I could deal with him but then he went and told my manipulative, bigoted, egotistical monster of a mother where I was. So now here she comes to take control of my life and brings Brittany, that bitch, with her for good measure. What else could go wrong?"

"Maybe it's really an accident that they're here," I said.

"Oh, please," she said, sitting up and staring out across the porch. "Mother won't be happy until I'm married. Sven and his money, as if I needed more money, were her choice, not mine. Apparently I don't get a choice in my life."

"What about your dad?" I asked. "What does he have to say about all this?"

"What about him?" she asked bitterly. "Mother and Brittany have him wrapped completely around their little fingers. He's never taken my side in anything, much less something as important as my so-called marriage."

"Then what about Brittany? If she's as smitten as all that, then maybe we can deflect her into Sven or something."

"Ever since she moved in with us after her parents died, she's been taking things away from me. It's as if she's blaming me for everything. I've lost dolls, homework, lunch money, boyfriends and even jobs because of her."

"That's very strange," said a voice which made me look up. Howard was standing near the porch. His pince-nez glittered in the sunlight.

"Oh," I said, "you've decided to quit running from a crying girl?"

He ignored me and came up and squatted near the front door. It was strange seeing him sitting there with his legs folded under him like that.

"My father says that Brittany and I are really twins," Anna continued, "twins born of different parents. I don't believe it. I'm the one who always did what they wanted me to do. She's the one who did whatever the hell she wanted to do."

"Sounds like twins to me," I said.

"You don't know anything, Danny."

"I have to admit it sounds like you're complete opposites. She's all dark and evil and you're all goodness and light," I conceded.

"I took economics and English Literature at Vassar," she said. "Brittany? She's some kind of freaking art major or something. She makes these stupid clay pots that Mother and Father ooh and ah over. I can explain the President's budget in detail while she can't balance a checkbook. I can drive Daddy's Lincoln through Midtown Manhattan in rush hour and she wrecks a car on a weekly basis. Yet, at all the parties, the guys want to hang around her, while I'm stuck off to the side against the wall."

"I think you're exaggerating," I said. "So what made you blow a gasket this time?"

"They were both trying to get me to marry Sven. Mother was telling me what a catch he was, and Brittany kept going on and on about how cute he is. Why she doesn't marry him, I'll never know. She's a 'free spirit' according to Mother, whatever the hell that is. I don't want to marry him, I have no interest in marrying him, and I am not going to marry him."

"I guess we could always aim Sieg at them," I said.

"Oh God, Danny," she exclaimed. "Don't even start with him!"

"Why? What has he done this time?"

Just then, Sieg came from around the back of the house. He had a butterfly net over one shoulder and a jar full of twigs and leaves.

"Now what have I done," he said after seeing our faces.

"You're helping them," Anna shouted. "I heard you talking about some kind of *love potion* you think you can make up. If you think I'm going to drink anything from your hand, you're crazy!"

"I don't know who 'them' is," he said, looking at her as if she had lost her mind. He put down his net and jar then placed his hands on his hips and glared at her. "I, on the other hand, was speaking to Mr. Dixon. I've agreed to try and help him win back the love of his ex-fiancé.

"Oh," I said, "isn't she the blonde with the cello?"

"Yeah, that's right. I was joking about the 'love potion' when I was discussing options with him. Although..."

"No, Sieg," I said.

"Oh, come on, Danny," he pleaded. "I can think of one or two different ways of working it out chemically."

"Which would only last as long as the chemicals did," I said.

"You're no fun."

"One of us has to think about these things," I said. "If I had done so last year, Mohawk wouldn't have burned to the ground."

"You just have to keep bringing that up, don't you?" he said.

"If I didn't, you'd forget."

"Well, I've got a couple of ideas I'm going to work on. I'm going to turn one of the unused bedrooms on our floor into a laboratory."

"You've got to be kidding me," I said.

"Hey," he said, "you've got all your books in the living room, and I need some space for my pursuits."

I had to admit that he was right about that. One small thing I had managed to accomplish while I was working between the resort, the house and Howard's shed was the cobbling together of a couple of bookcases out of old two-by-fours. They weren't the best, especially since they weren't painted, but they did hold the collection of books, including my Britannica, that I'd brought from home.

"All right," I said, "we'll discuss this later. I'm going

to have to bring up the rest of my stuff from home before the sale goes through anyway. Right now, I have other things to worry about."

* * *

Evening had finally arrived at Lake Weir. During the day, I had finally calmed down enough to go in and help out at the front desk, relieving Lisa for lunch. At the end of the day I had gone back to the house and found Anna sitting on the swing waiting for me.

"You didn't go back to work?" I said.

"No," she replied. "I told Cap I'd be down in the morning. He didn't seem to have a problem with it."

"He's probably just waiting for his chance to yell at you."

"Probably," she said.

I sat down next to her and we held hands and gently swung back and forth.

"You are going to have to go back to work, you know," I said.

"I know."

We sat like that for a while without speaking. At some point, Anna leaned over and put her head on my shoulder.

"I could get used to this," she said.

"Me too."

Mike and Sieg appeared out of the shadows and came up on the porch.

"Isn't that disgusting," Sieg said. "Here, we're doing all this work and there he is, canoodling on the porch."

"Shut up, Sieg," I said. He stuck his tongue out at me.

"Danny," Mike said, "I've heard a very disturbing rumor."

"Now what?" I asked.

"I was helping Lisa at the front desk after you left to carry up those towels to two-oh-nine when I heard Sven talking to Mrs. Charles about a big investment opportunity. He was saying that Big Ed was going to sell Lake Weir to some developer, and they're going to build condos throughout the canyon. He called it 'the next Vail.'"

I shook my head. "I don't think Ed would do that. He would let me know before he did something like that. At least I think he would."

"Why would he do that?" Mike asked. "Why would it be any business of yours?"

"He'd do it because I'm family. Trust me on this one."

"You don't pay attention, Danny," Sieg said shaking his head in disgust. "This is just like when he talked to me about working up here before he spoke to you. If Big Ed Jael thought he could make a buck by selling this resort, he'd do it in a flash, and you'd find out about it after he was done with it and we were both down in Cañon City."

He opened the screen door and went inside. I just watched him.

"Uh, Danny?" Anna said.

"Yeah?"

"Do you think you can unclench your fists? You're beginning to scare me."

I looked down and found that she was right. I brought one of my fists up and looked at it as if I had never seen it before. "What the hell is wrong with me?"

Without another word, I stood up and went down the porch stairs.

"Where are you going?" Anna said.

"I need to think," I said over my shoulder.

I walked down the trail, crossed the parking lot and climbed the steps to the resort's front door. I stopped with my hand on the handle for a moment and slowly thought about what I had just heard. Was Sieg right? Would Big Ed stab me in the back as if it were just another business deal? Sieg and I didn't just want to work at Lake Weir, we *needed* to. We had to keep our jobs to stay out of jail. Would Big Ed jeopardize our freedom just to make some money? I felt that I needed to call someone. I knew who it was going to be when I went into the lobby.

Lisa looked up as I approached the front desk.

"Back so soon?" she asked.

"Not really. Hey, do you know of someone interested in buying the resort from Big Ed?"

"Doug Assyrian," she said in a flat voice. The look on her face was not friendly.

"Who's Doug Assyrian?" I asked.

"He's a big name developer. He was leaning on the Bortero brothers when they owned the resort. He supposedly wants to tear it down and build a bunch of condos. 'The Next Vail' is the term I've heard bandied about."

"That's what I heard," I said.

"Apparently," she said, "he sees billions in this property."

I stood there for a moment and thought about what I had heard. It didn't make sense. If Ed wanted to make a profit on the resort from Doug Assyrian, why didn't he just sell it to him in the first place? Why try to make it successful if Assyrian wanted it so bad?

"Is there anyone else you can think of?" I asked Lisa.

"Not that I know of," she said.

"All right," I said. "I'm going to go into the coatroom

and use the phone."

"Sure, no problem."

There was one person I could ask about what Big Ed was up to who would not only know but wouldn't lie to me about it.

"Hi, Aunt Vera," I said when she answered her phone.

"Danny, it's so nice to hear from you," said Big Ed's wife. "How's life up at the resort?"

"It's fine," I said. "We're pretty busy right now. Uh, is Uncle Ed around?"

"No dear, I haven't seen him. Why?"

"I was going to ask him if he planned to sell Lake Weir to some guy named Doug Assyrian."

My ear was filled with the sparkling sound of Aunt Vera's laughter.

"Are you joking?" she finally asked. "Sell to Doug Assyrian? It would never happen. Your Uncle would rather go broke than do that."

"Why?"

"They went to school together," she said, "and they do not like each other."

"Would Uncle Ed sell to someone else?"

"I don't think so, Danny," she said. "He didn't tell you why he bought the resort?"

"I thought he won it in a poker game."

There was more sparkling laughter. "No," she said. "He bought Lake Weir from Don and Iggy Bortero right after your trial. He bought it because he knew you and Sieg were going to have trouble finding work after graduation."

"You're kidding me, Aunt Vera."

"No dear, I'm not," she said. "I was against his buying that rat-trap until he sat me down and explained it to me. We bought the resort so that the two of you can have a chance to straighten out your lives."

"Why would he do that? There had to be better ways."

"Daniel," she said seriously, "you do realize that with your father's death, you are quite wealthy?"

"I knew there was some money," I replied. "Mom and I never had to worry about it. I've just never found out how much we had."

"I don't know if I should tell you this, but you are quite possibly the wealthiest man in Mohawk County. Your grandfather divided the Bodie Jael fortune evenly between your father and his brothers. While Ray sits around in that hovel of his and Ed spent most of his creating his business empire, your father made several careful investments. I think the money you and your mother have been living on is just a small fraction of the interest from those investments."

"Bodie Jael?" I asked, confused. "How come I've never heard of him?"

"Mostly because if there was a black sheep in your family it was Bodie Jael," Vera said with a laugh. "He was your grandfather's older brother, and he came back from World War I and invested heavily in mining throughout the West. He made his real fortune during the Teapot Dome scandal and then killed himself. He left all his money to your grandfather, who divided it, as I said, between his sons."

"What about Mom? Isn't some of that money hers?"

"Your father left your mother quite well cared for. I think that's why she's moving to Nevada. This family attracts free-spirits, Danny, now you just need to free yours."

"What happens if the resort fails? Or succeeds, for

that matter?"

"I don't know, and I don't think Ed knows either. He took out a loan to buy Lake Weir but he didn't have to. He told me that he wants it to stand on its own legs and not need constant cash infusions from him. Is there anything else you need to know?"

"I guess not," I said.

"Well then, goodbye, dear, and call again. I want to hear more about your adventures up there."

We hung up together.

I came out of the coatroom in a daze. I was standing there, looking at nothing when I realized that Mr. Dixon was standing there, also.

"Oh, I'm sorry, sir," I said.

"That's all right," he replied. "I should have been looking where I was going."

"How are you doing? Are you enjoying your stay?"

"Yes and no. The resort is lovely, and I've already been out on the lake, which was great. I just have a problem I don't think anyone can help me solve."

"If you think of anything I can do to help…" I said.

"Actually," he said, "I have a question."

"Shoot."

"Do you think that other houseman, Sieg, is for real?"

"I've known him my entire life," I said. "So I have to admit that, yes, he is for real."

"He promised me he could do something about this problem I'm having."

"If he gave you his word, sir, he will do everything in his power to keep it."

"I'm just having second thoughts about it," he said, wringing his hands.

"I'll let him know and have him talk to you."

"Oh, thank you. Thank you very much."

* * *

I spent the rest of the evening hustling laundry up and down the elevator. I was relieved that the story about Big Ed selling out was false, but I was still concerned about my part in all of it.

Like I told Aunt Vera, money had never meant anything to me. I'd never needed it and my parents always lived kind of frugally. I had a roof over my head, clothes on my back and food on the table, so what else did I need?

I felt constrained ever since my father died. I suddenly felt an urge to break out of my shell and thought about what to do as I moved sheets and towels all over the resort. Then on the second floor, I came up with an idea as I watched Courtney rolling her cart toward the maid's closet. We arrived at the same time and she held the door for me. As I helped her put the fresh linen on the shelves and tossed the dirty linen in my cart, I turned to her.

"Do you mind if I borrow the Caddy?" I asked her.

"No, why do you need it? You don't have a driver's license."

"I want to take Anna to dinner," I said.

"Are you going to take her to the Alpine Haus?"

"I thought about it. How did you guess?"

"Because that where Sieg took me when he asked me to marry him," she said.

"What?"

I was surprised. I knew that they had been keeping secrets from me, including the after-prom party, but this came right out of the blue and hit me alongside the head. Courtney saw the expression on my face and laughed.

"He took me there when he asked me to marry him," she repeated. "That was before the prom, and I turned him down."

"Why?"

"I wasn't sure I wanted to marry him. After everything we've been through I'm not even sure now that I don't want to marry him. I just don't think it's time to make that decision. Are you going to ask Anna to marry you?"

"What? No!" I said. "I just want to take her to a nice restaurant. Maybe we'll just go down to the Sundowner in Nederland."

"I hear the Red Wolf in Weir is pretty good," she said.

Penny opened the door and squeezed in with us. She started exchanging dirty linen for clean and the pile in my cart was turning into a mountain.

"What are you two doing in here?" she asked.

"Danny wants to take Anna out, and we're just discussing where to go," Courtney replied.

"Ah, is this your first date?" Penny asked me.

"I don't know. I guess so."

"Start small then. Try Gregory's Hardware in Weir."

"You want me to take Anna to a hardware store?" I asked her. "Why?"

"It has a lunch counter," she said with a grin. She put some more towels into her cart. "Trust me, Mr. Gregory has the best food on the mountain, and that includes our kitchen. I think you'll find the store interesting, too. I'm surprised your buddy hasn't found out about it yet."

"Let me know how it goes, Danny," Courtney said. "I just might take him there. It sounds like a place he'd love."

"I didn't say I was going to take her there," I said.

Penny put a hand on my shoulder. "Trust me, Danny-boy, you won't regret it."

FIFTEEN

"It's in a hardware store?" Anna asked me for about the ninetieth time since I'd informed her of our destination. It had taken a couple of days but we finally found time to run off to lunch. I'd spent the time working while she spent most of hers hiding in her office from her family. I think both of us were ready for a little escape.

"I think you want to turn up at the sign," I said, pointing.

She was driving Courtney's Eldorado, since my license was still under suspension. She had cut a few corners short and banked into a few rocks while getting used to driving the monstrosity, but by the time we turned off the Peak-to-Peak and onto Main Street, Weir, she'd gotten the hang of it.

I was struck by the similarities between the resort and the town. Here and there stood gaily painted Victorian houses looking like bright wildflowers among the brown, sunburned weeds that were their neglected or abandoned brethren.

At one end of Main Street, the Baptist Church was nothing more than a memorial sign and a pile of rotting, white-washed timbers laid across a crumbling stone foundation. The Catholic Church at the other end of the town was built of stone and seemed to have fared better. Even its tiny graveyard looked well-tended.

The Fire Company was nothing more than a fading memory of weather-beaten wood and fading paint, and the adjacent Town Hall appeared to be abandoned, with tattered blinds and a heavy coat of dust on the windows.

Like a modern bride standing amidst her Victorian bridesmaids, one block of Main Street had been torn down and replaced by a completely modern strip mall. I noticed a small sign proclaiming it the product of the Assyrian Development Company. Inside it were the Post Office, a gift store, a florist, a pizza joint and a barber shop. Along one side of its parking lot stood an ancient narrow-gauge railroad car of undetermined origin with a sign for the Red Wolf Café attached to the roof.

Across the street from the mall stood a two story, gray stone building with the words carved above the door bespeaking of the long-vanished National Bank. In the window below was the colorful, almost carnival sign for Gregory's Hardware Store.

Anna brought the Caddy to a gentle stop in front of the store. We got out of the car and unconsciously holding hands, stood there staring at what we had found.

Dark green curtains shaded the bottom half of the display windows, which had a gilded design around the edges. Mannequins wearing period clothing and holding various hardware implements decorated the windows. There wasn't a single spot of dust to be seen.

We entered by the corner door and stopped, amazed. It was a moment before I found my voice again.

"Okay," I said. "I think this place beats the lobby."

Every square inch of the walls were either covered in jam-packed shelves or ancient pieces of hardware. All of it was very well cared for without a micron of rust. It was easily apparent that Gregory's was more than just a hardware store. Racks of clothing stood off to one side while fishing tackle and a few guns were displayed in cabinets near the center of the main room.

A young woman in blue jeans and a red-flannel shirt stood behind the cash register and looked up as we stood there.

"Can I help you?" she asked in a bored voice.

"We heard there was a lunch counter here," Anna said before I could speak.

"Yeah," the girl said. "Go down the Seeds aisle and turn right. Go as far as the ammo shelves and turn left."

The store had taken over its neighboring buildings, we found as we arrived at a place where one part of the old bank had been sliced open to make an opening into the store next door.

Sunlight streamed through windows covered in white and red checked curtains. There were several tables and a long, highly polished, mahogany counter that might have once served as the bar for some long-forgotten, mountain tavern. The room was deserted except for a tall woman wearing a yellow dress with a white apron. Her hair was arranged in a champagne-colored beehive that was in fashion back in the sixties. She looked up from her crossword puzzle and smiled.

"Come on in. What are you hungry for?"

We sat down at a table, and the woman came around the counter and put a couple of menus in front of us. While we were reading the menus she took a small notebook from her apron and started fishing around in her hair. After a second or two, her consternated look turned into one of triumph as she pulled a pencil out with a flourish.

"Ah, ha!" she said. "I need to do something about that. I keep losing pencils in there. What would you like to drink?"

Anna ordered an iced tea, and I asked for a Coke.

"Be right back," the waitress said and disappeared into the back.

"Okay, this is a bit strange," I said to Anna.

"Oh, I don't think so," she said. "It's kind of nice."

The menu, for the most part, was typical small town diner fare. There were a few things that raised my eyebrows though. While I didn't find the chilled monkey brains that I reflexively looked for, I did find Chateau Briand and lobster tails in garlic sauce.

The waitress came back with our drinks. I didn't recognize her at first, because she had somehow replaced her beehive do with straight red hair that hung in two plaits down her back. She ignored my look and pulled the pencil from the same pocket she pulled the notebook from.

"Have you decided?" she asked. "The Blue Plate today is tuna salad, and the Red Plate is the Deluxe Hamburger."

"I think I'll have the chicken fried steak," Anna said.

The waitress nodded and scribbled in her book.

"I'll have the Red Plate," I said.

"Good choice," the waitress said. "Do you want fries, mashed or baked potato with that? For fifty cents extra, you can have sweet potato fries."

"Just the regular fries," I said.

"All right," she said. "It'll be up in a jiffy."

With that she disappeared into the back again.

"You were right, it's very strange," Anna said.

"Told you so," I said.

As we sipped our drinks, a man in a gray, pinstriped business suit entered and sat down at a spot on the far end of the counter. He pulled a small, brown, paper bag from his coat pocket and placed it in front of him.

When the waitress came back, I was only moderately surprised to see that she now had curly black hair. She placed a large tumbler in front of the man, who stared at it blearily. The waitress gave a snort of impatience and pushed it toward him.

"Come on, Mr. Mayor," she said. "You know the rules. You have to pour it into one of our glasses."

"You'd think they reenacted Prohibition by the way you're acting," the mayor said.

"You know we don't have a liquor license," she reminded him. "I don't want to spend a night in that unheated, cinder-block shed your cousin calls a jail."

"All right, all right," he said, surrendering. "I never knew a woman so entranced by a bunch of meaningless rules. Don't you ever get tired of all this, Becky?"

"No sir," she said, "and neither should you. What kind of example are you showing people, where here you are, the mayor of our town, drunk as a lord before eleven in the morning? What would decent people say if they knew?"

"Decent people never come to Weir," he said. "As for my drinking, I blame both of my parents who gave me such a suggestive last name and this terrible thirst. On top of that, I don't think your so-called decent people would give a damn what I do. No one else in this town seems to. If they did, that idiocy across the street would never have been built."

"The town needed the money," Becky said. "Mr. Assyrian was willing to pay lots of it to build his mall. As for anyone caring about what you do, Mr. Mayor, Old Lady Murphy was in here for breakfast this morning. She wanted me to let you know that if you get into her trash cans once more, she'll be waiting for you with a shotgun full of rock salt."

"It's not my fault!" he protested. "It's a full moon, and I can't help that she always throws away those soup bones. You have no idea of how this affliction affects me. Every month, Becky, every month, probably for the friggin' rest of my goddamned life."

He took a long drink from the tumbler, examined the contents carefully and then pulled a flask from inside his jacket and poured its contents in. He took another long drink, covered his mouth with a fist and burped discreetly. He glared up at Becky.

"What's on the menu today?" he asked.

"Oh, my," she said. "Are you actually going to order food today?"

"You know I am," he replied. "I've been on the prowl all week. God, it's hard being a vegetarian at this time of the month."

"I've got a nice soy-burger already on the grill. Charlie over at the liquor store called and told me you were headed this way."

"Charlie's got a big mouth," the mayor said, "not that I'm complaining. Bring on the soy."

Becky went into the back and came out with three steaming plates of food. This time she wore a blonde pageboy haircut. She slipped a plate in front of the mayor as he drank from his tumbler again and then gave him a quick peck on his cheek. Then she came over and carefully laid our plates on the table before us.

"I'll be back with refills," she said.

I found that I was actually waiting with anticipation to see what color and style her hair would be this time. When she returned with another iced tea for Anna and another Coke for me, her hair was still blonde. This time it was in a long, Lady Godiva style that flipped over her shoulder like some early teeny-bopper.

We started eating and Anna looked up at me.

"This is pretty good," she said.

She was right. Mine had to be the best burger I'd ever eaten. The tomato was fresh, as were the lettuce, onion and pickle.

"So," she said. "Is Sieg still working on his little project?"

"Yeah," I replied. "I don't know what going on in his head. He won't tell me what he's up to. I think he and Court had another fight. When I brought up her name, he walked away muttering to himself. Maybe I should have just kept my big mouth shut."

She swallowed a bite of chicken fried steak before replying.

"Oh, I don't know," she said. "He always acts like he's smarter than everyone else. Maybe he's beginning to find out he's wrong."

"I doubt it."

We ate in silence for a few more minutes. Becky and the mayor were having a low toned conversation over at the counter. I noticed that she was holding one of his hands and speaking very earnestly even if I couldn't hear what she said.

I turned back to lunch and decided to venture into dangerous territory.

"So, what's going on with your mother and cousin?" I asked.

“Mother is still trying to set up a wedding here at the resort. I keep saying *no*, but she keeps plowing straight on. As for Brittany, I’d bet you anything that she’s sleeping with Sven every night.”

“Do you know that for sure?”

“Woman’s intuition,” she said. “Trust me on this. She’s been acting like the canary-eating cat.”

“I think you mean the bear-eating cat,” I said with a grin.

“Danny,” she said, “it may come as a surprise to you, but not every cat in the world is as bad as Edgar.”

“Prove it,” I said, and she laughed. Then she sobered and looked down at her plate.

“I guess Daddy’s coming in this weekend. I’m thinking about hiding in your attic until they give up and leave.”

I grinned at her. “I don’t think that would be too wise. Sieg’s laboratory is down the hall and you might not want to be right above his experiments.”

“Are they that dangerous?” she asked.

“Boy,” I said, “I’m torn. I could be loyal and say ‘Oh, no, he’s fine,’ or I could tell the truth. Sometimes his ideas go off the rails worse than mine. God knows I’ve screwed up more than my fair share. He seems to be so much more than that. It’s as if he was an elemental being who revels in chaos and destruction. He’s gotten away with it more times than not. Getting caught in one of his schemes can still mess up your day or your life.”

“I thought you were his best friend.”

“Yeah,” I said. “I guess I am, but every once in a while I slip and start seeing him as others do and forget the good things he’s done.”

“Our little fling has probably thrown your hormones out of whack,” she said with a small smile. Something about her tone upset me.

"Fling?" I asked. "Is that what you call it?"

"Oh, come on Danny," she said. "It's not anything serious."

It felt like a blow to the solar plexus. I sat back and looked at her. "It was serious to me," I said, stunned. I wasn't kidding. After we had made love for the first time, there in my bedroom, I had lain there with her head on my shoulder and dreamed of a life with her. I dreamed of a cottage with kids and maybe a cat or two running around. I dreamt of growing old with her. Now I felt like I did when my mother had called me. I felt like I did when Helen Shapely threatened to send me to jail. Worst of all, I felt betrayed.

I wiped my mouth and stood up. Without another word, I went up to the counter and paid the check, tipping the waitress.

"Come on back soon," she said.

I ignored Anna as I made my way blindly through the maze of shelves and back out onto the sidewalk. She followed me. When we reached the street, she tried to take my hand in hers. I jerked it away and turned my back to her.

"Do me a favor," I said, tasting the tears that were pouring unbidden from my eyes. "If it's not too much for you, please take the car back to Courtney."

"What about you?" she asked.

"Goodbye," was all I said.

"Danny! You don't have to be like this!"

Without looking back, I walked down Main Street toward the highway. I was being stupid and immature, but it seemed like a good idea at the time. After a few hundred yards, and climbing the hill back up to the highway, I began to regret my decision and started looking around to see if I could spot Anna and the car. She must have gone back by the long way since I never saw her. Every time I looked back and didn't see her, I would kick a rock and keep walking.

From the highway, it was only a mile or so to the resort. If you cut through the forest, it was barely a mile to the house. Lucky me, I found out the hard way it's a steep mile. I tramped through the forest, hoping against hope that I wasn't lost when suddenly Howard was walking next to me.

"Good afternoon, Daniel," he said. "How are you?"

"Not so good," I said. "Anna and I just had a fight."

"That's terrible. Fortunately, you're young and can heal from these little disappointments."

I didn't trust myself to speak as we continued up the hill. I knew eventually I'd either find civilization or the tree line and wondered which one would be first. We walked around a granite outcropping and stood in the clearing behind the house.

"Ah," Howard said, "you've found your way home."

I turned to him. "I thought I was following you," I said, puzzled.

"I thought I was following you," he said. "I didn't know where you were going but you looked as if you could use a friend."

"Does that mean we were lost?"

"I knew where I was," he said through a furry grin. "I just didn't know where you were going, since you hadn't told me."

"Sheesh," I said, "I guess it's true what they say about small children and fools."

"What is that?" he asked me.

"What do you mean?"

"What do they say about small children and fools?"

Howard asked me.

"You don't know?"

"If I knew, I wouldn't be asking," he said.

I started laughing. I couldn't help it. I leaned against the back of the house and let it all out in great spasms of laughter. I laughed until the pain in my throat stopped me. I laughed until I no longer felt the pain in my heart. I slid down and sat on the ground and shook my head. Then I stood back up and started walking around the house.

"What do they say?" Howard asked my retreating back.

"God looks out for them!" I replied without looking back.

Mike and Todd were sitting on the front porch as I came up the steps. Mike looked at me with a sad expression.

"I won't ask how it went since we already know. Anna came back alone and slammed the door when she went into the lobby."

I went inside and started up the stairs. Behind me, the screen door banged. I turned around. Mike was standing at the bottom of the stairs looking up at me.

"So what are you going to do?" he asked.

"I'm going to take a shower and go for a run."

* * *

Later, as my legs pounded on the trail, my thoughts spun around and around. I had no idea what I was going to do. Every time I reached a certain point in my thinking, the thought *I should have known Anna was out of my league* would intrude. She was beautiful, smart, educated and amazing in every way and I...I was some dumb teen-ager without much of a future except for the resort.

I had no illusions about the resort. It was nice, or rather, becoming nice, but it wasn't something that would attract a sophisticated woman like Anna. Maybe Doug Assyrian's idea was the best one. Maybe we should sell out and see what we can do afterwards.

There's only so much of that kind of thinking you can do before you realize what a pile of steaming cabbage farts it really is. I finally reached my fill long before the path dipped down at the upper end of the lake and crossed the swamps on a causeway.

Finally, I began to relax. By the time I strolled into the house, I felt a thousand times better, even as I dripped sweat from every pore.

Mike stuck his head out of the dining room and spotted me.

"Hey, Danny! Tell Sieg, dinner is served."

"All right," I said.

I found Sieg in his laboratory. He had added a makeshift lab bench made of an old door on a pair of saw-horses and a cardboard box cut up and taped to the window for a chemical hood to his store of equipment. He was busy working over the bench when I entered.

"Mike says dinner is served," I told him.

"Yeah, whatever," he replied.

I stood under the shower for a long time and let the water wash away the sweat, grime and dirt. Even some of the shame I had felt went down the drain, too.

After showering, I found that Sieg was no longer in his lab. Downstairs chili and biscuits were served and I sat down and began to eat.

"Do you feel better?" Mike asked me.

"A little bit, I guess. I'll get over it."

"Dude," Todd said, "what happened?"

"Nothing much, I just found out that I was just a

summer romance for Anna. I didn't take it so well."

Sieg looked surprised.

"What did you do?" he asked.

"We broke up, Sieg."

"Yeah? Well, I think Court's falling for you."

"I doubt it," I replied.

"Then why did she tell you about Prom?" he demanded.

"Maybe it's because I'm her friend. It could have been because you refused to talk about it. It could be a lot of things."

"I can fix your problem with Anna you know," he said with a small smile.

"No, Sieg," I said.

"I think you're too late," he said.

"What are you talking about?"

"I set off a pheromone bomb in the lobby this afternoon," he said.

"You did what?" I asked him in shock.

"I'm trying to fix Mr. Dixon's problem. I created what I call a 'pheromone bomb.' It's actually a combination of chemicals that increases ardor and lowers inhibitions. If anything is going to get those people together it'll be—"

"You moron!" Mike said, standing up. "Did it occur to you that there were other people in that lobby who'll be affected?"

"Uh..." Sieg said.

"That was totally irresponsible!" Mike continued. "What the hell is wrong with you?"

"I thought it was the best way to solve—"

"The best way to solve the problem was to leave it alone," I said. "Did it occur to you that people have been falling in and out of love for millions of years without your help?"

"I—uh..."

We were all staring at Sieg. We couldn't tell if he was serious or not. Getting freaked out wasn't going to fix the situation so I calmed down and took a deep breath.

"All right, genius," I said, "let's go over and see what the damage is."

"Dude, are you for real?" Todd asked Sieg, standing up and sliding his chair under the table.

"If he is," I said, "then we've got a big problem."

We ran over to the resort so fast that our feet barely touched the ground. We skidded to a stop just inside the front door and just stared at the tableau before us.

The lobby was filled with people—naked people. Clothes were strewn everywhere, hanging from trophies and piled on the floor.

Sieg's target, the blonde with the cello, was there all right. She was right in the center of the action, with her head bent and her bow moving as if there was no tomorrow. Sunlight streamed through the windows, making a halo around her head as if she were some kind of mad musical saint. I recognized the piece that she was then playing, it was the *Scheherazade*. She remained oblivious to everything around her, concentrating on the music that filled the air.

Here and there we saw busy couples that had separated and were doing their own thing away from the crowd. My gaze wandered down to where the polar bear stood, its face forever frozen in either a beastly snarl or an expression of sheer disgust. Behind it a couple was having their fun. With only mild surprise did I realize that they were Brittany and Sven.

Looking up, I found Mr. Monkey doing something or other with a stuffed lynx. I dropped my gaze immediately and looked away. Following Mike, we carefully picked our way around the crowd. With a shock, I realized the front desk had been abandoned and there was no sign of Anna, Cap or Lisa anywhere in the room.

Well, isn't that just wonderful, I said to myself. We stopped at the front desk and slowly turned around to take another look at the lobby. I think we were stunned, and I was a little bit disgusted. Everywhere we looked there were so many gyrating, sweating naked bodies that it was hard to see if they were human or not. Sieg turned to me with wide eyes.

"This isn't how it should have worked," he said. "The stuff should have made people a little looser, maybe a bit more likely to have a bit of fun, but this is nothing like I thought it would do."

"Dude," Todd said. He was more impressed that I was and he looked around with a huge grin that kept getting bigger with every second. "I can see it now: 'Instant Orgy! Just add a little of Dr. Sieg's Magic Formula!' Do you know how much they'd pay for this stuff up in Monterey?"

"This is horrible," I said. "Sieg, this isn't good, and it sure isn't funny. Think of the lives you've destroyed."

He stood there for a moment and then a smile slowly appeared on his face.

"I don't think it's as bad as you think," he said. "Sure, I have to admit that all those extra-chubby people should be doing this up in their rooms, but I have the feeling that we're not seeing a whole lot of adultery here."

I closed my eyes to the masses of flesh that were moving together before us.

"How long does this last?" I asked. "I hope we're not going to have a permanent orgy in here."

"I don't know," Sieg replied. "By the dosage I used, it

should end within an hour. However, as I said, it shouldn't have worked this way."

I opened my eyes only to spot Dr. Sybel. He had spread his jacket over a Navajo blanket next to the stuffed llama. A large, older woman had her legs wrapped around him. I quickly looked away, my face heating. He was surprisingly fit for an older gentleman.

"I don't see Cap or Lisa," Mike said. I glanced over at him and he was standing with his back to the spectacle with his brow furrowed. No one was behind the front desk and the office door was closed.

Glancing to the left, I realized that while Sven's office was closed, Anna's was not. Without a word I stepped over and peeked in, my jaw clenched against what I thought I was going to find. Fortunately, her office was empty and I quickly closed the door.

"I would have thought Anna would be back by now," I said to Mike. He ignored me and carefully knocked on Cap's door.

"Who's there," came a muffled voice from within.

"It's Mike."

"Are you dressed?"

"Yeah."

"Come in."

I followed Mike through the door. I let out a sharp breath of relief when I saw the situation inside. Cap was standing against the windows behind his desk. Lisa stood across from him, her back pressed against the bookcases next to the door. Between them stood every piece of furniture the office held, looking as if it had been shoved there in a hurry.

"I know I'm going to regret this," Cap said without taking his eyes from Lisa, "but do—"

"Do you know what's going on here?" Lisa said,

finishing his sentence. A film of sweat covered both of their faces and I noticed that they were trembling.

Mike looked at me, and I looked at him. It was as if we were trying to determine just how much to tell Cap. If we told him the truth, then I knew Sieg and I would get fired. At that moment I felt closer to Cañon City and prison than ever before. Mike finally shrugged.

"I have no idea. We just came in and found all of our guests having a lot of fun in the lobby."

I slowly let my breath out. Technically, Mike's statement was true, as we really didn't know what the hell Sieg had put in the air. His explanation, while interesting, was meaningless.

"What happened?" I asked.

"I'm not sure," Lisa said. Her voice wavered and she was clutching the shelves behind her with a white-knuckle grip.

* * *

"Anna stormed into the lobby," Lisa said. "Her face was red and there were tears running down her cheeks. She slammed the door to her office and I could hear her crying.

"Sven stepped out of his office to see what was going on. He looked at Anna's door and was about to knock. Ms. Hughes, the cellist, was crossing the lobby on her way outside to the Grand Stairs to practice like she does every day. The Hendersons were sitting by the buffalo, having their afternoon tea.

"It was as if a thunderstorm had suddenly gone off. The air became electric and Ms. Hughes stopped and put down her instrument. She opened the case and pulled out her bow. She dropped the case and kicked it away and started to play.

"It became hard to breathe, and suddenly people started coming down the stairs, out of the dining room and out from the bar. Mr. and Mrs. Henderson started taking their clothes off. Sven went over to tell them to leave the lobby. The elevator opened and Brittany came out. She ran over to Sven and then they were stripping at the polar bear.

"It just kept getting worse. People would come into the lobby, get that strange look on their face and then start dropping their clothes.

"The feeling came over me and I moved to the office door, my hand was shaking as I reached out and—

"I… I came in here to get Cap and…" she said. Her voice had been shaky as she related the story.

"Never mind that," Sieg said as he pushed his way past me and opened Cap's window. "I think it's a bit close in here and I think we'll all be better for a little fresh air."

"Did you see where Anna went?" I asked Lisa.

"No, her door was still closed when I came in here."

Somehow, I found that I was still calm. Bouncing around in all directions wasn't going to fix the problem. Oddly enough, I wasn't even mad at Sieg for endangering our freedom.

"Hey!" Sieg said. "Where's Courtney?"

"And where's Penny?" Mike added.

"Better yet," I said, "where's Todd? Wasn't he right behind you, Sieg?"

"I thought he was following us across the lobby."

I pulled the door open and we raced back outside. We looked all over the Orgy but didn't spot our co-worker.

"Why doesn't this affect us?" I asked Sieg. "And what's with Cap and Lisa?"

"We weren't here when the bomb went off," he said.

"The stuff only gets into the air for a short time before it dissipates. I think Cap and Lisa have more will power than we realized. Frankly, I'm surprised they weren't having a go on his desk."

"What?"

"Oh, grow up Danny," he said. "If you can't tell that there's a lot of attraction between those two, then you're blind."

"They're attracted to each other?" I said.

"And you wonder why you were only the secretary of the Science Club."

"We've got to find Todd and the girls," Mike said. "Follow me."

We moved away from the front desk and dodged around a group using pillows from some nearby couches for an impromptu bed. Suddenly the door to the back corridor opened and Todd stuck his head out.

"Dudes, in here!" he said.

We ran through the door and Mike was immediately grabbed by Penny. Todd closed the door behind us.

"I came back in here to see if I could find them and—" Todd said.

Before he could say another word, Courtney pushed past Sieg and aimed herself at me. I reached out and grabbed her arms, pushing her back.

"Stop it, Courtney," I said.

Behind her, Penny had Mike pinned to the wall. She was kissing him and had started to pull her top off.

I was about to say something when Courtney managed to grab my arm. The next thing I knew, I was looking up at the ceiling as she jumped on me and held my arms down with her knees. She reached for the buttons on her top as Sieg and Todd grabbed her arms and pulled her off me.

“Run for it, Dude,” Todd said. Even before I could move, Courtney turned and gave Sieg a knee to his crotch. Before she could do it again, Todd moved behind her and got a better grip on her. I rolled to my feet and made for the door. Somewhere in the background I could hear the cellist racing through the finale of the *Scheherazade*.

“Ow!” Todd yelped and I could hear Courtney’s footsteps behind me as I raced toward the front door. If I could reach it, I could probably find somewhere to hide.

“Gotcha!” Sieg yelled.

I turned around and saw he had tackled her. The effects of the bomb must have dampened her fighting edge because even though she fought like a wildcat, Sieg managed to keep her down on the floor. Finally, in desperation he sat on her back and there wasn’t anyone going to get up from that.

“I’ll kill you!” she raged.

“Trust me,” he said, “this hurts me a lot more than it hurts you.” I saw tears running down his cheeks and knew he was telling the truth.

I turned back to the door when something in the atmosphere changed. It was as if the storm had come to an end. Courtney stopped struggling and tears poured from her eyes. Sieg looked up at me, his expression unreadable. All around us the couples stopped moving and looked around bemused.

“I think it wore off,” I said. “Go ahead and let Court up.”

“Are you sure?” he asked.

“Yeah.”

Moving slowly, as if a sudden move would break Courtney, Sieg rose to his feet. She stood up and stared at me. Her eyes were wide and brimming with tears and her lips quivered.

"Why?" she asked me. "I wanted to love you."

"I don't love you, Courtney," I said. My voice was shaking, and I felt as if my heart was going to break again. "You're my friend, but I'm not in love with you. I'm not the guy you're looking for."

Without speaking another word, she turned and ran from the lobby. I could hear her crying as she took the stairs two at a time. I stood there for a moment, staring into nothing and wondering if I had made the right decision.

Mike and Penny came out of the back hall holding hands. They both looked mussed but they were at least wearing their clothes.

"What happened?" Penny asked. She looked around the lobby in amazement. Couples had started retrieving their clothes and a buzz of conversation began to rise. Ms. Hughes had retrieved her case and was carefully putting her instrument away. Her eyes were half closed, and a smile played across her lips.

"What happened?" Penny asked again.

"We'll tell you about it later," Mike said.

I glared at Sieg. "I don't suppose you can cook up something to make them forget this whole thing."

"I don't think so," he said.

"We're going to get fired, you know."

"Yeah. I thought I was doing Mr. Dixon a favor. Now it looks like I've screwed us up again."

Ms. Hughes had finished packing her cello and was walking toward the elevator. The top two buttons of her blouse were undone, revealing some cleavage that I couldn't help but look at. She moved the cello as if it weighed nothing. She waltzed past us and pressed the elevator's call button.

The elevator opened and she brightened to incandescence when she saw who was leaving it.

"Robert! It's so nice to see you!"

Mr. Dixon stepped off the elevator. My breath caught, and my heart dropped like a stone. Holding his hand and looking as mussed as he did was Anna. Dixon nodded to Ms. Hughes as he turned and held the elevator door.

"Oh, Sheila, it's nice to see you, too. May I introduce Anna Charles, my fiancée? Anna, this is Sheila Hughes, an old friend of mine."

"Fiancée?" Ms. Hughes asked.

"Yes," Dixon replied. "After a moment of passion, we've decided to get married."

"Oh," Ms. Hughes said, "how nice to meet you." Her eyes had widened, and she seemed to be staring at nothing. "I was afraid Robert would pine for me forever."

With a flash of insight I realized that Sheila Hughes wanted Robert to pine for her. She liked being pursued, and in that moment I realized that we were both crushed.

"So did I," he said. His eyes were bright, and a thin smile played across his lips for a second. He had the same insight as I did. "I finally realized that you're married to your music, and there's no room in your life for anything else. If you will excuse us, Anna and I are going to dinner."

"Yes," Ms. Hughes said as she watched them stroll off holding hands. She went into the elevator and pushed the button. As the door closed I saw the tears slowly dampening her cheeks. I turned away and walked out the front door.

With my own tears blinding me, I stumbled over to the house and threw myself into the porch swing. I sat there, slowly swinging and trying to control my tears.

There was a sound on the stairs and I looked up. Sieg was standing there, his face drawn and his eyes were red. I could see there were tears on his cheeks, too.

"I'm sorry, Danny," he said. "I never meant for any of this to happen. I've really screwed. I'm so sorry."

"Yeah," I said. "It's quite a day, Sieg. In one fell swoop we've managed to lose our girlfriends and our job. I'm almost looking forward to prison, now."

"I don't know," he said. "I think whatever Court and I had was dead when she went to Prom without me."

"Maybe we can fix this," I said.

Sieg came over and sat down next to me. "How? With the pheromone bomb, Court didn't even look at me except to clobber me."

"I don't think that bomb of yours works quite the way you think it does," I said. I swung back and forth and stared at the porch rafters. "I think you need to start with 'sorry' and work your way up from there."

"I don't think she's going to be visiting me in Cañon City," he said.

"Yeah, there's that."

We sat there in silence until Mike and Todd came up the trail. Todd barely nodded to us as he went inside. Mike leaned against the porch rail and crossed his arms.

"This had been one hell of a day," he said. "Sieg, if you ever pull something like this again..."

"I don't think you'll have to worry about it," Sieg said. "I don't think they'll let me have chemicals in prison."

"I wouldn't worry about that. It seems you've got a guardian angel or something. Everyone down at the resort seems to be happy. Apparently your little orgy was exactly what the doctor ordered."

"You've got to be joking," I said.

"No," Mike said, turning to me. "People have been coming over to the front desk and making reservations for next year. Sieg may have sparked a new boom for us. We haven't heard a single complaint, except for yours, of course."

Todd came out with a couple of beers. He passed one over to Mike and fished a bottle-opener from his back pocket. After popping the top he sat down on the top step next to Sieg and took a drink.

"Is this a private party?" Anna asked as she emerged from the trees. She was followed by Courtney and then Penny. Mike didn't look over as he waved to them.

"Come on up," he said. His voice seemed unnaturally loud in the evening stillness.

With deliberate steps, Anna climbed between Sieg and Todd and around Mike before sitting on the other end of the swing from me. I looked down and didn't say anything. I felt as if I'd frozen solid and I couldn't even look at her. I could smell her perfume, which only reminded me of the times we'd had together. On the edge of my vision I could see her reach out as if to touch my arm but she stopped just before contact.

"I should apologize," she said.

"There's nothing to apologize for," I said.

"Oh, Danny," she said, "I should have realized right at the first that this was just a summer romance, and I didn't even think about your feelings."

I looked up, straight ahead. Penny was leaning against the porch rail next to Mike and Courtney was sitting on the top step between Todd and Sieg. She was sharing Todd's beer and all three were talking in low tones.

"I'm sorry," Anna said.

"So am I," I said. "I just wish it could have ended

better than this."

"Yeah, I wish it had ended better, too. You have a right to be pissed off at me but I still want us to be friends."

"I'll survive," I said and forced a smile.

"Courtney is very fond of you."

"I said no, and I meant it." I was keeping my voice as low as possible. There was no point in embarrassing Court again. "I like her very much but she's more like a sister than anything else. It just wouldn't feel right."

I watched as Courtney took a deep drink from the beer and handed it back to Todd. She burped and wiped her mouth with her hand.

"Sorry," she said, "beer does that to me."

"Hey," Mike said, "I forgot something. Cap wants us to go into the attics and pick out any furniture we need for the house. We're supposed to go up there as soon as our guests leave next week."

"That sounds pretty generous," Anna said. "So, what's the catch?"

"He wants to motivate us to clean out the attics," Mike said. "Who knows what we'll find up there?"

"Probably just a bunch of old, broken-down furniture," Sieg said. "I'm going in for a beer. Anyone else want one?"

Courtney looked at me for a second after he had left. I shrugged and jerked my head toward the door. She placed her hand on the knob and hesitated for a long moment. Then she pulled the door open and followed in his wake.

"What was that about?" Anna said.

"I'm not sure," I said. "They needed a private conversation."

We rocked in silence for a couple of minutes. She

turned to me and lowered her voice so that I was the only one to hear her.

"I'm sorry, Danny. I never meant to hurt you."

"Don't be sorry," I said. "Just be happy. Will you be happy with Dixon?"

"I think so. I just didn't expect—"

"Look," I said, "we had our fun and I enjoyed every minute of it. All things come to an end eventually. I want you to be happy, and if Robert Dixon makes you happy, then be happy with him."

"Danny, I..."

"Look at it this way," I said, "I'm young and I'll heal."

I stood up and walked to the front door. Like Courtney, I stopped with my hand poised to open it and turned back to the woman I loved.

"Goodbye, Anna."

Inside, I wasn't too surprised to find Courtney pressing Sieg against the wall and kissing him for all he was worth. Smiling to myself, I squeezed past and into the kitchen. I grabbed a six-pack from the fridge and went back out to the porch. I wasn't surprised to find Anna had already left.

Penny looked into my eyes as I handed her a beer.

"Uh, Danny..." she said.

"It's okay," I said. "I'll live."

I sat back down on the swing and sipped my beer.

"We heard a bit of news before we came over," Penny said.

"Oh?" I said.

"Yeah, Sven's getting hitched to Brittany," she said.

I started laughing, and once I started I couldn't stop for a couple of minutes. Finally I had to stop and breathe.

"I hope," Penny said, "that that stuck-up, little,

conniving bitch will make him happy, because he'll be the only one."

"That's not nice," I said.

"Danny, I'll call her what I want. I'd tell you what I really think but it would cause you to doubt my lady-like qualities."

"I'd never doubt them, Penny," I said. "I like my arm in one piece."

"Jerk," she said with a smile.

I blew her a kiss and started drowning my sorrows.

SIXTEEN

I avoided Anna for the next couple of days. It wasn't as hard as it sounds since she spent all of her free time with Dixon and her mother. I would catch glimpses of them sitting and talking in the dining room or lobby. I would hurry past, trying not to think about the subject of their discussion. I wanted to be happy for Anna but, on the other hand, I wanted fire-demons from the darkest corner of hell to pop up and grab Dixon and take him to where he belonged.

The Robert Dixon voodoo doll that I made was a complete failure.

I spent most of my free-time fixing up Howard's shed or doing something for the house. By Saturday morning, however, I found myself at loose ends. I laid in my bed with my thoughts spinning around and finally decided to eliminate some of my mental baggage.

Forgoing my morning run, I pulled on a tee-shirt and jeans and jogged over to the resort. On the third floor, past all the guest rooms, I stopped and knocked at a certain door.

Courtney opened the door, sleepy eyed and tousled. She was wearing a long night-shirt that clung to her body, and I had to look away.

“Danny?” she said. “What are you doing over here? What time is it?”

“I need a favor, Court,” I said to a potted plant halfway down the hall from us.

“What do you need?”

“Can you give me a ride down to Mohawk? I need to go home one last time.”

“What? Why? I’m supposed to be here helping Penny. The new girls aren’t ready and—”

“They’ll live without you for a few hours. I just need to take some stuff out of my room before some stranger starts poking around.”

“That’s what you get for owning porn,” she said. “All right, I’ll drive you down as long as you’re the one who tells Penny where I’m going.”

“Get dressed, and I’ll meet you at your car. Penny’s over at the house with Mike.”

“Are you sure? I thought she was in her room.”

“My room is right above his,” I said. “Trust me. You can’t mistake the noise they’re making. I think she snores louder than he does. I left a note on the dining table for Mike. He’ll tell her where you’ve gone.”

“I just know we’re going to get into trouble.”

I grinned. “How is that going to different from any other time? I thought trouble was my name.”

“Hah,” she said and closed the door.

I went down to the lobby and was surprised to see Cap coming through the dining room door with a steaming mug in his hand. He looked at me with raised eyebrows.

"You're up and dressed early this morning," he said.

"I'm going down to Mohawk. Courtney's giving me a ride."

"Why does she have to drive? Oh, I forgot, you lost your license."

"Yeah."

"Stupid, really, as if your driving privileges led to the fire. You do know you're supposed to let me know if you're leaving the property."

"Uh, yeah," I said. I *had* forgotten, damn it. "I left a note for Mike. I thought I could get down and back before I was missed."

"Hah! Just stay out of trouble while you're down there. Try to be back before lunch."

"Right."

He went into his office and closed the door. The elevator dinged and Courtney came out. She looked around with a furrowed brow.

"Where's Sieg?" she said.

"He's probably still in dreamland. Why?"

"I thought you never went anywhere without him."

"That's what he thinks. I guess I do, too, but I don't need him on this trip."

"You're buying breakfast," she said as we headed for the door.

"Sure. No problem."

* * *

Even though Mom had left only a few days before, the house felt cold and empty as I let myself in. The effect was enhanced by the things she had taken with her. Here and there were missing photographs and knick-knacks, leaving only shapes in the dust. I felt a profound sadness fill me, and I couldn't even look into her room as I rushed by.

My room was untouched from when I left it. I stood in the door for a moment, taking it all in. I knew that no matter who Ed hired, they would carefully pack, label and store everything. A sound in the hall made me turn around. Courtney was standing behind me; she peered at me as if trying to see what was going on in my mind.

“I don’t think I’ve ever seen your room, Danny.”

“Yeah, I don’t think Sieg has, either.”

“I thought you guys did sleepovers,” she said.

“They were always over at his house. His mom thought she was helping mine by getting me out from underfoot.”

Court looked around as I started pulling the old posters off the walls. Most I just crumpled up but a couple, an old Frank Paul print and a Frazetta, I carefully rolled up and stuck into a mailing tube. I started filling a cardboard box with clothes and stuff I wanted to take with me when we heard another noise in the hall. Before either of us could react, Big Ed was standing in the doorway with an automatic in his hand. When he realized who it was, he quickly shoved it back into its holster.

“What the hell do you think you’re doing?” he said. “Mrs. Green called, saying someone had broken into the house.”

“I just wanted to get a few things,” I said.

“You should have let me know. It’s a ‘make my day’ state, you know.”

I pulled some old *Playboys* and *Hustlers* from under the bed and tossed them into the trash. I added my alarm clock to the box.

“I needed to go through a few things before it all went into storage.”

“You could have been arrested,” Big Ed said, “and

then where would you be?"

I froze at the thought. Some of the Mohawk cops would do anything to put me back in jail, and a phony trespassing charge would do the trick.

"I didn't even think of that," I said.

"I didn't think so," Ed said with a grimace. "Next time, try to think of it. Are you going to need more boxes?"

"At least one, there's some more things I want."

I went to lift the filled box and Courtney took it out of my hands.

"I'll take it down," she said. "And I'll stop in the garage and pick up another one."

"Are you sure?"

Ignoring me, she took the box, leaving me with Ed. He looked at me and sat down on the corner of the bed. I continued to open my dresser drawers and pull things out.

"So," Big Ed said, "how's it going up there?"

"It could be better," I said. "Then again, anything's better than prison."

"I heard that Sieg put his own stamp on the place."

"Yeah," I said, my thoughts going to Anna. "I tried to stop him this time. Fat lot of good it did me."

"Don't worry about it," he said. "Sven told me that word is getting around about all the 'therapeutic qualities' of the air at Lake Weir Resort. He thinks we're going to be busy for the rest of the summer."

"I have a question about Sven," I said.

"Shoot."

"How did you find him?"

"I advertised for a catering manager, and he applied," Ed said with a frown. "He has some experience and was willing to work for what we could afford to pay him. He seems to be working out."

"Is there a chance he could be working for Doug Assyrian?"

Ed's frown deepened at the name of his old adversary. He slowly rubbed a hand across his mouth before answering, as if trying to hold back a torrent of cuss words.

"Vera said you were asking about that bastard," he said. "What makes you think there's some connection between him and Sven?"

"I don't have anything concrete, but it was through him that I first heard the phrase, 'The Next Vail.'"

Ed's eyes narrowed. "Well, isn't that interesting. Thanks for bringing this to my attention. You couldn't believe what a menace Assyrian is."

"Oh yes I can. I saw that wonderful strip mall of his up in Weir. We don't need his brand of progress at Lake Weir. I'll be damned if it'll be ruined by a greed-head."

"I should never have let you read Hunter Thompson," Ed said.

"Too late now," I said. "Oh, and I need a favor from you."

"Now what?" he asked.

"I need you to take Dad's Pontiac and clean it up for me. I get my license back in a couple of weeks."

"I forgot about that," Ed said. "You know, I can always find you a new car. I was going to find you a Mustang for your birthday."

"I want the Pontiac. Dad left it to me, and I've never had a chance to drive it."

"All right," Ed said, "but you'll have to remember it's an old '61 Pontiac."

"Yeah, I know but it's the only car we've ever had. I want to keep it in the family."

Ed sighed. “I don’t know what condition the engine is in, much less the interior, the suspension or even the tires. “It might take till September before it’s drivable.”

“I’ve waited all this time, another few months won’t hurt.”

Courtney appeared at the door. She had another cardboard box in her hands.

“Hey,” she said. “Mr. Green wants to know what’s going on. I told him Danny was just picking up a few things but I don’t think he believes me. He’s still waiting out by Big Ed’s car.”

“I guess I’ll go and have a word with your nosy neighbor,” Ed said.

“Hey, if the house had been broken into...” I said, trying to defend Mr. Green.

“Yeah, whatever,” Ed said before stomping down the hall.

Courtney helped me pack a few more books into the box. We stopped and I looked around.

“Is this going to be it?” she asked.

“Yeah, except for one slight detour to the basement.”

“What for?” she asked.

“I promised Sieg that he could have my old chemistry set.”

“Oh, you have got to be kidding me,” she said.

* * *

We returned to the resort in plenty of time. Courtney helped me by carrying a couple of boxes. Sieg was sitting on the porch stairs, and I handed him the metal box containing the chemistry set and a smaller plastic case with a bunch of Erector Set parts I found on a dusty shelf in one corner of the basement.

“Here, genius,” I said. “Don’t say I’ve never given

you anything."

"Cool!" he said as he grabbed the boxes and sprinted up the stairs. At the top he stopped and called back down, "Thanks! Supremely cool!"

Courtney handed me the boxes she was carrying and glared at the screen door. "You'd think he'd at least give me a kiss."

"What are you going to do about it?" I asked her.

She looked at me for a second, stuck out her chin, and marched inside. When I reached my room, I could hear her talking to Sieg in his laboratory. I left the box on my desk to be dealt with later and changed into one of my uniform shirts.

I ran into Penny on the second floor landing, she was wearing one towel and had her hair up in another.

"There you are," she said. "Mike wants to kill you."

"He'll have to take number and get in line. I left him a note, and Cap knew where I was going."

"I think he wants you to inform him personally next time."

"Trust me," I said, looking at her up and down, "neither of you wanted me to inform him personally."

She blushed as I laughed. Then she slammed Mike's door in my face. I kept laughing as I went out the door and down the steps. Before I got to the trail, the screen door opened and Sieg called out after me.

"Hey! Wait for us!"

He and Courtney fell into step with me, and we headed down the trail.

"I see the two of you have patched things up again," I said.

"Yeah," Court giggled. Sieg had a slightly crooked smile on his face as if he wasn't sure where he stood with Courtney then he shook it off.

Lisa was busy on the phone as we came in. Anna came out of her office and almost walked into me again.

"Oh!" she said, "Hi, guys!"

"Hi, yourself," I said. "How goes the wedding?"

"My mother is involved," she said with a frown.

I chuckled. "Okay, that answers that. How's your fiancé handling it?"

"My mother is involved," she repeated in a deeper voice. "Guess."

"So, what's the problem?" Sieg asked.

"She wants us to get married at St. Patrick's and have this humongous wedding with everyone in New York State invited."

"What's wrong with that?" Courtney asked. "It sounds romantic. Kind of like Princess Diana."

"Robert and I just want to have a small wedding with a few friends and family."

"I might have a solution to your problem," I said.

"What's that?"

I told her my idea and she brightened up and kissed me on the cheek.

"That's a great idea! Wait until I tell Robert!"

She hurried off and I realized that Courtney was glaring at me.

"Yes?" I askcd.

"I don't know which is worse, you or Sieg. If she does what you suggested, it'll cause more trouble than any pheromone bomb."

"You might be right," I said, "but you have to admit, it's the best advice anyone could give her."

"Her mother is going to be livid," Sieg said. He had a thoughtful look on his face.

"Her mother can worry about Brittany and Sven's wedding instead," I replied.

"Like I said before--" Court said.

"Excuse me, guys," Sieg said. "I just remembered something I've got to do upstairs. I'll be back in a while."

"Oh, sure," Courtney said. "I've got to go back and find Penny. I hope she hasn't killed one of the new girls yet."

"You'd better get going," I said.

* * *

I helped Lisa at the desk for about half an hour when Sieg and Sheila Hughes came out of the elevator together. This time she was carrying the cello case and Sieg merely had the luggage. They stopped at the front desk.

"I need to check out," she said.

"Is there something wrong?" Lisa asked her.

"Oh, no, it's been wonderful. I just found out that I have a very important appointment." She hefted the cello case.

After checkout, I noticed that she and Sieg were deep in conversation as they went past. I stepped out onto the porch and found a taxicab waiting out front. The driver helped to put her luggage into the trunk. Sieg put the cello into the back seat and then held the other door for her. I saw him pass her something and she laughed and gave him a peck on the cheek.

"What was that?" I asked him when he came back up with the cart.

"Oh, just a parting gift."

* * *

Later that evening, I was sitting on the porch swing with my eyes closed trying to catch a breeze, any breeze from the lake. A noise made me look up to see Brittany coming up the trail. Her frown and the way she was muttering to herself told me that she wasn't happy. She stomped up onto the porch, grabbed one of the swing chains and yanked it violently. I reached out to steady myself and she grabbed my arm and pulled me to my feet.

"What did you do, you little—?" she said.

"Whoa! What are you talking about?"

"My cousin disappeared along with that jerk she's going to marry. I found a note attached to her office door telling us that she's run off to Vegas to get married. I thought Aunt Barbara was going to have a heart attack when Sven told her."

"So she took my advice," I said with a smile. "Good for her." I hadn't thought she would. Her mother filled a major space inside her head, and I despaired of her breaking away. To hear this from Brittany filled my heart with joy. At least Anna was growing up and being her own person.

"What did you tell her?" Brittany asked.

"Anna didn't want the huge wedding so I suggested that she take her husband to Vegas. I hear there's a chapel there where you can get married by an Elvis impersonator. Hopefully, it'll be a good one because there's nothing worse than a bad Elvis—"

Brittany slapped me across the face. It was so hard that my head rang. I swear, you could have heard the smack across the lake. I fell back down in the swing.

"You bastard!" she said. "Now that old bitch will take over my wedding! I had it all planned out. Aunt Barbara would be busy with Anna's wedding, that way Sven and I could get in some snuggle time and maybe elope. Now we're being followed everywhere as if I'm the one who wants to escape."

"Think about the advantages," I said.

"What advantages?"

“She’s already got half the work done already. You’ll be able to marry Sven in a hurry and live happily ever after.”

I stood up from the swing, mostly because her constant pulling on the chains was beginning to make me seasick. I don’t know what came over me, I just reached out and grabbed her arms and pulled her to me. Then I kissed her hard on the lips. She pulled away and slapped me again, this time not as hard.

“How *dare* you?” she hissed. “I’m telling Sven. Your ass is so fired!”

She turned and ran away as I savored the taste of her lips and rubbed the warm spot where she slapped me. *Nothing at all like Anna*, I thought to myself as I sat down and started swinging again.

SEVENTEEN

For the rest of the week I spent most of my time avoiding both Brittany and Sven. I wanted nothing to do with Brittany. She might have been as beautiful as Anna but there was something definitely dark and scary about her. On her part, whenever she spotted me she would make a point of coming up to me and deliberately leaning in a way as to expose as much of her cleavage as she could. It was the thought that *Anna* would find out that kept me honest. Sven, I wasn't worried about, so I was willing to let her flirt with me even if it started to bug him.

Sven was bugged, however, by something else entirely. We would set up the ballroom for a banquet or a dance and he would watch us as we set it up. An hour or so later, he would return only to find the place in total chaos again. He even resorted to hiring a security guard for a day and still the room was a shambles when he entered it.

On that Wednesday, he stood in the doorway and watched as Sieg and I worked to straighten the mess up.

“I don’t understand it,” he said. “Why does this keep happening?”

I ignored him, mostly because I was still feeling a bit guilty about kissing Brittany. Sieg, on the other hand, looked up from where he was working and smiled.

“I told you there was a poltergeist problem in here, but you didn’t want to listen.”

“What the hell are you talking about, Shultz?” Sven asked. Like a lot of people who dealt with Sieg on a regular basis he was beginning to sound exasperated. I began to wonder if my best friend was going to survive the summer even as he went over and spoke to Sven.

“A poltergeist is some kind of paranormal entity that likes to move things around,” Sieg answered slowly, as if talking to a child.

I rolled my eyes. *Don’t get us in trouble*, I silently prayed.

“So you’re talking about a ghost,” Sven said. He furrowed his brow as if trying to understand the concept.

“Sort of,” Sieg said. “The word ghost implies an entity of human origins. A poltergeist isn’t necessarily human. Some are attached to young men or women, while others, like the one in here, are attached to a certain place.”

“You have to be making that up, Shultz.”

“You can look it up in any parapsychology textbook,” Sieg answered seriously.

“Okay, I will,” Sven said. He stood up straight and glared across the ballroom at me. “Right now, you two need to get this place set up. Our luncheon is starting in half an hour.”

“We’re on it,” Sieg said. He slapped Sven on the back and came over. As he started moving chairs, I grinned at him.

"Nice patter of bullshit, my boy," I said.

"It wasn't bullshit, Danny. I was serious. I don't care if you believe me or not. The important thing is that *Sven* believes me, and that might save your ass in the future, especially if he decides to kick it for kissing his fiancée."

"Does everyone know about that?"

"She looks at you the same way Court or Anna does. I got curious and decided to ask her. I think you've attracted a new fan."

"Oh, great," I said.

"It's your own fault, lover-boy," Sieg said with a vicious grin. "If you didn't go around kissing them, they'd probably never notice that you're alive."

"I've never kissed Courtney, you idiot! What about you? Don't think I didn't notice you talking to Ms. Hughes. What are you trying to do?"

"That is none of your business," he said.

"Then stay out of my problems with Brittany."

"Oh, I know. I'm just saying that if you'd keep your lips to yourself then--"

"Don't you dare say another word, Shultz," I said. I could feel my ears turning red and my heart seemed to be missing a few beats. We worked in silence for a while and were just about finished when Sven came back.

"All right, Shultz," he said. He looked down at a piece of paper he held in one hand. The paper was covered in notes. "I called a friend of mine at Duke. He tells me that you're probably correct. I'm going to have some ghost breakers come in and see if they can get rid of this damned nuisance once and for all."

We both looked at him in amazement. I wondered if Sieg understood that someone else in the universe had just actually backed him up. The idea of breaking ghosts was something neither of us had thought of. We'd seen a few movies over the years, and I thought the idea was sound. The idea that someone actually made a living out of paranormal detection was a new one for me.

“Who are you going to get?” I asked. Sven glared at me as if I had just peed on his leg. Right then I knew Brittany had told him what had happened. Somehow, it didn’t bother me as much as I thought it would. On the other hand, I wasn’t going to repeat the experiment either.

“I don’t know yet,” he replied. “I’m going to make a few calls while I’m on my honeymoon.”

He left us to finish. When we were done and were leaving the ballroom, I looked over my shoulder and saw one of the chairs moving.

“Don’t you dare,” I yelled at it. The chair quit moving and we left in peace.

EIGHTEEN

Friday morning was moving quickly as both tour groups were leaving. Cap put on an old Duke Ellington record, and we hustled the luggage out to the buses to the sounds of "Take the 'A' Train" and "Mood Indigo."

Things were going smoothly until I turned around and found Brittany standing there with her suitcase in hand. We stood there for a long time, neither of us speaking until she broke the silence.

"I guess this is good-bye, at least for now."

"For now?" I asked.

"Of course, when Sven and I are married we're coming back here to work."

"Well, good luck," I said.

"Thanks."

Then she was gone.

* * *

We spent the rest of the afternoon running dirty laundry down to Mr. Chang while Penny and the remaining housemaids covered furniture in old sheets. With both groups leaving, the North Wing would go back to sleep, at least for a while. A new, smaller group was due on Monday morning, which gave us the weekend to clean up and do a few odd chores.

"You've done a good job," Cap told us that afternoon. He'd inspected the rooms and had returned satisfied. "I have one more little chore for you." He handed a ring of keys to Mike.

"I want you guys to go through the attics and throw out everything unusable. I want whatever is left to be organized as much as possible. Big Ed and I are going to do an inventory sometime next week.

"Hey, Cap," Mike said, "you promised that we could—"

"Yeah, if you find anything you want for your house, grab it. I don't care what it is. Now get to work."

* * *

It turned out that our earlier estimate of the quality of the junk in the attic was perhaps a bit generous. In the North Attic, we just opened a window and started tossing broken pieces of furniture out onto the lawn. Mike and Todd had roped the area off to keep people from being killed by falling trash. While we swept up, Sieg shook his head disgustedly.

"This is a waste of time," he said.

"At least the clean-up is easy," I replied.

Todd and Mike entered the attic.

"Uh, Danny," Todd said, "you know we've got to load the dump truck when it gets here on Monday."

I smiled at him and kept sweeping.

"Don't bring me down."

* * *

We walked through the mezzanine on our way to the South Attic when the elevator dinged and opened. We turned and stared in surprise as Howard stepped off. He smiled when he spotted us.

"Ah, that's a jolly bit of luck."

"Howard!" I croaked. I think we were all dumbstruck. "What are you doing here? Where have you been?"

"Oh," he said, "I am sorry, gentlemen. I began to find those pesky tourists underfoot every time I wished to leave my home. Since my presence here is supposed to be something of a secret, I decamped to the abandoned mine at the upper end of the canyon."

"There's an abandoned mine?" Sieg asked.

"Yes. That's where I have been hiding for the past week or so. I came down when I saw the buses leave. Did I miss anything interesting?"

"Just Anna dumping Danny and then running off with some guy she met here at the resort," Sieg said.

"That wasn't very kind of her," the Sasquatch said. He placed a hand on my shoulder. "I am sorry to hear that, my friend."

"That's okay," I said, "I'm over it."

"Still..."

"Don't worry about it," I said, perhaps a bit more forcefully than I wanted to. "Why are you inside the resort? Aren't you worried that someone might spot you?"

"Oh, there are fewer people around and the odds of running into someone are considerably lessened."

"How did you get by Lisa without her noticing?"

Howard merely flicked his necktie and grinned at me.

"It seems that people assume that I am just a tall, hirsute human."

"A tall, hirsute human with a nudity fetish," Mike laughed.

"No one seems to notice that, or if they do, they are too polite to mention it. So what adventure are we up to today?"

"Not much of an adventure," I said. "We've finished cleaning out the North Attic and we're going into the South side to do the same there."

"If you don't mind, I think I will join you. You never know when you'll need a strong pair of arms."

The four of us looked at each other and made a collective shrug. If our friendly neighborhood Sasquatch wanted to tag along with us, who were we to discourage him? He followed along as we went over to the South Attic. At the top of the stairs, Mike fumbled with the keys and then opened the door.

"We were only in here briefly," he said. "I didn't see much we could use."

"Then we toss it out the window," Sieg said with a shrug.

The attic was filled with dozens, if not hundreds of white-sheeted shapes. The air smelled and tasted of dust, rot and age.

"Dudes, where do we start?" Todd asked.

Mike pointed at a tall, sheeted figure near the door.

"Begin at the beginning," he said.

We moved into the space. Howard had to duck under the rafters as he walked. We lifted up sheets and looked under them. It seemed that every piece of useable furniture that had been retired was stored in the low ceilinged room. What had started as a junk hauling expedition had turned into an antique hunting expedition.

I watched as Mike uncovered an old sideboard. It was made of highly varnished dark wood. Even though some of the polish was gone, I could tell what a magnificent piece of furniture it had once been. We stood there and admired it.

"I think that's an actual Wedgewood," he said.

"How would you know?" I asked.

Before he could answer, Todd stuck his head into the aisle from where he was looking under a sheet.

"Dudes, come see what I found!" he said.

As we walked over, he started taking the sheets off a pair of couches. They were huge and looked as if a million yards of mauve fabric had gone into covering them. The arms were high and the backs were almost as tall as I was. They were facing each other and as I stood there looking at them I started to laugh.

"All we need is a Gump head," I said.

Sieg came up from behind us. "Oh, yeah, and a few palm fronds, some rope, a Scarecrow, a Sawhorse and..."

"What are you talking about, Dude?" Todd asked.

I laughed at his confused look. "It's a *Land of Oz* joke, don't worry about it."

Mike stood there staring at the couches and slowly shaking his head.

"There's no way, guys," he said.

"Oh, come on, Mike," Todd said. "I love them. They're fantastic, ugly and wonderful all at the same time."

"I have to agree," I said. "Besides, we've got plenty of room for them."

"Yeah," Sieg chimed in. "Not to mention that there's enough room on one of these for two, if you know what I mean." He nudged Mike in the ribs with an elbow. Mike looked at him acidly.

"There's almost enough room on both of these for everyone who was in the lobby. On the other hand, did any of you think of how we're going to get them down the stairs and across the parking lot? I'm certainly not going to carry them on my back."

I reached out and pushed against one. It didn't move. "They're damned heavy. I think the four of us can move one."

"I'll carry the other," Howard said from behind us. We turned and stared at him. "You helped me with my new home so it is only fair that I help you with yours."

Mike looked around and realized that we had him outnumbered. He shook his head in disbelief. "All right, let's give it a try. Sieg, I want you and Danny to clear us a path to the door. Todd, help me with the sheets."

Fortunately for Sieg and me it looked as if whoever had placed the couches in the attic had decided enough was enough, so they were pretty close to the door. We moved a few things out of the way, creating a runway, and came back to find Todd and Mike testing the weight of the one we were going to carry.

"I just hope the floor doesn't give way," Mike said. He was biting his upper lip and looking at the couch dubiously.

"At least we'll get them downstairs fast," Todd said.

"I'm not worried about *them*," Mike said.

I took one end, Sieg and Todd took the sides and Mike took the other end. With a mighty groan we lifted the couch and shuffled over to the door. Even though the flight of stairs from the attic to the hall was short, they weren't much fun. We managed to get into the hall without mishap and Howard followed us with a Tiffany lamp clutched in one hand. He marched over to the elevator and stood it up there and hit the button.

"There's no point in wasting a trip," he said.

Then we heard a noise and Howard ran back up into the attic. Before anything else happened, the elevator opened and Dr. Sybel stepped out. He held a finger to his lips. A second later, Mr. Monkey came bounding up the stairs and right into his arms. He screeched but Dr. Sybel held him tight.

"Now quit being a bad monkey," he told his pet.

They walked back down the stairs and we shoved our couch inside the elevator and hit the button for the lobby. Howard came back with the other couch tucked firmly under one arm.

"Last one down is a rotten egg!" Sieg said. He stepped into the elevator and pressed the close door button.

We turned and raced down the stairs but he reached the lobby first and the elevator was standing open. We dragged the couch out and the doors closed. The elevator groaned as if it knew what the next load would contain.

We stood there trying to muster up the energy to lift our couch when Howard exited with the lamp held lightly in his free hand. He strolled across the lobby and solicitously held the door open for us. In his hands the couch was a mere toy but in our hands it was like carrying the *Titanic*.

We staggered down the stairs and were slowly making our way across the parking lot and were about to enter the trail up to our house when a hand fell on my shoulder.

"What's going on, guys?" Courtney said in a loud voice. Startled, I dropped my end of the couch, which pulled it out of everyone else's hands. I turned around and saw that she was standing there looking surprised.

“Oops,” she said. “Are you all right?”

Sieg flexed his hand. Mike winced as he rubbed his shoulder.

“We’re fine,” Sieg said. “How about helping us?”

“I don’t think so,” she replied. “Have fun.”

She skipped away up the trail, and I turned to Sieg.

“What was that all about?” I asked him.

“I have no idea.”

Groaning again, we picked up the couch and struggled up the trail. When we got to the house, Courtney was standing there, holding the door for us. In the living room, Howard was already dusting off his couch and had plugged in the lamp. For once, the room looked like somewhere people actually lived.

After we put our couch down, Mike sank gratefully onto it and crossed his ankles.

“We’ll go back tomorrow.”

I fell down between him and Todd, while Sieg sat across from us between Courtney and Howard. The couches held all of us comfortably. Courtney bounced up and down on the cushions for a second.

“I like them,” she said. “They’re positively hideous.”

“That’s what I said,” Todd said grinning.

“They don’t make them like this anymore.” She bounced again. I was too tired to be in a good humor about it.

“There’s a reason for that,” I said. “There are laws against it.”

Court stuck her tongue out at me, and I returned the favor. For once, everyone seemed to be loose and happy. There was a knock at the front door, and then Penny came in and stopped.

“What’s going on here?” she asked.

“Come on in,” Mike said. I scooched over, and she

sat down in his lap.

"Where did you get them?" Penny asked. "They look like you looted an Ugly Couches Limited store."

"We found them in the South Attic," I said.

"Oh, yeah," she said. "Cap wants you to finish that soon. The truck is supposed to be up here Monday morning."

"Yeah," Mike said into her neck, "we know."

"The North Attic is cleared," I said, "but the South is going to take a bit more effort. With any luck, we'll be done before Monday morning."

"Why are you guys taking so long?" Courtney asked.

"Because the South Attic isn't filled with junk," Sieg said. "Cap will have to come up and see if he wants to keep any of the stuff up there. We can probably sell the rest as antiques."

Penny turned to me. "So, are you getting better?"

I had to think about the question for a moment. "Are you asking if I'm getting over Anna? To tell you the truth, I don't know."

"Well, don't worry about it," she said. "Summer flings happen all the time. I remember my first one."

"You had a summer fling?" Mike asked. His eyes had widened, and his brows were twitching.

"Yeah," she said, "with you, you big goof!"

"Oh, oh yeah."

They started laughing, and I stood up and walked out to the kitchen for a glass of water. Moving the couch had wiped me out, and now I was pretty damned thirsty. Penny followed me, and I turned to find her standing in the doorway.

"Danny, I'm sorry," she said. "I shouldn't have brought her up so soon. Trust me though, you'll get over her."

"Yeah, that's what everyone keeps telling me. It just hasn't happened."

"It hasn't even been a full week yet," she said. "Give it time."

"Right."

She went back to the living room, and I stood in the darkening kitchen drinking my water and thinking.

NINETEEN

The next morning came, and I found myself running the lake trail again. For some reason it wasn't as much fun as it used to be when Anna was running at my side. I caught myself speeding up, trying to punish myself. I think I was trying to wear myself out so that I would be too tired to think about her. It didn't work. I found myself back at the resort in record time, drenched in sweat. Anna's face still hovered in my vision, and as I reached the parking lot. Sven came down the front stairs.

"Hello, Danny," he said, nodding cordially.

"Hi. Are you ready for the big day?"

"I can't wait. I think I was pursuing the wrong cousin. Will you be coming to the wedding?"

"I have the feeling Mrs. Charles won't want me within a mile of the proceedings, especially after my little talk with Anna."

"Oh, she'll forgive you eventually."

"How goes the ghost breaking plan?" I asked, trying to change the subject.

"I'm still working on it," he said. "It seems that people who do that kind of work are few and far between."

"Maybe they don't like to advertise."

"That could be it. I think I'll try a few of those psychic shops I spotted down in Denver when I was last there. Maybe they can point me in the right direction."

"Well, good luck with that," I said.

"Thanks," he said. "Oh, before I forget, there's one more thing I need to tell you."

"Yes?"

"If you ever kiss my fiancée again, I'll kill you. No joke."

"I don't think you'll have to worry about it," I said.

He laughed. "Oh, I'm not going to worry about it. I'll make sure you get an invitation to the wedding."

His smile changed to one that made me, deep in the back of my brain, want to wipe it off his face. I gritted my teeth and jogged back to the house.

The guys were already in the middle of eating breakfast as I came down from my shower. I slid into my seat, poured some juice and started munching some toast.

"So, what's the plan today?" I asked, spitting bits of toast.

Mike pursed his lips. "We've got to finish the attic today. There's some more guests coming in Monday, and Cap wants the dump truck to be gone before they arrive. He's paying extra to have them come up as early as possible."

"Cool!" I said. "Maybe we'll find some more neat stuff."

"Like my couches, Dude?" Todd said.

"More like those lamps," I replied. "We ought to take

a couple down to Cap and see if he wants them in the lobby. They're better than the ones down there."

Whatever modernistic impulse had occurred back when the lobby was last remodeled, it resembled a train wreck. Another genius idea came to me, and it must have shown on my face, because Mike turned to me.

"Now what are you thinking, Danny?" he asked.

"I'm going to run this past Cap first, but I was thinking about restoring the lobby so that it looks like a fancy hotel back in the 1920s."

"Why?"

"Why not?" I said. "I like Art Deco, and I thought I saw a few pieces in the attic that would match."

Sieg glanced at the kitchen as I mopped up some egg with a bit of toast.

"Who's doing the dishes today?" he asked.

"You are, Dude," Todd said. "It's your turn."

"Are you sure?"

"Yeah, I'm keeping track."

We found Howard swinging slowly back and forth on the porch.

"How now, gentlemen?" he said.

"We're going back up to the attic," Mike said, nodding. "You can tag along if you want to."

"I certainly shall. You needed my help yesterday, and I think I can be useful today as well."

I didn't know how he did it, but there were times when Howard could be damned clumsy, cracking sticks and rustling in the bushes. Other times, he could be as silent as the fog. A couple times, as we crossed the parking lot, I had to look back to see if he was still following.

On the second time I checked, I almost tripped and fell across the steps. Sieg reached out and caught me.

"What are you doing?" he said.

"I'm trying to figure something out."

"What?"

"I'll tell you later."

We gathered at the foot of the steps, and I looked over at Howard. He was smiling pleasantly and twiddling his tie like Oliver Hardy.

"Okay," I said, "please explain this for us, Howard."

"Explain what?"

"Why is it that you can be absolutely silent most of the time except for when you're out in the woods?" I said. "Out there, you make more noise than a troop of blind lumberjacks."

"Ah, you must understand that, as a member of the Sasquatch tribe, I have a...a...well, a reputation to maintain." He waved a hand in the direction of the lake and the forest. "Out there, I need to make a bit of noise so that people think that maybe I am there. In here, I would rather remain incognito, so I keep quiet. Trust me, a Sasquatch in the woods can be more silent than any deer—when they want to be."

I had to admit that it was a good explanation, if it was true. There being nothing gained by arguing right then, I followed the others up the steps and into the lobby.

Sven was standing at the door, a coffee cup in hand.

"Good morning, boys, I..."

He stopped when Howard stepped into view behind Todd. He and Howard stared at each other for a moment.

"Uh, oh," the Sasquatch said, breaking the silence.

"Hey!" Sven said.

Howard faded back through the door, and Sven pushed his way through us. We didn't make it easy for him, and it was a few seconds before he finally got out onto the front porch. We followed and discovered no sign of our furry friend. Sven stood there, looking around.

"Where did it go?" he said.

"Where did what go?" Sieg asked.

"The Bigfoot that was just here!" Sven said

"Bigfoot? I didn't see a Bigfoot. Did you, Mike?"

Mike shook his head. "Nope." I guessed that my view of telling the truth to superiors was shared by my co-workers.

Sven paced back and forth and stared out at the surrounding woods. "Oh, come on!" he said. "How could you guys miss it? It was right behind you!"

"What was behind us, Dude?" Todd asked.

"There was a Bigfoot behind you!"

"We didn't see a Bigfoot, Dude," Todd said.

"It was right behind you!" Sven wailed.

While we found this incredibly amusing, Mike and I were both getting tired of it. Besides, there was always the chance that one of us would slip up and let the cat out of the bag.

"Look, Sven," Mike said. "We haven't seen a Bigfoot. We haven't seen a UFO, nor have we seen Elvis lately. If you have nothing better to do, why not go out and see if you can find all three today. Maybe you could start a scavenger hunt or something. We've got work to do, and we're going to go and do it."

"I've had enough of this!" Sven yelled. "I've seen poltergeists, orgies, and now a Bigfoot! I'm going to find someone who can help me figure out just what the hell is going on around here."

Sieg shot him a nasty gesture as he tromped down the stairs and got into his car. Sven sped away in a cloud of dust even as I pulled Sieg's hand down.

* * *

When the elevator doors opened for us on the third floor, Howard was standing there, waiting for us as if he were merely another guest waiting around.

"How did you get here?" Mike asked.

"I ran around the building and took the back stairs, of course," he said. "I have to admit that it was a bit more athletic than I'm used to. What did that person do when I left?"

"Sven's gone off to find someone to help him," I said. "I've got a bad feeling that we're going to have idiots all over the canyon for a while."

"I do apologize, my friends. I should have known to avoid the front door."

"Look, Howard," I said shaking my head, "you're our friend, and if you want to come in the front door, I'll be damned if you can't. We'll just have to figure out a way to get rid of any Bigfoot hunters—"

"I'm *not* a Bigfoot," Howard corrected.

"We know that," Sieg said. "You know that. They don't know that. Don't let that distract you."

"Very well, I'll not be pedantic. So, what shall we do now?"

Mike pointed down the hall toward the attic stairs. "We continue our job."

The cleaning of the attic turned into an archeological expedition. There was furniture that was at least as old as the resort, maybe older. I found a couple of heavily carved china cabinets with etched glass fronts. They were empty except for dust and so heavy that, like the couches, I couldn't even budge one without help. Deciding to stay out of Doc's clinic, I went off to examine some boxes stacked up in the shadows behind the cabinet.

“Uh, guys?” Sieg called. He’d been poking around in a dusty nook, and he was standing there, waving at us.

I looked up from a box of cracked dishes. There was something about the way Sieg looked that made me stop and go to where he was.

“What now?” Mike asked.

“You need to come over here,” Sieg replied.

That was easier said than done. After crawling around and over a bunch of tattered, overstuffed chairs, sideboards, headboards and side tables, we gathered where Sieg was standing, looking at what he had found.

Howard turned as white as a sheet when he saw what it was. “Please, please, say it isn’t so.”

Sure enough, under a sheet, and a film of dust, was a stuffed Sasquatch. It was moth-eaten, but it was still pretty clear what it was. Howard began to sob.

“I was afraid of that,” he finally said after catching his breath. “Uncle Ernie disappeared when my grandfather was but a lad. I came to Colorado to see if I could find any trace of him. I had hoped…”

I had stooped down to examine the plaque attached to the trophy. Before Howard could continue his histrionics I started to laugh. Everyone looked at me as if I had once again lost my mind.

“It’s a fake,” I told them.

“What? Are you sure?” Howard asked.

“The plaque says that this is a representation of a creature seen by natives in the area. It was created by Nathan Keller and presented to the Weir Canyon Lodge in 1923. I think it’s like one of those ‘Jenny Hanivers’ I’ve read that sailors used to make.”

“But it looks just like Uncle Ernie,” Howard said.

“I suspect that Mr. Keller might have known your uncle. Oh my, could it be that simple?”

"What?" Sieg asked.

"I think it's a decoy. If Nathan Keller had met Uncle Ernie and befriended him, the way we've befriended Howard, then his knowledge of taxidermy would have been useful in making a fake Sasquatch. Maybe he did it to throw off the curious."

Sieg stood there and stared at the stuffed Sasquatch. A strange light came into his eyes.

"I bet we can use this to fool that idiot Sybel. If he wants to find a Bigfoot—"

"I'm not a Bigfoot."

"Shut up, Howard," we said in a chorus.

"Maybe we can use Uncle Ernie here as a decoy," Sieg said with a broad smile.

"Before we do that," Mike said, "we need a battle plan. Let's put Uncle Ernie somewhere before someone sees him."

We shoved Uncle Ernie back into the corner and recovered him with a sheet. Then we shoved a couple of the tall sideboards over to hide him. In the shadows, it looked as if there might be an old dressmaker's dummy or mannequin back there, nothing more.

We spent the rest of our time gathering up what we thought should be salvaged and pulled the wrecked stuff to a window and began tossing it onto the lawn. We started making a contest out of it. Who could drop the heaviest piece without help? Who could get the best distance? Who could get Cap to charge up here to ask—?

"Ahem. What the hell are you doing up here?"

We stopped and looked at Cap. Then we looked at each other and started laughing.

"We're clearing out the attic like you asked," Mike said.

"You almost broke one of the windows in the dining

room. Be more careful."

"Yes sir."

Cap just looked at us, cursed under his breath and turned to leave. He stopped and took a look at one of the lamps we had uncovered.

"That would look good in my office. Do you guys mind if I take it downstairs with me?"

"Go ahead," Mike said.

"Oh that reminds me," Cap said. "There should be an old trunk somewhere with a bunch of photos and stuff. Keep an eye out for it."

"We will."

Cap took the lamp and headed down the stairs. I turned around and saw that Howard was standing very still behind something under a white sheet. As the attic door closed, he stepped out from his hiding place.

"I believe I have found that trunk," he said. He reached back into the space behind the door and hauled out a battered steamer trunk. The lock was broken, and Howard gently pushed the lid open. It was filled to the top with papers, photographs, and bits and pieces of resort ephemera.

Todd knelt next to it and began slowly taking things out. "Oh, wow," he said. I squatted on my heels next to him and carefully peered in.

"Let's take it back to the house," I said. "This really isn't the place to be looking at it." We carefully replaced what we had pulled out.

"I will carry the trunk over to your house," Howard said. He gently closed the lid.

"Be careful of Sven and Sybel," I said.

He picked up the trunk and stuck it under one arm. He reached over and picked up a fairly nice armchair with his free hand. "Oh, don't worry. They'll never notice that I'm there."

How he planned to pull off that trick was beyond me, but he seemed confident enough as he left. We finished dragging the actual junk to the window and disposed of it. Then we went downstairs and gathered all the broken junk together with the stuff from the North Attic. We put it where the guys with the dump truck could pick it up. Standing there, I was amazed at some of the things we had found. Sieg stood next to me as I surveyed the carnage.

"Sure is a bunch of crap," he said.

"It didn't start out that way."

"Yeah," he said, "now look at it. What's going to happen to the rest of the stuff up there?"

Mike looked up from where he was working. "Cap's going to let the other employees look it over and see if there's anything anyone wants. We'll probably end up carrying it all down to the ballroom. He gave us first shot because we're the ones tossing it out."

"Dude," Todd said, "I hope they don't find Uncle Ernie."

"They won't be the only ones who'll be surprised if they do," Mike said.

* * *

Back at the house, Courtney and Penny were sitting on the front porch with Howard. They were all drinking lemonades. As we came up to the house, Courtney held her glass up.

"Come on up and get some lemonade. I've added a bit of vodka to mine, but you can add whatever you want to yours."

I was starting to become concerned with this sudden onset of drinking by myself and my friends. You could buy 3.2 beer in Colorado, but you had to wait until you were twenty-one for the hard stuff. They had just changed the law, and soon you'd have to wait until twenty-one for any alcohol.

"I think I'll stick to just lemonade," I said.

Courtney looked at my expression and laughed. "I was joking about the vodka. You can be such a prude sometimes."

"She's got you there," Sieg said. He took a glass and sat down next to her. She kissed him on the cheek, so I assumed their relationship was "on" again. I wondered what was going to turn it "off" the next time.

Mike sat down on the swing between Penny and Howard. "We found a few more interesting things."

Todd and I leaned against the porch rail and sipped our drinks. Penny took a deep drink of hers and smiled.

"I saw the trunk when Howard brought it up," she said. "What else did you find?"

We told her about "Uncle Ernie" which earned a "yuck" from all of the girls until Mike explained that it was a fake.

"Do you think you can fool people with a fake Bigfoot?" Penny asked him.

Mike had to think about it for a moment. "Maybe we can. What I think we'll have to do is try and convince them that *we* have been fooling people."

"Good luck with that," Courtney said. "How about if we look in that trunk you guys brought home with you?"

"Sure, why not," Todd said.

Together we trooped inside and began to wish we hadn't. It was hot and stuffy. Cap had promised to get us a swamp cooler soon, unfortunately at the moment we only had a bunch of fans blowing air through the house. I turned the one in the dining room to point out the window. I didn't want whatever was in the trunk to be blown all over the place.

Mike and Sieg hauled the trunk from the front room, and Howard brought in one of the armchairs and placed it in the corner where he could watch the front hall and the kitchen without being seen from outside. The rest of us arranged ourselves around the table. I found myself with Sieg sitting next to the trunk. Mike glanced over at us.

"Danny," he said, "I'm appointing you to be our secretary."

"Why me?" I said, looking up at the ceiling. When I didn't get an answer, I shook my head. "Fine, I want everyone to glove up."

"What?" Penny asked. Her eyes had widened and her brow had furrowed with her surprise.

"These documents will probably be falling apart," I said. "I need everyone to wear gloves so that the acid in your skin doesn't add to the damage."

"I guess that makes sense," she said.

Sieg left the room and returned a few minutes later with a box of thin, latex gloves.

Penny looked at them incredulously. "Where did you get those? They look just like—"

"I snitched them from your storage closet," he said. "I needed them for my chemical experiments."

"Why you little..."

Mike laid a hand on her arm. "Save it for later, Penny. Shultz, you and I are going to have a long talk about this."

"Yeah, whatever, boss," Sieg said. "Here, take some gloves and put them on."

When we were all properly gloved—even Howard was able to stretch a pair over his hands—I lifted the trunk lid, and we peered inside.

Newspaper clippings filled every corner, along with old photographs. I carefully lifted out a stratum of paper and gently laid it on the table.

"All right, guys," I said. "Let's assume that we're going to find the newest stuff at the top. We'll figure out the filing later."

Slowly we all picked up various articles and looked at them. Sieg carefully made a couple of piles in front of him. I looked at him quizzically.

"The left pile is articles that actually pertain to the resort," he explained. "The right pile is articles that don't."

"The right one seems to be the larger one," Mike said.

"It is. From what I can see here, it's a bunch of stuff clipped out of *Fate* magazine and other odd places. They all seem to deal with ghosts or séances."

Penny looked up from her own pile.

"That's weird," she said. "I have a bunch of clippings here from the 1920s, and they're all about séances up at the resort."

That struck me as odd. "They were calling a resort by then? Everything I've seen here is from the turn of the century. Everything then refers to it as the '*Weir Canyon Lodge.*'"

"I was assuming it meant the same thing," she replied.

Howard looked up over his pince-nez. "Make a note of that, Daniel. Let's see if we can discover when people started calling it a resort instead of a lodge."

"Do you think it's important?" I asked.

"It may be. It will also give us a dividing time to sort the papers around."

Slowly we worked our way through stacks and stacks of clippings, photographs and a few saved administrative documents. I couldn't believe how many cancelled checks we found strewn through the bottom of the trunk. I could have insulated both attics with them.

Todd looked up and waved a handful of clippings in the air. "I think I've found something."

We all craned our necks to see.

"What is it?" Courtney asked.

"It's a bunch of old clippings from the *Rocky Mountain News*, the *Denver Post*, the *Mohawk Courier* and the *Weir Journal*."

"Weir had a newspaper?" she asked.

"Apparently," he replied. "It's not a groovy picture I'm finding here."

He laid the clippings in order across the table.

* * *

Henry Weir was a prospector who claimed the canyon on both sides of the lake. He had found a place to mine, so he then purchased all the land in the canyon and built a house for himself, his daughter, Mary, and a couple of servants.

In 1893 he sent Mary to a finishing school in New York. While there she made friends with Archibald Nieuport, an apprentice architect in the firm of McKim, Mead and White. McKim, Mead and White would later become infamous as the firm of Stanford White. White would be killed by Harry K. Thaw for sleeping with Evelyn Thaw in the so-called "Crime of the Century."

Nieuport came to Colorado, and Mary talked her father into hiring him to design the lodge that they planned to build on the shores of their lake. The idea was to establish him with his own firm and get away from

McKim, Mead and White. Mary would return a few months before he did. That's when the big trouble began.

Mary brought Nieuport's plans for the Lodge with her. The architect was under contract with his employers for a series of projects back East, so he stayed to work on them. After her arrival in Colorado, Mary met Horatio Knack, a local contractor that Henry Weir had hired to build the lodge.

* * *

Howard cleared his throat. "I think I've got some pictures here."

He carefully laid them on the table above the clippings. One showed a large man in a leather jacket standing in front of a mine hoist. A donkey stood nearby, cropping grass.

The next photograph showed a beautiful young girl with dark hair. She wore a white dress with a parasol and a large-brimmed hat. She was standing next to a tall man in a suit with a waxed moustache and a derby. It was taken in front of a strange building that looked like...an elephant.

"Hey!" Sieg pointed to Mary's portrait. "That's the old Elephant Hotel on Coney Island."

Mike leaned over to take a better look. "How do you know that?"

"I've seen pictures of it in an old book about amusement parks. My Dad brought it home from a business trip when he still worked for Astrocom. I must have read that thing cover-to-cover a thousand times."

"Okay," I said, "that's probably Mary with Archie Nieuport."

The final photo was of Mary again. This time she was standing out on the front lawn of the resort, and with her stood a young, stout man with short-cropped blonde hair, holding a derby in one hand. The resort was covered in buntings and American flags. A small crowd of people were standing off to one side as if watching the festivities.

I reached out and tapped the photo. "I'll bet that's Mary and Horatio."

Penny nodded. "You're probably right. So we know what the principals looked like."

* * *

The Weir Canyon Lodge was built, and quite quickly. Henry Weir spared no expenses. It was almost finished by the time Nieuport finally arrived the day before the Grand Opening. As he stood there with Mary anxiously talking in his ear he felt his entire world falling away.

Not only was she pregnant with Horatio Knack's child, but the contractor had managed to build the lodge backwards. Nieuport had designed the Grand Stairs to sweep a visitor up and through the doors and into the lobby. The building was meant to embrace the lake and now instead it embraced the clearing.

There was a Fourth of July ball that night. Nieuport spent part of it drinking. Suddenly, Mary swept in with Knack on her arm. The architect could restrain himself no longer, and he marched up to them and slapped the contractor's face.

"You bastard!"

"Excuse me," Knack said, rubbing his cheek, "but do I know you?"

"I'm the man who you've made a laughing-stock!"

"I dare say, old sport, it's a woman's prerogative to change her mind."

"I wasn't speaking of Mary, you dog! What have you done to my beautiful lodge? Couldn't you follow a simple blueprint?"

"I did!"

"You built it backwards!" yelled Nieuport. "You've ruined me!"

"It's not that bad—"

Before Knack could get out another word, Nieuport reached inside his coat and pulled out a long dagger. Without another word he plunged it into the contractor's chest and fled the room.

As Horatio Knack died in Mary Weir's arms, a wordless cry was heard outside. Archibald Nieuport had gone up into the tower and thrown himself off.

With a heavy heart, Mary would bury her lovers side-by-side in her rose garden, which would also become her last resting place seventy years later.

* * *

"Yuck," Courtney said. She screwed up her face and stuck her tongue out. "It's like *Romeo and Juliet* but without the romance."

"Yeah," Mike said. He snapped his fingers. "I'll bet you that's the source of our poltergeist."

"Could be," Sieg said.

"Whoa," I said.

"What's the matter?" Courtney asked.

"Take a look at the date," I said. "It all happened almost ninety years ago tomorrow."

TWENTY

High Country Waste's dump truck slowly nosed its way away from the resort. It was fully loaded with all the trash and junk from the attics. It had barely disappeared around the curve in the road when a pair of ancient ex-Greyhound buses emerged from the dust cloud. Each was emblazoned with the logo for New Frontier Tours.

We were already wiped out from loading the dump truck and could only watch in disbelief as the buses wheezed to a stop and began to disgorge their passengers. Sieg took one look at them and hung his head.

"Oh, my God," he said. "Are you sure we're going to survive this, Mike?"

"Damned if I know," our fearless leader said. He grunted as he tried to stretch his back. "There's no point in crying about it. Let's get to work."

Proving that there really was a God, most of the New Frontier people carried their own bags to the front desk. I ended up behind the desk, and the guys had to help only a small handful carry luggage to their rooms. I looked up to see Mike wheeling a luggage cart through the front door.

"I should have known this was going to happen," he said.

"What was going to happen?" I asked.

Two men followed him inside. The first one had a couple of camera bags slung around his neck, and in his hands he carried a Nikon that looked as if it cost quite a bit. He stopped just inside the door and did the usual double-take everyone did on their first time in the lobby.

His companion was busy doing the same thing. As he was looking around, he was also scribbling furiously in a small notebook without looking at what he was writing. Finally his eyes came to rest on me behind the front desk, and they took on a calculating look as if I was some kind of opponent.

"Welcome to the Lake Weir Resort," I said.

The scribbler walked over and held out a hand to shake. "Hi, I'm John Train, and this is my partner, Carl Local. I believe we have a reservation."

"Let me look," I replied.

My nose twitched as I smelled Train's cheap aftershave, sweat and stale liquor. He wore a black and white checked sport coat with a light blue shirt and no tie. He also wore a pair of badly stained blue slacks. While I looked up the reservation, he and Local perused the trophies and stuff.

Local was dressed in a multi-pocketed, khaki vest filled to overflowing. Another camera and several small satchels dangled from belt-loops and tie-offs sewn onto his vest.

It didn't take me long to find their reservation, it being at the top of the ledger. There was something about them that didn't sit right with me. It reminded me of when I checked in Dr. Sybel. Ignoring my misgivings, I pulled the correct keys from the board and slid the register over to them to sign.

"Here you go," I said as they came back to the front desk. "Mr. Train, you're in number 201. Mr. Local, you're in number 203. As you requested, there is a connecting door between the rooms."

They followed Mike over to the elevator, and as the doors closed, Mike flashed me a quick thumbs up. I didn't feel like smiling as I finished the paperwork.

"Are you okay?" Lisa asked me.

"There's something about those two I don't like. The photographer seems to be pretty normal, but his buddy acts a lot like Sieg."

"I think Sven said they were reporters," she said. "Or at least Mr. Train is. They work for the *Midnight Star*. When they called to confirm their reservations, they told me they were coming up here to hunt for a Bigfoot. I thought I'd better pass them over to Cap. He said that if we didn't accept crazy-people money, we'd be broke in a week."

I wondered how they ended up in the rooms directly across from Sybel's. I noticed that both their and Sybel's reservations had been put into the book with Sven's handwriting. They were the only ones our catering manager had filled in himself. It was something to file away for later. Then my brain caught up to my ears and a shock ran through me like a jolt of pure energy. As Lisa went back to work on her paperwork, I sat there and stared at the stuffed polar bear in the lobby.

The *Midnight Star* was one of the biggest tabloids in the country. Usually they covered celebrities and their diets, but there was a section in the middle that was always reserved for strange news stories. They ran stories like one about a man in India who could lift a car with his tongue or a family in Brazil who worshipped a golden crocodile. They also had a Loch Ness correspondent and a whole bunch of reporters running around the country checking out cryptozoological leads.

Was it a coincidence a pair of *Midnight Star* reporters now appeared along with the mysterious Dr. Sybel? I didn't think so.

"Danny!"

With a start I realized Lisa had been trying to get my attention. I looked up at her and smiled.

"Sorry," I said. "I was just thinking about those two reporters. Sieg and I had some pretty nasty encounters with the press over the past year."

"I understand, but we've got some more guests coming in."

I looked up and found most of the crowd was gone except for three people standing in front of us. The first was a large woman in a flower-print muumuu and a big straw hat with a flower garden wrapped around its crown. Beside her was a skinny man wearing a blue flannel shirt and carrying a couple of hard-plastic cases. Behind them was a young woman, about my age, wearing a white tee-shirt and blue jeans. She was carrying a backpack over one shoulder and dragging a huge suitcase on wheels behind her. Another huge suitcase stood nearby.

"Sieg," Lisa said, "could you help with these bags? I've assigned rooms up on three."

As the three signed the register, Lisa handed the keys over to Sieg. He stared at the girl as if he had seen her before. He saw me watching and winked. From that I knew something was up. He stepped over to the man and held out a hand.

"Can I help you with those?"

"No!" the man barked. Thinking better of it, he threw up his hands. "I'm sorry, I didn't mean to snap but these are very expensive cameras and I'm responsible for them. Jennifer will probably need a hand with the rest of the luggage, though."

Jennifer was the girl. She had long brown hair and blue eyes. She smiled warmly as Sieg came over.

"Thanks," she said.

"Oh, Danny," Lisa said. "Could you take over for me? I'm supposed to have lunch with Gwen, and I think I'm running late."

"You could ask Mr. Monkey for a banana."

"You're so adorable," she said. "Can I eat lunch with my sister before I drop in my tracks?"

"Yeah, sure, go ahead," I replied.

She left as the lady and the skinny man got on the elevator. Sieg and Jennifer waited while it closed and rose with its usual high-pitched whine. I started to scan the register, trying to figure out how many rooms we had in service when Sieg turned to Jennifer.

"Okay, what the heck is going on, Jenny?"

"What do you mean?" she asked.

"Don't tell me those two are your parents."

"Hardly, Madam Keeply is my employer, and the guy is her assistant, Bernard. We're ghost hunters."

He shook his head slowly. "I can't believe you're hunting ghosts with a psychic and a cameraman."

"Do I know you?" she asked.

"I thought you were more scientific than that. For someone in Sci-apa, you're sure hanging around with some unscientific people."

She gave him the same look everyone did upon

meeting him and then her eyes narrowed.

"You're in Sci-apa?"

"Yeah, I'm Sieg Shultz."

"Oh, yeah! You're the guy who burned down Mohawk! That was incredible!"

I found that to be surprising. Usually, Sieg was pretty quiet about our exploits, and here he was talking to someone who seemed to know all about them. I was going to speak up and ask a question when I became aware of someone standing nearby. Turning, I found Gwen standing there. She was smiling sadly and was dressed in her usual black dress. The dress made her look older than she was, even though it set off her platinum hair spectacularly.

"Hello, Danny," she said in a voice that was deeper and richer than Lisa's. A thrill ran through me when she spoke. "Have you seen Lisa?"

"Yeah, I think she's waiting for you in the dining room."

"Thank you."

Once again I was struck by the thought that there was something infinitely sad about Gwen. It wasn't something that you could put a finger on, and I sighed as she disappeared into the dining room. When I turned back, Sieg and Jennifer had gotten onto the elevator and the doors were already closing. My questions would have to wait.

Sven came down the stairs and looked around.

"Did everyone in New Frontier Tours get in all right?"

"Yeah, the last three just went up."

"Good. Were the two guys from the *Midnight Star* with them?"

"Yeah, they came in just a little while ago. Mike's

taking them up to their rooms. Do you know them?"

"No, not really. John Train called right after I booked New Frontier and asked if we still had some rooms. I checked the bookings and didn't see a problem, so I okayed it."

"Hey," I said, "do we have a pet policy around here?" I pointed up where Mr. Monkey was shagging the stuffed lynx again.

"Why don't you ask Anna about our pet policy when she gets back from her honeymoon?" he said sarcastically. "Better yet, ask yourself how many customers this place can afford to turn away. If someone brought an alligator, as long as it was on a leash, I'd allow it."

"You don't have to get all worked up about it," I said. "By the way, your ghost hunters arrived, too."

"They did?"

"I'm assuming you hired Madam Keeply and her crew."

"They were highly recommended by Denver Psychic Industries," Sven said. "If they can do something about Shultz's poltergeist, then maybe I can have them do something about the Bigfoot."

"Shouldn't Sybel be doing something about the Bigfoot?"

"He's looking into it, but I'm not sure he's going to be able to do anything about it. We need to take care of it, since I heard a rumor about it while I was mailing a letter down in Lake Fork yesterday."

My blood ran cold. It was bad enough to have Sybel wandering up and down the canyon. Now we had the two *Midnight Star* reporters and Madam Keeply to worry about. There could be nothing good about Sven's interest in Howard.

“Well,” I said, “I don’t think we really have a Bigfoot in the canyon. I think someone’s playing a trick on you. Anna thought she saw one when we first started running together, but it turned out to be a deer.”

“She did, really?” he asked. “I would have thought she’d have told me about that. Maybe some of the natives are putting me on.”

“Yeah, they might do that, especially with a city slicker like you.”

Sven snorted and went on into his office. I had time enough to double-check the reservation list before the elevator opened again with Sieg and Jennifer coming out. They were chatting like old friends, and I looked up and waved.

“Hey stupid, come over here for a minute!”

They came over, and I motioned with a crook of my finger for him to come around the desk. When he got close enough, I grabbed the front of his shirt and pulled him closer.

“You told her about the dragon?” I asked in a hoarse whisper.

He pulled away from me and looked as if I had lost my mind.

“Yeah, we were discussing the problems of control. Some of the guys came up with some great ideas for next time...”

I grabbed his shirt again. “There isn’t going to be a next time, idiot!”

Jennifer laughed and held out a hand. “You must be Danny Jael. Sieg has written so much about you.”

I let Sieg go and shook her hand. “None of it good, I’ll bet,” I said.

“You’d be surprised. I’m Jennifer Danthis, Madam Keeply’s summer intern. I was just explaining to Sieg that

I'm trying to make some money before I go to CU in the fall. She needed a scientific expert, and Bernard hired me."

"Why does she need a scientific expert?" I asked.

"She needs someone to come up with a scientific reason why none of her séances seem to work. I also have to keep her from sticking a nail file into a light socket to see what happens."

"What?"

"That's just something that Bernard says. He's always teasing her and pretending he doesn't like her. She pays for the equipment, and he'd sell his soul for the night-vision camera she bought him. I suspect that there's something else going on between them though. I haven't been able to catch them at it, but a girl knows."

"So, what's your big plan?" Sieg asked.

"I've been ordered to scout out a good place for our first séance. Madam Keeply sees this as a way to convince people that she's not a fake. We usually have these long meetings to plan out everything. When the lights go out, we get lost, freak out and accidently scare Bernard. So far, it's been fun and interesting, if not very illuminating."

"I have a feeling your luck is about to change," Sieg said. He was smiling broadly, and I could see the wheels turning in his head. Thinking about the poltergeist I had to agree with him.

* * *

After Lisa came back, Sieg and I took off. All the way back to the house, he was whistling to himself. I wasn't in quite as good a mood. Mike and Todd were getting lunch on the table as we came in.

"Oh, look what the cat dragged in," Mike said. He

was glaring at us. "Why can you two never be found when work needs to be done?"

I looked around and then back to him.

"What are you talking about?"

"Lunch," he said. "Is it only coincidence that you two show up after all the work is done?"

"Well, actually, yeah. I was watching the front desk for Lisa. Sieg, on the other hand, was busy with our new psychic and her crew."

"New psychic?"

"Yeah," I said. "Not only do we have Mr. Monkey and his keeper, we have those two reporters from the *Midnight Star* and now a psychic. It's as if someone was setting us up for something bad."

"Oh, that's great, just what we needed."

"It gets better," I said. "Assisting the psychic is Sieg's new girlfriend."

Sieg kicked me hard under the table. "She's not my girlfriend. I'm just in an apa-zine group with her. I still can't believe she's hooked up with a phony psychic."

"What makes you think she's a phony?" I asked. I glared at him while I rubbed my shin.

"She claims to be a psychic, therefore she's a phony. Trust me on this one. If she could read minds, she'd have slapped me several times."

"Right."

As we ate, Sieg told Mike and Todd about the ghost hunting trio. Mike put down his glass of milk and looked thoughtful.

"The ballroom sure spooked Sven. I wonder if you're right about it."

"If I am," Sieg said, "Madam Whatsis won't find out. On the other hand, I've got an idea."

"Oh, great, here it comes," I said.

"Shut up, Danny," he said. "I think I can come up with some real equipment, and we'll see who hunts the ballroom ghosts."

There was a knock at the door and Mike went out to answer it. He came back with Courtney.

"It looks like Madam Keeply gets the first round," he said. "She's holding a séance in the ballroom tonight. Sven wants us to set it up right now."

* * *

The ballroom was arranged according to Madam Keeply's instructions. Tall candles had been brought from her room and placed at the edges of a pentagram she had chalked on the ballroom floor herself. We were unhappy knowing that we were going to have to clean it up later.

A round table was set up in the middle of the pentagram with five chairs. Madam Keeply brought in a white tablecloth with a dark green Celtic design around the edges. In the center of the table she placed the largest crystal ball I had ever seen. Next to the ball she laid a silver rose and a gold knife.

Outside the pentagram we put seating for about fifty people in two large semi-circles, leaving an aisle that led to the doorway.

Sieg came over after setting up the chairs while I was helping Bernard with his cameras.

"Now I know she's a fake," he whispered in my ear.

"Shhh."

When Madam Keeply reappeared, she was wearing a long, white, lace dress with a long veil trailing from the golden comb in her hair. Sven, dressed as if he was going to a funeral, followed her. Then came Jennifer, and to my surprise, she was followed by Gwen.

Both Jennifer and Gwen wore black dresses. Gwen's

was funereal and severe. She also wore a wide-brimmed hat with a black veil. My breath caught when I saw her.

As beautiful as Gwen was, Jennifer was my highlight of the night. Her dress was tight in all the right places. It had a high collar and was touched here and there with black lace. If Gwen looked like she was going to a funeral, Jennifer looked like she was going to cause one. Sieg let out a slow breath and looked over at me.

Madam Keeply watched the audience file in with an air of smug satisfaction. I was sure, whatever the outcome, we were going to get one heck of a show. She waited until everyone was seated before speaking.

"You may stay, or you may go," she said. "The circle holds only five, and I can offer protection only to them."

Sieg smiled. "I'll take my chances out here," he whispered. "There's more room to run."

I shrugged, and the others just looked at him. Whatever Sieg had planned was going to be interesting. The group within the pentagram sat down while Madam Keeply glided around the circle, lighting the candles with a taper. She turned to Mike.

"Would you be so kind as to dim the lights?" she said.

Mike went to the switch and turned the dimmer until the ballroom was lit only by the flickering candles. Madam Keeply sat down at her place, bowed her head and held out her arms.

"Take my hands," she said, "and those of the person next to you."

As the participants did so, Sieg gave a tiny snort. I nudged him to silence and watched breathlessly as Madam Keeply began. You could feel the electricity in the air and could have heard a feather drop.

"We call upon the spirits of this room to come

forth!" she said. "In the name of Solomon's Seventh Seal, I call thee!"

From the way Madam Keeply acted, I suspected there was even more to be said but before another word could be spoken, the candles began to flicker.

"What is she doing?" whispered a voice to my right.

"I think she's trying to call the ghosts," I whispered back. Then my brain kicked in, and I realized that I was sitting on the end of the row, and there wasn't anyone sitting to my right. I turned and looked through the man standing next to me.

He was somewhere in his thirties and had a waxed moustache. He was wearing a Victorian suit and a mild look of disapproval. I knew exactly who he was, since I'd just seen his photograph the day before.

"Good evening, Mr. Nieuport," I whispered to him.

He looked down at me. His eyes widened as he realized that I had addressed him by name.

"You can see me?" he asked.

"Yeah, it looks like we're into a special night."

The silence in the room caught my attention, and I turned around and realized that I had the attention of everyone else. People were standing, and a few were making their way to the door. Madam Keeply stared at me. Then her eyes rolled up in her head and she fell, hitting her head on the crystal ball.

"Can all of you see this?" I asked.

Sieg and Todd nodded, and Bernard quickly left the circle to turn the camera. Just as he reached it, a hand appeared out of nowhere and slapped the power switch.

"None of that, Boyo!" a voice said from nowhere.

Like a cloud growing out of a clear blue sky, the rest of Horatio Knack appeared. He looked down at Bernard, and the psychic's assistant stepped back.

Chaos ensued as the crowd left the room as fast as they could without trampling someone. Bernard stood there with his eyes bulging and his throat working as if trying to swallow.

"Uh, oh," Sieg said.

"What?" I asked.

"Do you realize what tonight is?"

I thought back to the papers that we had uncovered from the attic, and a chill caught at my heart. I tried to scramble away from Nieuport. Sieg caught me before I fell and helped me stand up.

"I forgot," I said. "It's their anniversary isn't it?"

Sieg's eyes widened. "Oh. Yeah."

Knack nodded and slowly began to solidify. "That's right, boyo," he said in a voice that was much closer and louder. "Over ninety years ago on this night that son of a French dog put his blade into my heart."

I heard a growl and turned to see Nieuport becoming more real, too. His hands flexed as he started toward Knack.

"You stupid bastard! It was you who ruined my masterpiece! You stupid, stupid bastard!"

"Oh, aye? An' tell me, who it was who forgot to simply mark 'north' on his blueprints? It was you, Mr. Snooty Architect! A cold fish who couldn't even warm up to a pretty lass like—"

"Don't you dare! Don't you dare speak her name! How dare you defile the name of someone so pure with that vile tongue of yours?"

In horror I watched as Nieuport pulled a shimmering knife from under his coat. I suddenly realized that we were watching a reenactment of the crime that had taken place on the first night the Weir Canyon Lodge had been opened. With a flash, the knife was buried in Knack's breast. As he fell to the floor, Nieuport looked at the blood on his hands and raised his face toward the ceiling.

"Why? Why must I kill him every time?" he cried in an anguished voice. I felt as if someone had taken a hold on my heart.

Nieuport ignored all of us and glided through the doors into the lobby. Somehow I knew that he was going up to the observation platform at the top of the tower, to throw himself into the rose garden one more time. I turned and saw that Knack had faded away.

Sieg and I were halfway to the door in pursuit of Nieuport when Bernard's cursing stopped us. Turning around, we saw him dancing around the video camera, cursing and pulling at his already sparse hair.

"Dammit! Dammit! Dammit! First time we've actually encountered a real ghost, and the damn lens cap is still on! Damn it!"

"I took the lens cap off," Jennifer said. "Besides, didn't that one ghost shut the camera off?"

"I turned it back on when the other appeared. You must have forgotten to take the cap off."

"No," she said, "I know for a fact that I did."

She pulled piece of paper from her back pocket and peered at it. "Yeah, I marked it on my checklist."

"You must be wrong," Bernard said, "the lens cap is on."

Mike turned the lights back on. Bernard ran over to Madam Keeply while Jennifer looked around the camera.

Gwen stood up and removed her hat and veil. She let out a long sigh and sat back down, shaking her head. "For a moment I hoped that it was Steve who would come tonight."

"Steve?" I asked.

"My husband," she said matter-of-factly. "He promised that he would come back."

She began to sob, and Jennifer went over to comfort her. Sieg looked at me and raised his eyebrows. Suddenly Madam Keeply sat up. We braced ourselves for trouble.

"Ohh, Bernie...what happened?" she said in a dazed voice.

"You don't remember?" Bernard asked.

"Remember what?"

"We found two ghosts! If that incompetent intern of ours hadn't forgotten to take off the lens cap, we would have had proof!"

"And we didn't get it on film?"

"No."

"Oh, damn! Damn! Damn! Damn!" she said. With each exclamation she slammed her head against the table. Then she stood up and imperiously strode out of the circle and through the doors into the lobby. I could hear the curses streaming under her breath. Lisa helped Gwen leave, both of them with tears filling their eyes. Jennifer and Bernard started to take down the equipment, all the while arguing in whispers about whose fault the lens cap was. When they were done, Bernard looked over at us.

"If you would be so kind as to leave my equipment, I need to check on Madam. I'm sure she's all right, you know. It's just that I wish to make sure."

"Go ahead," Mike said.

We still had chairs to stack and a table to put away. Jennifer helped us, and I found that there was something about her that I liked. After we were done with the chairs we headed into the lobby. At the elevator, Jennifer held out a hand to me.

"Hey, I just want to thank—"

She was interrupted when a sudden noise made us turn. It seemed to come from the main staircase. We headed over to see what was coming down the stairs. As we approached, the noise became louder. From around the corner of the landing, something came rolling, bouncing off one of the walls and then falling down the last flight of stairs. We jumped back to keep from being clobbered by a small wine cask. It skidded across the marble floor and smashed into the pillar under the stuffed moose head.

Cautiously, Sieg approached it. There came a grating sound as if something was being unscrewed, and then the top of the cask popped open. I goggled as Mr. Monkey stumbled out. He staggered around in looping circles for a moment.

"Mr. Monkey?" I said. "What the hell is going on now?"

From above us came a noise. Looking up we saw Dr. Sybel peering over the mezzanine rail.

"Yahoo! Mr. Monkey, we have to do it again!"

We watched with astonishment as he came bouncing down the stairs. By this time, Mr. Monkey had steadied himself by leaning against the pillar and was looking at his owner. He hissed loudly and jumped into Jennifer's arms. Dr. Sybel took one look at him and shook his head sadly.

"Oh dear," he said, "I guess that wasn't nearly as much fun for Mr. Monkey as it was for me."

"Huh?" I asked in my usual witty manner.

"You've heard about how much fun a barrel of monkeys is? I thought I would perform a little experiment and see how much fun a barrel of monkey would be. Then I would extrapolate my findings. I think I'm going to abandon my research, though. If this is any indication, a barrel full of monkeys would probably result in the death of the researcher."

"It wasn't much fun for Mr. Monkey, at least," I said.

"Ah, well," Sybel said. "Failure is a byproduct of science."

"Animal cruelty is also a byproduct of science," Jennifer said. "You should be ashamed of yourself for putting such a cute little monkey into danger like that."

Dr. Sybel looked down and sniffled. For a fleeting moment I felt sorry for him.

"I know, I know, I'm so wretched. It's terrible how I treat Mr. Monkey. How about I make you a banana daiquiri, Mr. Monkey?"

Mr. Monkey looked up at Jennifer, smiled his monkey smile and then jumped to the floor. He grabbed Dr. Sybel's hand and began leading him toward the elevator. Dr. Sybel looked back at us and winked. Jennifer turned away.

"That was disgusting," she said.

"He could have at least invited us along for drinks," Sieg said with a snort.

I decided it was time for the question I wanted to ask.

"So," I said, "how did Sieg know what you looked like?"

"Oh, my picture is part of the header on my apa-zine. I call it 'Science and Intuition' since I like to think I bring a bit of feminine intuition to the hard facts of science."

"Snappy," I said. "What's Sieg's 'zine like?"

Sieg looked away, and I could see his ears beginning to turn red. Jennifer watched him for a moment and then laughed.

"You didn't want your best friend to know about all

that poetry, did you?" she asked.

"Shut up."

"Poetry?" I said. "Does Courtney know?"

"You can shut up, too."

"Oh, come on, Sieg. I'd think she'd love to hear some of your poetry."

He turned to Jennifer with a pleading look. "Now do you understand? This is the kind of crap I get from my so-called best friend."

She held a hand to her mouth but we could see her shoulders moving with suppressed laughter. Something else caught my attention though, and I held up a hand.

"Do you hear that?"

They stopped and we stood there silently for a moment. Somewhere behind us came the sound of a woman sobbing. Turning around we saw a gorgeous blonde woman in an antique dress sitting in one of the chairs and sobbing into a handkerchief.

There were two things that made me swallow hard. One was the fact that we could see the chair through her, and the other was that I knew who she was. Like Archibald Nieuport and Horatio Knack, I'd seen her picture recently.

"Good evening, Miss Weir," I said.

She looked up and through me as if I wasn't there. I realized we were witnessing yet another part of the reenactment. We stood there, transfixed, for at least five minutes. Then Mary Weir stood up and started walking toward us. I could see the tears still streaming down her cheeks as she began to fade away. Before she reached us, she disappeared.

"How did you know who she was?" Jennifer asked. Her eyes were wide, and her hands were shaking.

"It's a long story," I said. "We'll tell you about it in

the morning." I noticed Sieg looking around and sniffing the air like a bloodhound. "What's the matter?"

"Do you smell flowers?"

TWENTY-ONE

If there was one thing I learned over the summer, it was that you can't expect the unexpected. The morning after the séance, I came home from my usual run around the lake. Just as I arrived at the foot of the porch stairs, the screen door popped open and Edgar flew past me, his paws scarcely touching the ground. With a wild caterwaul, he tore off down the trail in a flash of fur. Almost before I could catch my breath, the door burst open again, and Sieg charged out, brandishing a spray bottle.

"You goddam bastard," he shouted. "I'm going to kill you!"

Screaming like a banshee, he tore off after the cat. Against my best judgment, I followed. There was a good chance that I would have to apologize to any innocent bystanders caught in the maelstrom of Edgar/Sieg chaos. When I reached the parking lot, Sieg was already clear down by where the road started. He hit the underbrush at the edge of the lot at full steam. With a sudden scream, he fell from view.

I let out a long sigh. "Oh, good grief."

I ran over to where I had last seen him. At the back of my mind was the fact that the mountains were riddled with old mining claims. You never knew when an old pit or shaft would appear at your feet. Part of me feared for Sieg's life, another part just didn't want to have to run back to the house and inform the guys that "Sieg's fallen in the well." When I reached the point where he had disappeared, I found him in some bushes, slowly rolling over into a sitting position with scraped elbows and bloody holes in the knees of his new jeans.

I looked down at him and shook my head. "What the hell is going on, now?" I asked him.

"The little bastard peed in my shoes," he said in a grim voice. "I'm going to turn him into a goddam muff."

"Yeah? Come on. Let's get you back to the house and fixed up."

"Well, that was certainly smooth," said a voice behind me. The voice was sweet, feminine and familiar. I closed my eyes and slowly turned around. When I opened them, Anna was standing there, one hand on her hip, with a suitcase in the other. All I could do was stare. She turned around and looked behind her.

"I'm sorry," she said. "Have I grown an extra head?"

"You're back," I said. I could hear our voices but what I was saying wasn't coming from anywhere near my brain.

"Yes, Danny," she said carefully, as if anything else would break me.

"I thought you were getting married?"

She frowned, and I got the feeling that I'd stepped on a nerve. "So did I," she said in a flat voice.

"What happened?"

"My, aren't you full of questions today?" she replied. "In short, it's a long story but I didn't get married, and I think your buddy there had something to do with it."

Sieg staggered to his feet and held up one hand. "Hellooo! I'm still bleeding over here."

"Shut up, Sieg," we said in unison. Then we looked at each other and started laughing. He started limping toward us, pushing the bushes aside with a disgusted look on his face.

"Fine, fine," he grumbled. "I'll just go home and tend to my own wounds...in the dark...by myself."

"Oh, don't be so melodramatic, Sieg," Anna said with a smile. "Oh, and by the way, I think you've just found the tennis court."

We turned around and looked. Sure enough, the ground where Sieg had fallen had been flattened and you could see the remains of the shattered surface of what must have been a tennis court. Here and there you could still make out the faded lines and both net posts were swallowed up by thorn bushes but you could get the general idea if you looked hard and squinted.

"I wonder how long this has been here," I said.

"Centuries," Sieg said. He shook his head and started limping for home again. "Can we go now so that I can get some first aid?"

Anna and I each took an arm to help him. She seemed to be sad, and more than once I heard a sigh escape from her lips. I wanted to hold her again, but somehow I knew that the last thing she would want was to have some horny teenager pawing at her, even if that horny teenager was me.

"Are you going to be all right?" I asked her.

"Yeah, I guess it's not important. Breakfast is important."

"Are you hungry?"

"I'm famished," she said.

"Well, come on then."

* * *

After I had taken my shower and Sieg had been attended to, Anna took the place of honor at our breakfast table. Mike put on a feast. There were plates of pancakes, ham, sausages and potatoes enough for everyone, even Sieg and Todd.

As we ate, I related the story of our little adventure with the tennis court. Sieg told Anna about finding the fake Sasquatch when we were cleaning out the attics. When he was done we all looked over at Anna expectantly. She looked back at us, blandly.

"Now, what?" she asked.

"What happened?" I asked. "I thought you were in Vegas getting married to Dixon."

"Yeah," she said, "I thought that too."

"So what happened?"

"Why don't you ask Sieg?" she said.

I turned to my partner in crime and raised an eyebrow. He hated that because it was a trick he couldn't do.

"I guess Sheila Hughes used my little going away present," he said.

"What going away present?" I asked.

"Well..."

"Spit it out!"

"I, uh, made up a...let us say 'diluted' version of the chemical in my pheromone bomb."

"And?" I said through clenched teeth.

"I gave a small squeeze bottle of it to Sheila Hughes," he said quickly as if trying to sneak it past me.

"You did what?" I yelled.

"Calm down, Danny," he said. "I gave her a bottle of the stuff and told her that she might be able to catch up with Anna and Dixon in Vegas. That's all."

"What was it about not interfering that you didn't understand?" I asked.

"Look, man," he said, "I knew I screwed up with that stupid bomb, and I thought I could sort of fix it."

"What about innocent bystanders? What if Hughes had decided not to use your bottle of crap? What if she used it on the wrong person? Did you think about the consequences? No! Of course not! You never do. If you keep this up, we're going to end up in Cañon City."

"She promised me that she was only going to use it on Dixon," he said.

"Yeah, and she used it," Anna said, "on the steps of the Elvis-o-rama Chapel of Contemplation. One moment I was getting married, the next, my fiancé only had eyes for another woman. Do you have any idea of what that's like?"

"Uh, yeah," Sieg said.

"At least he was gracious enough to leave me our hotel room. So I blew some of Daddy's money on the roulette wheel and caught a plane back to Colorado."

"Welcome back, anyway," I said.

"Thanks. So...how's Howard doing?"

"Oh, he's fine," I said, "except for the guys from *Midnight Star*, the phony psychic and our good friend Dr. Sybel. If it gets any more crowded out in the woods, he's going to have to find a new place to live."

"Oh, no!"

"Yeah," I said, "that was my reaction. I'm hoping something will happen soon so that all of them will go home."

"I can understand Dr. Sybel," she said. "He's pretty harmless. I think he's using his search for 'Bigfoot' as an excuse to get out of the house with his monkey, but what's this about a phony psychic?"

"She was Sven's idea," Mike said. "She showed up along with a girlfriend of Sieg's—"

"She's not my girlfriend!"

"Anyway," he continued, "we had a spectacularly successful séance last night. It looks as if our poltergeist might be old Nieuport and Knack fighting it out in the ballroom."

"Don't forget Mary Weir," Sieg said.

"That was different," I replied.

"How was it different?" he asked.

I sat back and thought about it for a moment before speaking.

"Remember, Knack and Nieuport were able to interact with us even as they were reenacting the murder and suicide. Mary Weir never acknowledged our presence, and I think she's just doing the same thing over and over."

"You're talking about two different kinds of ghosts, Danny," Mike said.

"Dude, I think he's talking about three different kinds."

We all looked over to where Todd was sitting. He looked back at us in bewilderment.

"What?" he said. "I thought it was obvious."

"Not to us," Mike said.

"Think about it, Dudes. Knack and Nieuport seem to be ghosts that are stuck here because of what they did when they were alive. Their spirits are wandering the earth. Mary Weir's ghost seems to be a recording of some sort. I'll bet she does her little crying bit every single day at the same time. We just don't see it normally but thanks to Madam Keeply, we did. Then there's the poltergeist."

"I thought we decided that Knack and Nieuport were the poltergeist," Sieg said.

"No, Dude, we don't have any evidence of it. The poltergeist may have been pushed out of the ballroom last night by all the other ghosts that showed up."

"This all sounds like a bunch of gobbledygook to me," Anna said.

"Yeah," Sieg said, "I wish someone would do a serious scientific investigation of this stuff so that we could talk about it intelligently."

"That's something you two could study in college," Anna said brightly.

"If we ever get to go to college instead of jail," I replied.

"Oh, I think you'll go," she said. "You have to stay positive."

Todd stood up and wiped his mouth with a napkin. "Dudes, as much fun as we're having with this stuff, I've got to run down to Lake Fork and pick up the mail. Cap handed me a list last night, and I've got a couple of errands to run. Is there anything you guys need?"

"Psychotherapy for Danny," Sieg said. I kicked him under thc table, and he let out a yelp because I nailed his skinned knee. He tried to retaliate but I'd been smart enough to pull my legs up where he couldn't reach. Since there were no other takers, Todd shrugged and left the room.

Anna stood up and stretched languorously. "I guess I'd better get over to the resort and see what kind of disaster I have to fix. Cap's been writing checks without me for almost a week."

"That's a bad sign," Mike said. He stood up and

started clearing the table. Sieg started helping him, and I went out with Anna onto the porch.

"I'm glad you're back," I said.

"So am I," she replied. "I'm sorry, Danny. I wish all this with Dixon hadn't happened. Of course, if Sieg hadn't done what he did, then I would be happily married, but I don't think it would have ended happily. I think I was just trying to escape my mother, and he was trying to escape from his feelings for Sheila. In the end I think we all got what we needed."

"Yeah, maybe," I said.

"Oh, come on. It'll all work out in the end."

"We can hope."

Suddenly, Sieg yelled from inside the house.

"I guess I'll have to be going," Anna said and kissed me on the cheek.

"Yeah, I should go in and see what's going on."

She took her suitcase and went down the stairs. I went back inside. I found Sieg standing in the living room looking all around with a disgusted expression on his face. He glared at me as I came in and I glared back.

"Now what is your problem?" I asked.

"I can't find my other shoe."

"Didn't you bring it back with you?"

"It didn't leave the house! Damn it, this is my old pair that I'm talking about. I don't want to have to work in a shoe that smells of cat urine."

With a sigh I helped him look under and around everything. There was no sign of the missing shoe.

"Did you check your bedroom?" I asked.

He just glared at me.

"Of course I did!"

"Well, let's go look again."

Upstairs we found the offending shoe lying in the

middle of the hallway.

"How the hell did this get up here?" Sieg asked.

"Damned if I know. I'll wait for you downstairs."

As I reached the end of the stairs, there came a short knock at the front door. Howard stuck his head inside. His pince-nez was askew and his eyes were bright.

"I say, is there anyone at home?" he asked.

"Hi," I said. "What's going on?"

He smiled and entered the hallway. He had a newspaper tucked under one arm, his fur standing on end.

"I found Uncle Ernie!" he said.

"What? Where?"

"Right here!"

He held up the newspaper, which turned out to be a copy of the latest *Midnight Star*.

"That's not your usual *New York Times*," I said.

"No, I found this in the trash behind the resort when I was stalking those two reporters."

"You've got to be careful about that," I said. "There's always Dr. Sybel and his monkey running around."

"I don't see them very often," Howard replied. "They almost never come out of the resort."

"That's very interesting," I said.

"What's very interesting?" Sieg said from behind me.

"That's not important," Howard said. "*This* is important."

"Let's take it into the dining room," I said.

Mike was just finishing cleaning up the dining room as we came in. "What's going on?"

"I found Uncle Ernie!" Howard said. He spread the newspaper on the table. The cover was a black-and-white photo of a beach with a bunch of people standing around looking at something that had washed up on shore. The headline read: "*Sea Monster Washes Ashore in Florida*."

"Oh, you can't believe this," Sieg said. "What they did was take a picture of a crowd watching something and superimposed the fake sea-monster on it."

"No!" Howard said. "Look at the back of the crowd!" He jabbed at the newspaper with one furry finger.

The photograph was blurry because of the reproduction method, and I had to look hard. However, standing at the back of the crowd was a figure that was clearly taller and hairier than the rest. He was wearing a straw hat.

"You can tell its Uncle Ernie by the hat," Howard said. "We've heard stories of a supposed 'Florida Skunk Ape' and until now dismissed them as products of overworked imaginations. This is proof that it exists and it's Uncle Ernie."

"How do you know he's the skunk ape?" I asked.

"Uncle Ernie always did sweat a lot in summer. I think that's why he left home."

"Howard," Mike said, "this is the *Midnight Star*. Trust me, they're not definite proof of anything."

Sieg picked up the newspaper and idly flipped through it. Then he stopped and stared at an article.

"Oh, crap!" he said. "I know one thing that it's definite proof of."

"What's that?" Mike asked.

"We're in trouble." He spread the newspaper back across the table. The headline screamed "Bigfoot Attack in Colorado!" and the article below wasn't much better.

"It's by those two reporters," Sieg said.

"Yeah," Mike said, "they're claiming there's been a series of Bigfoot attacks in the mountains around here. I haven't heard of any attacks, have you?"

Howard picked up the newspaper and looked at it with an outraged expression on his face.

"Bigfoot attacks?" he said. "I know that they get a bit rowdy at their toga parties and are a bit vulgar but still..."

I glanced out the window and saw Courtney running full speed up the trail.

"Oh, this can't be good," I said.

She ran into the house and slammed the door closed behind her.

"We're in trouble," she said, gasping.

Mike went into the kitchen for a glass of water, and Sieg put an arm around her shoulders.

"What's going on, Court?" he asked.

She kept gasping for breath, and when Mike returned, she grabbed the glass with both hands and gulped the water down. When she was done, she handed the glass to Sieg and wiped her mouth with the back of her hand.

"You guys need to get over to the resort. Everything is going to hell."

"What?" Sieg asked.

"Penny and I were working on the second floor when we heard someone talking on the house phone. Dr. Sybel's door was open, and I looked in. He was the one on the phone but it wasn't his normal voice he was using."

"What was he saying?" I asked.

"He was yelling at someone to calm down and that everything was working out fine."

"I thought there was something fishy about our Dr. Sybel," Sieg said. "He was just a bit over the top to be real."

"I'm not done," Courtney said. "When I went downstairs to talk to Anna about Sybel, I passed Sven's office and saw Brittany there, sitting on his desk."

"When did she come back?" I asked.

"I don't know. I don't think she or Sven saw me. I stepped over toward Anna's door but I kept listening to them. Sven was talking to someone on the phone, and he hung up and told Brittany that 'it' was all taken care of and that they should 'see some action soon.'"

"Damn it," I said. I smacked my fist into my hand. "Damn it! I knew we should have investigated both of those weaselly bastards sooner! Damn it! Damn it! Damn it!"

"Danny, calm down," Sieg said. "This isn't the time for histrionics."

"Calm down, Sieg? There's something bad going on and—"

"And why did Courtney come running up here now? We knew there was something going on with Sven and Sybel."

He had me there. We all turned to her and she nodded.

"Those two reporters, Train and Local, have called in some reinforcements. There's two more down at the resort."

"Oh, that can't be good," Howard said. He looked as he fumbled and fidgeted with his spectacles. "Those reporters are going to be the death of me. They are cleverer than we thought, and they've managed to hide near some of my favorite places. If they've brought reinforcements, I may have to leave the canyon for greener pastures."

"Just wait a minute," Sieg said. He was looking pissed off as he turned back to Courtney. "Who are the two they brought up?"

"I don't know. I have no idea at all."

* * *

On the way back to the resort, I asked Courtney, "Do you have any more great news?" Everyone had finally calmed down and Howard went into hiding. We decided the best course for now was to brazen it out as if everything was normal.

"Lisa and Penny are planning a party," Courtney said. "They want to commiserate with Anna, and they also want to have a party."

"That was fast," I said.

"Yeah, well, there's nothing that goes on at this resort that Lisa doesn't hear about, and if Lisa thinks someone should know—"

"Then they'll know," I said.

"Speaking of Anna, how do you feel about her? I mean, your girlfriend went off to marry someone else and then came back unmarried. Do you think you'll get back together with her?"

"Hell, Court," I said, "I don't know. Where do I begin?"

"Well, I find it interesting that the first person she went out to find was you."

"I think she just saw me following Sieg and decided to see what we were up to."

"I don't know about that," she said with a smile. "She could have waited for you up at the house, instead she followed you."

"Tell you what," I said, "I'll burn that bridge when I get to it."

We had arrived at the resort and found Brittany sitting in one of the new outdoor chairs on the porch. She smiled and stood up.

"Well hello there, tall, dark and handsome."

"Hi," I said. "I thought you'd be busy planning your

wedding."

"I'm letting Aunt Barbara do all the work on that. She's been planning Anna's for so long that she needs a little release for all that energy. Especially since the little tramp went and eloped."

"You may have spoken too soon, Sweet-Cheeks," I said. My temper had flared with her description of Anna as a tramp. "Anna's back and very unmarried. I'll bet you she's inside cuddling up to Sven even as we speak."

"There's no way!"

"She was over at my place for breakfast earlier this morning. She cuddled up to me quite nicely. I can bet you she's in there with Sven right now."

"Oh, no she isn't!" she said. She flung open the front door and charged into the lobby. The door slammed behind her. As I went to open it, Courtney caught my arm.

"I can't believe you just did that. That's something Sieg would do."

"I felt she needed some doubt," I said. "That ought to slow her down a bit."

"You know you just started another fight between her and Anna."

"Yeah," I said. "Then again, after talking with Anna at breakfast, maybe a fight is exactly what she needs right now."

"I take it back. You're worse than Sieg."

"I'm standing right behind you," Sieg said. He was standing at the foot of the stairs. I smirked at him.

"We know."

* * *

Inside the lobby, I turned to Courtney. "Did those new reporters say anything to you when they came in?"

"No," she said, "I never even saw them. Lisa told me about them when I came down for breakfast."

"I wonder if they're investigating these so-called 'Bigfoot attacks' that the *Midnight Star* keeps blabbing about."

"All I know is that they're some older guy and a woman."

"Great. I wonder who they are."

"Lisa said she thinks the older guy is those reporters' babysitter. I have the feeling that their newspaper was tired of paying for their vacations."

Lisa looked up as we arrived and smiled. "Hi guys. Danny, could you watch the desk for me for a few minutes? I really need some coffee."

"Sure, no problem," I replied.

She headed over to the dining room while I took over her station behind the desk and opened up the register. Courtney peered over my shoulder.

"What are you doing?" she asked.

"I thought we might get a name or two for our mysterious guests. Ah, here it is: *Mr. and Mrs. Horace Bedfarther, Chicago, Illinois*. Hmm, they paid cash for their room."

"Is that odd?"

"No, just interesting. Isn't the *Midnight Star* headquartered in Chicago?"

"Yeah, I think so," she said. "Daddy always picks it up when he buys groceries."

Cap opened his door and frowned when he saw us looking in the register.

"What's going on out here?"

"Uh," I said intelligently, "Lisa asked me to watch the desk while she went for coffee."

"So, where are the rest of the slackers?"

"I don't know," I said. "I think Sieg followed us inside but he might be off checking the ballroom. Todd went down to Lake Fork for the mail and supplies and Mike is probably helping Penny with something or other."

"'Or other' is right," Cap said with a smile.

"You know, Cap, we're kind of shorthanded right now. I thought we were all going to die yesterday when New Frontier came in."

"Yeah, I'm sorry about that," he said. "I've been trying to find someone, but so far I've struck out."

Right then the elevator doors opened, and Madam Keeply, Bernard, Jennifer and Sieg stepped out. For a moment it seemed as if an argument had just exploded into the lobby with Madam Keeply and Jennifer yelling at each other.

"You ungrateful child!" the psychic said. "After all I've done for you!"

"All you've done for *me*?" Jennifer said with her voice going up several octaves. "You've dragged me all over the country on these stupid séances, and when we actually do find a ghost, you want nothing to do with it. I'm telling you, this is the place where we can get some solid scientific evidence of the paranormal.

"You don't know what you're talking about," Keeply said. "There's no money in the paranormal. What we do is give the people a show, make them think they're talking to a dead relative, make them feel better about themselves and then move on to the next sucker."

"Now, Madam," Bernard said trying to be the peacemaker, "please remember that we're in public. Jennifer has some good points here and we can use this—"

"I'm not interested, Bernie! The little fool has got to

go before she blows it for all of us."

"But Madam—"

"She's fired, Bernie! Fired with a capital Fi! Make sure she gets her things and send her on her way. Now if you'll excuse me, I have an appointment with someone for a personal reading."

With that she stomped off and Bernard looked down sadly at Jennifer.

"I'm sorry, Jennifer," he said in a kindly voice. "There's nothing I can do."

Jennifer shook her head and looked at him with tears glistening in her eyes.

"I'm sorry, too, Bernie. You know I'm right."

"Yeah, but the problem is that she's the boss. Go pack your stuff, and I'll cut your last paycheck."

"Where am I going to go?" she asked.

"I'm sorry, Jennifer, but this is as far as you're going with us. Just remember that we had the best of times."

"Damn it, Bernie, I needed that money for school."

"I know, I know. There's nothing I can do."

Sieg looked over at Cap, and a smile suddenly spread across his face.

"Hold on, Bernie, I think I may have come up with an idea. Let's see if we can kill two birds with one stone."

He turned to Jennifer, and they spoke for a few moments. Although we couldn't catch what he was saying, Jennifer started to smile. She and Bernie got on the elevator, and Sieg came over to where we were standing.

"Just what did you do?" Cap asked him.

"Uh, I hope you're not going to get mad at me, Boss."

"I will if you don't tell me what you just did."

"You know how you're always saying that you can't

find another new houseman?"

"Yes?"

"I, uh, kind of took it upon myself to hire Jennifer as a houseman."

"You did what?" Cap said. His voice had lowered into a dangerous tone.

Before Cap could say another word, and while we stood there looking at Sieg in disbelief, the two reporters and the couple I assumed to be the Bedfarthers came out of the bar and made a bee-line toward us. Mrs. Bedfarther's bee-line was more bee than line, and occasionally her husband would steady her with a hand.

Horace Bedfarther was somewhere in his fifties, with thinning gray hair, long sideburns and a walrus moustache. He was wearing a tight-fitting green suit with a yellow shirt over his short, egg-like frame.

His wife was a brassy blonde with dark roots and too much makeup. She was stuffed into a Rodeo shirt and blue jeans at least one size too small. Her face was angular and hard, with a look in her eyes that seemed to create a personal force-field around her. It was like she had sold her soul to get where she was and once there, found out that she didn't like it much.

Bedfarther came up and tapped Cap on the arm. I held my breath for an explosion but Cap merely looked at him blandly. Bedfarther ignored the silent rebuke.

"Hey, do you work here, pal?" Bedfarther asked.

Cap's lips tightened, and I could almost hear him editing his first couple of responses. Finally, he swallowed and smiled slightly.

"Yes, sir, I'm Cap Hayes, the General Manager. Is there something I can do for you?"

Bedfarther drew himself to his full height, which brought him up to my shoulder. "I'm Horace H.

Bedfarther, editor-in-chief of the *Midnight Star*, America's most-read newspaper. I'm the man who put up the money for the Great American Bigfoot Hunt, and so far it's been a bust. Every week, some poor sod sends us what he thinks is the best picture ever taken of a Bigfoot, and every week I have to tell them their picture is no good."

"I'm sorry to hear that," Cap said.

Mike came out from the back hall and came up to where we were standing. He put his hands behind his back and straightened up. Meanwhile, I was trying to keep the rising smile from my face. It wouldn't help anything to tell Bedfarther that the best picture of a Sasquatch ever taken had already graced the front page of his paper, and he didn't even know it.

Bedfarther pulled a cigar from an inside pocket of his jacket and then chomped it between his teeth. He fumbled around for something light it with, patting his pockets and mumbling around the cigar. Mrs. Bedfarther rolled her eyes while he was doing this.

"Oh, for Pete's sake, Horace," she said and pulled a slim, green, disposable lighter from one of her back pockets. I had to admit it was an operation worth watching. Then she pulled the cigar from between his lips, put it in her mouth and lit the end of it. After a couple of puffs, she put it back in her husband's mouth, and he pulled it out and jabbed it at Cap.

"Where was I?" he asked. "Oh, yes. I really want my boys here to get the money, since I can just slip it into their paycheck when the time comes, and that'll keep the accounting simple."

Local and Train shared a startled glance, which made me instantly suspicious of Bedfarther's accounting methods. Bedfarther, on the other hand, ignored them as he continued to speak.

"So my wife—wave at the yokels dear—and I have come West for what you might call a working vacation. My boys told me that they liked what they saw. Now I don't know if you are aware of it, but you've had a bunch of Bigfoot sightings in this canyon."

Cap winced as he tried to move out of Bedfarther's smoke. It took everything I had to keep from choking. The smell was something akin to old tires and wet leaves in a garbage fire. It reminded me of Ray and his cigars; a brief wave of homesickness washed through me.

"I wasn't aware of anything like that," Cap said carefully, as if trying to keep from breathing in. "Frankly, I don't care too much about them. What does any of this have to do with my resort?"

"Let me see if I can explain this," Bedfarther said. "You've got a Bigfoot. I want the boys here to take pictures of said Bigfoot and write the story of the year for my newspaper, a newspaper, I might add, that's read by millions of Americans from coast to coast. You play ball with me, I'll play ball with you. Trust me, this could turn out very good for the Lake Weir Resort. I'm so impressed with that polar bear of yours that I'm thinking about doing a spread on this resort for the newspaper. Do you think we can make a deal?"

"I'm not sure what you want from us," Cap said.

"I told you they were going to stonewall us, Horace," Train said. "Hell, I'll bet they want the money from the Hunt for themselves. I could smell a story here when Carl and I first arrived. This is going to be better than those stupid kangaroos in Topeka."

"John, my boy," Bedfarther said, "we have time for all that later. Besides, that was a damn fine story the two of you turned in about those rogue Kansan kangaroos.

It'll probably make our Best of the Year issue."

"Only if these yahoos don't stop stonewalling us about the biggest story of the year."

Cap looked at Train as if the reporter was something found on the bottom of a shoe. Mike held up his hand to forestall any explosions from our side.

"Honestly, I can't think of what you're talking about. I'm sure we'll give you all the help we can but you'll have to be careful about wandering around our house, up on the hill. We have a killer cat that likes nothing better than to ambush the unwary."

"Kid," Train said, "do I look like I'm worried about a stupid cat? Do I? Can you understand that I've just spent the past month leaping over backyard fences in Kansas? They have dogs there, you know."

Local looked at the floor and shook his head. "Big dogs with teeth," he said slowly. "I thought that Shih-Tzu was a real killer."

"Shut up, Carl," Train snapped. "They get the picture. Their cat isn't going to stop me from getting this story. Besides, we can always write a story about the stupid cat if we think it's warranted."

"I hope you use Edgar's name," Sieg said with a laugh. "He likes to see his name in print."

"Oh, I'll bet he does," Train said.

"Gentlemen," Cap said to us, "I want you to assist Mr. Bedfarther to the best of your abilities. They're paying guests. If I remember correctly, your job is to do what I tell you within the limits of the law and morality. Unless any of you can prove that helping them wouldn't be either, I suggest *strongly* that you do so."

"All we're asking," Bedfarther said, holding his hands up in supplication, "to begin with, is a little tour of the resort."

Mike frowned at this but Cap shook his head warningly.

"What are you guys waiting for? You heard the man."

"We're hoping for a last minute reprieve," Sieg grumbled.

"Fat chance. Get to work."

"Where do you boys want to start?" Bedfarther said with a wave of his cigar.

Mike sighed. "How about the observation deck? From there you can see the whole canyon."

"That's an excellent idea, lad."

Mrs. Bedfarther tugged at her husband's sleeve. "Horace."

"Not now, dear," Bedfarther said.

She tugged even harder. "Horace!"

Sighing, Bedfarther turned to her. "I'm busy dear. What is it?"

"I'm bored," she pouted. "I'm going up to our room for a nap."

"You wouldn't be so bored if you quit drinking all those three martini lunches."

"I think you might be right," she said in a brittle voice, and with a bright smile. Bedfarther winced as if realizing he'd gone too far. "Maybe I ought to call my lawyer about my lunches," she continued. "I'll bet he'd find your observation very illuminating."

"Oh, Maddie! Don't be like that!"

"Just remember who's the boss, Horace dear."

"I should have traded her in a long time ago," Bedfarther muttered as she walked away.

"I heard that," she called back to him.

"Danny," Cap said, "when Jennifer comes back down, send her in to me. I'll have to discuss with her where she wants to work. Despite Sieg's best intentions, she might not want to be a houseman around here. If she's any good, maybe she can work with Penny and Courtney."

"Sure, Cap," I said. "No problem."

"Good," he said, going back into his office.

Mike and Sieg had already led their little tour group over to the stairs. I had the feeling they were going to try and wear out their new friends by walking them all over the place. Just the thought of all that walking made me shudder. Then a door behind me opened, and Sven came out of his office and looked around.

"What's going on, Danny?" he asked.

"Not much," I replied. "We're just giving those reporters and their editor a tour of the resort. It looks like they're going to be here for a while."

"Oh, good. We can always use publicity."

"Sven," I said, "it might not be good publicity."

"There's no such thing as bad publicity," he said. "Well, I'm going out. I've got a few things to do in town. Brittany ought to be showing up in a few minutes. If anyone else is looking for me, let them know."

"No problem. I'll tell Lisa when she comes back."

"Thanks."

As he started across the lobby, the elevator opened. Brittany, Jennifer, Dr. Sybel and Mr. Monkey came out. Brittany grabbed Sven's arm and pulled him toward the door. Dr. Sybel fell into step on his other side.

"Hey, mister," he said to Sven, "do you want to pet my monkey?"

Jennifer had her backpack slung over one shoulder as she came over to me.

"Whatever you do," she said, "don't ever ride in an elevator with that man. He kept talking about that monkey, and you can't imagine the smell."

"Too late," I said, "been there, done that. Cap wants to talk to you."

"Do you think he'll hire me? I was just fired from my last job."

"Jenny, he hired me and Sieg, and we haven't been fired. Yet. Trust me on this, he's pretty tolerant of everything except laziness."

"Can you watch my bag?"

I put her backpack behind the desk, and she knocked on the door and went in. I decided to start checking the register to see who was parked in which room. As I did this, various members of the New Frontier group came and went. Some wandered into the bar, some into the dining room. A couple of adventurous souls actually went outside. It was kind of interesting to sit back and watch the ebb and flow. With a small group there weren't the huge knots that had filled the lobby back when we were full up.

Excepting the guests, I pretty much had the place to myself, and I pretended that I was in Cap's shoes. *Would I want to hire Jennifer? Sure I would.* As shorthanded as the housemen and housemaids were, I'd hire Helen Shapely if she wanted a job. Hell, I'd hire Mr. Monkey if he would dust those hard to reach places up in the rafters. He could even groom the hunting trophies. I stopped then because the thought of Mr. Monkey in a maid's outfit made my head spin.

Bernard came off the elevator and walked over to me.

"I'm here to pay off the room that Jennifer had. We're letting it go since she doesn't work for us anymore."

"Yeah, we kind of saw that," I said.

"I'm sorry you had to witness that. Frankly, I think Jennifer was right, there's a good chance to get some serious paranormal evidence in this building, and Madam is just throwing it away. Unfortunately, Madam is paying the bills..."

"Yeah," I said. I really wasn't all that interested in the secret workings of fake psychics but something made me ask: "So, what was this 'reading' she mentioned?"

"Oh, that woman who helped us with the séance, Gwen, I think her name was, wanted a personal reading. I understand there was some kind of tragedy in her life, and she wants Madam to contact the spirits for her."

Something about Madam Keeply making money off of Gwen pissed me off to no end. I glared so hard at Bernard that he shrunk back.

"You think that's okay?" I asked. "Do you think that cheating a widow is right?"

"No, I don't," he said. "However, like I said, Madam is the one paying the bills, and I like to eat once in a while, too."

"You mock their tragedy, you exploit them, you—"

"I know, I know," he said holding up his hands. "I'm ashamed of myself but I really haven't got a choice. Let us just say that Madam knows all and won't tell if I do what she wants. Besides, if you're so concerned, why don't *you* tell her yourself?"

He had me there. Since I had nothing else to say, he paid the bill, and I went back to checking the register. I found myself thinking about it as I leafed through the book. While I didn't like someone taking advantage of a friend, there really wasn't anywhere for me to jump in and not be doing the same thing Madam Keeply was. At least I knew Lisa was keeping an eye on her sister. If Keeply went too far, she'd find herself facing a very angry desk clerk. I shuddered at the thought.

Apparently Sven had learned his lesson and didn't double book the resort again. I dusted around the back of the desk and waited patiently for Lisa to return.

The front door opened, and I looked up. I was stunned to see Big Ed and Aunt Vera enter the lobby. I stepped away from the desk and hugged my aunt. She smelled vaguely of lavender and motor oil, a combination that was oddly comforting. It reminded me of the car lot and the long days I had spent working there. For a flashing moment I felt homesick again.

"How are you, Danny?" she asked.

"I'm okay, I guess. What brings you two up here?"

Ed smiled and I knew something good was about to happen. "Oh, we decided to take a couple of days off before the big Fourth of July weekend. Ray's back home, watching the lot."

At that moment, Lisa finally came back from her coffee. My suspicion of what she'd actually been up to was confirmed when Gwen and Madam Keeply followed her. Madam Keeply was in an animated conversation with Gwen.

Lisa took my place at the desk, and I waited until Gwen and Madam Keeply had passed out of earshot before turning back to Big Ed.

"Uncle Ed, there's some strange things going on around here."

He laughed and clapped me on the shoulder. It hurt.

"With you and Sieg involved?" he said. "I don't wonder."

"No, I mean things beyond that."

For a moment I debated telling them about Howard and the ghosts, but at that moment, the elevator arrived, and Sieg, Mike and their new friends stepped off. Train and Bedfarther were arguing about something while Local just looked bored. Sieg walked over to us.

"Hi, Big Ed! Hi, Vera!" he said. "What brings you up here?"

"As I was telling Danny," Big Ed said, "Vera and I wanted a couple of days off before the big weekend."

"Oh, yeah, the Fourth of July is coming up. You guys are always busy then."

"Yep, especially when it falls on a Friday like this one. Do you two remember what happens today?"

I thought about it for a moment and then felt excitement rising from the pit of my stomach.

"I forgot! We get our driver's licenses back today!"

"That's right," Big Ed said, beaming at us. "I'm taking the two of you down to get your licenses, and then we've got another surprise for you."

"Oh, good," Sieg said, grinning like a maniac. "I like surprises."

I looked at him as if he'd lost his mind. "No, you don't."

"Well, the nice ones I do."

Cap came out of his office with Jennifer. He waved Mike over and spoke to him quietly. Mike smiled as he and Jennifer came over to where we were standing.

"Well guys," he said, "we have a new houseman."

"That's houseperson," Jennifer said.

"The official title is houseman," Sieg said, "we don't expect you to be a 'man' but that's the title."

"The title will be houseperson when it's applied to me," she informed us, "or don't apply it at all."

"All right," Big Ed said with a laugh, "I hereby proclaim that it's 'houseperson' from now on. If you don't like it Sieg, you can always go and find another job."

"Gee," Sieg said, "thanks Big Ed. Thanks awfully."

"Don't get sarcastic with me, young man, or you can walk all the way down to Mohawk for all I care."

"Aw, don't be like that. All right, Jennifer is a 'houseperson,' even if I think it sounds silly."

"There's one problem, though," Mike said.

"What's that?" I asked.

"Where are we going to put her?"

"She could stay upstairs with Court, Lisa and Penny," Sieg said.

"I don't know," Mike said. "I'd like all of us to be in the same house together. It builds camaraderie, and I can assign jobs easier."

"Then she can have my old room," Sieg said sourly. "I've already moved all my stuff over to the room across from the lab."

"You have a laboratory?" Jennifer asked.

"Yeah," Sieg said, puffing himself up. "It's not too much right now but I'll eventually fix it up."

"Cool," she said. "I can't wait to see it."

"Trust me," I said, "you can. Besides, the boy-wonder and I have places to go and things to do today."

"Huh?" Mike said.

"Sieg and I are going down to Mohawk to get our driver's licenses back."

"Oh, God, then what?"

"They'll find out," Big Ed said.

"Great! I can't wait," I said.

"Well, let me and Vera check in first. I was serious about the vacation."

They went over to the front desk. Mike went over to where the *Midnight Star* group was patiently waiting and spoke to them for a few minutes. He came back without a trace of a smile on his face.

"They say they can handle it from here without us," he said.

Sieg smiled. "Good. I wasn't looking forward to helping them all day."

"I told them that you two were going to take the afternoon off and I had a new trainee," Mike said. "Todd should be back soon in case anything else needs to be done. I'll just run Jenny down to the laundry to get her new shirts, and we'll go over to the house. She's getting the room across from Danny's, right?"

"That's right," Sieg said. He turned to Jennifer. "If you want, I can take your backpack over to the house and put it in your room for you."

"I don't think so," she said. "I might be dumb, but I'm not letting a bunch of boys paw through my stuff."

"We wouldn't do that," I said.

"You're boys," she shot back. "Trust me, you'd be tempted."

"Okay then," Sieg said, "we'll leave it to you."

"Wow," she said, "you can learn."

Before the discussion progressed further, Mike took her arm and led her into the back. I thought about the shirts that Mr. Chang had given Courtney and began to snicker. Sieg looked at me.

"What's so freaking funny?"

"Wait until—"

The front doors burst open, and a couple of the New Frontier guests came running in. The man was wearing an orange and white Hawaiian shirt, white and red checked Bermuda shorts, black socks and flip-flops. The woman was wearing shorts the color of lime sherbet and a matching tank-top that was at least a size too small for her. They both looked scared out of their wits.

"We saw it!" the man shouted. "It tried to kill us!"

Sieg and I exchanged a look.

"What are you talking about?" I asked.

"Sharon and I were walking on a trail when this big hairy thing jumped out at us, roared and took a swing at me! We turned and ran but it chased us."

"Was it as bear?" I asked.

"I think it was Bigfoot!"

* * *

Ed's big surprise was waiting for us at the car lot. Sieg and I were already excited about getting our licenses back and having lunch with Big Ed and Vera. Then we pulled into the lot and saw Ray polishing a car next to the office. I about freaked out.

It was Dad's Pontiac.

I could almost see Big Ed grinning behind me.

"I guess Matt kept that car in better shape than I thought," he said. "It needed an oil change and I had to replace all the rubber. I sent it to a guy I know who restored the paint and interior for me. It took a lot less time that I thought it would."

Ray was grinning from ear-to-ear as we got out of the car. He hugged me and even shook Sieg's hand. "All right, you two. You're forgiven, but the next time you're in a parade, forget about the flame-thrower, okay?"

"There's going to be a next time?" I said. "What's this next time you're talking about?"

He laughed and hugged me again. It felt good that he wasn't pissed off at us anymore.

Then I noticed that Sieg had wandered off. I turned around and he was standing at the rear of the lot, looking at one of the old cars that Ed had taken in trade and hadn't had a chance to get rid of yet.

Some of those cars would be fixed up and sent off to

auction, others would become a supply of needed parts and others would be sent to the crusher as is.

Sieg was looking at an old yellow Ford Mustang II hatchback. The hood was painted flat black, and it was obviously a homemade job. The yellow paint had faded to a very pale pastel color that clashed horribly with the rust spots. He shaded his eyes with his hands in order to look inside. I came over and did the same on the passenger side. The bucket seats apparently came from another car and didn't match the rest of the interior. The radio had been installed by someone using the old "leave the wires out so I can fix it again" school of installation. Frankly, I couldn't understand why he was looking at it. He stood up and looked over at Big Ed.

"Hey, Big Ed," he said, "what do you want for this Mustang?"

Ed walked over and looked at the car and then at Sieg. "What are you? Nuts? Your mom and dad would kill me if I sold you that piece of junk. Come on over here and let me show you—"

"Nah, this is the one," Sieg said stubbornly. "This is the car I want. How much?"

I recognized the look on his face. It was the one he had when I tried to talk him out of the flame thrower. It was the one he had when Mrs. Garvey told us there was nothing she could do to help us. It was his stubborn look. I sighed and shook my head.

"You might as well tell him, Uncle Ed," I said. "He won't rest until you do."

Ed apparently recognized the look, too. He also let out a big sigh and turned to Vera.

"Dear, how much are we selling that Mustang for?"

"You must be joking, Edward Jael! That car has been driven to death by at least four different owners.

The valve-cover gaskets are shot and the water pump, fan clutch and fuel pump are all about to give out. I wouldn't even try to sell that...that...car to my worst enemy."

"How much dear?" Big Ed repeated.

Vera's lips thinned as she knew she was beat. "At least show the boy one of the other cars," she said.

Sieg looked over to her and grinned. "Vera, dear, I don't want one of the others. This is the one for me. Mom and Dad aren't buying this for me. I'm spending my own money on it. So how much?"

"Five hundred," she said. "I'd sell it for less, but that's what I can get for scrapping it."

Sieg grinned. We had stopped at the bank on the way over from lunch, and he'd gotten some money. I didn't realize how much he had until he walked over to her and counted out twenty-five twenty dollar bills. Vera held the money in her hand and looked up at him for a moment. Her face softened for a second before returning to her businesswoman expression.

"I'll pay the taxes on it, just because it is such a piece of junk. Come on in, and I'll fix you up."

She opened the door for him, and after he'd gone inside, she looked at Big Ed, who nodded back to her. Somehow I knew that the five hundred dollars would find its way back into Sieg's hands again in the near future. Ray smiled at Big Ed.

"He's like his old man, isn't he? Remember that old Oldsmobile he bought from Conrad's that time?"

"The one he painted with a brush? Oh, yeah. Remember those zebra-skin seat covers he put in it? Oh, my God, they were awful."

"I thought the paint was worse," Ray said. "Looked like he painted it with a broom. Fast car though."

"Yeah, fastest in town. I remember when he beat

some kid in a souped-up '57 Chevy. The kid wanted to know what he had under the hood, and Bob Shultz opened up and showed him that old 'ball of grease' engine just sitting there throbbing away."

They both started laughing. Sieg and Vera came out of the office. Vera carried a temporary license plate for the car. She affixed it to the rear, and Sieg opened the door with his new keys and slid inside. A moment later the engine turned over, and he rolled down the window.

"I like it already! If we're done here, I'm going back up."

Ed shook his head as Vera handed the paperwork to Ray.

"Raymond, file that for me, will you?"

"No problem, Sweet-cheeks. You two go and have fun. I'll see you in a couple of days. Clyde and Jim will help me with the bunting and balloons for Friday."

"You do that," she said. "Are we ready, dear?"

"Whenever you are, Dear," Big Ed said. "Daniel, be careful. We don't want to find either you or Sieg in Mohawk Creek today."

"Don't worry," I reassured him. "I've waited six months for this, and I'm going to be very careful to keep my license."

"You'd better, boy," he said.

TWENTY-TWO

“Come on, Sieg,” I said. “We’ve got a Bigfoot sighting to work on.”

“Oh, yeah, I forgot. Do you think they bought the bear story?”

We were walking back toward the house the night after we had gotten the cars. There had been three “Bigfoot” sightings reported, and at least six other guests had come back inside with strange looks on their faces. We knew one thing, whatever it was out there, it wasn’t Howard—he was hiding at home.

“To tell you the truth,” I continued, “I think most of them would have believed just about anything we told them.”

“Yeah, but I hope we won’t have a game warden or forest ranger coming up here to find that ‘bear’. It might become a bit...sticky.”

“Tell me about it.”

At the house, Jennifer, Courtney and Penny were sitting on the porch swing talking and giggling to each other. Anna was sitting in a chair, and it seemed as if she was only partially listening to them. Her face lit up as we came up the trail. Mike and Todd were sitting on the stairs and stood up as we approached.

"Have you heard?" Mike asked.

"About the so-called Bigfoot attacks?" I said. "Yeah. It's getting tense down at the resort. A couple of the New Frontier people have checked out and left. Cap isn't very happy about it."

"Are you sure it isn't Howard, Dude?" Todd asked.

"Pretty sure," Sieg replied. "Can you really see him jumping out at people or chasing them down a trail?"

"Good point."

Courtney came down the stairs and took Sieg by the arm.

"Sieg, when am I going to get that ride in your new car? You did promise."

"Right now?"

"Why not?"

Anna smiled as we watched them go down the trail, then she bounced down the stairs and took my arm.

"Are you busy, Danny?"

"We're just trying to figure out this whole Bigfoot thing. It's nothing that can't be interrupted."

"Good, let's take a walk. The lake is pretty in the moonlight, and we need to talk."

"All right," I said.

"Dude, we'll keep a light on for you," Todd said with a huge grin.

Anna and I walked into the gloaming and soon found ourselves sitting on the Grand Steps behind the resort, watching the moonlight play across the ripples in the lake. She was holding my hand and sitting close. I breathed in her scent and sighed contentedly.

"So," I finally said, "what do you want to talk about?"

"When I was flying back, I thought about how I treated you. I'm sorry. I'm ashamed of myself."

"Why?" I asked. "It wasn't your fault. The pheromone bomb was Sieg's fault. Besides, you had fun, I had fun, and we left as friends."

"You wanted it to be more than that."

"Anna, let's face it, I'm just a kid. I'm not even dry behind the ears, yet."

She stared out at the lake, and I was surprised to think that she looked a bit like Courtney when she was telling me about the after-prom party.

"I think you're more mature than that, Danny," she said. "I don't know what happened to you after I left but you aren't bitter and you've been nice to me since I came back. I never meant to hurt you. I just didn't think."

"Would it help if I told you that you're forgiven? I'm not holding a grudge. Robert could have given you things that I can't. He has a college education, and I'm *persona non grata* with higher education right now. Perhaps in a couple of years I'll be able to try again. Besides, Robert isn't a criminal; I burned down my hometown."

"Danny, he snores. Personally, I think I've gotten the better part of the deal."

We sat and stared out at the water again. Then suddenly from somewhere in the distance we could hear the underbrush rustling. The acoustics of the lake prevented us from figuring out where the commotion was coming from. I drew in a long breath and let it whistle out from between my teeth.

"So," I said. "What are we going to do now?" I knew what I wanted. I wanted her in my arms again. I wanted to feel the cool heat of her body on warm sheets. I wanted to be hers again. During her absence I had begun to wonder if that was too much. I could feel the saliva drying in my mouth as I waited for her answer. She rested her head against my shoulder. Perhaps it wasn't everything, but it would do for a start.

"Can we start again?" she asked. "Can we start over?"

I put my arm around her shoulders. "Anna, I—"

The bushes at the bottom of the stairs parted, and Howard appeared, his tie askew and his pince-nez thrown over his shoulder. He had a wild look in his eyes as he charged up the stairs at us.

"Help!" he said. "They're right behind me!"

"Oh, crap!" I said, standing up. Anna looked down to where Howard had emerged and was suddenly on her feet.

"Come on!" she said.

She grabbed one of Howard's arms and started to propel him up the stairs. I took his other arm, and we managed to get him into the resort. I slammed the door behind us and looked back through the window. Train and Local emerged from the bushes.

"They're at the foot of the stairs!" I said.

"We've got to hide him," Anna said.

"Where?"

"Upstairs, in my room."

"Oh, I say..." Howard said.

"Shut up, Howard," I said. "We could take him down into the laundry. I think Mr. Chang already knows all about him."

"Steam ruins my fur!"

"Shut up, Howard," Anna said. "No, my room's the best option. I can keep them out of it."

I watched as Train and Local searched along the

base of the stairs. Train was banging at the bushes, and Local was busy looking through his viewfinder. Somehow, I knew it had to be a night-vision camera. I looked over my shoulder at Anna.

"Your room is a freaking postage stamp."

"We've got to do something," she replied.

Local looked up the stairs. I dodged out of sight.

"They're coming this way," I said, sighing.

"You're repeating yourself," she said. "Let's go upstairs. Maybe we can lose them."

Anna led Howard through the door, and I followed behind them. We took the stairs two-at-a-time.

"Damn it," I said, "I need Sieg!"

"He's not here," Anna said. "We're going to have to do this without him."

Anna opened the door to the second floor and pulled Howard through it. I shut the door and leaned with my ear against it. I could hear someone coming up the stairs.

"We've got to hide in one of the rooms," she said.

"What good will that do?" I asked.

"We need to buy time until we can figure something out."

"That's why we need Sieg," I said. "He can think faster than we can."

"He's not here, Danny. He's also an idiot. Use your brain."

"Let's hit the elevator," I said. "Maybe we can find Penny and get her keys."

"Why?"

"I'm not sure..."

The elevator bell rang, and we watched in horror as the arrow began to turn inexorably from the lobby.

Howard grabbed my shoulder. "Someone's on the elevator," he said.

“Tell me about it,” I said. I grabbed a doorknob and rattled it. It wasn’t locked, and I looked up in wonder. Anna smiled at me.

“That’s some luck,” she said.

I opened the door and pushed Howard inside ahead of me.

“What about—” Anna said, but I stopped her and pushed her inside the room after Howard. I slammed the door behind us and then looked up.

“Oh, no!”

We were in the Bedfarther’s room. There weren’t any other guests in this part of the resort, and you could tell it didn’t belong to one of the reporters or Dr. Sybel by the assortment of feminine clothing and toiletries all over the place. It was obvious that Madeline Bedfarther was used to maid service. I could almost imagine the words that Penny or Courtney would be saying under their breath in the morning.

I peeked out of the door and saw Bedfarther trying to guide his wife out of the elevator. He would pull her one way and she would go along and then just keep going until he managed to stop her. Then he would try to turn her in the direction he wanted her to go in. Somehow he managed to point her in the general direction of the hall and gave her a slight nudge to get her going. She staggered out and walked five feet forward and about eighty from side to side. It was kind of like what I imagined tugboats did with really big barges, only without the precision.

A sound from the fire door at the end of the hall made me change position to look in that direction. Train and Local came charging out into the hall. They spotted the Bedfarthers and jogged over to them.

“Damn it, Horace,” Train said. “We had it! We had

the picture, except the damn thing—"

"Watch your language in front of my wife."

"Sorry, sir," Train said contritely. "We had the picture. It must have spotted us or smelled us or something, because it took off running before Carl could snap the picture. We chased it to those big stairs behind the place, and it disappeared."

"So then what did you do?" Bedfarther asked. He was distracted as he tried to keep Madeline upright. She was swaying more than a pine tree in a windstorm and reached out and wrapped her arms around Train's neck.

"My, you're so big and strong," she said in a voice that was thick and slurred.

Train tried to untangle himself. Bedfarther and Local tried to help because she seemed to have a grip of iron. For a minute it looked as if all four were dancing.

"Come on, Maddie," Bedfarther said. "We've got to get you to bed."

"Don't wanna. Wanna stay and play with Mr. Big and Strong."

I turned around but didn't see either Anna or Howard. I looked around in a panic. "Where are you?" I whispered.

The curtains moved slightly, and I came around the bed and found a pair of huge, hairy feet sticking out from under them. I peeked behind the curtains and found Howard and Anna pressed hard against the window.

"You two try to figure a way out of this room," I said. "I'm going to call for reinforcements."

"What?" Anna asked. She was looking at me as if I had lost my mind, yet again.

"Just do it."

I picked up the house phone and put it to my ear. Fortunately, Bedfarther wasn't such a cheapskate that he had the phone turned off. Gwen answered it on the first ring.

"Front desk, how may I–"

"Gwen," I said, "it's Danny. I need you to connect me with Mike. He should be over at our house."

"What are you doing on this line?"

"Don't ask, just connect me. *Please!*"

The phone rang a few times before I heard Mike's voice.

"'lo?"

"Mike, help!"

"Danny?" he said. "What's going on?"

"No time to explain," I hissed into the receiver. "Howard, Anna and I are trapped in Bedfarther's room. I need you guys to get us out of here."

"Holy cow! We're on our way."

We disconnected just in time. I heard the key scraping in the lock, and I dove under the bed. I peeked out and whispered to Anna.

"Any luck?"

"No," she whispered back. "The window's painted shut."

"Damn incompetent bastard!"

"Who?"

"Me. I painted the windows on this side of the resort. I should have been–"

I shut up as the door finally opened. I held my breath as I watched three sets of feet trying to move a fourth set into the room.

"I don' wanna go to bed."

"Dear," Bedfarther said in a reasonable tone of voice. It was as if he were speaking to a small child. "You've been up all day..."

"Don' wanna! Don' wanna! I want to stay with dear,

dear, dear, dear, dear John. Isn't that a funny name? Dear John, like I was leaving him or something."

"There had better be a good explanation for this," Bedfarther growled at Train.

"Boss, I don't know what you're talking about."

"We come up here, and she's all over you like a cheap suit, that's what I'm talking about."

"Boss, if Carl had been in front..."

"Oooh, I don't feel so good," Madeline said. I could hear the disaster in her voice.

"Quick!" Bedfarther said. "Get her in the bathroom for Christ's sake!"

"Too late, Boss," Local said. He was standing in front of me, and I saw him jump away. I scrambled back a bit as the vomit hit the carpet in front of me. I ground my teeth together to keep from joining Madeline in making a mess.

"Goddam it!" Bedfarther shouted. "Get a goddam housekeeper up here!"

I watched with mounting terror as Train walked around the end of the bed to the small table where the phone was. He picked it up and jiggled the receiver button for a second.

"Hello? Yes, this is Room 206. We've had a little accident here. Someone got sick all over the carpet."

While Train was on the phone, Local and Bedfarther managed to get Madeline into the bathroom and prevented more damage as she had another eruption. I was praying for something, anything, to intercede when a knock came to the door. Train nearly fell over the bed trying to answer it, and I almost sobbed with relief.

"Hi," came Mike's voice.

"Hi, uh, I'm sorry...she threw up all over here by the bed."

"Oh, they didn't tell me that downstairs. I'll have to get stuff from the maid's closet. Shouldn't take a moment."

Mike's feet disappeared. I wondered where the other guys were. The moment felt like eternity before Mike returned. He stood in the doorway and surveyed the scene.

"Is there any way that you folks can leave the room for a bit?" he asked. "The stuff I'll have to use is pretty nasty."

"Let me check," Train said and went over to the bathroom.

"Boss, the house-guy wants us to leave for a while. Apparently he's going to use some chemicals or something."

"Damn it," Bedfarther said. "Dear, can you stand up, Maddie?"

"Yeth."

"We're going to go outside for a few minutes while the nice houseman cleans up that mess. Do you think you can make it?"

When she spoke, her voice was stiff, as if she were trying desperately to keep the rest of her stomach inside her body.

"Prob—ab—ly."

"I'm sorry but I'm going to need your help again," Bedfarther said to his employees.

I watched as Local's feet hurried over to the bathroom.

"No problem, Boss," he said.

It took a few moments before they managed to get Madeline out of the room. As soon as Mike closed the door behind them, I rolled out on the clean side of the bed and stood up.

"Danny?" Mike said. His eyes were wide with amazement. "You were under there?"

"Yeah, from about the time you quit talking to me."

"Where...?"

Anna and Howard stepped out from behind the curtains. I moved over to the door and peeked out.

"How are we going to get out of here?" I asked.

I peeked again. "Ah, hold on, they're taking the elevator downstairs."

"They're going to have time to compare notes," Anna said.

I nodded and turned back to the door. "Yeah, then they're going to figure out that we disappeared on the second floor, and they'll come back."

Mike was already moving around us.

"I've got to clean this mess up."

Someone knocked on the door. I was about to have a heart attack until we heard Penny's voice.

"Housekeeping," she said.

Mike opened the door. Penny stepped inside and stopped.

"What's going on, some kind of party?" she asked. "You didn't invite me?"

"Long story," Mike said, "no time. I'll stay and help you clean up the mess and then—"

"Mess?" she asked. She looked down and saw she was standing with one foot in the puddle.

"Oh, God! Ick!" She tried to shake the vomit off her shoe.

"Lady had one too many. We've seen that before."

"Yeah but I didn't step in it that time."

I didn't have time for banter and opened the door.

"We've all stepped in it this time. If they're down in the lobby, then the only way we can go is—"

“Up,” Anna said, pointing at the ceiling.

“We’d better hurry,” I said. “Where’s Sieg?”

“He and Courtney haven’t come back yet,” Mike replied. “I left Jennifer guarding the elevator.”

Penny grabbed the rubber gloves and the bottle of cleanser that Mike had been holding.

“So that’s what she’s doing lurking in my supply closet,” she said. “You guys get out of here, and I’ll fix this mess. I don’t think you’ve got a whole lot of time.”

“I’ll stay,” Mike said.

She placed a finger across his lips. “No. We’ll talk later. I want to hear all about this. Right now, though, you need to get Howard out of here.” She kissed him and then turned away.

I looked out into the hall one more time. The coast was clear. “Come on, it’s now or never.”

They followed me out into the corridor, and we started toward the elevator. My heart leapt into my throat as the elevator arrow was almost back up.

“Oh, not again,” I said.

The door to the maid’s closet opened and Jenny waved to us.

“In here!” she said.

While the maid’s closet was huge—mostly used to hold extra blankets, sheets, towels, lamps, bulbs and so-forth—four humans and one Sasquatch definitely filled all the available space. Mike and I competed for space near the door. Howard squeezed himself into the back of the closet, while Jennifer and Anna perched in an open spot on one of the shelves.

I was the last one in. When I peeked through the crack in the door, Train and Local were getting off the elevator. I could tell Train was pissed off and was looking around as if he had X-ray vision. I was glad that Lisa had put the New Frontier people in the other wing. The last thing I needed right now was for a bunch of guests to wander in and complicate things any more than they already were.

"I'm telling you, Carl," Train said, pointing a finger a Bedfarther's room, "there was something fishy about that kid."

"Oh, sure, he shows up after we call him and—"

"He showed up damn quick! I'm pretty damn sure we told them downstairs that Maddie had thrown up, and he didn't know about it."

"That reminds me," Local said, giving a sly look to his partner, "how come you're so close to Maddie Bedfarther, huh? Are you trying to get us fired? I mean, I can get a job just about anywhere because everyone's looking for a good photographer but you writers are a dime-a-dozen."

"Oh, hardy har har. Very freaking funny. I'm going to get some answers around here. As for Maddie, let's just say I was the one who introduced her to Horace and let it go at that. I should never have let her within a mile of that greasy son-of-a-bitch."

They went to the room and opened the door. Penny was on her hands and knees, cleaning up the mess, and she looked up at them with a frown.

"Hey!" Train said, pointing at her. "Where's the other kid?"

"I sent him back," she said. "I'm the head housekeeper around here, and I'll be damned if I'll let one of those housemen do my job for me."

Train let the door close and then looked at his partner. "I knew it! I'll bet you they've got that Bigfoot hiding around here somewhere, and we're going to find it!"

“What are those idiots doing?” Jennifer whispered in my ear.

“I don’t know, but it can’t be good,” I whispered back.

The maid’s closet was becoming hot and stuffy and filled with the smell of wet pine needles. I looked back at Howard but he seemed to be preoccupied with the contents of one of the upper shelves. He was looking at it as if there was something hidden there that could help us. If I didn’t know better, I would swear that he was embarrassed about something. I went back to the crack in the door to see what Train and Local were up to. They had started walking down the hall, fortunately away from us.

“You take that side, and I’ll take this one,” Train said. He pointed to a door. Local walked over and tried the knob. It was locked. So was the first one Train tried. They moved down the hallway to the next set of doors and rattled the knobs.

“They’re going door to door and trying each one,” I whispered to Mike.

“Eventually, they’re going to come back to us,” he said.

“Can we lock this door?” I asked.

We both quickly examined the lock. It was a deadbolt that had a keyhole on both sides. Mike looked at me and just shrugged.

“I don’t have a key,” he said. “Penny does, but we’re cut off. It sounds like they suspect me. Take a look and see where they are right now.”

I peered out into the corridor. “They’re about halfway down the hall and...all right!”

“What?”

“The door to 216 was open,” I said, “and they’ve

gone in. Let's get out of here."

"I hope that's not an active room."

"If it is, we'll get fireworks a couple of days early."

"Yeah," he said, "just what we need. Come on, let's go."

We hurried out of the maid's closet and headed for the elevator. Mike made a quick detour across the hall to the Bedfarther's room.

"What are you doing?" I whispered after him.

He ignored me and went in. I heard muffled talking and looked up to see Anna, Jennifer and Howard waiting for us at the elevator. Jennifer was bouncing from one foot to the other as if she had to go to the bathroom. Their eyes were riveted on the arrow as it slowly climbed. I looked back down the hall, worried that our intrepid reporters would come out before we got Howard under cover. From Bedfarther's room I could hear Penny's voice as she spoke to Mike.

"Oh, all right!" she said in exasperation, "You'll have to give them back ASAP."

Mike came back out and held a ring of keys triumphantly. There was a fresh smear of Penny's lipstick on his cheek but I ignored it. He grinned at me as we ran to the others at the elevator.

"She gave me the master keys," he said.

"I don't even want to know what you're going to have to do to pay for those."

"Yeah," he said, "you don't. Ask Anna someday when you're all grown up."

"What took you so long?" Anna asked when we arrived at the elevator. The doors were beginning to open and you could feel the tension in the air. Jennifer and Anna were the first to dart into the elevator. Jennifer looked at the buttons for a second then looked out at me.

"Up or down?"

Anna reached out with a hand. "We've got to get out of here. Down."

Howard squeezed into the cage as I caught Anna's hand and held it back.

"No good," I told her, "the Bedfarthers are in the lobby. We'd never be able to get Howard past them. Especially since Bedfarther's going to be looking for those two. He's the kind of guy who sees things that are really there."

"Damn it," she said.

Jennifer cocked her head to one side as Mike and I both squeezed in. She then pressed a button decisively. "I guess we go up."

The doors began to close. To my horror, Train and Local came out of 216 and looked right at the elevator.

"Hey!" Train shouted.

They ran toward us as the doors closed. I banged my head on the inside. "Crap!"

Howard was pressed against one side of the cage, which still made him as inconspicuous as a giant at a midget's convention.

"Did they see me?" he asked. I could see the panic in his beady, black eyes. I could only nod.

"Oh, yeah," I said. "I'm pretty sure they did."

Jennifer looked first at him and then at me. "Now what?" she asked.

"Now we try to hide upstairs. I hope Anna's room can hide us. Mike, where's Todd?"

"I left him with Gwen in case we need a reserve," he said.

"We're going to need him," I said.

"Where the hell is Sieg?" he asked.

"I don't know," I replied. "He's always got an idea of

what to do."

"That's not necessarily the best thing, you know," Anna said over her shoulder.

"Right now it is," Jennifer said. "I hope one of you geniuses have a plan."

I glared at her. She was biting her lower lip and looking worried. I turned to Anna and saw the exact same expression on her face. I think I fell in love with her all over again in that moment.

She looked back at me. "Well?"

"Why are you asking me?"

"Because you're the one who always has a plan. We're going to need one right now."

"Are you nuts?" I said. "I haven't got a clue."

"You'd better start thinking, Danny," Jennifer said. "We're going to get trapped on three if we're not careful."

"Can we shut off the elevator?" I asked Mike when we got off on three.

"No," he replied. "I don't have a key. Besides, they'll just use the stairs."

Jennifer looked from Mike to me and back. I could tell she was enjoying the excitement, and somehow, I knew she was going to fit right in with the rest of us. She glanced up and down the corridor. "What are we going to do?"

"Don't panic," I said. "Let's get over to Anna's room."

"Her room is smaller than the maid's closet," Mike said shaking his head.

"Yeah, but it's right next to the stairs up to the attic."

"What good is that going to do?" he asked.

The doors to the elevator closed and we watched the arrow start on its way down. I went around to the back of the elevator and listened at the top of the stairs. I returned to the others in a hurry.

"We'd better think fast," I said. "Someone's coming up the stairs. I could hear Train cursing."

Howard slid slowly down the wall and put his head in his hands.

"Oh dear, my nerves are in a complete disarray. Maybe I should just give myself up. I know it would be a blow to my people but maybe we can have some understanding instead of all this harassment."

Jennifer grabbed his arm and tried to pull him to his feet.

"Don't bet on it," she said. "First they'll take your picture and the next thing you'll know, some rich idiot will want a genuine Sasquatch skin for their floor. That's how those bastards think."

"Yeah," I said. "Once those imbeciles prove that you exist, the forest will team with poachers and hunters all trying to get something of yours that is an aphrodisiac in China."

"What would that be?" Howard asked with bulging eyes.

"Damned if I know, but they'll think of something. The point is, we can't give up."

"First," Anna said calmly, "let's get down to my room. Maybe we can call Todd for help or maybe find Sieg or something."

After getting Howard back on his feet, we raced down the hall toward the staff bedrooms. One door opened and a green-faced demon stepped out and looked at us.

"What's going on?" the demon said with Lisa's voice. She was wearing a fluffy purple bathrobe and had her hair up in pink curlers as well as having some green stuff plastered on her face. I just nodded to her as I stopped at

Courtney's door. I was hoping for a miracle, or Sieg, and hammered on the door. There was no answer.

"Damn it. I'd hoped she and Sieg were in there."

"Why would they be in there?" Jennifer asked. I just looked at her for a moment. "Oh," she said, blushing.

I decided to ignore her embarrassment. I turned back to Lisa but Howard was already on his knees before her with his hands folded together as if in prayer.

"I seek sanctuary. Those reporters are right behind us."

She looked down the corridor. You could now hear their footsteps and Train's cursing on the steps. Lisa pushed her door all the way open and jerked a thumb over her shoulder.

"Get in here."

She stood to one side as Howard, Anna and Mike squeezed past her. Unfortunately, I had been right. There just wasn't enough room for all of us inside. Jennifer looked at me and I looked at her. We were the odd ones out.

"Now what are we going to do?" she asked.

"Mike—keys—now!" I said and held out my hand.

Startled, Mike tossed the keys in our direction. I caught them and pointed toward the attic stairs. Before we could move, I reached past Lisa, pulled Anna to me and kissed her.

"Thanks," I said, then I pushed Jennifer in the right direction as the door closed behind us. I could hear someone on the landing as we took the stairs two at a time.

"There they go!" cried Train. I fumbled with the keys and finally managed to slot the correct one into the lock and opened the door. Jennifer stood there peering into the dark hole.

"What are we going to do in there?" she asked.

"I'll think of something. Just get in there, damn it!"

She started inside when Train and Local came to a stop at the foot of the stairs behind us. Train pointed his finger at me.

"Stop!"

In her scramble to get inside the attic, Jennifer's arm came back and hit my hand. That's when I dropped the freaking keys. They hit the edge of the stair and bounced all the way down and landed at Local's feet.

"Just great," I growled. I pushed Jennifer inside and slammed the door closed behind myself. Fortunately, there was a latch as well as the deadbolt, and we both sighed with relief as I shot the bolt home. I sagged against something and looked over at her.

"Now what are we going to do for an encore?" I asked, unconsciously repeating what I asked Sieg as we watched Mohawk burn down.

Jennifer started laughing. "I have to admit, this is way more fun than chasing fake ghosts with Keeply. Is your friend a real Bigfoot?"

"He claims to be a Sasquatch," I replied. "Trust me, he thinks there's a difference."

"I'll try to remember that."

Train and Local tried to force the door but it was made of seasoned oak and the latch was formidable. They rattled the hell out of it but the latch never moved or gave an inch.

"So what are we going to do now, Butch?" Jennifer asked.

"I'll think of something, Sundance."

I hadn't turned on the lights but the full moon shining in the windows let us see where we were once our eyes adjusted. A wisp of memory made me turn slowly around and look at what I had been leaning against. It was one of the china cabinets we'd found on our last foray into the attic. The beginning of an idea came to mind, and I started to try and push the cabinet out of the way.

"Here, give me a hand," I said to Jennifer. She came over and it took both of us to move the cabinet to one side. Then I pulled Uncle Ernie from the shadows behind it.

"What the hell is that?" she asked.

"It's a fake Sasquatch. I'll explain later." I started looking around, and she came over to help me.

"What are we looking for?"

"I'm trying to find the house phone," I replied. "Try over there."

She found the phone in a small box attached to the wall next to the door.

"Who is this?" Gwen asked. She didn't sound happy. "What are you doing in the attic?"

"It's Danny again, Gwen. I need you to connect me with Lisa's room."

"Don't you people ever sleep? I've been trying to finish this crossword puzzle for an hour. Right now I have that Bedfarther guy and his lush of a wife down here. She's passed out on one of the couches but he keeps pacing back and forth as if she's giving birth. He's making me nervous. Todd's been sitting in here with me, eating crackers and trying to help with my puzzle—oh, and Sieg wants to talk to you."

I never thought I would feel as much relief as I did when my best friend's voice came over the phone. We both started talking at the same time.

"Danny!" he said. "We spotted the fake Bigfoot! I'm sure it's someone in a costume and—"

"Sieg!" I said. "We're trapped in the attic. Howard

and the rest are hiding in Lisa's room and—"

I suppose that he stopped and looked at the phone in consternation at the same time I did. I put the receiver back to my ear.

"What?" we both said at the same time.

I took a deep breath. Some of what Sieg had said filtered into my consciousness.

"All right," I said, giving up. "You win. What are you talking about now?"

* * *

"So this is it," Courtney said. She stood behind the Mustang and looked at it as if it was going to infect her Cadillac with rust.

"Yeah," Sieg said. "Isn't she great?"

"Why did you buy it?"

"What's wrong with it? I like it."

With a sigh, Courtney realized that her boyfriend had a new love in his life. Gritting her teeth she smiled at Sieg.

"It's okay, I guess," she said. "I just didn't think you were going to buy a car yesterday."

"Well, neither did I until I saw it sitting there. Can you imagine it? Vera and Big Ed didn't want to sell her to me."

"I couldn't possibly imagine why that would be," she said without a trace of a smile.

"My point, exactly. Well, let's go."

"Where are we going?" Courtney asked.

"Ah, we'll just run down to Lake Fork and back."

The ride down and back was pleasant. They had the windows down and she liked the feel of the wind in her hair. She had to admit that the car ran well. She looked over at Sieg who was concentrating on the road and suddenly she felt...happy. She realized then that she was in love with Sieg again, and she was all right with it.

They drove slowly up the road to the resort and pulled back into the spot where they had left. Sieg paused as he stood up out of the car.

"What the heck is that?" he asked and pointed toward the rose garden. There was a tall figure lurking in the shadows near one of the dining room windows.

"Could it be another ghost?" she asked.

"We'll find out," Sieg replied. He reached into the car and pulled out his flashlight. Holding a hand up for silence, he started walking toward the rose garden. Courtney followed silently behind him. They got within twenty feet of the figure when Sieg held up the flashlight and turned it on.

"Hey!" he shouted. "Whoa!"

Standing there was a Bigfoot, and it was definitely not Howard. In a minute, both Courtney and Sieg realized that it was a fake.

* * *

"How did you guys know it was a fake?" I asked.

"We've been hanging out with Howard long enough," Sieg replied over the phone. "Trust me, no self-respecting Bigfoot is going around with a shiny new zipper running down the length of their body. Also, while it was tall, it was still too short for a real one. I think we have evidence of some skullduggery going on around here."

"Okay," I said with a laugh, "so where is this fake right now?"

"I don't know," Sieg admitted. "That's why I was trying to find you guys. Court and I chased it around the building. We think it got inside. Somehow I managed to lose her, and now I can't find either of them."

"Just great. Well, while you've been doing all that, those damned reporters somehow spotted Howard."

"Oh, no."

"It gets better," I said. "Anna and I brought him inside, and right now, Jennifer and I are stuck in the attic with those two idiots at the door, and the rest of our friends are hiding in Lisa's room."

"What are they doing in Lisa's room?"

"You had to be there. So here we are, stuck in the attic with our stuffed Sasquatch, Mike and Anna are in Lisa's room with the real Sasquatch, and there's someone running around the resort dressed up as a Bigfoot."

Sieg was silent for a moment. Then he smiled. "You know, when you put it that way, this really sounds like the best episode of Scooby-Doo ever written."

"Great," I said. For one fleeting moment I wanted to reach through the phone and strangle him. "Sieg, if I could reach you, I would hurt you. All right, so what are we going to do about this? I would really like to get out of this attic and get Howard home without being photographed. If we're still here at daylight, it's going to be impossible, and I don't think those reporters are going to give up too easily. They can smell the story of the century."

Sieg was silent again. I was hoping he was coming up with something. I wanted and needed him to have an idea.

"I've got nothing, Danny," he said. My heart sank. "I'm just too worried about Court right now. It's not like her to disappear like this."

"All right," I finally said, "we'll go with my original plan."

"What's that?" Sieg asked.

"Have Gwen connect me with Lisa's room."

"Why?"

I put my forehead against the doorframe and bit back about a thousand sarcastic replies. "For once, Sieg," I said through gritted teeth, "just do what I want. After that, I want you and Todd to start looking around for Courtney and that fake Bigfoot. Try around Sven's room or maybe Sybel's. Brittany's room might be a good choice, too."

He was quiet for yet another moment. I hadn't heard him this quiet in ages. "You know," he said finally, "I didn't connect those dots. Yeah, I think you've got the idea, all right. If I can, I'll try and herd our phony Bigfoot toward the lobby. Let's get you connected to Lisa."

I grinned to myself. Now we were clicking on all cylinders. A moment later I was listening to Anna's breathless voice.

"Are you all right? Where are you?"

"We're fine and up in the attic. We're kind of trapped at this moment. I need to talk to Mike, I think I've figured a way out of this fix."

"What's going on?" Mike said when he came on the phone.

"Train and Local are pounding at the door right now. I think I've come up with a plan, but I need them to go away. Can you make a lot of noise and lead them back toward the elevators?"

"Probably. You've still got those keys?"

I winced. That was one question I didn't want to answer right then. "They're on the stairs or in their hands. I kind of—uh—dropped them when we were getting into the attic."

Mike cursed.

"Whatever you do," I said when he was done, "keep

Howard in Lisa's room. Keep him undercover while we try to work this out."

"That's easy. He's sitting on the bed eating cookies. If I leave him long enough, the girls will probably be painting his toenails or something."

My mind reeled at that.

"I think Anna and Lisa should stay here," Mike said, "and keep him company but I'm going to get those keys back. Penny will kill me if anything happens to them."

"Yeah, think about what she'll do to me."

"No," he said, "*you* think about what she'll do to you. I'm more worried about my own hide."

"All right but hurry up. I want you to run down the hall, make a bunch of noise and then hide in one of the rooms. If they follow you, call Gwen and have her connect with this phone. Oh, by the way, Sieg, Courtney and Todd are running around somewhere inside. They're trying to track down that fake Bigfoot. I gave Sieg a couple of ideas of where to look."

"What fake Bigfoot?" Mike asked.

"The one attacking people," I answered. "It's someone in a costume."

"That makes sense. Well, here goes. I hope we know what we're doing."

I stared at the phone after I hung it up.

"Yeah," I said to myself, "so do I."

"What are we going to do?" Jennifer asked. I'd almost forgotten she was standing there and when I turned and grinned at her, she took an involuntary step back.

"We're going to play a game," I said in a very calm, level voice.

"What game?"

"It's a game called Sasquatch, Sasquatch, who's got

the Sasquatch."

"What?" she asked.

I pointed at the stuffed Sasquatch standing there in the shadows behind her.

"Uncle Ernie here is going to help us finish this little fiasco once and for all."

She looked back at Uncle Ernie and then looked at me. Then she slowly turned around and looked at the Sasquatch again. When she turned back, she was smiling the same way I was.

* * *

Mike looked out from Lisa's room and peered down to where the stairs to the attic were. Sure enough, Train and Local were standing there at the foot of the stairs, arguing.

"Come on, John," Local said. "Those kids are probably long gone. I'll bet there's another way out of there."

"No, I don't think so," Train said. He climbed the stairs and Local followed him.

Looking down the corridor, Mike could see something metallic glinting in the light. With a smile he slipped out of the room and quietly moved down to the base of the stairs. He flattened himself against the wall and peered around the corner.

Train was standing with his ear pressed against the attic door while Local watched him intently. With a grin, Mike reached down and grabbed the keys. He deliberately shook them to make some noise and both reporters looked down to where he was standing.

"There's one of them!" Local shouted.

"Oh, crap," Mike said loudly. He turned and ran down the corridor, past Lisa's room and the stairs down.

"After him!" Train called out from behind.

Mike knew the keys almost as well as Penny did, and he knew which one he wanted. He slotted the correct key into a lock and disappeared through a door, locking it behind him.

* * *

Jennifer and I went over to Uncle Ernie and moved him to just across from the door. I put an ear to the panel and didn't hear anything.

"Should I take a look?" I asked Jennifer. She shook her head. Then the phone buzzed. I picked up the receiver.

"Okay," Mike said, so low that I could barely hear him. "I'm in 301, and I managed to get the keys. Now what?"

"You're not going to like this," I said.

"What?"

"I need you to go out and lead them into the other wing. Jenny and I have some special help here, and we need to get it to the elevator."

"You're killing me, man," he said.

"Trust me," I said.

"Yeah, right."

I opened the attic door a crack and found the stairs deserted. Grunting and swearing under our breath, Jennifer and I managed to get Uncle Ernie down the stairs and into the hallway. Lisa's door opened and Anna stuck her head out.

"What are you doing?" she asked.

"Decoy," I replied. "Give me about thirty minutes. I'll have Gwen call you when the coast is clear and you can get Howard out of here."

"Is this going to work?"

“I damn well hope so,” I said.

“Well hurry up,” she said imperiously. “We’re running out of ginger snaps.”

Ignoring the implication of Lisa’s and Howard’s taste in snack food, Jennifer and I picked up Uncle Ernie and struggled down the corridor to the elevator.

“There he is!” came a voice from the depths of the north wing.

“Wait a minute,” Local shouted. I pressed the button for the elevator and prayed that our timing would be right.

It wasn’t.

Before the elevator had even reached the second floor, Mike came tearing down the hall.

“They’re right behind me!”

I looked at the elevator arrow and then down the hall. Train and Local were just coming around the corner.

“Help me take him downstairs!” I said.

Mike and I grabbed Uncle Ernie, and we headed around the elevator to the stairway. Jennifer followed us. On the first landing, I pushed us aside so she could go on ahead.

“Go down and scout for us,” I told her. “We need a way down to thc lobby.”

“Right,” she said and took off. When we got Uncle Ernie down to the second floor, she was waiting for us.

“Sven and some girl are coming up the stairs,” she said.

I looked over at Mike. “Well, that leaves only one last suspect on my list.”

“No time for that,” he said. “We’ll have to hide in one of the rooms again.”

“We can’t,” I said. “Sven’s room is just down the hall.”

The elevator doors opened, and I thought the end was near. However, Sieg and Todd came out. Sieg grinned when he saw us.

"Hi! We still haven't found Courtney—"

"No time!" I said. "We need to hide!"

Sieg looked one way and then the other. Then he pointed to the north wing. "This way."

"What about the guests?"

"Do you have a better idea?" he asked.

I looked over at Mike. "Do you still have those keys?"

"Of course I do."

"Good," I said. "Let's stick Uncle Ernie in the maid's closet."

Mike grinned at me, and we ran over to the closet door. He pulled the door open. Penny came out, not looking to happy.

"Hey!" she said. "You're not putting that filthy thing in here!"

Mike and I exchanged a look. Behind us, we could hear Train and Local pounding down the stairs. Without a word we headed down the hall and around the corner with Sieg, Jennifer and Todd on our heels.

Just past the corner, a door opened and Madam Keeply stepped out into the hall. She was wearing a pink chiffon nightgown and a peach housecoat. There are some things that you can never un-see, and God knows I wish I could un-see that one. She saw us coming down the hall and drew herself up to her full height.

"What's with all this noise?"

I don't know why I did it but some impish impulse made me stop and stand Uncle Ernie on his feet. Mike and Sieg looked exasperated as I bowed to the psychic.

"Madam Keeply? May I introduce Uncle Ernie?

Uncle Ernie, this is Madam Keeply."

She recoiled when confronted with the stuffed Sasquatch. One hand came up as if to protect her face or perhaps to scream. Mike and Sieg grabbed Uncle Ernie and hurried down the hall. I shrugged and followed them.

Mike stopped at a door and started fumbling with Penny's keys. He opened the door, and we all went inside. Sieg slammed the door closed and slid the latch in place.

The room had once been an office. There was an ancient roll-top desk, a couple of chairs and a pretty damned thick layer of dust. I looked around in surprise.

"Where the hell are we now?"

"It's the old manager's office," Mike said with a smile. "Back in the old days, the resort was so busy that the front desk had its own manager. That's the office that Cap uses. I spotted this when we were cleaning up the north wing for the guests." Then he turned to me, and he wasn't smiling anymore. "What the hell were you thinking, Jael? Those idiots were on our heels when you stopped."

"Sorry," I said, "I couldn't resist."

Jennifer started laughing. "Oh, did you see her face? That was priceless!"

"Merry Christmas," I said, "I did it for you."

"Thanks."

Sieg was busy ignoring us and listening at the door. He unlatched the door and it burst open. The fake Bigfoot stood there. He looked at us and we looked at him.

I could understand why people might think that it was a real Bigfoot in the dark. If you didn't see the zipper and were surprised, it would be pretty realistic, if short. On the other hand, it was more like some artist's conception of what a Bigfoot might look like based on vague accounts.

The phony Bigfoot stood there, and I could tell he was looking at Uncle Ernie. Slowly he backed into the hall and pointed at the stuffed Sasquatch.

"That's...that's..." was all he could say. I thought I recognized the voice, but before I could say or do anything, and before the Bigfoot could take another step, a figure flew into sight and slammed into it hard.

"Gotcha!" Courtney shouted.

The Bigfoot lost his balance, and the two of them rolled across the floor. The Bigfoot managed to get to his feet and take off back toward the stairs. Courtney rolled to her knees and cursed.

"Damn it," she cried. "I had him!"

I ran into the hall and watched the Bigfoot knock over Madam Keeply, who had come back out into the hall to complain. I turned to Mike as he and Jennifer came out into the corridor.

"Lock the door!" I said. "Let's get him!"

Jennifer went over to Courtney and helped her to her feet. Sieg and I took off after the Bigfoot. He had regained his feet after his encounter with the psychic, but we were right on his heels as he went around the corner.

Train and Local were coming back from the north wing, and we all watched as the Bigfoot knocked over Sven and Brittany and headed down the stairs. Sieg and I almost collided with Train and Local but we managed to push them back and took the stairs three at a time.

The Bigfoot was apparently scared and was trying to find an exit. It hit the polished floor of the lobby at full speed and was arrowing toward the front door. Suddenly, out of nowhere, one of the wooden chairs was *thrown* through the air and tangled up with the Bigfoot's legs.

"*None of that, boyo,*" seemed to drift across the

lobby followed by a ghostly chuckle as the Bigfoot slid across the floor until its head slammed into one of the pillars. It lay still, and Sieg and I stood over it, breathing heavily.

"Thanks," I said to the ghost. Sieg tapped my shoulder and pointed behind me.

Looking around, I spotted the Bedfarthers over on one of the couches. Madeline sat swaying with a cup of coffee in her hands while Horace looked at us. His eyes were wide, and his mouth was shaped into an "o". He walked over with an outraged expression and pointed at us.

"Hold it right there!" he said.

I turned around and saw Train and Local coming down the stairs behind us. Behind them I could hear a crowd coming. I knew we were out of options. Bedfarther came up to us and pointed a finger at the fake Bigfoot.

"What is that?" he demanded.

"Uh, well...I...uh..." I said.

Sieg saved me from sounding even more like a fool. "It's a fake Bigfoot. We were chasing it upstairs, and I think your reporters were chasing it too."

The reporters finally reached us. Local unslung his camera and started snapping pictures. The Bigfoot slowly got to his hands and knees, woozily shaking his head. Mike, Courtney and Jennifer came running up, followed by Sven and Brittany. Courtney reached down and pulled the Bigfoot to his feet. Jennifer grabbed one of his arms to help steady him, and Courtney took hold of the other one.

Mike reached over and grabbed the zipper pull. "How about we find out who this is. This is probably why there are all those rumors about a Bigfoot in the canyon."

While this was going on, I quietly stepped around

the crowd and moved back behind Sven and Brittany. I wanted to keep them in sight, as I still had some suspicions and wanted to see if I was right.

Before Mike could pull the zipper down, the Bigfoot tried to push his hand away. Jennifer and Courtney struggled to keep his arms at his side.

From behind us, I could hear the elevator opening. I turned and panic rose up in my head. Cap stormed off the elevator, followed by Aunt Vera, Big Ed and Todd. Todd was being propelled by my uncle.

Cap was wearing a red bathrobe and blue pajamas. He was tightening the belt of his bathrobe as he pushed his way through the crowd.

"What in the name of all that is holy is going on around here?" he said.

My uncle and aunt followed in his wake. Neither of them looked very happy as they pushed Todd ahead of themselves. Todd caught my eye and shrugged helplessly. I began looking for escape routes.

"Bad news, Horace," Train said. "This one isn't as good as the Swanberger Hoax back in '78."

Local looked up from his camera. "Does this mean we don't have a story?" he asked his partner.

"Nah," Train replied, "I'll come up with something."

"This has been a colossal waste of time," Bedfarther said. He was quivering and his hands twitched. "I should fire both of you, especially you, Train. All Maddie can talk about is how big and strong you are."

"Now Boss," Train said, He held up his hands in self-defense. "We thought there was a story here. There is one, just not the one we thought. We don't know what kind of story it is right now."

"What kind of story could there be?" Local asked.

Train looked up at the ceiling, and when he lowered

his eyes to Bedfarther again, he was smiling.

"We'll tell the story of the *Lake Weir Hoax*. It'll be bigger than the Swanberger. We'll sell millions of copies. If there's one thing people like more than a real Bigfoot, it's a fake Bigfoot, exposed. I can see the headline now: 'Weird Canyon Hides Phony Bigfoot'. Snappy, huh?"

"Maybe," Bedfarther said grudgingly. "If we take out the word 'phony' I think you're onto something. Yeah, maybe we can do that."

Cap and Big Ed were watching this exchange with rising impatience. The elevator opened again and Penny came out, carrying her cleaning kit. She walked over to Mike, and he wordlessly slipped the keys into her hand. By this time, everyone was ignoring us in preference for the reporters and the fake Bigfoot.

"All right," Cap said, grabbing the zipper pull, "let's see who's been wreaking so much havoc around here."

The Bigfoot struggled to get away. However, Courtney and Jennifer were more than a match for it. Big Ed reached over and pulled the head back and away.

I smiled grimly to myself as the wrinkled features of Dr. John Sybel were revealed under the Bigfoot mask. He winced at the light and tried to get away again.

"Why, Dr. Sybel," Cap said with narrowed eyes, "what is the meaning of this?"

While I watched, I kept one eye on Sven and Brittany. Sure enough, a look of panic appeared on both of their faces. It confirmed what I had been thinking. Sieg looked across the crowd at me, and I slowly nodded. He returned the nod, and then something Big Ed did caught our undivided attention.

He reached into a pocket and pulled out a handkerchief. He wiped Dr. Sybel's face, and I was surprised when some of the wrinkles disappeared. Big Ed began laughing.

"Well, well, well," he said to Dr. Sybel. "How nice to see you again, Doug. Using the old collodion for wrinkles trick, eh? And you said there was nothing in Drama 101 that could be applied to the real world."

"It doesn't matter," Doug Assyrian said. His face twisted into a snarl. "When the story gets out, no one is going to visit your little resort, Ed Jael. The value of the property will plummet, and you'll be begging me to take it off your hands. Soon this whole canyon will be mine!" He started laughing and raised his face to the ceiling and laughed even harder.

A cold chill gripped my spine until I saw Sieg pushing his way through the crowd. He had *that* look on his face again. He walked up and stood next to Big Ed.

"I've got some very bad news for you, Mr. Assyrian," he said. "You saw that old Sasquatch statue that we were toting around? That's going to be the centerpiece for the new Lake Weir Bigfoot Tour. We're going to get every romantic and adventurous couple on the planet to come here and try their luck at finding a Bigfoot. We're going to be minting money. I thought of it almost a month ago, and now you've given me the opportunity and the advertising that I needed."

Assyrian's triumphant look drained away to be replaced by one of horror. He was a natural showman, and he could see better than anyone what Sieg was doing. Even I could see it plain as day, and not for the first time. I was proud of my best friend. Big Ed clapped Sieg on the shoulder.

"That's a great idea, Sieg. Now, Doug, we could always hire you to wear that suit and run around for people."

"If you like," Sieg said, grinning even harder, if that

was possible, “you could even wear that and stand in the driveway entrance and wave at people on the highway.”

Assyrian‘s face twisted into an expression of rage. “I’ll see you in hell first!” He gathered up his costume, shook off Courtney and Jennifer, and stormed over to the elevator. Cap looked over at Big Ed, who merely shook his head.

“Let him go,” Big Ed said. “He can leave in the morning.”

Bedfarther had been watching this eagerly. He took Cap’s arm and turned him around even as Assyrian disappeared onto the elevator.

“I want this story!” he said.

“Then write it,” Cap said wearily. “I’m pretty sure neither I nor Mr. Jael will have any objections to it. As Sieg said, this is going to be a publicity boon for us. I’m going to have to hire more people, and I’ll be able to get this place fixed up properly. Now, if you’ll excuse me.”

He, Big Ed and Aunt Vera walked over to the elevator, speaking softly among themselves. Vera turned around and winked to me. I grinned back. Then I turned around and realized that I’d lost sight of both Sven and Brittany. I wasn’t too worried, though, since I knew I had plenty of time to deal with them later.

Bedfarther, on the other hand, had other things on his mind. He had turned to Train and Local and put and arm over each of their shoulders.

“Look guys,” he said, “help me get Maddie back to our room, and we’ll hammer this out.”

“You mean we’re not fired?” Local asked.

“Hardly,” he said and turned to Sieg. “That statue that you mentioned, I supposed that was what my boys here were chasing.”

Mike hung his head and assumed a hang-dog look.

"Yeah," he said, "sorry about that. We were trying to hide it to keep you from writing a story that there was an actual Bigfoot around here. We were just trying to—"

"You were trying to keep the *Midnight Star* from getting embarrassed," Bedfarther said. "Thank you. This is going to become one hell of a great story. We might not have our Great Bigfoot Hunt winner, yet, but if you guys can bring that statue from wherever you hid it and put it over here, we'll take some pictures of it in the morning. This story is going to sell millions of copies."

"Yeah," Mike said, "I guess we can do that. If we're going to start having Bigfoot tours, I guess we'll have to put Uncle Ernie on display."

"Why do you call him Uncle Ernie?" Train suddenly asked.

Mike shut up as he realized that he had gone too far.

"He looks like my Uncle Ernie, down in Florida," Sieg said. "Uncle Ernie wanders around with his shirt off which isn't a good thing for someone so big and hairy."

"Oh, I guess that makes sense."

With that, Bedfarther and his two reporters walked over to where Madeline Bedfarther was passed out with an empty coffee cup dangling from her hand.

"There are going to be book rights," Bedfarther said to no one in particular.

"Book rights, Boss?" Train asked.

"Oh yeah. I can see you writing the book about this one. There may even be a movie."

They got Madeline back on her feet and dragged her over to the elevator. For once, when the doors closed, I was able to let out a sigh of relief. Then Gwen stepped out of the PBX Office, her crossword puzzle book in one hand.

"What the hell is going on?" she demanded. "Doesn't

anyone around here sleep anymore?"

We all laughed, and Penny turned to her. "Trust me, you don't want to know."

Grumbling, Gwen went back into the office as Mike turned to me.

"What about Howard?" he asked.

"I think we can safely get him outside now," I said smugly. I was proud of the way things had worked out. "If anyone asks, we're just moving Uncle Ernie."

"Bigfoot Tour?" he said to Sieg. "How are we going to hide Howard with all that going on?"

"Simple, we'll be running the tours. Since he's on our side, we'll just coordinate with him and take the tourists to places where he isn't. In fact, Assyrian did us a favor. Now if anyone sees Howard, they'll just assume that it's someone in a Bigfoot costume."

"Dude," Todd said, "we'll have to get a costume made."

"We can do that," Sieg said. "Only a better one, with a hidden zipper."

"You know," I said, "this isn't exactly how I thought this was going to work out."

"No battle plan ever survived contact with the enemy," Jennifer said.

"Todd," Mike said, "I want you and Sieg to move Uncle Ernie down here. Danny and I are going to get Howard out of here. With any luck no one will ever know that there are two of them."

TWENTY-THREE

I was waiting at the front desk the next morning when Assyrian came down. Mr. Monkey was riding on his shoulder, and when they came up, the monkey flipped me the bird. I just smiled at him. Assyrian looked at me disgustedly.

"You should be careful of the enemies you make, youngster," he said.

"So should you," I replied. "Just remember, when you take on one Jael, you take on all of us. Oh, and remember that job offer is still open. We could always use your help with the Bigfoot Tour."

"Go to hell."

"Aren't you adorable? Well, thank you very much. I hope you have a great time. Goodbye, Mr. Monkey."

I handed Mr. Monkey a banana but he just flipped me the bird again. I guessed there was no pleasing some people, or monkeys, but he did eat the banana eventually. Then he placed the peel like a hat on his owner's head. Oddly enough, I found I was going to miss that miserable little beast.

I walked over to the front windows and watched as a long, black limousine pulled into the lot and Assyrian got into the back. He rolled the window down and looked up at me as his driver loaded his luggage into the trunk. Suddenly, he called the driver over and spoke to him for a moment. The driver pulled a large box from the trunk and came up the stairs. I met him at the door.

"Mr. Assyrian wants you to have this," he said. "He says you'll find more use for it than he will."

He went back and soon the limo drove away in a cloud of dust. I put the box on one of the side tables and opened it. When I saw what was inside, I started to laugh and couldn't stop for more than five minutes.

It was the Bigfoot costume.

* * *

Jennifer came over to the resort a bit later. Watching her cross the parking lot, I suddenly had an idea. I knocked on Anna's office door.

"Yes?" she called out.

"Come on out," I said. "I'm about to do something evil."

"Oh, that should be different."

"I'm going to do it to Sven and Brittany."

She was at the door in a microsecond. "You have my undivided attention."

When Jennifer came into the lobby, I went over and spoke quietly with her for a moment. She giggled and agreed with me. We hung around in the lobby for a short while until Sven and Brittany came down the stairs. They were holding hands, and she was whispering in his ear. I almost called off my plan but then my hand touched the box with the Bigfoot costume. I nodded to Jennifer, who ran across the lobby and jumped on Sven, wrapping her arms around his neck.

"Oh, Svenny," she said in a decent imitation of a vapid schoolgirl's voice, "It's so good to see you again! I've been looking everywhere for you. Mama has the whole wedding planned, and Papa is talking to the priests at St. Patrick's. I just can't wait!"

She kissed him hard on the mouth and then jumped back. Brittany drew away from him and then slapped him across the face. I could hear the smack all the way to where Anna and I were standing. For a moment I felt sorry for our Catering Manager.

"I should have known," Brittany said. "You're still screwing around on me!"

"No! I've never seen this girl before…"

"Oh, Svenny," Jennifer said, going further than I had anticipated, "don't tell me that you love this girl, too! Oh, what will we do?" She pouted. "They don't allow polygamy in Utah anymore!"

I couldn't help it. I just started laughing and saw that Anna was biting her handkerchief to keep from being heard. Sven looked at Jennifer as if she were a snake that was going to bite him. Brittany looked at her in disgust.

"You can have him," she grated.

"No," Jennifer said, shaking her head sadly, "it'll be a blow to Daddy, but I think you deserve him. He tastes like onions."

With that she walked over to where Anna and I were standing. Brittany saw the look on her cousin's face and then turned on her heel and stormed back up the stairs. Sven turned around as if to follow.

"Sven!" I called in a loud voice.

He turned back toward me. "What?"

I walked over to him. "You know," I said in a low voice, "there were times when that fake Bigfoot was spotted when Assyrian was right here in the lobby. I tried to figure out who was helping him, and there were times when it was spotted and you and he were both here. Then I figured it out. There were three of you in on it."

He looked at me warily. Sometime in the past twenty-four hours, it had finally dawned on him that I was more than just Big Ed's nephew. I smiled widely at him.

"This was just the down payment," I said. "Cross me again, and you'll live to regret it."

"What are you going to do? Are you going to tell Cap or Big Ed?"

"No. At least not for now. You've done a pretty good job around here. If you keep doing that job, you'll keep it. Mess around like that again, and I can assure you that you'll wish they'd fired you."

"I'll keep that in mind," he said.

"Good. Now go catch up to Brittany. She's probably in tears by now."

With that, I turned my back on him and walked over to where Anna and Jennifer were waiting for me. Anna kissed me on one cheek, and Jennifer kissed me on the other.

Yeah, it was going to be a good day.

* * *

That evening, Sieg and I sat on the front porch by ourselves. A cool breeze blew from the direction of the lake.

"Well, Old Son," I said, "I guess Brittany forgave him. At least she didn't leave the resort."

"Yeah," he said. "You know, we've only been out of

school for a couple of months, and despite the probation, our world has really changed."

"I think we changed it a long time before that, Sieg."

My best friend looked over at me with a sly smile. "So, is this what we're doing for an encore?"

I started laughing. "Damned if I know. It's a weird canyon after all."

THE END...?

About the Author

The son of a printer and a waitress and born in Colorado in 1967, **A.M. Jordan** grew up camping throughout the Front Range. He is married to Laura, who somehow puts up with him, and is owned by three cats. They all live together in the not-so-wilds of metro Denver. He is passionate about books, railroads, history, and baseball. *Weird Canyon* is Mr. Jordan's debut novel.

More Fascinating Fiction from
Thursday Night Press
An imprint of DX Varos Publishing

M.L. Grider
Bitter Vintage

Sourdough Jackson
That Old Science Fiction
Torpedo Junction

A.M. Jordan
McGuire's Luck

Karen A. Morrissey
Fisher King: Percy's Descent

CPSIA information can be obtained
at www.ICGtesting.com
Printed in the USA
LVHW031319230222
711788LV00001B/33

9 781955 065443